The Mender

Book 1 of The Mender Trilogy

Jennifer Marchman

Stående Bjørn Press

Edition 1.0

Cover art by Oliver Bennett of More Visual Ltd.

Print ISBN: 9798397298322

Stående Bjørn Press
Austin, Texas, USA

For my husband,
who has shown me what real love is.

And for my children, K, D, and A,
who are just relieved I didn't write this entire thing
in GIFs.

Contents

Content Warning

This novel is intended for an adult audience, deals with mature themes, confronts age-old conflicts, contains some language, and occasionally depicts violence, including brief scenes of sexual violence.

Any misplaced commas are unintentional but probably deserve a warning as well.

7 And God dwelled at the Source, Axis Mundi, for eternity and a day.

8 At the dawn of time, Chaos rose from the Abyss and broke the holy Vessel of God, shattering what was once whole and pure into material existence, multitudes upon multitudes, false reflections of the True line.

9 Verily, I say unto you, each shard traps a spark of the divine, separated from the Source.

10 This evil creation will not end until the Vessel is mended.

Book of Lisha 4:7-10

Chapter 1

Eva

Sanctum, Axis Mundi, the True line, 1997

The quantum strings bent to her will. She gave them no choice. Each countless strand in her body, each in the tree, sang an octave higher at her command. The thick, diamond-patterned bark of the ancient ash transformed under her touch, and she glanced one last time over her shoulder. "Ready?"

"No… wait," Tophe said, rummaging in their shared knapsack.

"I didn't forget anything."

"I just want to double-check," he said.

Impatient to proceed, she huffed and held the portal open. "Extra water?" she asked.

"Yes." He gripped the bag at arm's length, peering into its open mouth, and his dark hair fell forward. "What are we missing?"

She scanned his Mexican officer's uniform and thought through the items she had packed. "Nothing," she said. "It's not like we're going to be there a week. We've done this exact mission a million times in a million Goliad copies."

Tophe nodded and retied the pack. "You're right. Let's go."

With a parting glance, her gaze skipped up the hill to the sanctum of the True line, a safe haven for all those she loved, the only free and conscious beings in the multiverse.

"Come on. Now who's dawdling?" he asked and bent to kiss her cheek. "Last one, then better things." His sight turned inward, and he widened the doorway beside her.

She focused on the vibrating energy found within all quantum particles. There was nothing magic about their abilities. As a sixth sense, real humans could move freely through space and time simply by changing reality at the quantum level. After taking a deep breath, she spliced each wiggling snippet into a loop, changing the pitch of the cosmic choir. Free now to move, she sensed the inseverable tether of her lifeline, a thread woven across dimensions, anchoring her to the one true reality, Axis Mundi, the navel of the universe, and strong enough to bring her home.

Since the mistake of creation, Axis Mundi, the True line, had shone as a holy light through the shattered pieces of a broken mirror. Briefly, gratitude flooded her chest to be one of the chosen, for only her people, the Lux Libera, could move between worlds.

A soft haziness enveloped them both, and the evergreen wavered, unsure of its place in space-time. She gathered her existence up like skirts from the mud, keeping herself separate from the tree and Tophe.

Fully between dimensions, she sought the beacon set by her people's scouts on previous missions to guide them. The worlds floated around her, a near-infinite shimmering sea. Without difficulty, she located the signal, but as she drew closer, the target split into two diverging lights. Her thoughts flew to Tophe. Uncertain where he would go, she knew she must choose before her strength wore out.

As she exited the portal, a dark world greeted her, and her stomach dropped. She should be standing in a sheltered grove outside the embankments of a military camp with the rising sun streaming into her eyes. Ocean waves should be crashing beyond the dunes. Instead, the inky blackness reminded her of the Abyss, and horror clutched the back of her neck. Sound stretched, telling her of trees and an expanse filled with the layered, whirring drone of cicadas. Her heart beat a swift staccato in her throat.

She shut her eyes, swallowing panic as dry as cotton, and inhaled to the bottom of her lungs to regain control. The rest of this timeline was forever closed to her now. Once she entered a line, she could only travel forward as part of the time-stream. When she exhaled, her shoulders shook. The air swirled hot like a cooling oven, remnants of a blistering day rather than the damp chilliness of the early spring she had expected. The scents of summer grasses, of ash juniper and sycamore, surrounded her.

She reached back to the trunk and placed her hand on its bark, willing it to be solid for her. A gust of dry wind danced through the leaves and swept down to brush her hair across her cheek. Abruptly, she thought she heard breathing and spun her head toward the sound.

Her eyes strained through the moonless night. She waved a hand in front of her face but saw nothing. After a moment, she crouched, searching the ground within her reach. A twig snapped.

She lowered her voice. "Tophe?"

The canopy sighed above her. She stood, ignoring her fear, and took a step. The ground disappeared beneath her feet, and she pitched forward into a midnight void. Terror catapulted a shriek from the back of her throat, and she threw out her hands, training forgotten, and tumbled through branches and thorns with increasing speed. Too late, she remembered to tuck her head and shoulder.

As she watched, her mother spread butter on extra thin slices of white bread to make cheese toast for spaghetti. They stood across from each other in the kitchen of her childhood home. Years had passed since she had last seen her, since she had left her birth timeline without a word, and a longing for her abandoned family welled and tugged at her like an unexpected riptide. She cleared her throat to speak but realized her mother was spreading mayonnaise on the bread instead of butter. With a smile, she turned the piece of bread as if it were a photo she wished her daughter to see and shoved it in her face.

The sensation shocked her awake, and the dream faded as she found herself nose to snout with a large brown and tan dog. A man grasped the dog's scruff in his fist to pull it away. With the heel of her hand, she rubbed its lick from her eyes and nose and tried to sit up, but her head exploded. She tapped at the back of her skull with feathered fingertips. Under her crusty hair, the tender skin oozed. The bed creaked as she shifted her sore body, and she registered a rope lattice pinching her numb hip. Pain shot through her wrist.

"Lo siento," the man said. He pushed the dog out of the cabin and fastened the door. Firelight illuminated him. As he moved about the stuffy room, his silhouette splintered and rejoined when she attempted to focus on him. "Está acostumbrado a estar adentro," he said.

The amount of effort required to speak confused her, but she understood him. "It's all right. I like dogs." She prodded the words over a swollen tongue, and an inner voice told her she should have responded in Spanish, but she couldn't remember why.

The animal's scratching at the door increased, loud and insistent. He whined in confusion.

"If he's used to being inside, please let him back in... I really don't mind."

The man raised an eyebrow as he handed her a gourdful of water. "People don't usually think dogs should be in a house."

She rolled to her side and lifted her head to drink.

"I'm Jim," he said, opening the door. "This is Wokweesi."

The dog barreled past his master's knees, rocking him back on his heels. He stopped next to her head and yawned in canine irritation, baring yellow teeth. As his great furry head sniffed her from shoulder to foot, she fell to her back and twisted her head away.

She opened her mouth to express gratitude for the water, but her stomach heaved. With a cautious pause, she sipped a breath and swallowed. When that didn't help, she closed her eyes, and after another moment, tried again. "I..."

Water and the remains of her last meal spewed across his wool blanket. Pain exploded through her neck, head, and shoulders. She felt him remove the covering. Bile caught in her nose and burned her throat, and her cheeks and ears grew hot with embarrassment. Her eyes watered, wanting to close, but she forced them open and found his face. "I..."

"Shh. Just tell me your name and then sleep." He wiped her chin and tucked a clean but musty blanket around her. "You're not ready to be awake yet."

"Eva," she said, shutting her eyes against the pain. "My name is Eva."

She had little sense of the sunlight moving along the cabin floor, of the small fire being built up and burning down. Sometimes it would be dark when Jim offered her a stew or light when he helped her to the outhouse. The heat of the day oppressed her;

the nights smothered her. She wished someone would release the clamps from around her head. Moving was agony. Jim tried to ask her a few questions, but her thoughts would not stay in one place.

Sometimes she remembered Tophe, and a twist of loneliness would settle in her belly. Worse, her knives were in his knapsack. If she wasn't careful, anxiety would consume her as she imagined angering the Elders over a failed mission. Fears collided in her head like billiard balls, unable to be caught and sorted, and she groaned until sleep eased her pain again.

Throughout the day, Wokweesi would climb up on the bed next to her and lay himself out like a person, head on her pillow, back along her side. Her body protested at the extra heat, but she was too tired to do anything about it. She rested her cheek against him. He smelt of skunk, and she slept. During the hottest part of the day, she was alone.

Eventually, the pressure on her head eased, and she thought she might be able to sit up on her own. Low, golden light filtered into the cabin. Wokweesi blinked his eyes, sneezed all over her, and jumped down. After she pushed herself upright, she swung her feet over the side and braced both hands on the bed frame as she gathered her strength. Yawning, the dog slid his paws across the floor in a stretch and then sat on his haunches.

She could smell herself and wrinkled her nose. Old, sticky sweat coated her body. As she inspected her hands and arms, she found them scratched, but clean, the scabs flaking off. She rolled her wrist. Though sore, she didn't wince until she pressed her weight on it. She remembered Jim removing cactus quills with slow, gentle fingers.

Wokweesi sighed, watching her from the floor.

At his scrutiny of her, Eva smiled. "We're friends now, aren't we?"

The tip of his tail waved, brushing dirt and debris back and forth across the floorboards. He dropped a heavy paw on her knee, and she scratched his chest and under his foreleg. The moment she stopped, his claws curled, digging into her skirt until he gave up and let his leg slide back to the floor.

"Yes, okay. I'm getting up."

She stepped out onto the dogtrot of a homesteader's rough-cut log cabin, and Wokweesi vanished. Under the eaves, the late afternoon sun hung low enough to be visible, and she shaded her eyes against the glare. She had known days like this in her childhood timeline and as unbidden thoughts of her former family surfaced, she pushed them away. A gust drawn through the open-air corridor between the two rooms of the house lifted her hair from her sweaty neck, blowing cool and then warm again. In the distance, the leaves of the cottonwood and sycamore trees were still green.

Out of breath, she sat down on the step leading to the yard. She explored the back of her crusty head and sniffed her hand. Not dirt, she thought.

"It's yarrow."

Eva jumped.

Jim strode toward her from the other end of the dogtrot. "It helped stop the bleeding. Some of it may be from the juice of the prickly pear pads I put on it." He lowered himself beside her. "Sorry I couldn't do much else for you besides the corn husk tea I had you drink. I haven't been given the right kind of medicine you probably needed."

"No, no," she said, lifting her hand. "Thank you. I… you… you've been very kind. I mean, I threw up all over your bed. You've had to help me to the bathroom." When a look of confusion flashed across his face, her thoughts tripped. "The privy, I mean, the outhouse," she said, waving in its direction, embarrassed as much by her lapse in correct word choice as anything else.

His face cleared.

Her embarrassment puzzled her. It shouldn't matter to her because he wasn't real. There were many copies of him in the multiverse.

With a toss of his hand, he dismissed her concern. "I hate to push you, ma'am. I'm glad to see you up. But I am powerfully curious to know how you fell into that arroyo. It's fifteen feet at least. You managed to hit the only cactus on the way down."

Below her dangling foot, Eva watched large red ants meandering through the dry grasses. An accent laced his words, but she couldn't place it.

When she didn't respond, he said, "Somebody must be missing you."

She should have anticipated Jim's questions, but her thoughts had only strung together long enough to make her way out here onto this porch. At the reminder of Tophe, she pictured him suspended between dimensions. He couldn't even know they had been separated yet. "What year is it?"

Jim furrowed his brow. "1835."

"And is it about September?"

"I think so." Jim looked at the sun and back at her. "I don't really keep track. I don't have a calendar. It's another moon… month… at least before the weather cools."

Eva counted in her head. She was six or seven months too early for her mission in El Copano with the Angel of Goliad. "And where am I?"

"Austin's Colony in the Mexican state of Tejas y Coahuila. That's the Brazos River," he said, pointing toward the distant line of trees.

Fingerlings of pain crept along Eva's scalp, and the more she concentrated, the deeper the pressure built behind her eyes. She couldn't think of anything clever or reasonable to explain how she ended up in that dry creek bed.

"I'm guessing by your questions you don't know how you came to be here."

She shook her head.

"But you remember your name."

She nodded.

"Do you have a family name?"

"No." Her old, forbidden last name fluttered to mind, then faded.

Jim sighed and ran his hand over his face and through his hair. One of his eyebrows swept upward. He rested his cheek in his hand, elbow on knee, and studied her. "I was surprised you spoke English," he said. "You're dressed more like a Tejano lady than an Anglo one."

Eva looked down at her embroidered skirts, stained and torn, and the small movement retightened the vise around her head. "I think I'm going to go back to bed," she said.

Jim opened his mouth to speak, but then only nodded and helped her to stand. When he stepped free from her, she swayed, and he caught her arm. For a moment, they stood frozen, and she was struck by the strangeness of depending on a Fated one who could choose no action for himself.

"Where have you been sleeping?" she asked. "I've obviously taken your bed."

"I sleep outside in the arbor this time of year. It's too hot in there."

You could say that again, she thought.

As if summoned, Wokweesi materialized from under the cabin and led the way.

"He's been taking care of me."

Jim chuckled. "You're just an excuse for him to lay about all day." As he eased her down onto the bed, Wokweesi hopped up behind her, edging into the center. "Move, kaayʉkwitʉ." Jim pushed the dog to make space. "He's the one who found you, you know," he said, scratching behind the dog's ears. "I imagine he thinks you're the best prize he's ever brought home."

Eva smiled and wrapped her arm around Wokweesi, almost laughing at the irony. Neither of them could have ideas of their own. Her own thoughts turned to the Elders and what they would have to say about the cascading changes she must be making to this timeline, like a branching domino track she bumped with an elbow and now couldn't stop. As the compounding threats multiplied in her mind, fear crept into her heart. She couldn't stay here long.

Chapter 2

Jim

Nʉmʉnʉʉ Sookobitʉ (Comanchería), 1832

P asahòo chuckled at his nephew, Tʉe Kahuu, who jumped in place next to his father, arms outstretched, wanting to be held in the crook of his father's elbow like his baby sibling.

Deep in conversation with one of his wives, mother to Tʉe Kahuu, Pasahòo's brother placed a reassuring hand on the top of his oldest son's head. Though the boy calmed for a moment, he returned to jostling against his father with more insistence.

"Come here," Pasahòo said, opening his hands, and Tʉe Kahuu bounded to him, grinning wide enough to show every baby tooth in his mouth.

Once in his uncle's arms, Tʉe Kahuu slapped him on the cheek.

"*Yehh*, what was that for?" Pasahòo plastered a stern expression on his face, but his eyes glittered when his nephew snickered in answer.

Tʉe Kahuu lifted his hand to give another playful slap, but Pasahòo caught his nephew's small wrist.

When Pasahòo had been a very young child, as young as Tᴜe Kahuu, and before he had been adopted by the People, his blood father would have spanked him for such behavior. Over the years, Pasahòo had learned one should never hit a child, and so instead, he pretended to eat each finger, one after another, and back again, as Tᴜe Kahuu squealed and tried to escape. Pasahòo started to set him down, but the boy tightened his grip around his uncle's neck.

"Shoulders?" Pasahòo asked. Tᴜe Kahuu bucked against his uncle, nodding in silent assent. After he hoisted his nephew over his head to straddle his neck, he grasped the boys' ankles and stepped toward his brother's youngest wife to say farewell.

"May you bring back many horses," she said.

Pasahòo smiled down at her lovely round face, then pressed his forehead against hers.

"Yes, and a new kettle," his brother's chief wife said. "There's a thin spot in the bottom of ours. It'll be a hole soon."

"I'll see what I can do," Pasahòo said, embracing her in turn. "I will trade for one with the Comancheros if I have the opportunity." Depending on his success, it might be worthwhile to visit the New Mexican traders for many things besides a cooking pot before heading home.

"And make sure you don't forget to leave my son behind."

Tᴜe Kahuu squirmed against the back of Pasahòo's head. "I'm going, too."

"Not this time," Pasahòo said, "but when you're big enough, I will take you on your first raid."

At this news, his nephew deflated, curling over his uncle's head and laying his hands across Pasahòo's eyes.

"Don't worry. I won't leave until after the dance tonight. Until then, you can stay with me."

Tнe Kahuu sat straighter, and Pasahòo pulled at the little boy's hands.

"I do need to see, though."

"Good hunting," his brother said, hugging him with his free arm.

"You should be going with me to Mexico."

His brother shrugged. "I'm content to raid closer to home this summer."

As if to confirm his words, a cooling breeze swirled into the kahni. His brother's wives had pulled the buffalo skin sides up from the ground earlier that morning.

"Regardless," Pasahòo said, "you will be missed."

"I'll have a food pouch ready for you this evening," his brother's chief wife said.

With Tнe Kahuu still astride, bouncing his heels, Pasahòo nodded his thanks and turned toward the door. When they reached the opening, he realized his mistake. "Son, scrunch down like the Little Mouse you are so we can fit through the door."

His nephew collapsed against him with all his tiny might, squeezing his uncle's head to make himself as small as possible.

"Perfect," Pasahòo said and crouched to exit.

Outside, the midday heat met him. The late spring sun always lightened his chestnut hair and darkened his pink skin, but he hardly noticed.

"Where are we going?" asked Tʉe Kahuu.

"To say goodbye to Hʉwʉni."

"Yehh," his nephew said in a credible mimic of the word only men used.

"What? Don't you like Hʉwʉni?"

"She's a girl."

"Your mothers are girls. What do you think of them?"

Pasahòo could feel his nephew pondering. Eventually, Tʉe Kahuu said, "They're not girls."

"Ah, you're right. You have me there, Son. They're women, not girls, but both kinds are good to be friends with."

Tʉe Kahuu huffed, unconvinced.

As they wound their way through the village, they came to his adoptive father's lodges. "Let's say farewell to your grandfather and grandmothers first."

Rather than responding, Tʉe Kahuu wiggled to be let down and ran off in search of grandmotherly hugs and treats. Nearby, Pasahòo's father sat beneath the shade of a burr oak, straightening shafts for arrows, and Pasahòo approached him with a confident stride.

"You have everything ready?" his father asked by way of greeting.

"Yes."

"Good. You will do well this season, just as you have since I took you on your first raid."

Pasahòo glowed under the praise, his chest swelling. There was no man he admired more than his father, who was a renowned warrior in his own right, and now, as a respected elder, had earned the trust of the People to serve as one of the peace chiefs. His war deeds and strength of character were unparalleled in Pasahòo's mind. Thoughtful and reserved, his father rarely dispensed unnecessary words. To hear the older warrior's confidence in him spoken aloud surpassed the entire village cheering his return.

With a nod, Pasahòo bent to grasp his father's forearm and touch foreheads. He noted that his father's spirit seemed lighter than it had in a year, ever since his sister had been raped and murdered by an Anglo who had strayed into their territory. Pasahòo and his brothers had avenged their sweet sister's death, taking many Anglo scalps. Even now, he had a hard time thinking about her, remembering her laugh and the silly pranks she pulled on him when they were younger. Just the day before the attack, she had agreed to marry the man she loved, and then she was gone. Her passing left a hole in Pasahòo's heart, and he missed her still. Fresh rage and grief rose within him but withdrew again like a snail into its shell just as quickly. By the time he straightened, he had reburied his pain.

After a brief word with each of his mothers, he made his way, finally, toward Huwuni's kahni. She noticed him approaching and stood from the hide she was scraping to wash her hands. Pasahòo grinned, her beauty taking his breath away.

"I wish you were staying here this summer," Huwuni said.

It pleased him to the tips of his toes that she would miss him while he was gone. "When I return, I'll have enough horses to make a gift to your parents worthy of you."

Huwuni's eyes sparked with a mischievous flash. "Unless Tatua has more success."

Pasahòo darted his hands to her waist in a rough tickle. "Don't even think about him. You wouldn't want to be his woman. He snores."

Huwuni pulled him nearer and wrapped her arms around his neck. "I prefer you, Pasahòo."

"I don't know that I believe you," he said, nuzzling her neck. "I'm just glad Tatua will be with me and not back here with you. Why would you want me anyway?"

She giggled, lifting her shoulder to her ear to protect against his kisses. "Well, for one thing, you're very handsome. For another, your list of war deeds is long." She dodged away when he tried to move to her other side. "I know you would take care of our children and protect me."

"And?"

"Did I already say you're very handsome?"

"Yes, but you can say it again." Tingling shivers spread through his body to hear her regard for him. When he had been just a captive boy, he'd never dreamed he'd win the heart of a high-status woman like Huwuni. But the respect he had earned within the band hadn't been by luck. From the moment his father had adopted him, he had vowed to be the bravest and strongest Numu warrior he could be. His collection of horses numbered in the hundreds, and marrying Huwuni would only increase his status.

"You're very handsome," she whispered in his ear.

"You could come to Mexico with us," he whispered back. "You're a better shot than me sometimes, but don't tell anyone I said so."

Huwuni laughed and then raised her voice. "Pasahòo says I'm —"

He clapped a hand over her mouth and growled low in his throat, placing his forehead against hers. "I think I will just kidnap you."

At his serious tone, her demeanor shifted. "I wish I could. My mother is not improving, and I fear she won't last the summer. I can't leave her."

"I know, but that doesn't mean I don't wish I could just steal you away."

"This fall, we will be together, and nothing will separate me from you then."

That night, the dancing to send the warriors off lasted longer than any dance in recent memory. Pasahòo plopped next to Kuhtu, a man as close to his heart as a brother, hiding from the whip wielders who spurred the dancers as needed. Huwuni, his partner for the night, landed next to him, rattle in hand. Her chest rose and fell in deep heaves, but then she placed her hand on Pasahòo's arm and said, "This is my favorite song."

At her encouragement, Pasahòo joined his chanting voice with the other men's, his gaze fixing on hers.

Going away tonight;
Be gone a long time.

While I'm gone,
I'll be thinking of you.

Huwuni snuggled closer, and Pasahòo encircled his arm around her. Excitement warred with impending loneliness, clenching his heart.

"I'll miss you," he said into her ear. "I'll be thinking only of you." It took all his restraint not to be unseemly and flaunt his affection for her.

Kuhtu cleared his throat. "Good hunting, Haitsi. I regret I won't be by your side where I belong," he said, looking down at his broken and splinted leg.

"I raid for both of us. What I win will be yours, too," Pasahòo said. "You may have first pick of the new horses when I return."

With a swift puff through his mouth, Kuhtu expressed his impatience with that plan, but Pasahòo pushed forward.

"Your injury saved my life."

"Of course, I saved your life, just like you've saved mine other times. You are my true friend, my haitsi."

"Then you shouldn't have a problem sharing in my bounty. Maybe I will bring you back a woman."

Kuhtu smirked. "Bring a pretty one, not a smelly, old one like that woman from the Anglo farm with all the pigs."

At the reminder, Pasahòo wrinkled his nose but then rolled a shoulder. "How am I to know what you will find pretty? I make no guarantees."

Kuhtu whipped his arm around his true friend's neck, trapping Pasahòo in a headlock. "You know perfectly well what I like."

Laughing, Pasahòo wrestled him to his back and worked his way out of Kuhtu's hold, a feat only managed because his friend's injury gave him an unfair advantage. "If you're not careful, I'll find you in the Old Men's Smoke Lodge when I come back."

"Not likely. I'll be healed and raiding the Anglos before you return. I'm quite certain you will be asking horses of me."

Pasahòo clasped Kuhtu, concealing his disquiet at having to leave his staunchest ally behind. The other warriors would be slipping away soon to form the traveling party. Pasahòo would join Tatua, two visiting Wichita men, and another warrior from the Nᵾmᵾnᵾᵾ village along with his woman. Though their party was small, Tatua had told him they would be joining forces with warriors from other bands once they reached Mexico.

With one last caress, he bid Hᵾwᵾni farewell. "I will return. I promise. And we will be married in the fall."

Hᵾwᵾni smiled at him, the firelight glowing against her cheek and painting the lightest strands of her black hair a dark gold. "I know you will."

The war party traveled in the coolest parts of the day, changing horses frequently to keep a good pace. Pasahòo had been pleased to be invited by Tatua on this expedition. They had been close friends as boys, but a rivalry had developed over the years.

As he thought back, Pasahòo couldn't put his finger on the moment things had changed between them; he just knew they had. Where Tatua had been warm, often now, he was cold and dismissive, arrogant beyond even the most expected behavior of a true Nʉmʉ warrior.

That Pasahòo had ever allowed such a relationship to deteriorate in the first place unsettled him, and he had spent many hours replaying old interactions. In none could he find where he had been at fault. Over time, he'd decided to act as if they were friends and stop worrying about it. Not being real friends didn't preclude them from being loyal brothers-in-arms.

So Tatua's invitation to join him for a summer campaign in Mexico surprised him but also gave him hope. Pasahòo remembered their boyhood days with fondness and welcomed a return to mutual friendship.

The only thing that bothered him was how Tatua circled Hʉwʉni when he thought Pasahòo wasn't around. No, that wasn't true. He had also bristled when Tatua had introduced him to the Wichita men as a Nʉmʉnaitʉ, a man living as a Comanche, rather than just as Pasahòo, a fellow Nʉmʉ warrior. The qualification irked him more than he wanted to admit.

But he reminded himself that for his father and his brothers, he was as Nʉmʉ as they were, no extra words needed. That's what mattered. In fact, he felt so completely Nʉmʉ that he struggled to remember his original Anglo name before he had joined the People, the Lords of the South Plains, a population more powerful than any people this land had ever seen, including Anglos.

Eventually, he brought the syllables to mind. His Anglo father had called him James McCullough, but his mother had called him Jim. He mouthed the words, rolling the foreign sounds around his mouth like pebbles, then spitting them out. He had no connection to that soft boy from a soft people, let alone his Anglo father. Pasahòo's Nʉmʉ father had been the one to raise him, to show him kindness and what it meant to be a man.

On they rode, day after day, skirting wide of Anglo and Tejano settlements. At first, Pasahòo tried to chat with the other men, but as the trip ground on, their lukewarm responses and eventual dead silences unnerved him. By the fourth day, he regretted agreeing to this venture. His familiar anxiety of not measuring up threaded through his sinew, tightening him like a bowstring.

Only ridicule waited for him at home if he turned back early from the warpath. Enduring the village's mockery would be intolerable; therefore, he had no choice but to continue. He had experienced worse. Years ago, he had survived being a slave, and look at him now: a free man and a valuable Nʉmʉ warrior. But his desire to renew a friendship with Tatua had dissolved into numb disregard before regrowing as active disdain.

As they approached San Antonio the next day, Tatua called a premature stop for the night to make camp. Pasahòo tamped down his irritation at prolonging their journey more hours than necessary.

He'd rather push on, not to mention put more distance between themselves and the most extensive enemy settlement bordering their territory. Really, it made no sense.

He unsaddled his traveling mount and checked on his prized war pony, one of the largest stallions in the band. With significant effort, his father had helped him catch the wild horse and train it over many months. When Pasahòo stroked the velvety neck, he sent gratitude to the great warrior.

Around him, the other men busied themselves with starting a small fire and searching for water. Another reason this was a bad place to camp. They all knew there were no springs nearby. Pasahòo puzzled over Tatua's stupidity. What a terrible raid leader he was turning out to be. If he wasn't careful, he'd get them all killed.

With that thought, Pasahòo decided he'd rather travel alone. He no longer had faith in Tatua, and in such a case, he could split ways with the man at any time without any loss of respect from the People. He just couldn't go home.

Unwilling to wait another moment, he picked up his saddle but turned when he heard multiple footsteps crunching over the scrubby grass. Each man wore an enemy's face, emotionless and hard. Instinct kicked in, and he dropped his saddle, breaking into a run for his war pony to make a desperate barebacked escape. Within several strides, someone tackled him from behind. He succeeded in rolling his assailant, but before he could get away, Tatua reached them, raising the blunt end of his tomahawk above his head. Pasahòo tried to duck the downward blow, and though his brain registered the strike, he knew no more.

Chapter 3

Eva

Jim's Farm, 1835

Eva stared up through the canopy of a majestic pecan tree, listening to the wind playing through the leaves. Green husks of ripening pecans studded the branches. She hadn't the strength for much more than turning her head. When she closed her eyes, dappled light skittered across her face, cool, blistering hot, and cool again. She had never liked Texas summers, but then again, she had never had a gigantic pecan tree to spend the day under. Nearby, Wokweesi hunted lizards under the stack of firewood, his great snuffling head knocking the split wood loose from its arrangement. Jim shouted something unintelligible at him, and her gaze lazily followed the dog as he took off at a reluctant trot.

From her vantage point, she scanned the homestead. A broken plow lay next to the barn with a gouge in its timbers, showing fresh golden wood grain beneath the weathered remains. Weeds sprouted taller than the picket fence, enclosing what she assumed was a kitchen garden. Slats hung loose or were missing entirely. In contrast, the smokehouse door looked freshly repaired and lined true, and a sturdy brush arbor stood neat and new, many of the leaves still green. Chickens wandered the yard. A solitary ox chewed cud in his pen. She shook her head, lost in dismayed thought at the scene, a far cry from the rows of military tents she should be standing amidst.

On impulse, she lifted her arms to stretch and felt the trunk behind her. She tried again to focus on closing her particle strings into loops, but an empty, silent dullness continued in place of her sixth sense. The more she pushed herself, the deeper the nail points forming at her temples dug. When her vision blurred, she gave up. Her chest tightened at the thought of being stuck here, waiting for Tophe. There was nowhere safer to go; it was all too soon.

Before she could snowball further, she closed her eyes. Patience. Time. Blending in. They were her only escape. The Fated, like Jim, could kill her easily; they just wouldn't know they had done so, insentient beings as they were.

As if summoned, Jim appeared on horseback in the distant pasture with Wokweesi loping ahead, and she watched, thankful for the distraction, as he galloped the horse, then stopped before kicking its flanks again. Right turns. Left turns. Run. Trot. Whoa. After a while, she bored of the repetitiveness, and even Wokweesi wandered back to her side. He panted a cheerful grin at her before plopping in the powdery dirt and stretching out full-length in the sun.

Within moments, a shrill whistle floated toward them from the training field. Wokweesi raised his head to peer over his shoulder with a grunt. When hoofbeats approached the pecan tree, the dog hopped to his feet. "You're in trouble now," Eva said, mouth twitching in amusement.

Jim leapt lightly to the ground. Next to him, his horse sidestepped, sweat matting its dingy white breast and chest. Around its lower jaw, Jim had tied a lead rope rather than using a halter.

"Your horse responds well without a bridle or reins," she said.

"She's learning." He loosened the belly strap. When it slapped the dirt, he removed the light saddle, placed it on the fence rail, and turned his horse loose in her corral.

"Better than your dog."

Jim quirked an eyebrow. "Wokweesi usually knows best. It was time for a break."

Eva's brow wrinkled. "You don't mind that he didn't obey you?"

"Why would I?"

"Because men…" of this time period, she started to say but caught herself, "because men like to be obeyed."

"I expect that from my horse, but not him." After a moment, he revised. "Well, I would expect it from any other dog but him," he said, gesturing at the sun-toasting hound. As if on cue, Wokweesi rolled to brown his other side. "He usually obeys me unless he wants a nap."

"I noticed you live alone," she said. "I mean, except for Wokweesi."

"Yes'm." Jim joined her against the tree. "The fellow I was partnering with died of lockjaw about six months ago. In the early spring. The fellow before him on this land had died about two years before that. Got kicked in the forehead by his horse."

Eva gasped and turned her head toward him.

"The mare popped him with her front hoof while he was shoeing her, and he was deader than a doornail. So they told me."

"Without any warning?"

"He probably didn't pay attention to her warnings."

Eva ran the mental image through her mind and warily eyed the horse. "What are the signs?"

"Well, pinned back ears... swishing tail..."

The horse swished her tail to remove a fly. "Like that?"

"No, more agitated like... Like mad swishing. They'll stomp around sometimes. You really want to watch for a cocked hind leg." Jim glanced at Eva's worried face. "Are you nervous around horses?"

"Wasn't until now."

He laughed. "I call her Nɨena. Means wind." As he spoke, he re-rolled the loosened sleeves of his shirt. "She's even-tempered. Takes a lot to make her mad. She mostly just wants to eat."

Eva thought through the several languages she knew. "I'm not familiar with the word Nɨena. What lang—?"

"Nɨmɨ tekwapɨ. Anglos call it Comanche."

"But you're not Comanche," she said, tilting her head and looking at him with fresh eyes. His chestnut hair hung below his chin, longer than customary, but he wore cloth pants and a vest. Moccasins covered his feet, though that was not unusual for a frontiersman.

Jim colored slightly but didn't respond. He plucked a blade of grass and split it along its veins into tiny threads.

Odd, she thought. This was the longest, unscripted conversation she'd had with one of the Fated in nearly ten years. She didn't know if she should care that he seemed uncomfortable or ignore it. Either way, it didn't matter. He wasn't conscious, not like her. He had no true feelings for her to hurt. Still, she chose a safer question, "What does Wokweesi mean?"

Jim tipped his head at the sleeping dog. "Cactus. His full name, Muubiwokweesi, means Nose Full of Cactus or Cactusnose. He can't resist a lizard or a mouse, no matter where it goes." Jim held the shreds of grass up in his open hand and let the wind take them.

"Does he also chase skunks?"

"Mmm," he nodded. "Mortal enemies." Jim rubbed the back of his neck. "Speaking of skunks." He peeked at her out of the side of his eye, uncomfortable again. "I don't know how to say this delicately."

"I smell."

"Yes!" he said, a little too loudly. "I mean, yes, ma'am." One corner of his mouth lifted. "Do you feel like you could make it as far as the river today? We could take a swim."

In answer, Eva nodded and slid her back up the tree. Sparks swam in her periphery. When she closed her eyes to wait for her double vision to resettle, Jim scrunched his eyebrows and looked her over, head to toe.

"I'll be fine," she said. "Just give me a minute."

With a last uncertain glance, Jim stepped toward the cabin to retrieve what they would need.

Spanish moss festooned three enormous cypress trees on a thin spit jutting out into the river. Pine and sycamore lined the burnt orange, sandy banks, and Eva followed Jim to the edge.

"You can bathe here, and I'll be on the other side," he said. "If you have any trouble, just holler for me." He handed her a pair of his pants and a spare shirt, along with a cloth for drying.

She nodded her thanks and laid his clothing on a thick tree root above the damp loam. Since he was nothing more than a pre-programmed reflection, Eva didn't care if they bathed together, but his cultural script expected her to want to preserve her modesty. She didn't even really care if he thought she smelled, but nothing sounded better at that moment than being clean again.

The muscles in her legs twitched from exertion, and she sat for a moment to slow her breathing. She balled up the worry over her weakened state before it could expand and tossed it in the river. There was no reason she wouldn't regain her strength in time to complete her mission in El Copano six months from now.

She had never washed clothes by hand before and suspected that rinsing them out and banging them against the rocks would not be sufficient, but it would have to do. Even with laundry soap, she couldn't have managed more. She removed her boots and her stockings and set them on the bank.

When she had wrung out the last piece, she paused to recuperate, arranged the clothes on bushes to dry in the sun, then tiptoed over the sharp gravel to the edge of the bank. Using the old tree's roots, she stepped carefully into the river. The slimy mud squished up between her toes, and a swarm of minnows darted out of her way. As an afterthought, she reached back to the root and focused on her quantum string snippets, the smallest bits of vibrating energy that made up every single particle in the tree and herself, then frowned at the stubborn silence in her body. She shouldn't have even bothered. She just needed to accept she was too injured to travel.

Silt bloomed around her as she waded farther and farther toward the middle. Startled, sunning turtles dropped into the water from their logs. For a moment, she spread her arms and floated on her back, face in the sun, dunking her head, happy to be cool for the first time in… days? had it been a week? more? She sighed with contentment, every exhausted muscle relaxing, and the throbbing in her head subsided. She'd give anything for an inner tube and a nap.

From the corner of her eye, she noticed a black vine drop from a tree on the opposite bank. Before her mind even registered the snake gliding toward her, she screamed. Eva windmilled her arms behind her to swim to the bank, afraid to turn her back on the water moccasin. The surface rippled as it skimmed across the river, and her hands scrabbled against the river bottom, groping for anything to use. She kicked wildly with her feet, but the reptile flew across the water, undeterred. Adrenaline coursed through her, but her sight tunneled, increasing her panic.

She couldn't see, she couldn't see, she couldn't see.

Eva pitched a rock the size of a baseball, but missed, displacing a fountain of water a foot into the air. With the snake less than a yard away, she found another stone and threw it with all her might, hitting it squarely on the head.

Eva scrambled the rest of the way out of the river, stumbling over the roots. Jim stood panting at the edge, a stick in hand, mouth gaping.

"Did you see that?" she asked as Jim shouted, "Tsaatu!" Eva could hear the admiration in his voice, and they stared at each other in speechless shock. Wokweesi emerged, shook himself, and dropped the carcass between them.

"I can't believe you hit that," Jim said.

Eva shrugged, and a wave of nausea threatened. She might have missed. She couldn't believe she might have missed. Suddenly, she wasn't just worried about her predicament, she was scared. "I can't believe I hit it either." Her lungs pumped double-time.

First to realize they were both naked, Jim pivoted in place. "Apologies, ma'am."

Eva watched in fascination as a blush spread, further darkening his broad upper back and neck. A decorative tattoo outlined an old scar on his side; she had seen similarly marked scars across his chest.

"I didn't think… I know Anglo women care about…" His words trailed off. He noticed the clothing he had loaned her near his feet, scooped them up, and threaded his legs through the pants.

"Jim, please, I think shyness could have been deadly." Suddenly, tears welled, blurring her vision. Surprised by her reaction, she sniffed and dashed them away, but he heard her and turned back to look.

He grabbed a cloth for drying and draped it around her shoulders. When he crouched beside her, he stared into her eyes, concern peering back at her.

"Sorry, I don't mean to cry." As she suppressed her emotions, her head throbbed anew. She glanced up into his face. "I'm fine, really." She shivered theatrically. "See, all better."

Jim cradled her cheeks and brushed his thumbs under her eyes. Strangely, his touch calmed her. Her heart slowed as he continued to hold her face. Her hands and knees shook from the adrenaline, but she hardly noticed, completely drawn in by his attention, not wanting the connection to end.

"Hello the house!" A faint voice echoed across the field to them.

Jim spun in the barn's direction. In the distance, a tiny Wokweesi greeted the approaching figure. Eva had been so absorbed she hadn't noticed the dog leave. Jim grinned, shouted a hello, and caught up the snake's death-curled body before rounding the peninsula to retrieve his high-cuffed moccasins.

After a minute, he returned and tossed the loaner pants back to Eva, and his gaze turned toward the visitor. Jim remained shirtless but now wore buckskin leggings and a breechcloth. As he jogged away, the muscles in his back and the swinging fringe and tassels mesmerized her. Slowly, her senses returned, and she shook her head to break the unwelcome spell.

Chapter 4

Eva

When Eva returned to the house, Jim and the newcomer were in the barn unhitching the team from a heavily laden and tarped buckboard. She slipped into the shadowed space just as the men led the horses out to Nʉena's paddock.

"And who do we have here?" the man asked. He removed a sweat-stained hat from his balding scalp.

Jim introduced Eva and recounted the adventure of Wokweesi's discovery and the difficult time he had in dragging her home.

"And you are?" she asked, lifting her chin.

"Ah, apologies, ma'am!" Jim coughed. "This is Pumphrey Brunet. Pump for short."

"How'd you do?" Pump said, bowing over his hat and showing the top of his shiny head.

"Pump's been a good friend to me these last couple years," Jim said, reaching up to clap the man on his thin shoulder. "He's also a trader in these parts. He'll earn his supper by telling us the news."

Pump winked at her.

elle

Jim fed the small fire that had kept a black-eyed pea and venison stew simmering most of the day in the outdoor kitchen. Eva watched the muscles in his arm knot as he stirred up the coals. An off-hand comment from him earlier in the week made her realize he had kept a hearth fire going in the cabin for the sake of her health. Given the heat, she felt lucky to have survived his efforts to ward off fever.

"You're a quiet little thing, aren't you?" Pump asked. His words called Eva back, and she shrugged. Tophe would disagree with you, she thought, and her partner's face rose in her mind, causing anxiety over their separation to twist her stomach into knots all over again. Though she had no other choice, every interaction with Jim, and now Pump, had the potential to create major, unknown changes to this timeline's future. The punishment she and Tophe would face when they returned — she touched that thought with icy self-discipline to freeze it in place, unwilling to let her imagination take her any further.

"Don't let him fool you, Eva. He prefers a… what's the word… racked audience."

"Rapt," Pump said.

"Rapt audience," Jim repeated. "He's usually the one doing all the talking."

Pump's smile widened. "I'm not sure I'm the one who had her attention."

Eva frowned. Her rescuer had been nothing but a gentleman, but that could shift in a heartbeat, and the last thing she wanted was to give either of these men the wrong signals. Without anywhere to go until March, she needed Jim's goodwill, but not his interest. Such a thing would only worsen her fate with the Elders. She nearly stood, her legs itching to move, to run away, but she forced every muscle to relax, the picture of half-bored innocence. A woman waiting patiently for her dinner. Nothing more.

Jim had his back to them, deaf to Pump's last comment, blowing on the molten stew. When Pump gave her a warm, fatherly smile, she thawed a little, despite her reservations. He reminded her of a favorite elderly neighbor she had once had long ago, long before she had left her family for Lux Libera.

"I see your cotton's coming along nicely, if a little neglected," he said, turning to Jim.

Jim groaned as he mixed up cornmeal batter. "You can talk of anything but that."

"Let's get this out of the way," the older man said. "I think you're gonna need help getting that crop in. I already inquired at the McMullen's. All you have to do is ask."

"You know how I feel about the Anglos' slaves," Jim said.

"You can compensate the slaves along with the owner."

"If slaves show up here, I'll supply them and point them to Mexico or the Saltwater Tribes."

"And if you do that, your neighbors'll burn you to the ground. And then hang you," Pump said, his voice rising. "And I don't doubt they'd scalp you while they're at it just to make a point."

Jim glowered at the coals. A stony, uncomfortable silence fell over the group as he scattered ashes on a flat rock, then ladled out the batter. Eva's mouth watered. She was only half-listening, suddenly hungrier than she had been in days.

"I'm sorry, boy," Pump said. "I worry about you losing your holding this year with your partner gone. Even though you feel Comanche, you have the blood of plantation owners in you."

"Nʉmʉ, not Comanche."

"Yes, yes."

Emotion drained from Jim's features, leaving them blank. Pump pursed his lips. It seemed to be an old argument.

"I only got a few acres planted before the plow broke. I'll be able to get it in on my own," Jim said. "I can catch wild beef cows for the rest of the dues." He flipped the ash cakes. "Tell us the news of the world."

Pump sighed in defeat and stroked one of Wokweesi's silky brown ears. "I only want what's best for you."

Jim nodded, jaw tight.

Pump composed himself for a moment and shifted in his seat. He drew a breath, ready to recite.

"Why do you feel Nʉmʉ?" Eva asked, giving voice to an unformed, niggling thought.

Pump clapped his mouth shut and tucked his chin, but Jim's demeanor softened. Before he could answer, Pump said, "He lived with them from the time he was eleven until three years ago." He looked at Jim and then back at her. "He was captured with two of his sisters when his family took a wrong turn on their way to Austin's Colony."

Jim bowed his head and gestured toward the older man, yielding the floor.

As Eva connected this conversation with their earlier one on the porch, the ground shifted beneath her feet. She recalibrated. "I didn't think the Comanches… sorry, the Nʉmʉ took captives." *This early*, she wanted to add but stopped herself. It was at least a decade earlier than the Parker Massacre set to take place this coming May in other similar timelines. She would have expected them to prefer raiding Mexico instead. If the Anglos had been enduring attacks all this time, then Parker's Fort would probably be better defended, and Cynthia Ann wouldn't be taken. Eva's thoughts arced from cause to effect with lightning speed. Did it matter? Maybe not. Still, it was unsettling to discover her intel skewed. Every new detail she heard from this moment on might be important. What else had they gotten wrong? Damn scouts.

"The word is Nʉmʉnʉʉ when you intend more than one person," Jim said. "It just means 'people.' Human beings. But to answer your question, my people have taken esitoyanʉʉ, er… Mexican captives, as slaves since the Spanish conquered the peoples there and made them weak. They are never armed; they're not allowed to have weapons," he said. "But I was one of the first Anglos. Pump helped me when I returned to San Antonio. Secured this place for me here," he said. He stared into the fire. "To 'recivilize' me."

"And your sisters? The rest of your family?"

"My parents and their slaves were killed in the attack. The youngest Negroes with us were captured and traded. My captor eventually separated my sisters and me. I don't know where they are now," he said.

"You haven't gone to search for them? To rescue them, too?"

"I wasn't rescued." Jim's face darkened. "If my adoptive father didn't have other sons, I would return to provide for him." He stabbed at the embers. Sparks popped. "My little sister was six. A woman who had lost her daughter adopted her. She became quite spoiled." He smiled to himself. "She forgot how to speak English. The Nʉmʉnʉʉ are her family now." Jim handed her a bowl of stew and an ash cake. "My older sister was given to a friend of her captor. The last I saw of her, her nose had been burned off by her mistress, and she was being sold to the Hʉpenʉʉ, the Timber People." Jim sat down with his own bowl. "She's most likely dead."

Eva didn't know what to say. He looked up at her. Concern must have shown on her face — or pity. She felt both, inexplicably.

Jim hastened to add, "I didn't know her well. She was much older than me." Dusk shadowed his granite form.

As Eva continued to stare, the fire crackled, filling the growing silence, and cicadas droned in the trees overhead. From the river, frogs joined the chorus.

Pump cleared his throat and clapped his hands. "Well… how about some news?" When neither of them responded, he proceeded. "Stephen Austin is back in the Colony," he said. "He was released from prison, and they say he's no longer trying to be a peacemaker. He's had it with Mexico. They never did give him a trial."

Jim raised both of his eyebrows. This appeared to be a surprise. "The Anglos are upset that Mexico outlawed slavery and won't keep extending the deadline that Anglos have to get rid of theirs, isn't that right?"

"Yes, but that's an overly simplistic way to look at what's goin' on right now," Pump said. "Has more to do with how much power we have here versus everything being mandated from Mexico City. And the constitution being abolished."

Jim snorted.

"And you need to start thinking of yourself as Anglo if you ever want to be fully accepted."

Jim gave no answer to that. They ate in silence for a moment, then Pump continued, "A Mexican soldier beat a man to death in Gonzales a couple weeks ago. No word on why. Add that to the tales coming up from the state of Zacatecas, where Santa Anna allowed his soldiers to loot the capital city, and people are getting stirred up. Thinking the soldiers are being given license to do as they please."

"What kind of tales?" Eva asked.

Under the kettle, a log snapped, eaten away by the hungry blaze, and Pump squirmed. "They're not for a lady's ears, ma'am."

Eva tamped down her irritation. "Okay," she said, slitting her eyes. The next moment, she cast them down, knowing better than to push, and instead, held out her hand to collect his bowl.

He gave her a speculative look and darted a glance at Jim.

Chapter 5

Jim

Jim stopped Eva from washing the dishes and sent her to bed. He had seen her rubbing her head when she probably thought he wasn't looking. The walk to and from the river, the scare in between, and Pump's arrival were more activities than she'd had in over a week. He would start expecting more of her soon, though.

"So, no idea where this girl came from?" Pump asked when he and Jim were alone. "Who her family is?" He blew a trail of smoke rings into the fire's corona.

"No. Every time I've asked, she's told me she can't remember and doesn't want to search." Jim stirred the coals. "She's asked to stay here for a while."

Pump puckered his lips, gaze distant. After several minutes, he asked, "Have you thought about marrying this girl? Seems you could bake two pies with one crust right there."

"How so?" Jim stretched his arms to their extent, then cupped his head and sat with his back against a log.

"Well, for starters, with that black hair and blue eyes, she's pretty enough to make a man plow through a field of stumps, and there aren't that many available women in the Colony. Furthermore, if you default on your land dues, the state *might* grant you an extension if you're married."

Jim tried, in that moment, to feel concerned about the land dues. The ten-year tax-free grant expired this year. He listened, but his heart echoed dull empty silence.

Pump continued without pause, "You haven't found another fellow or two to help you work the land, and I haven't gotten any indications you're planning to recruit. You've made it abundantly clear you're not willing to buy help. Married means you'll have a woman to help you in the fields, future children to spread the work. Sounds like she might appreciate a permanent home."

"It would be nice to have help with the chores. I'm hardly a man here." Jim extended his legs out beside Wokweesi. "But I don't need to marry her for that, no matter how long she stays."

Pump bristled. "Of course you have to marry her if she's going to stay here."

Without turning his attention, Jim twitched a shoulder. "I hope she will warm my bed soon, but she's free to go when she's well." He buried his forehead in the dog's scruff and waggled it to and fro. Wokweesi jumped into a play bow. "I'd rather find a way to get more horses. I've been thinking about catching a wild pony or two."

"Are you listening to me?"

"Yes." Jim calmed the dog.

"She can't warm your bed unless you marry her. She would be shunned by the women here."

Jim scowled. "I know Anglo women are different than Nʉmʉ women, and there are different rules, but it's confusing."

"Nonsense. Regardless, you have no people. You're lonely; you don't socialize."

"They don't trust me. The women hide their children from me. The men stare."

As if patiently displaying wares to an indecisive customer, Pump spread his hands. "You haven't exactly gone out of your way to earn their trust, and you needed to be working double hard since the day you first stepped foot here." Jim stared into the crackling embers, and Pump continued, "I've stood silent long enough, watching you these many months. Have you offered any neighborly aid? Have you made visits?"

Jim shook his head. Heat burned his cheeks, and not from the fire.

"Neighborliness is like money. You have to earn it in order to spend it. For instance, the farmer I left today, Mr. Allen, was building a new hog pen. Plenty of work for two men, and he only has little'uns. If you have time tomorrow, you could go over there and offer to help. Understand what I mean?"

"Well, how does marrying Eva help me with that?"

"If you have a woman here, that will set the men more easy about you. Their wives will want to visit her. Right now, they think you're a half-savage living alone, ignoring his crops, ignoring his repairs, ignoring his neighbors, wandering away from his farm for days, training his horse like a Comanche war pony. They talk. You scare them. What are you planning on doing? Raiding?"

Jim held his smile in check.

"There are rumors," Pump said. "I've been able to squash them, but tell me I'm not a liar."

In the flames, Jim saw Anglo houses alight, people screaming, manes flying. "You're not a liar," he said. At Pump's silence, Jim glanced up. He had paused too long. His friend gazed back at him, mouth pressed to a skeptical line. "My brother found me. His raiding party was in the area a month ago."

Immediately, Pump straightened, eyes like full moons. "How did they know you lived here?"

"They didn't. They were trying to make off with Nʉena when I shouted out to them. Pure luck that my brother was with them. They moved to an area farther south from here."

When Pump's skepticism turned to stiff, icy judgment, Jim threw up his hands. "I didn't go with them!"

"Good. The sooner you accept that you are Anglo, for once and for all, the easier your life will be. You aren't Coman — Nʉmʉ anymore. Never were, really. And people aren't going to accept you until you believe it yourself."

The night pressed in on Jim, and he stared at his feet outlined by the firelight. "People around here, they think they know what I've done. They're right to be afraid of who I was, but I had justification every time because of something an Anglo or an enemy did." For a moment, he sat astride his stallion once more, his brothers and true friend beside him. "But I'd be lying if I said I didn't miss my life with the Nʉmʉnʉʉ."

A long beat passed as Pump furrowed his brow, but Jim could tell he didn't want to engage in another deep discussion about the rightness or wrongness of blood feuds. Avoiding his gaze, he stared into the flickering coals. Jim's self-righteousness dissolved into a deep loneliness, a gaping hole that expanded at the thought of each person who loved him. His brave father, his loving mothers, his loyal brothers and their welcoming wives, their children — little ones he called "son" and "daughter" as if they were his own, and each of his friends. Snug nights in their kahnis. Exhilarating days on the plains. Hunts. Games. Laughter. For a moment, he crouched next to his boyhood friends as they prepared to pull a prank on the old men in their Smoke Lodge. He searched for the Anglo parts of himself, wishing to please Pump, but finding only scraps of memories, all of which felt as if they belonged to someone else, someone not of the People, some child who no longer existed. His thoughts turned to the never-ending list of farm chores.

"I'm having trouble seeing the benefits of all the toil I'm expected to do here," he said, looking at his lap. "I've given it a year. Like you wanted."

"Almost. Almost a year. A wife could change things for the better. Think on it. That's all I ask."

At a memory, Jim jerked to meet his mentor's gaze. "And, to your other point, I haven't neglected things. I built the arbor." Like any sane Nʉmʉ. He left that part unsaid. Anglos didn't build arbors like the Nʉmʉnʉʉ. They built sweltering cabins and contented themselves with a patch of dirt as if there wasn't a whole world to inhabit. "And I repaired the smokehouse."

With the barely audible sound of a tongue being bitten, Pump lowered his chin to peer directly at him over his spectacles, then opened his arms wide, taking in the entire homestead.

Jim looked away.

Nʉmʉnʉʉ Sookobitʉ (Comanchería), 1821

Jim was too busy being terrified about falling off the galloping horse to be terrified of the Indian who held him in place across his lap. He tried to see where they were going, but all he could see were flying hooves. His older sister Mary screamed somewhere behind him, and he thought his little sister Anne had been taken, too. His captor gripped his father's scalp in his hand. Another Indian had his mother's. Others had the slaves'.

Sitting around the hearth back home in Tennessee, he'd heard many a hair-raising tale about wild Indians and what they would do to children. Some folks called them Cherokee or Chickasaw or other names he couldn't remember and had said they did no such thing, don't you believe a word of it, but most folks just called them all Indians and said absolutely they did do such things, don't you be a fool, boy. With a dig of calloused fingers into Jim's bony shoulder, they'd tousle his hair, adding, "And don't tell your mother I'm telling you such stories. She'd have my hide."

Since the moment they had loaded their household goods onto wagons, his mother had been worried about the Indians. Every morning, she'd asked about the Indians, had scanned the horizon for Indians all day, and at night when she thought he and his sisters couldn't hear, she had whispered in low tones about Indians. With bored grunts, his father had mumbled for her not to worry. All these feelings flashed through his mind as one composite picture: his mother's stricken face. She had been right.

For a few miles, the raiding party rode at breakneck speed, but then the Indians seemed to feel it was safe to slow their pace. There was no one left to chase them.

Without warning, Jim's captor dropped him to the ground. His feet connected with the dirt, and his momentum drove him to his bottom, where he rolled onto his back. Somehow, he avoided hitting his head. As he looked at his scraped hands, his rear end screamed in protest. It had endured a whipping from his father just that morning.

Two little slave girls about Anne's age clung to each other with wide eyes. They had been deposited on a blanket with an Indian woman who was setting up camp. The next moment, Anne was added to the group. Jim stood and surveyed his surroundings. Another Indian rode up with Mary in front of him. She kicked and flailed. He discarded her, then leapt down. He grabbed her as she fixed to run and bound her hands and feet. When she yelled, he slapped her. The Indian knocked her legs out from under her and then left her struggling against her bonds and crying. Around them, the Indians made camp, chatting amongst themselves. In the center, the Indian woman pet the little girls and cooed in reassuring tones.

Though none of them were looking at him, he knew they were aware of his movements. Anne nodded to the kind woman, allowing a cautious smile to spread across her tear-stained cheeks, but Mary cast frenzied eyes about, each breath coming shorter than the last. After a glance around, he risked sitting beside her. She was older than him by five years, practically a woman in his mind, and he put his hand on her shoulder, wishing he was grown. Sensing her captor's eyes on him, he was careful not to touch her ties.

"Mary, calm down." Her agitation alarmed him, but he didn't know what to do about it. "It won't do any good to fight them," he whispered.

At first, she just gawked at him, each eye rimmed in white, her loosened hair wild around her face, but then she said, "We have to get away."

The warrior didn't like that she was talking and came back to gag her. With a forceful tug, he completed the knot, jerking her head forward, and the rawhide dug into her cheeks. Jim didn't dare loosen it.

For the moment, the raiders seemed most interested in the scalps they had taken. They spent the afternoon chanting, scraping, and sewing them onto small willow hoops. When they finished, they smoked them over the fire. After a while, the slow process numbed Jim to the horror of his parents' hair being turned into something he didn't recognize, and he crept to the blanket to sit next to Anne.

The Indian woman smiled at him when he arrived. She talked to him as if he could understand her and gave him water and a bar of a strange kind of food. He found the taste pleasant and wanted to eat the whole thing, but she indicated that he should share it with Anne and the other two girls. No one gave anything to Mary.

After the sun set, the Indians began to dance. They placed the scalps on their lances and sang. At various intervals, the woman laughed and cheered along with the men. Jim watched in fascination, wishing he could understand the stories they were telling.

Eventually, Mary's captor untied her feet, grabbed her up by the arm, and led her to the fire. He freed her hands, then tore off her clothes. He hit her when she fought him. The sight sent all thoughts flying from Jim's mind and rooted him in place. At the same time, the Indian woman covered the three little girls with a blanket, and she spoke to them in a muffled singsong tone. Jim wanted to hide under the blanket with his tiny sister, but a voice told him he shouldn't. Instead, he gaped, unable to look away.

Though he understood what the man did next, he didn't understand why. Mary screamed and screamed around her gag. When he was done, she was bleeding and crying, but she wasn't screaming anymore. Jim wanted to go to her, but he didn't know what he could do to help.

Without warning, his own captor strode toward him. Fear propelled him to his feet, and he stared down the Indian as he approached. Jim thought his arm would pull out of its socket when the man yanked him forward and half-carried, half-walked him to a tree where he tied him. Rawhide thongs cut into his wrists, and his shoulders strained. The man undid his pants, pulled them down, and walked back to the other warriors.

Jim sought Mary with his eyes, but she was oblivious to what was happening to him and writhed in a crumpled heap at the edge of the firelight. He didn't want to cry out and scare Anne. Another warrior unsheathed the knife at his belt and took aim at him, holding it overhead by the tip. Too startled to react, Jim froze, and his lungs stopped working. When the blade sunk into the trunk well above his head, he took a gasping breath. Within moments, his own captor copied his friend, the edge coming closer to Jim's scalp this time.

Jim told himself not to scream. He would not cry in front of these men. A third warrior ran roaring at him, battle-ax raised, and Jim roared back in return, his fear becoming a fierce thing beyond his control. The warrior grabbed his forelock and chopped through his hair, skimming the scalp. He held the sandy hair aloft for his friends before releasing it to the dark wind.

After his captor retrieved his knife from the tree with a jerk, he said something to his companion, who laughed and shrugged. The one who had spoken put his blade under Jim's most private place but didn't do more. Jim did his best to keep his eyes open and focused on the Indian watching him. They were eyeball to eyeball, and Jim couldn't understand a word of what he was saying, but the other men smirked and yelled encouragement.

His captor shouted over his shoulder, and another man brought a burning stick over to him. His tormentor took the firebrand and drew it slowly toward Jim's groin. To focus on something else, Jim bit his cheek, tasting blood. He hoped the man would stop short of actually hurting him as he had before.

When his captor tossed the stick back into the fire, a wave of relief washed over him. One of the other warriors untied him and pushed his head toward the woman's blankets. Under his feet, the ground floated, and he stumbled a step before the world righted again. Jim pulled his pants back up and went where he had been directed. The men paid him no more attention until they tied him to a tree for the night, foiling his plans to flee with his sisters to safety.

Chapter 6

Eva

Jim's Farm

The next morning, Eva woke to Pump telling Jim goodbye somewhere outside. Along with their dim voices, blue light filtered through the window, not yet truly dawn. She threw a blanket around herself, stuffed her feet into her boots without lacing, and ran to the cabin steps.

Jim sat astride Nuena, but he smiled when she appeared. Pump stood below at his stirrup, giving the younger man's thigh a farewell thump.

"Where are you headed?" she asked.

"Help a neighbor with a hog pen. Pump will be here with you." Nuena sidestepped, and Jim gave her bitless reins a sharp jerk. The horse froze. "Feel up to helping Pump with the animals?"

Eva nodded without thinking. Used to teamwork and following orders, her ready response hid the misgivings tightening her chest.

"Good. I may not be back until tomorrow."

With those words, Jim sucked his teeth and nudged his heels in Nuena's sides. She broke into a trot.

Wokweesi ran ahead of him, and Pump and Eva watched until he passed beyond the bend in the road. In the distance, a low mist hung over the adjoining pastures, the heavy atmosphere muffling the river. Rows of little droplets lined the tough blades of grass at her feet. The sun would burn it all away once it was up. Her thoughts drifted to the chores Jim expected her to know how to do.

"So, gal," Pump said, turning to Eva. "Which timeline are you from and when?"

Eva stared at Pump in abject shock, her mind reeling, completely blank. She could sense her face giving her away. "You're direct, aren't you?"

"The best way to get the truth!" Pump grinned, triumphant. "I knew it!" he said, slapping his thigh.

"How? What? Are you a Lux Libera?"

"Ah, now there's a name I haven't heard in years. Not a Lux Libera, no. I didn't complete the novitiate. But I can travel."

"How is that possible? Only Lux Libera can travel." The mist blew a lock of hair across her eyes. "It's our gift and calling." With her fingers, she combed the strands back, dragging them free from her damp eyelashes. "How did you not lose your ability?"

Pump's smile flattened, and he didn't reply at first. "As to how I recognized you, after years of traveling, you pick up on the signs when something isn't quite right. Your dark hair, for instance. Your blonde roots are beginning to show. Certain types of women here dye their hair, but the color isn't as natural, and your boots look factory-made."

Eva stroked her hair and examined her feet as they walked. More time must have elapsed than she realized. She had dyed it for this series of missions, but she was never around the Fated long enough for these little details to cause concern.

"I wasn't sure until you used the word 'okay' last night. Not in the lexicon here yet, I'm afraid. I used it myself with Jim once. Such a useful word. Impossible to get rid of once you learn it. English isn't really Jim's native language anymore, though he speaks it pretty good now, so that slip-up didn't matter."

Eva grimaced, wondering what other mistakes she had made. She knew better. "I guess it's safe to ask you… what day is today? Jim doesn't have a calendar."

Pump shut his eyes, calculating, then popped them open. "September 18th, a Friday. Go get dressed, and we'll start the chores."

Walking to the cabin allowed Eva time to think. If Pump could travel, it could only mean he was blessed like her. She sat for a second on the edge of Jim's bed and noticed her thighs shaking. This was no different than any other mission, she told herself. She just didn't have a script this time. What else could she do but what she always did: watch and wait, listen and follow. She rubbed her hands along the tops of her legs, then stood to dress. In truth, she had an ally now, someone who understood and could think and choose for himself. A real person. Honestly, could she be any luckier? Out of the whole multiverse? To land in the wrong place and run into another traveler?

When she came back, he studied her skirt for a moment, his eyes roaming to the cut of her Mexican-style blouse, and then nodded to himself. They walked to the well, and he lowered the bucket. After Eva took the handle from him, he filled a second before pausing and looking her directly in the eye. "I'll be honest with you. I supposed you were a whore on her way to San Felipe de Austin who had somehow come to harm. You stood unashamed in front of me yesterday in the clothes of a man you barely know. This situation you got here with Jim, it doesn't look good. Not for these people, for this time. Understand what I'm saying?"

Eva sighed. She had assumed that already and said so.

As Pump picked up his bucket, he smirked. "And I'm guessing you have no clue what the animals need?"

Eva laughed. "None." The rough rope cut into her hand when she hoisted the heavy bucket. "I'm usually mingling with high society."

"Is your timeline like this one?" Pump asked.

"My birth timeline, yes, more or less exactly — at least what I can recall of it. I left when I was twelve and never returned. I think there are only minor differences between my original timeline and this one. But from Axis Mundi, the True line, there are significant differences."

"And what year did you leave from?"

"From Axis Mundi: 1997." Water sloshed in the trough. After switching the empty bucket to her other hand, she peeked at her reddening palm. It stung. They returned to the well.

"You're obviously American. State?" Pump drew up another bucketful.

"Born in Texas."

"Makes sense to use you for missions here."

Heat crawled over her ears at his implication, and she set the bucket down with piqued emphasis. "I usually go on missions in North America and Europe, and I've been to ancient Rome and Greece several times."

Pump raised his brows and pursed his lips in a soft, genuine whistle. After a moment, he jerked his head for her to follow him.

"So, what happened here? How did you get injured? Been playing the role of the amnesiac, I take it."

"There was a guidance beacon leading here. I confused it for my actual target, the one our own scouts set. It was pitch dark, and I didn't see the cliff. Jim told you the rest." Eva glanced down at her splashed skirts, which now clung to her ankles.

Pump widened his eyes. "A beacon? Here?"

"Not yours?" Eva's mind stopped arranging the pieces she had thought were fitting together.

"No, not mine. Remember, I was never fully inducted as a Lux Libera. I left them." Pump pointed to the hay and grabbed up an armful. Eva copied him.

"Then how do you travel?"

"I choose randomly. I don't care where I go, though I skim along a line to catch a glimpse before I commit to entering. And you know, since we're tethered to our point of origin, we don't need a beacon to return home."

"But you seem to live *here*. Why?" She halted in place, itchy hay forgotten in her arms.

"This is home. My family is here, in this time."

"Plumbing? Electricity?"

Pump shrugged and tossed the hay for the ox. "What are creature comforts when you will never see your loved ones again?"

As she added her armful to the pile, Eva's heart twisted. He could have no idea his words pierced like an indictment. She hid her face.

"Have you been further than 1997?" he asked.

Startled, Eva shook her head, looking at him again. "No, of course not."

She seemed to confirm something for Pump, and he nodded. "Yes, well, there are some fascinating wonders past 1997."

Just the suggestion churned Eva's stomach. All Lux Libera avoided traveling forward. Repairing the world meant untangling the lines of the past. What was he if he was not working toward reuniting the one True line of Axis Mundi with its unholy splinters?

"Why haven't you left yet?" he asked.

Her reply froze on her tongue as she scanned his kind, open face. Eventually, unable to conceive of how he had the ability to travel if he was unworthy, much less dangerous, Eva pointed to her head. "I can't hear the strings since my injury. It's like I'm deaf. I can't retune the snippets into portals if I can't find them. I've debated staying until my original target time or returning home to the True line, but I'm not getting that choice at the moment. At least, not until I finish healing."

Pump locked her gaze with a vacant stare for a second, then nodded. "Ah, yes, I remember. Everyone has different words for things. It's been so long since I was in Lux Libera, I had forgotten."

Eva knitted her brows.

"Strings. Snippets. Your words for the smallest particles of our existence; that vibrating essence at the quantum level we manipulate," he said. "What do you travel through? I never made it that far in my training."

"Trees. Why? What do you travel through?"

"Nothing." Pump smiled serenely, savoring a secret behind his lips.

"Nothing? Like nothing–nothing?"

"Trees just help you focus. Some Lux Libera use water, though they don't call themselves Lux Libera. But you don't actually need anything. I'll show you how when you're better."

Now Eva's churning stomach plunged. "I've never heard of any others who can travel." She stood on the edge of a crevasse, terrified to look down. Only his straightforward demeanor held her anger and disbelief at bay.

"I imagine not," he said.

"Do you belong to one of these other groups?"

"No. I am a free man." Pump never dropped his eyes, but conflicted emotions flitted behind his pupils. She could see him rolling unspoken words around in his mouth like marbles. "What was your mission?" he asked.

Instantly wary, Eva hesitated to answer. It was surreal to be having this conversation with a man who claimed to be able to travel but was not Lux Libera. Such a person didn't exist. Shouldn't exist. She chose the tiniest sliver of information. "March next year."

"Ah, of course, the revolution," Pump said.

Without another word, he motioned for her to spread feed for the chickens, and then they peered into the coop together. When their arms brushed, Eva tensed.

Pump tsk'd in disapproval at the uncollected eggs. "Does Jim eat eggs? I thought Comanches ate eggs, too."

Eva wrinkled her nose. "I don't know. I haven't seen him eat any."

"Do you like eggs?"

"Love 'em."

"Well, here you go," Pump said. He gestured toward the full nests. "You should eat these. See if you can get Jim to eat any."

He reached for a dusty, neglected basket and started gathering eggs. With smooth efficiency, he turned and chucked the ones covered in waste and frowned at those that were a cracked, smelly mess. "Maybe get him interested in taking care of his chickens. If nothing else, he needs a rooster, so the eggs don't just rot. I'm amazed the critters haven't cleaned him out."

"I've seen him close the hens up at night," she said. The muscles in Eva's shoulders relaxed as Pump grumbled about Jim under his breath. There were too many unknowns here, and she was happy to avoid more questions for now.

"Well, at least he's been doing that," Pump said. "He's lucky this isn't a nest full of egg-stuffed snakes."

In just one day, the homestead looked better than Eva had seen. Pump showed her how to do all the daily chores and encouraged her to encourage Jim. She wasn't sure she wanted that responsibility. The man seemed cut out for another kind of life. When she said so, Pump turned serious.

"It's his only chance at a normal life, Eva, among his own people. He has to make a success of this. He has no other trade skills."

"He seems pretty handy," Eva said, thinking of the repairs she had seen about the place. The craftsmanship was meticulous.

"Yes, he has a natural talent when he uses it." Pump hammered a nail into a fence picket. Nearby, he had set Eva to work weeding the garden. She would periodically ask him what was weed and what was keep. Destroying plants was well within her comfort zone. Her life's purpose didn't leave time for hobbies, and she imagined she had a black thumb.

"Would that count as a trade skill, his handiness?" Eva asked.

After a quick puff through his cheeks, Pump lifted his hat and wiped his sweaty head with a handkerchief, hammer still in hand. "I suppose so. Part of his problem would be getting people to trust him enough to give him work. He'd probably need to apprentice with someone, but he's a bit old for that.

Not impossible, though. Or set up a shop of some sort in San Felipe. He'd need funds… Could work as a freighter…." Eva had sent him off on a trail of potential lives for Jim.

"Why do you care so much about what happens to him?" she asked. "He's not real anyway."

"Hmm? Oh…" Pump placed his hat back on his head and returned his attention to her. "That's a bitter tale to tell."

As she waited for him to elaborate, Eva wrestled with a plant Pump had called prickly lettuce. It was nearly as tall as she was. He had shown her how to wrap leather around her hands and then grasp it at the bottom. Since it did not want to come out, she paused to rest. In a moment, she would take it unawares when it least suspected. She lifted her eyes to Pump. Several minutes slipped by before he leaned both arms on the fence.

"I'm the reason Jim lost his family in the first place. His father and I were good friends in Tennessee, and I gave him bad trail advice for their journey here." Instead of facing her as he spoke, he addressed the horizon. "I didn't know it at the time, of course. I got landmarks mixed up when I wrote him, and they ended up lost. We reckon, reckoned at the time, that rather than turning back, Jim's father pressed on and into Comanche territory… or at least, close enough."

Eva tried to generate empathy for Pump. He seemed to be a good man, and clearly, his mistake cut to the heart. But why? It didn't make any sense. The death of Jim's family was an immutable fate. Is the person reading a book responsible for the terrible things that happen to fictional characters? Or the viewers for the characters on a television screen?

He turned his focus down to her. "How do you know Jim isn't real?" he asked.

"These are just shadow worlds of the True world. None of this is real."

"Does this line *feel* like a shadow? Does it truly feel different from the Lux Libera's 'true' timeline? From what you call 'Axis Mundi?'" Pump's eyes bored into her.

Eva considered Pump's question. When she was a novice, she had asked the Elders why other lines didn't feel more like shadows. She couldn't remember their exact answer, but it had made sense at the time. "The True line feels more real."

"Does it?" Pump raised his eyebrows. "Does it really? It sounds like you have traveled extensively. Has any timeline ever truly felt any less real than any other?"

Once her novitiate was over and the Elders allowed her to travel, she had been well past her initial misgivings. She had never thought about it again, but his question plucked at a loose thread she had ignored.

"How do you explain the millions and millions of Jims? They can't all be Jim."

"I agree with you. They can't all be our Jim. They're each their own Jim with their own consciousnesses," Pump said.

"Or they are just reflections in a mirror."

"Does Jim seem like a reflection in a mirror? Does he make choices? Are there ideas rumbling around in his head?"

As the younger man's amber eyes came to her mind, Eva reflected on her brief time with him. Was there a light inside him? A spark of true feeling? Heavy weights pressed down on her shoulders, and she blocked the new impressions. How could he possibly exercise free will? His future was fixed.

"Are you so sure you are the only Eva able to travel or there are no Jims who can do so as well?" Pump tossed his hammer on the ground to gesture with his hands. "Do you know how hard it is to know I can travel to any timeline and save Jim's family from destruction, but I can't save this Jim? This is the Jim I care about." Pump took his hat off and hung it on the fence with such force that Eva expected him to put a hole through it. "If you were to visit another timeline with another Jim, would he recognize you? No! Because that Jim wouldn't have any shared interactions with you. Oh, I know what you've been taught by the Lux Libera, but how do you know, for sure, Jim isn't real? What proof do you have?"

The strength of his argument pushed her back on her bottom. Once she had become a full member, she had never seriously contemplated such a thing. The Fated, indeed all creation, were trapped in a slavery of determinism. Each world occupied a separate broken shard of space-time, every creature ignorant of its mindless nature. Only the chosen of Lux Libera exercised free will and moved between shadows. Her duty was to restore the world to a state of wholeness. But prove this was true? No one had ever asked her.

Eva searched for a pertinent verse among the many she knew by heart, then took a breath to speak.

"Lux Libera scriptures don't count," Pump said, holding up a finger.

"But what other proof could I give you?" How did you prove another creature experiences or doesn't experience consciousness? With her only counterargument declared irrelevant, she shifted to sit cross-legged in the dirt, stiffening her spine and drawing up straight.

Pump tilted his head, leveling his gaze over his spectacles. After a while, he said, "You think about it. You think about how you can prove to me that Jim doesn't experience consciousness or free will. That he is just an automaton." With marked deliberateness, he picked his hammer up and sorted through his collection of nails.

Watching Pump as he tossed aside bent nails, Eva's mind sought a counterargument outside of Lux Libera's teachings, but she floundered, speechless.

Chapter 7

Eva

Multiverse Copy
Haarlem, Netherlands, Summer, 1943

As Tophe pulled his sleeve below his jacket cuff, Eva ran her thumb over the Totenkopf of his black-brimmed hat. Rain pounded on the barn roof.

"I'm not used to being the bad guys," she said.

Tophe frowned. "We're not, ma crotte," he said, shaking his arms. He glanced up and combed his fingers through his dark, greased hair. "You know we're not."

Disquiet made her fidget with the satin inner lining. Eva chewed her lip, then set the peaked cap on his head, twisting it askew.

"Hey!"

She grinned as Tophe repaired the damage to his hair. His red armband folded over on itself in the process, but Eva couldn't bring herself to touch it. After a moment, she killed the flashlight and listened to the drumming. Dawn would arrive in another hour or so. Wondering if her coiled braids had come unpinned in the dash for shelter, Eva patted the back of her head, then brushed ineffectively at her drenched dress.

"Scouts should have to serve as Menders first. Did they not know it was going to rain, or did they just not care?" Tophe asked. He stood in the wide-open doorway, facing the night. "Look at this. What the fuck?"

"And would it kill them to put the beacon in town?" Eva asked, examining her stylish heels. "Or at least allow us to jump there from here."

The smells of cow, horse, hay, and mice competed with damp earthiness. Minutes passed, and the rain steadied; little frogs peeped to each other in the distance. She found a milking stool to sit on, and Tophe paced in the gloom with little anxious huffs. Going home unsuccessful was not an option.

Eva's own anxiety blossomed in her gut, and more than once, she caught herself chewing at a cuticle. Much time had passed since the last time they had failed the Elders. She didn't want a repeat of the punishment... or worse. Every minuscule decision she and her partner made during the mission could mean the difference between success and failure, mercy or wrath.

After some time, the shower turned into an erratic sprinkle.

"I was beginning to think we would have to devise a plan B before the farmer woke up," Tophe said, renewed hope in his voice. He lit the flashlight under his chin, deepened his voice, and said, "Time to go," then shone it in her face.

"Stop it, Christophe."

He illuminated his stuck-out tongue with a teasing snicker and switched it back off. As their eyes adjusted, they could see shimmery puddles in the darkness. The full, distant moon drizzled a pale glow over the yard.

Eva rose and stuck her head out. When she reached out an open hand, she felt only mist.

"Have you decided if you will be German or Dutch?" Tophe asked.

"German, I think. My Dutch is still only passable." She stepped back from the entrance. "I really thought it would be simple to pick up. At first blush, it seems like a German dialect, but it's really very different."

"Mmm… Mhmm…." Tophe gathered their satchels.

Eva peered into the blackness at him. "You always ask me questions and then only half-listen to my answers."

"Maybe your answers are too long." He inspected the floor for loose items. "Your Dutch is fine. Better than mine. It's the one thing we don't need to worry about. But we can both be German if it makes you feel better." With a grunt, he stooped to retrieve something. "Besides, it's probably safer, given the scouts have already fucked up the weather intel." He stood upright and closed the knapsack. "They were telling me to be Dutch." He shook his head and pointed a finger at her. "I knew, though. This timeline might not have an organized Waffen-SS Regiment for the Netherlands. It should, but they might not have the full, glorious uniform, comme ça." He waited, hands spread, for her to comment on his dashing good looks.

She smiled at him, taking a bag. "Yes, very handsome."

He twitched an eyebrow at her sarcasm. "On y va."

After skirting around the deepest potholes, Eva lengthened her stride to keep up. The dawning sun lit everything from below. She tried to see the uniform through Tophe's eyes. Head-to-toe black, well-cut, flashes of red. The effect was impressive if she laid all her associations aside. Hugo Boss designed the regalia to intimidate, and he succeeded. She shivered.

"Tophe, I know you didn't have Nazis in your birth timeline, but in mine..." She didn't know how to continue. Her question fell off the tip of her tongue, landing in the mud, and she lapsed into silence, concentrating on her feet crunching the wet gravel. Her mission partner seemed to be in his own world.

"If it starts pouring again, we could use the rain to our advantage. Duck into the watchmaker's shop, no? On pretext of escaping the storm." After a beat, when she didn't reply, he slowed to a standstill. "Qu'est-ce que c'est, Eva? You're never this hesitant. Or this quiet." He lifted one corner of his mouth. "It's nice, I must say." As he took in her face, his smirk faded.

She turned to him but didn't know what to say. Why was this different? How could she put it in a way he would understand?

When she didn't say anything more, Tophe placed his hands on her shoulders. "You look beautiful. You look like an Aryan princess with your golden hair and blue eyes."

Even though that was her goal, Eva flinched at his description.

"Your German is perfect. Most importantly, today, you have a handsome German boyfriend."

She rewarded him with a punch.

Tophe rubbed his arm. "You have nothing to worry about. We are making the world whole again, and you are the best, the most dedicated Mender I have ever seen." Before releasing her, he kissed her on the forehead. "Sister Eva," he said, using her official Lux Libera title and clicking his heels with a shallow bow.

Eva forced herself to appear reassured. She wasn't worried about the mission, at least not how Tophe thought. They had done many similar tasks together, but seeing him in a Reich uniform from her childhood history books jarred her conscience. Just a disguise, she reminded herself. Not real. Shadow world.

Over the years, Tophe had told her of his home timeline, one so different from her own, and she rifled through the pictures she had imagined for him in her mind. No World War I or II. A strong European Union leading the world through the Cold War. A weak United States to which no one paid much attention. He only vaguely knew about the Americans' decades-long eugenics program and apartheid system. His had been a charmed upbringing in France, closest ally to the world's leader, Germany. He spoke reverently of the German space program, which put the first man on the moon in 1956; of their love of representative democracy and civil liberties, and their perseverance in uniting all of Europe in peaceful confederation after centuries of petty wars between kings.

"You know, when I was still with my birth family, I read about our targets in school," she said. "The scene I remember most vividly from Corrie ten Boom's book is where her sister is ill — deathly ill, in fact — but she shares out the last drops of her medicine with the other women in the barracks of their concentration camp. And it lasts a miraculously long time and helps many more women than just herself to survive."

Tophe shrugged. "Their lives are preprogrammed. Just distorted images of reality."

What he said was true; she knew it, but in that moment, childish wonder sparked in her chest. Oh, to be eleven again, before she had learned the truth, reading about an act of selflessness in the face of so much death, even if it hadn't been real.

For the rest of the walk, Eva lost herself in memories, while her partner trudged beside her in silent lockstep.

When they reached the town, it started raining again, much to Tophe's delight. "This makes things so much easier." The watchmaker's storefront sat three doors down on the corner. They had made it all the way to Barteljorisstraat before they had needed to pop under an awning.

"Merde!" Eva had tripped in a puddle, swamping her foot.

"Nein, 'scheisse.'" Tophe said, correcting her French profanity to German.

"Ah…" Eva pulled the brown pump from her foot to shake it dry, but cleaning would require her palm to smear the filth away. "Ja, mein lieber," she said, giving up and clutching his arm to steady herself. Her toes were a little pinched in the borrowed shoes, but they would do.

"And no more English. Only Deutsch or Hollands from now on," he said.

"Ready?" she asked in German.

"Always."

"Wait, wait, wait… take your jacket off."

"Oh, good idea." Tophe suspended the makeshift umbrella over her head.

As they dashed through the puddles, Eva's heart soared, exhilarated, and the tediousness of their journey dropped away. These were the parts she loved: entering the stage, crossing the threshold, stopping the carriage, or bumping into the target — a moment of anticipation before aligning the worlds a little bit more.

The shop bell rang above them, and they laughed as they shook the water from their sleeves.

Chapter 8

Eva

Jim's Farm

Eva winced as she opened her cracked and bleeding palms. She'd have given anything for a pair of gloves. They existed in this time, but none resided on the property. Pump's hands were roughened and tough, and she suspected Jim's were as well.

Pump had worked her until sunset. With a new appreciation for this way of life, she definitely could not see the appeal. She missed Tophe. She missed hot showers, ice, her bed, shampoo, air conditioning. Missions were like camping trips, and returning to the comforts of home and the warmth of friends was as dear to her as the adventure itself.

Pump approached her with a crock in hand. "Here, this salve will help."

Eva held out her hands as he gently smeared the greasy substance on her wounds and bound them under a clean rag.

"There," he said, smiling at her.

"Thank you." She turned her hands over to inspect his knot work and sniffed at it cautiously. It smelled like bacon fat with something faintly herbal.

"That'll keep your skin soft so it can heal more easily. Let's eat."

Eva followed him to the outdoor kitchen. Pump used an iron hook to lift the lid from the stew pot hanging from a tripod, and they both peered in to check its steaming contents. Earlier in the day, he had retrieved meat from the rafters of the dogtrot and shown her how to set a bean porridge going with salt pork. It would simmer all day with some periodic attention and could be added to for the next day. All in all, he'd given her a crash course in pioneering.

"Now, Jim doesn't eat pork on account of the Comanches think it's a dirty animal. It lives in water and mud. But he's got all these provisions his partner put up last fall, and they're going to waste. Anglos eat hog. You get what I'm saying? He needs to get used to eating it again if he wants to fit in, so be sure you use it."

Eva nodded.

"And speaking of hogs, he's got a few that've been foraging acorns all summer. He'll need to round them up and slaughter them come the first cold snap. I'll come round to help. It's a multi-day affair."

When she commented on how much she had learned, thanking him, Pump said, "We'll make a proper Anglo wife of you yet."

She knew he intended it as a joke, but she also had a hunch he hoped these skills would come in handy for her. The night before, snippets of

Pump's matchmaking had wiggled through the cabin timbers to her ears, but Jim's lack of interest reassured her the idea would remain simply an old man's wishful thinking.

Though she had every hope of finding Tophe in the spring, spending the next six months hauling water, weeding gardens, tending stock, and creating every bit of foodstuff from scratch, let alone cooking every meal to earn her keep, made her heart sink. Any further suggestion she might be playing a settler's wife forever was unbearable. Though she knew Lux Libera Menders who had failed to return from missions, she had always assumed they had been killed. She had never imagined they might just have been... stuck.

"Tomorrow, I can show you how to wash clothes by hand," Pump said.

Eva groaned to herself, and all the little buildings of the farm telescoped toward her, pressing her soul against the grove of trees at her back. To push through the crush, she forced a breath, focusing inward, taking Pump at his word that one could travel without a tree, but heard only silence where she should have heard the song of the universe. No matter. She only half-believed him anyway. His mere impossible existence demanded she keep an open mind, but that didn't mean one could travel without using trees. She'd try again the old-fashioned way as soon as she could.

In the meantime, Pump showed her how to mix the ash cakes Jim had made the previous night. Simple enough, she thought. Cornmeal, salt, water. "Is this all you eat?" Eva asked aloud.

"It's a common meal, but we eat other things. My wife is a marvelous cook." Pump looked up at her from where he crouched, ladling out the batter. "She could teach you."

Eva wondered how that would appear. A grown woman like her who didn't know how to cook in their manner. "What would your wife think of me?"

Pump considered for a moment. "Mmm. Probably nothing good. She would come to my initial theory about you as well, I'm sure. Still, it's not a bad idea." Pump stood back up. "If you find the need."

"I will keep it in mind," Eva said.

Pump chuckled at her lack of enthusiasm. "I know your world is very different, but a person can find a lot of contentment with this life. Besides, Jim will give you a safe place to stay if you need, so long as you pull your weight."

With a final stir, Eva served up beans for both of them. Pump called it "pot licker" or "pot liquor;" she wasn't sure which he meant, and he liked to dip his corn cake in the juice, so she followed suit.

"Jim speaks English very well," Eva said.

"Yes, he has a good ear and a better memory. Oration is important among the Comanches, much like the ancient Romans. His English came back very quickly after he returned. Though his accent is still thicker than folks like, and he can't read a lick. Well, that's not true. He remembers most of his letters but has no patience to pick it back up again." Pump wagged his head in disapproval.

At these words, Eva envisioned Jim's life with the Comanches, where he wouldn't have needed to know how to read. Pump had opened her eyes to the fact that Jim might have a real, conscious life, like hers; that he was not an unfeeling shadow. Or rather, not shadows, plural, because if Jim was aware, it meant everyone in this world was aware. She suspended her disbelief for a moment, and the compounding logic of universal consciousness rose like an unexpected tide at her chest, threatening to overwhelm her before she could move to higher ground.

From her perspective as a healer, her mind swam through the coming years, jerking her heartstrings in tow. A bleak future lay in store for the Comanches. "Should we tell him what happens to his people later this century?"

"My, gal," he said, furrowing his brow. "You switch topics like a horse going from full gallop to full stop." Pump stared at the fire as he thought about her question. "I've pondered this myself," he said. "There are lots of things to consider." He held up a finger.

"Number 1: will this timeline lead to the Comanche wars and, ultimately, the removals I've seen in other futures? There's no way for me to know, and there's no way for *you* to know since neither of us can travel to any other point in time from here in this thread. It's not like killing Columbus will do us any good here. We'd just be changing a different timeline somewhere else."

"But we know what will happen from other timelines," Eva said.

"Yes, but I've also been to other futures where their histories record that all the Plains Indians, and the displaced Indians from the East, and the Indians in the Rockies and the West Coast, they band together to form an impenetrable wall against new settlers. The United States never realizes their 'Manifest Destiny,' and the Indians build their own larger confederate nation. Some futures even have that confederate nation pushing the Europeans back into the sea."

Eva had seen those as well. "But do you see that happening here?"

Pump shrugged. "It's hard for me to see from my little plot of land in Tejas and through my travels in this colony. It's hard for me to see all the many, infinitely many, tiny choices individuals make that create a different future."

Eva set her bowl down on the ground, then leaned forward, forearms on her knees, deep in thought. "Is there anything we could say to him, though? That could warn him? That would let him warn his people?" She threaded her fingers in her hair. This morning, before Pump had revealed himself to her, before he had compelled her to question the irreality of this shadow world, she hadn't cared about the destiny of one man, much less of an entire people. Aligning this timeline with Axis Mundi was her job. To mend what had shattered at creation. To cleanse. To heal. Now, she didn't know what to believe.

For a moment, Pump tilted his face to the sky, then shook his head slowly. "No, I don't think there's anything we could say. He would think we were crazy, and that would be just the first hurdle. He'd then have to convince his people that he wasn't crazy. The hurdles after that are massive. I think change must come through many people choosing similarly at the same time or over a long period of time. It can't just be one man."

"Sometimes, it is just one man, and all it takes is a phone call or a bullet," she said.

Pump looked at her for an eternal beat. "It's always easier to destroy," he said.

As heat blossomed at the base of her neck, Eva darted her eyes away, wanting to argue but unable to form the words.

"Number 2," Pump continued, "and this is a selfish reason not to warn Jim; I admit it, but I don't want him to return to his people. He belongs here. We're his people. Anglos. Always have been. Jim should have grown up with my own boys." Buried anguish punctuated his words. "Would have if he hadn't been taken because of my bad advice. There's a very good chance that the Comanches are doomed in this timeline, and he might be unlucky enough to live to see it and die on a reservation. And any children he has."

This was the real reason he would never say anything to Jim. "And you're okay with what will happen to the Native Peoples? All of them? Not just the Comanches."

Pump didn't answer. He dipped down and placed a twig in the fire. "I try not to think about it very much," he said, tossing another. "I've been to so many different worlds with so many different futures. They all exist, every one of them, every single possibility, and infinitely so." He found her eyes. "But this is the one I was born into; this is my home. I'm caring for my family as best I can among the options presented to me and what I have the power to do."

Something didn't sit right. His very presence in front of her as a traveler, but not a Lux Libera. His experiences. His assertions. Rationale grabbed her by the back of the neck, forcing her to look at herself, and a subtle nausea bloomed like the tiniest seed at her core. Suddenly, Eva needed to stand. Within moments, her feet were moving, but her thoughts sputtered and then seized, too alarmed to proceed. She shook her head in slow denial, watching the ground pass beneath her feet. She was a Mender, not a destroyer.

Pump rested his elbows on his thighs. "I think only a Comanche — or another Indian person — a person they felt had what they call 'strong medicine' and they trusted, someone who could travel and then saw for themselves what could happen... I think only someone like that would be able to convince them," Pump said. He bent down and threw another twig into the fire.

Deaf to Pump's final musings, Eva's imagination had moved well beyond Jim and the fate of the Comanches to fly with increasing speed through every world she had ever altered. She crossed her arms over her cramping stomach. "No, no, no, none of this can matter. It's all just reflections, refractions of probabilities off the True line."

"Is everything perfect in your True line? Is Axis Mundi completely without flaws?" Pump asked. "Those exist, you know. And their opposite. Like static paintings, unable to change to be anything else. Good and bad need each other because... well, otherwise, nothing really happens." He gazed at her with concern and took off his hat, turning it around and around by the brim.

Eva had never examined the True line from that angle. Was it without sin? Without evil? Without suffering? No, not at all. The realization brought her up short.

"Why are you working to match all other timelines to that particular one? If it is the True one, shouldn't it be perfect? A heaven on earth?" he asked.

While she paced, Eva stared at him, clutching her belly all the harder, as if she would spill out if she let go.

Pump laid his hat beside himself on the log, then squared his shoulders, tilting forward and lacing his fingers between his knees. "It's not perfect, is it? And I can vouch that Lux Libera is not the only group of people who can travel. Far from it. I've met others, and I'm living proof myself." He displayed his lanky frame with spread hands. "Just because you, Eva, can step out of time and, in a way, see all the outcomes all at once of all the choices ever made — that doesn't mean that the individual souls of people who can't travel didn't make their own individual choices in each individual moment of their lives. Every single choice and possibility exists on some timeline somewhere, but it's the individual souls that chose the path they will navigate. Each tiny choice *creates* a new timeline and a branching soul. Right now, ongoing."

What he described — it was too much. The implications were horrific. If what he said was true… my god, what had she been doing with her life? She was a monster. She came to a standstill, staring into the gloom beyond the campfire. For a moment, she floated above herself, looking down, lining up pieces, memories, teachings, years-old questions that had gone unanswered by the Elders, but which she had dismissed as beyond her comprehension. Was this a bad dream? There was no one here to ask, to tell her what to think.

Wokweesi bounded up through the night, appearing in their circle of light out of the complete darkness. Eva screeched in alarm. She tried to laugh when she realized it was just the dog, but her throat closed, and tears threatened. Jim shouted something from the corral, but Eva couldn't understand what he was saying.

She spun around to face Pump. Worry creased his face with oaken lines. She dashed away the brimming tears, swallowed, and slapped her cheeks.

Pump smiled at her, his eyes tender. "All will be well, girl."

"Will it?" she asked. "Do you have any idea what I've done?"

He nodded once, solemn.

Jagged sobs rose in her chest, but she shoved them down. With the briefest exchange of hollow smiles, they turned to greet Jim.

Chapter 9

Eva

**Multiverse Copy
Barteljorisstraat, Haarlem, Netherlands,
Summer, 1943**

The expressions on Meneer ten Boom's and his daughter's faces haunted Eva. Outside, under a shop awning, she and Tophe watched soldiers pack eleven people into a military truck. Despite knowing this wasn't the real version of Corrie ten Boom, she had been a bit starstruck meeting an author from her childhood. Corrie appeared younger than the photo she remembered on the back cover. Though homely, kindness lit her face with its own kind of beauty.

When the bell above the door rang, Corrie had greeted them warmly, and Eva had felt an unexpected rush of nostalgia for her sixth-grade class, her birth parents and siblings, her bedroom in her family's home where she liked to read, even the dormant grass and bare trees of her front yard in winter.

Corrie's white-bearded father had sat behind the counter, working on a watch. He examined Eva and Tophe over his jeweler's loupe as if they were a pair of brass gears. His daughter raised her eyebrows, asking if she could help them. Ever considerate, Tophe shook his jacket outside the door before fully entering.

After that, everything fell into place. Small talk about the incessant nasty weather. Inquiries regarding a watch repair — now that they thought about it, having hopped in from the rain and all — then pretending to hear a noise and commandeering their phone to call the Gestapo headquarters.

Eva had held them at gunpoint. She knew where the secret place was. All she had to do was direct the SS officers.

Corrie had pleaded; her father shouted. The authorities hauled nine human beings out from hiding. Corrie's sister was not at home, and Nazis would not cart her away today. Corrie's sister would never see her family again, and Eva and Tophe had prevented her from saving future fellow prisoners in this timeline.

Though Corrie had focused her dry-eyed attention entirely on her elderly father, before she had stepped up into the truck bed, she found Eva and held her eyes with a stare of such intensity that it felt like a punch. Eva gasped, marveling at the recognition, the condemnation. Surely, it was her imagination. The SS officer pushed Corrie, making her stumble, and she disappeared into the tarped darkness.

The next moment, Tophe jarred Eva with a suggestion. "Let's stop by a café for bitterballen and a beer before we head home. Deal?"

Eva nodded, distracted.

An officer approached them to shake their hands, thanking them for their service and complimenting Eva on her good instincts and quick thinking. At his sweet words, she smiled demurely, shifting her loving gaze to Tophe's face. The officer bid them good day, and they returned his sieg heil with crisp enthusiasm.

She stared after the vehicle as it drove away. Her body stood next to Tophe, but her mind followed Corrie to Ravensbrück.

"Well, that was simple. The Holocaust makes it so easy. No blood! No mad escapes." Tophe peered down at his smart uniform, picking a wet leaf from his sleeve and rotating to check his appearance in the window glare. "We even have time to take in the sights if we want to." He extended his arm to Eva. "Which we do."

She shook herself. Tophe was right. This was an easy job. They had done what the Elders had tasked them with doing; they had mended another timeline, set it a bit more to rights. Because Germany won the war in the True line, Corrie ten Boom couldn't be allowed to continue in the Dutch Resistance before being arrested, and the hidden Jews couldn't escape detection completely. Corrie only continued her compassionate work in timelines like Eva's birth line, or this one, and therefore needed to be fixed. The Dutch Resistance didn't even exist in Tophe's birth line. No Nazis to fight. That would also need to be fixed. Eventually.

But it wasn't about Nazis. It was about the holy work of alignment. She might look and act like a Nazi in this moment, but that didn't make her one.

It was for a higher cause. Corrie, her idol, would never feel a thing. Eva took his arm and matched his stride, but her usual satisfaction at accomplishing their sacred purpose eluded her, despite the voice in her head reassuring her.

Jim's Farm

"Did you leave me and Wokweesi any supper?" Jim's cheerful voice lightened the mood, distracting Eva and allowing her a moment to bury her horror deeper. He carried a jar with a leather lid.

"Didn't Mrs. Allen feed you? There's none left here," Pump teased, but he was already preparing a bowl for him.

Eva privately reeled, her entire worldview upended, but was grateful Pump was there to interact with Jim. She had been sent to repair this universe, to bring it back in line with Axis Mundi, merging something that should never have been separated from the Source back into a state of spiritual unity, and thereby ending its material existence. But instead of combing the barbules of a feather back into a sleek vane, she had been snipping each barb from the shaft with a pair of scissors. Or something like that. She didn't know. She needed time to think.

Jim settled on the ground, back to one of the logs, and placed the jar beside him. Wokweesi sniffed at it, but Jim brushed him away with a firm hand.

In answer, the dog turned to Eva for attention, thumping Jim in the face with his tail as she petted him. She hid her welling tears in the scruff of Wokweesi's neck.

"What do you have there?" Pump asked.

"Honey!" Jim beamed, pushing his dog's rump away. "Mrs. Allen said it was payment for work well done."

Pump clapped his hands. "Ash cakes with honey?"

Jim tilted his head down and back up in exaggerated formal consent, "Yes, sir!"

At Jim's childlike face, Eva laughed in spite of herself, anxious to cover the turmoil inside her soul, and began mixing up the batter as Pump had shown her.

While she worked, Jim took a spoonful of stew, paused mid-chew, and then looked at Pump with narrowed eyes. The older man's line of sight slid away as he busied himself mending a piece of harness. With disgust curling his lip, Jim studied the tabooed salt pork floating in his bowl for a long moment. When he continued to eat, reluctantly and sullenly, his spoon made the journey at half-speed.

Eva watched him from the side of her eye, curious to see if he would confront Pump. After his third mouthful, he put the bowl to the side, and Wokweesi took over. Eva passed him two hot ash cakes, and he smiled up at her with gratitude.

"So, tell us, boy. How did it go?" Pump asked.

"At first, when I rode up, I think Mr. Allen was tempted to shoot me, but he let me help him with the pen. In the afternoon, I noticed one of his horses was tender-footed and showed him how to trim back the heel and put a rawhide boot on it." Jim used his tongue to chase a runnel of honey down the side of his hand, then took another mouthful, talking all the while. "Looks like that hoof tends to grow strangely. He knows what to do now." Eva could barely understand him through his full mouth. "After that, he warmed up considerably. His wife even let the little ones come near." Jim grinned, ear to ear, honey glistening on his chin.

Pump might have been the younger man's reflection, tinged with pride. "What did I tell you, boy!" Pump took a gigantic bite of cake and honey.

Jim concurred, obviously pleased with the day overall.

When Eva collected the men's bowls, Jim caught hold of her wrist. "What happened to your hands?"

A frisson ran up her arm. She glanced at Pump before turning to meet Jim's eyes. "They experienced a world without gloves today."

Chapter 10

Eva

Jim's Farm

The following day, Pump bid them farewell, and Eva's epiphanies the previous night faded beneath the climbing sun. A thick brush of shame coated her from head to toe, scolding her weak faith.

Who was Pump? a voice in her head asked. *A stranger.* But another voice, a still, small voice, sat in the back of her mind and did nothing more than switch on a lamp. Eva hid her eyes from the brilliance, unwilling to see.

Pump's words had entered her conscience and set up permanent residence, impossible to evict. As the days ticked by, she replayed their discussions while she tended stock, swept the floor, and washed linens.

For the first time in years, she allowed herself to think of her abandoned family. She tried to recall their faces, the color of their hair, her grandparents' home. How long did they live in her birth line after she had left? She had disappeared without a trace. She could imagine her mother's fear now, her whole family's, her friends'.

Her Lux Libera teachers had promised her that her loved ones would have felt nothing. The memories swirled, carving an expanding, bottomless well into her heart. When she caught herself crying, she rubbed her cheeks and forced her thoughts to other things. Tophe. Her Lux Libera friends. Her respected Elders. Her mission in El Copano.

Finally, she strangled the quiet voice and knocked out the light. She just wanted to go home to the sanctum. To Axis Mundi, where everything made sense.

One morning, Eva stirred boiling sheets, mind numb and body overheated. She wore Jim's spare clothes, but the shirt consumed her, and the sleeves kept getting in the way. Annoyance and anxiety sat like an undigested meal in her stomach, swelling in the steam billowing from the kettle. Jim's farm was as good a place as any to wait for Tophe, but that didn't stop her from feeling trapped. Her irritation burst through her skin, and her hands, acting of their own accord, abandoned their work and chucked the paddle as far as she could throw it.

Wokweesi brought it back to her covered in live oak leaves and dirt. With a sigh, she took it from him, and he trotted beside her to the well to rinse it off. Without breaking stride as she passed the oak, she pressed her palm against the bark and listened for strings, but silence echoed back. She gripped the paddle and ignored the urge to take a swing at the next thing she saw.

Choice stolen, she permitted the laundry task to calm her, and when she finished hanging the wash on every bush and low limb near at hand, she went to the pasture to watch Jim train. He waved to her, and she waved back.

Eva studied her well-healed and toughening hands, then fiddled with her earring as she followed the horse and rider, the bow and arrows, with her eyes. She reveled for a moment in the beautiful fall day with its blue sky and perfect temperature, and she turned her face to the sun, eyes closed, smiling despite the heaviness in her stomach.

Over the past weeks, a pattern had formed in her days: chores, meals, and watching Jim. Jim did the heavier tasks, hunted, trained… and watched her. One morning, he took her foraging for wild grapes, calling attention to other useful or edible plants as they rambled. Wokweesi kept his own inscrutable schedule, disappearing and reappearing at will. Increasingly, Eva found reasons to be near Jim, and Jim included her in jobs he could easily do alone, both enjoying a budding friendship.

She heard hoofbeats approaching and turned to see Nꙋena. When they reached her, Eva stood and handed up a dipper of water from the bucket Jim had set nearby. He wiped his mouth and smiled at her. Her time alone with Jim, week after week, made it difficult to feel separate in nature from him. A light shone behind his eyes.

All formality had dissolved between them, and Jim had given up calling her ma'am soon after Pump had left. He had also long since seemed to realize she didn't require modesty like Anglo women and sat shirtless and barelegged above her in a breechcloth with only his medicine pouch around his neck. Every starved sense of her being drank in his broad chest and muscular arms, but she concentrated her eyes on his face.

"Teach me to ride," she said. "And shoot."

Jim's eyebrows rose behind the dipper of his second drink. He swallowed. "Have you not ridden before?"

"I've been on a horse many times, but I wouldn't say I know how to ride. Not like you. I can shoot a bow, though," Eva said, replacing the dipper in the bucket.

"Oh?" he said, dismounting. "This I'd like to see."

Eva inclined her head, pointing with her hand and foot. "Lead the way, sir." She couldn't wait to surprise him.

Arrayed across the open meadow, he had several rawhide and straw targets of various sizes. He halted about five yards in front of the first.

Insulted, Eva paced off another ten. "This is a better warming-up distance."

Jim smirked and rolled a mild shoulder. He started to hand her his bow but stopped short. "Um, you're not bleeding, are you?"

"What? Where?" Eva glanced down at herself and her arms and touched her face.

"No, I mean…."

"Oh," she said, puzzled. "No, not right now."

"Okay, good." Jim handed her the bow, turning red. He had picked up the word from Eva and now used it as if he had always said it. Curiosity tempted her to ask for an explanation, but she was too eager to show off her skills. She inspected one of his metal-tipped, triple-fletched arrows.

"What type of feather is this?"

"Red-tailed hawk. The shafts are dogwood."

When she noted the lack of an arrow shelf on the bow, trepidation threaded through her mind, but she brushed the doubt aside. Those doubts resurfaced when she had trouble keeping the arrow in place, and she began to rethink her arrogance. The heavy point drifted away at an angle whenever she took position. She peeked back at Jim, who waited with his arms crossed. "It's not like the kind of bow I'm used to using." Though she was an excellent shot, she had never specialized in archery and its many bow styles. Another Mender would have been unfazed.

"You're also shooting from the wrong side."

Her cheeks burned as she recognized it was the wrong side, even for her with a modern bow. How had she made that mistake? To his credit, he seemed to want to instruct rather than tease and demonstrated how to press the arrow against the bow with a bit of tension, loaded from the left. The arrow rested on her crooked index finger; then, he adjusted her thumb to lie along the belly of the bow.

As she watched his fingers adjust her hold, his forearm muscles rippled under his skin, and her thoughts seized on gummed gears. He moved to her draw hand, and amusement played on his lips. He teased her then for the strange way, to his thinking, she tried to curl her thumb around her index finger to grasp the nock.

"Here, this is easier." Jim encircled her, placing his hand over her bow hand and pinching the string with his other as if it were a slingshot, three fingers pulling beneath. Eva could feel the hard muscles of his bare chest and belly leaning into her back. The pleasant, complex smell of him enveloped her. He placed his cheek next to hers, talking her through the draw and release, but his words mushed in her ears. Together, they hit the edge of the target. "Now, you try," he said, handing her an arrow.

After taking a moment to compose herself and kick her mind free of her body's forbidden reactions, she spread her feet to stand straight and aligned. When she drew back, she took a breath in and released the arrow on the out-breath. The bowstring smacked her arm, and the arrow struck the target well away from the center and fifteen degrees from where she had intended.

"Good," he said. "Better than I thought you would do."

Eva puckered her lips and shook her head, then gazed down at her arm. Typically, she wore a protective padded sleeve. She noticed that he wasn't wearing one and said so.

"I don't hit my arm," he said.

"How?"

"You were holding it out too straight," he replied.

Eva pondered, eyes to the side, then looked at him. "But how do you keep your aim?"

"Stance doesn't matter when you're on a horse. My adoptive grandfather used to say to think of it like sending your heart to your target." Jim took the bow from her and held it in front of him. "Your body is in constant motion on a horse." He moved his arms in a fluid line as if he were riding, bow canted at an angle. "Your arm is mostly straight, but you can bend it just enough to keep the string from hitting it and still aim true." He drew back but didn't release the empty bowstring. After a moment, he relaxed and handed it back to her.

"And the cuts from the fletching on my finger?"

He shrugged. "If you line up the cock feather, it won't do that."

"But how do you have time if you're shooting quickly?"

"It becomes second nature. You also just toughen up if you forget," he said, his grin growing wider.

Even though Eva shot a few more times and her accuracy improved with each round, Jim was not as impressed as she had hoped. Realizing she had another option, she glanced at his belt and then returned his bow with a thanks. With deft precision and no warning, Eva darted her hand to his hip, pulled his knife, and sent it spinning toward the target, where it buried itself north of the center. "Heart," she said.

Jim stared at the rawhide in disbelief. Mouth agape, he turned and scanned her up and down. A stream of Comanche flowed as he gestured at the target. She gave him her smuggest smile.

He switched to English. "God damn, woman."

"Now, teach me to ride."

Jim studied the ground and shook his head before looking back up at her. "I see you are a woman I should never cross."

"You would be correct, sir," she said, giddy.

Eyes bright, he shook his head again. They walked together to retrieve his knife and find Nuena. Inside, Eva glowed, elated, but she shifted her outward demeanor to studious attentiveness as Jim shared pointers on the ground before helping her mount.

"Mind you, remember she's not a dog. She's not interested in pleasing you. She just wants to do whatever you want her to do as quickly as she can so she can get back to eating," Jim said. "Right now, though, I'll lead her, and you can shoot."

They spent the rest of the afternoon with Jim guiding Nuena on foot while she shot, accompanied by hunting lost arrows in the grass. Blood ran down the top of her bow hand by the time they were ready to quit, but she didn't care. The setting sun's glare cast long shadows across the grass, making it harder and harder to distinguish the shafts on the ground. Tired and with stomachs rumbling, they gathered the last of the arrows, and Eva paused to watch the wind ripple across the pasture as it created a golden sea.

Jim tugged at Nuena's rope when the horse made a desperate grab for a last bite or three before heading back to the corral. "See, what did I tell you?" he said, jerking at her muzzle and catching Eva's eye.

When he didn't look away, the distance between them shrank, and Eva's heart warmed in her chest.

Sparks flew up the chimney as Jim propped a log on the fire the next evening. Eva rose stiffly from the bench, levering herself up like a pregnant woman. "Ow-wow-wow." Her legs weren't cooperating.

Jim laughed at her. "I think the Anglos would call you 'green.'"

"And what would you call me?"

Jim focused his eyes inward. "There may be a word for it, but the People put their children on a horse as soon as they can walk." He sat back on his heels. "No one ever has to learn. I was still young enough that if I was ever sore, I don't remember it." Poker in hand, he turned back to the fire, rearranging it, to Eva's eyes, from the perfectly acceptable configuration she had built to something exactly the same. "Our women don't need carriages or wagons either," he added, glancing up at her.

Eva examined him from the side of her eye, hands on hips.

He grinned an arrogant challenge.

What would he think of cars? she thought. Eva squatted in place, stretching. The move didn't help her hips, and she regretted the position the instant she realized she needed to stand back up. Eva had woken up this way, and the pain had only eased during the day while she worked. She tried to straighten but was stuck.

One corner of Jim's mouth lifted as he suppressed his amusement. "Would you like help?"

They were now eye to eye, Jim cross-legged on the hearth in front of her, Eva contemplating her options. "Yes, please."

Once standing, Jim lingered with her hands in his. "I could rub your legs for you. That can help."

His amber eyes bored into her, and Eva let her gaze fall. For the first time, she didn't know if she should trust him. Until this moment, she had ignored her growing attraction and felt an easy companionship with him, not unlike her partnership with Tophe, and for Jim's own part, he had acted as nothing other than brotherly toward her. She couldn't pinpoint when she had started to feel as if she had always known him.

Jim's thumbs skimmed the backs of her hands. For several heartbeats, he stared into her eyes until he dropped her left hand and cradled her right, his thumb caressing her palm.

She should stop him. Instead, she nodded.

Chapter 11

Eva

Jim led Eva to the bed and positioned her on her belly. When he started with her foot, she melted into the quilt. No one had ever touched her like this. The little muscles in her sole came alive, and Jim laughed at her muffled moan. Dazed, she followed his thumbs along her calves, up and down, but as he moved to her overworked thigh, her grunts of contentment turned to higher-pitched squeals of agony.

"Never mind!" She drew her arms up to escape.

Jim pushed her back down. "Don't." Distaste at her inability to take a little pain laced his voice, but he massaged more gently. "It will help, I promise."

Eva closed her eyes and steadied herself. Releasing a jagged breath, she tried to send her thoughts elsewhere. The next moment, he nudged her dress above her waist, revealing her bare bottom, and the surprise brought her back. She opened her mouth to protest but was mesmerized by his warm hands kneading across her buttocks. Eva marveled she didn't stop him even as her conscience chanted the Admonishments. As proscribed, her missions with Tophe never involved intimacy, of any sort — not with her partner and certainly not with a Fated one. She should stop him. *Would* stop him.

Instead, she enjoyed his hands circling her waist, squeezing but not quite meeting. He explored the line of her hips before pulling her skirts down. "Roll over."

Unable to ignore her burning curiosity and make herself do otherwise, her body turned, rebelling against her mind, and Jim moved to sit closer to her knee on the edge of the bed. Her skirts flowed over both of his wrists as he traveled higher, locking his eyes on hers. He rubbed the top length of her thigh.

As Jim stroked the most tender inner muscle, his fingertips dipped between her legs and inched further up. Eva winced at first, but soon heat rushed to her core. Jim watched her, his face growing serious. When he crossed to her other thigh, Eva noticed her dress bunched around her hips again, nearly exposing herself to him. Her breath hitched as he advanced, his hands reaching deeper underneath and drawing back up in a rhythmic motion. A strange dampness caught in his fingertips, and she gasped in embarrassment. Had she started her period? No, couldn't have. It was too early.

Suddenly, Jim halted and yanked her skirts down over her legs, turning his head away.

Panic filled every crevice in her mind. His shift in attitude, her lack of self-discipline. What had just happened? She had let herself — and him — go entirely too far.

In a blink, he stood up, back to her. "Better?"

"Y-y-yes." Her breath came in short, shallow beats. When had she started panting? Eva swallowed and took a deep breath. "Thank you."

Already moving and halfway out the door, Jim mumbled over his shoulder, "I need to tend to something outside."

The instant the door banged shut, Eva checked between her legs. No blood. Reassurance flooded her.

Jim

As the cabin door slammed behind Jim, Wokweesi swept past his legs. Jim's walk sped into a run. Closed to any other possibility, he could only interpret Eva's face as terrified, and it floated in his mind's eye, rebuking him. In his triggered memory, it merged with other female faces, Anglo and Mexican. He opened the gate and whistled for Nɥena, who trotted to him as he ran toward her. He grasped her mane at the withers, threw himself onto her back, and, using his knees, pointed her down the lane away from the homestead. The ghostly faces trailed behind him, chasing him. Enemy women he had played with on the journeys home once they were well into their own territory.

_ee_

Colorado River, Nʉmʉnʉʉ Sookobitʉ (Comanchería), 1832

Pasahòo (Jim)

A favorite gathering place for all the Tribes, the familiar grove of cottonwoods alongside a spring welcomed the travelers. For many hours, the party of raiders and captives had not paused to rest or eat as they put ground between themselves and any pursuers.

The baby had been crying for the last hour. Pasahòo sensed his true friend losing patience. Since her capture, Kuhtu's woman had had trouble keeping up and had slowed the entire group down. A horse-warrior typically left an infant when he stole its mother unless he killed it out of mercy or to remove nits from a lice-infested land. Kuhtu had made her dismount once they were beyond danger, and she had jogged behind him barefoot. Still attached to his saddle by a long rope, she sat where her captor had stopped, the bottom of her feet a red mat of burrs. Knowing she would have had to put her baby down to escape, he had tied her at the waist.

Kuhtu paced, his visible exasperation rising in tandem with every movement. Even the other men wearied of the incessant noise, casting annoyed looks

at the warrior. The captive woman tried to nurse
her baby. It calmed for a moment before taking up
its ragged cries again. Pasahòo suspected she was
dehydrated and out of milk, and he had taken her a
sip of water before he had tended to his own horses
and captive.

Without warning, Kuhtu grabbed the baby from
its screaming mother and, seizing it by the ankles,
dashed its head against a pecan tree. Relief appeared
on two of the men's faces, though most did not
approve. Infants were a mixed prize; better were older
children who didn't need the intensive care of a
woman on the journey home. Some childless wives
would have rejoiced in a baby, and his true friend had
already brought it this far.

The mother howled in anguish.

Looking at Rutsima, Pasahòo saw his brother's face
was carefully blank. He knew Rutsima thought their
close friend could be heavy-handed and wasteful, and
Kuhtu had only become more ruthless in the months
since Anglos had murdered his adoptive father. After
turning his back on the scene, his brother strode off
to dispatch their evening meal from the remuda.

Pasahòo led his pony to graze and loosened its
saddle. He tried to block the wails from his ears. In
contrast to Kuhtu, he had only seen Rutsima torture
and execute a female captive once before. That act
had been in response to the rape and murder of his
sister by a far-wandering Anglo settler. The monster's
scalp now hung from his brother's pole. Pasahòo
had accompanied Rutsima on the rage-driven trail

of vengeance for their sister, and he had relished the captive's misery.

Pasahòo set his saddle at their campsite, laid the blanket out to dry, and threw a glance at his little captive. She hadn't moved. Rʉtsima squatted in front of his own woman to offer a bit of raw horse meat, his hands gory from the butchering. The captive turned her head away, but his brother forced her mouth open.

His brother's opinion of Kuhtu irritated Pasahòo. As a full-blood Nʉmʉ, Rʉtsima had nothing to prove to the People. He didn't understand the stakes for adopted men like them. There could be no doubt where their loyalties lay. Ever. Sometimes they had to be more brutal.

At another screech from Kuhtu's captive woman, Pasahòo's shoulders tensed. He kept his eyes averted. Kuhtu was his haitsi, his true friend, close as a brother and sworn to fight to the death and never to desert the other, but Rʉtsima was right. He was getting worse. Worried, he turned his head to see what the crazed woman was doing. His friend's captives rarely made it back to the village anymore, and they never died easily.

The distraught mother stood, bawling gibberish. Pasahòo darted his eyes to Kuhtu.

When Rʉtsima came to help him clear the ground, the skin around his brother's eyes was tight.

"If she keeps doing that, she will remind Kuhtu of his cruel mistress," Pasahòo said. "The one from when he was an Indio child in Mexico."

Rutsima's jaw tightened in agreement. Their friend no longer distinguished between a Spanish overlord or an Anglo settler immigrating from the East.

Pasahòo stopped building camp. He would rather have enjoyed his own captive first, but this woman was pushing her master too far. While Kuhtu and another man were distracted making sport with their spears and the little body, Pasahòo dragged the woman away into a stand of brush.

She bellowed and struggled with wild, ineffective abandon. Pasahòo's own irritation took over. He clutched the back of her neck and jerked her ear to his mouth. "Him kill you," he said. He searched his memory. "Quiet."

Shock silenced her. "You speak English," she said, and he could feel her eyes scanning his hair, his nose, his cheekbones, his jaw, his skin. "You're Anglo like me."

Pasahòo ignored her. Being one of the People had nothing to do with birth or appearance.

She pleaded with him, but he couldn't follow her words, only the tone. He knew this woman's fate if she didn't cooperate. He had seen it play out countless times. If he could subdue her before Kuhtu got to her, she might have a chance.

When she realized what he intended, she shrieked and flailed again. Tears streaked her face, turning dust into mud.

He lifted her body and slammed her to the ground, knocking the wind out of her and almost slipping on the thick bed of oak leaves under his feet. He added two controlled punches for good measure. After that,

"Why?" was all she said, more to herself or her god than to him.

When he finished, she was quieter, weeping silently. Captives usually were after the first time. He hauled her up, more roughly than he meant to do. He chewed over leading her back to camp where she would see the body of her child or tethering her here where she might stay calm until Kuhtu wanted her. In the end, he picked leaving her, thinking it was the safer bet.

Pasahòo returned to camp alone. Kuhtu questioned him with his eyes, and Pasahòo reluctantly directed him back to the woman over his shoulder. His true friend could have rebuked him for taking his captive without asking, but he didn't — a benefit of their relationship he didn't want to overuse. He had hoped Kuhtu would have forgotten about her for the time being. Bloody screams rose from the thicket, and his heart sank. The woman was not as subdued as he had expected, or Kuhtu may have been inflicting pain deliberately, regardless of whether or not she cooperated.

When his true friend came back with her, her cheeks had been slashed. She dropped where he left her.

One of the youngest horse-warriors built a fire, and they spent the rest of the evening dancing and recounting the raid. Having split off into different directions, the men had joined back up at a designated rendezvous.

One man had cut the rope of a mule standing next to the wall of a farmhouse. When he tried to mount it a secure distance away, it had bucked him off. In anger, he shot an arrow after it and hit it in the nose.

"I'm sure it headed straight home to its stake," his friend said, earning laughter at the other man's expense. "Imagine the Anglo's face in the morning."

As his brother Rʉtsima reverently passed a pipe, Pasahòo reclined and soaked in the camaraderie. His heart glowed with pride at their exploits and love for his brother, his true friend Kuhtu, and the other men. In his head, he summed up the horses and scalps he had taken with his ones at home and imagined the cheers of the women and old men when they returned victorious.

His woman crouched beyond the ring of light. With an appraising eye, he considered her qualities. He was sure he could trade her for two, maybe three horses, in another band. He never kept females for long, only older boys to watch his expanding herd.

Rʉtsima stood and stretched. When he walked toward the women, they squealed and pressed their shoulders against each other. He pulled his captive to her feet. She was the oldest of all the women they had taken. If they owned one, the other horse-warriors took their own women by an arm. Pasahòo stripped his girl. She stood in silent terror as he did.

Thoughts of his elder sister had long since been locked in a dark box. He understood the purpose of the hazing process for new captives of the People. The round, uncomprehending eyes of the captive children watched from the perimeter. No Nʉmʉ woman traveled with them this time to cover their innocence with a blanket, but he put them out of his mind. With various games, the captors tested the Anglo women's courage. The captives protested, cried, and begged, save for Pasahòo's girl, who shook and shivered in the summer heat. Kuhtu's captive railed like a cornered animal.

Rutsima asked to borrow Pasahòo's more attractive captive instead, and Pasahòo gave her, with his blessing. She seemed pliable and quiet, which would help her survive the trek home, but he wished for her sake she had a little spark remaining to defend against the women's initiation. If she didn't, the whipping she received upon entering the village would not be her last. She'd be the lowest in the hierarchy of females. Pasahòo's stomach flipped. Nothing was more disgusting or dangerous than cowardice.

When they tired of the women, they slept for a few hours, then rose well before first light for the last leg home. They would stop again just out of sight of the village to dress for a grand entry, fix the scalps to the bridle of the bravest warrior's pony, and announce their complete victory, all men safe, with a volley of skyward gunshots as they approached. None of the captives had been retied during the night. There was nowhere for them to go except the parched hill country and death.

Pasahòo's own captive stood, head bowed, waiting for his direction. By design, she was exhausted and resigned to her fate. He placed her on a horse, and she flinched at the contact to her raw thighs from the previous days of hard bareback riding. Mesquite thorns had scratched threading lines across her arms and face. He debated tying her on so she didn't fall off, and when she swayed on the pony's bare back, he decided in favor of securing her.

Kuhtu's captive had not moved from where he had deposited her the night before. She stared ahead, seeing nothing. When the warrior tried to pull her to her feet, she refused. As Pasahòo watched, disappointment wrapped another wet sinew around his bound and hardened heart. Captives either adapted, or they died. The only question would be if Kuhtu chose to drag her all the way to the village or kill her now. Kuhtu retrieved his tsepuhtuhte lance, the eagle feather of its shepherd's crook spinning in the wind, and drove it through her chest with the absentminded efficiency one would use to douse the campfire.

Chapter 12

Jim

Outside Jim's Farm

Nʉena soared through the night as Jim sought the life he'd had before he came to this confusing place. Adventures with friends, raiding enemies, counting coup, taking horses, women, and children. Moonlight shone down, lighting his way. The ghosts of his war party galloped beside him, scalps dancing from shields on their arms and the miles flying under their feet. When needed, revenge felt righteous. Justified. Riding back into camp, the praise of the women and old men made every hardship worth it. Everyone respected the Nʉmʉnʉʉ, and that respect kept them safe.

Sometime later, he passed the road leading to the Allens' farm and tallied the unguarded horses, the children. The wife. In the past, he would have collected each as an anonymous thing for profit, free for the taking, a boon to the People and his own reputation. But he had eaten at their table, shared a laugh, helped them. They were anything but enemies. He squeezed his eyes shut, uneasy at their vulnerability. Beside him, Wokweesi kept pace, mouth agape and tongue lolling, but Jim kicked Nʉena faster, leaning over her neck.

The only woman he had ever wanted to marry was fading from his memory. As his eyes watered in the headwind, he called her up, but Hʉwʉni shunned him, taking the hand of the man who was her husband now. Tatua. Tiring, he let Nʉena slow to a walk and then signaled her to stop. They stood together in the center of the path, listening to the crickets. Finally, he rested his head along her neck and draped his arms down her lathered, heaving breast.

Everything was upside down in this Anglo world, and Eva didn't act like Anglo women. He didn't know what he wanted from her, what he should expect, demand, or even ask. Who was she to him? Not captive. Not enemy. Not relative. Not his.

He thought about the sizable herd he had collected from the largesses of his war leaders and his own skill. Who had them now? Who had his favorite pinto stallion? He had acquired enough horses to make an impression on the family of the woman he loved. She had nearly been his. Tears burned in his eyes at the memory of his humiliation.

The haunting spirits caught up with him there under the night sky. They assaulted him from all sides, and he buried his face in Nʉena's mane. Their features had all blurred together, but now they coalesced into Eva's. Into her fear-rimmed eyes. For how else could she react to his unwanted touch except with terror, and he never wanted to see that look on her face again.

Shortly after he had arrived in San Antonio, an Anglo woman had been ransomed back to her people. When he had tried to talk to her, she had cowered and would speak only English. The mission brothers had flown into a rage when they saw him. Pump told him later that her husband had refused to take her back. His words rang in Jim's ears: "She should return to the United States where no one will know she's been defiled." A few months later, he told Jim she had died.

The cooling night shifted the heat of the day and blew the specters away, but they struck home with their lances before departing, skewering him. Jim inspected the twinge pressing on his heart, stinging like a buried splinter in a thumb, and his stomach heaved, leaving the taste of bile in his mouth.

Eva

The moon hung higher when Jim slipped into the cabin. Eva had gone to bed but cracked an eye while watching him spread a pallet on the hearth. Since the nights had become chilly, he had begun sleeping there. Wokweesi spun several circles, pawed at the blanket, circled again, and slid down Jim's back for maximum contact. Jim said something to him in Comanche, to which the dog grunted and blew through flapping jowls.

Eva snickered at the sound.

Jim tilted his head to her. "He barks in his sleep, too."

"I know. I've heard him. Right next to my ear."

Jim huffed in amusement and settled back, head resting on the crook of his arm.

Eva bit her lip, desire and guilt wrapping themselves around her with the bedding. She couldn't desire him. What did that even mean? The mere thought tangled with her beliefs.

But the distance between them stretched and yawned like an unbearable chasm, and her body tossed in place, uncomfortable, unsettled, urging her logic to just shut up and pull him across.

Then, her heart made a perfectly innocent suggestion. For weeks now, she had been better but still took his bed. "You should sleep up here... with me. There's room for both of us." The words tumbled out of her mouth before she could catch them.

Jim didn't respond. Maybe he hadn't heard her. Eva pulled the quilt tighter and shut her eyes. Unable to keep quiet, she lifted onto an elbow. "It's silly for you to sleep on the floor. This is your bed, after all."

Jim rolled to sit up. "Are you sure?"

"Yes, of course. I should have asked you sooner." Immediately, with her heart happy, her confusion eased, content at righting a wrong — an injustice even. She had been selfish, that's all. She scooted over to make room for him, and the ropes of the bed frame creaked and popped under his added weight. "Will the bed hold us both?"

"I hope so," he said.

Away from the glowing coals, Eva could only see his teeth and the whites of his eyes. The next moment, he pulled the covers over himself. A drafty edge appeared on Eva's side, and she tugged on the blanket to reclaim an inch or two, giving her back to him.

Her guilt melted away, and she relaxed into his presence beside her. She hadn't lain next to anyone since she had left her family as a child. Even if she and Tophe shared a room, they always slept separately. She inched closer to Jim's warmth, the novelty irresistible, and he rotated toward her, curling his knees up behind her own. Exhausted from the day, she closed her eyes and let her mind drift.

At a gentle brush on her shoulder, she roused but decided she must have dreamed the touch until she felt it again. When she turned to face Jim, he cupped the back of her head and placed his forehead and nose against hers. His breath smelled of lemony wood sorrel. As he stroked her hair, her hands found his waist. She explored his back, tracing the scars, then brought her hand to his chest, transfixed by the muscles moving beneath his skin as he caressed her.

The more they touched, the more the desire to kiss him became too insistent to ignore. Eva lifted her chin to bring their lips together.

Jim drew back in shock.

"What?"

Jim blinked at her. "I'm sorry, Eva. You just took me by surprise, is all."

She propped herself up on her elbow. "Why? It seemed so natural. I've never kissed anyone before. Did I do it wrong?"

"I've never kissed anyone before either. My people don't kiss like that."

"Which people? Anglos kiss, don't they?"

Jim canted his head, seemingly confused that she didn't know the answer to that question herself. "The Nʉmʉnʉʉ," he said.

"You were kissing my shoulder, weren't you? When my back was to you."

"Yes, but we don't kiss on the mouth. It's… strange. I just didn't expect it."

"Didn't your parents kiss?"

"If they did, it was never in front of me. I was only eleven when they died."

Eva sat up in bed, spell broken, and threaded her fingers through her hair. "This is for the best. I shouldn't have let it go this far. I should never have been touching you."

Jim reared back as if she had scalded him. "What do you mean? Because I'm a 'filthy Injun?'" He spat the epithet in a tone she imagined had been spat at him.

"What? No! Nothing like that. Why would you think that?"

"Because that's what Anglo women think."

"I'm not Anglo."

"Of course you are." He scanned her, head to foot. "What else could you be?"

"I can't touch you because my people are celibate."

"Like a nun."

"Yes, like a nun."

"But you're not a nun." His deadpan words confirmed rather than questioned.

"No."

"Wait." Jim's eyes sparked, catching the meager light from the fireplace. "Who are your people? Do you remember your family?"

Eva didn't know how to respond. "Yes and no. I just know I'm not Anglo."

"And you're celibate."

"Yes."

"And that's all you remember?"

"Yes." Eva was glad it was too dark for him to see her expression. "It's part of a vow — a vow that gives me the ability to do what only we can do."

Jim inhaled sharply. "A vow for puha? For power? You made medicine. On your own. Without a husband? How is that possible? You're too young. And you're not a widow. Are you a widow?"

Eva was unfamiliar with what he meant. "No? Yes? I mean, no, I'm not a widow. Our people don't marry."

"And this vow, does it include touching? Are men allowed to touch you? What happens to men if they touch you? You shouldn't even be speaking of it. Should you?" Jim's voice reached a pitch higher than she would have ever expected to hear from her.

"Or is puha different for your people? You shouldn't even have it. What happens to it when you bleed? Does your woman's power not wash it away?"

Unsure which question to answer first, Eva took them in order. "Nothing. Nothing happens to men if they touch me. And I don't know. I'm not even sure we're talking about the same thing."

When she finished speaking, Jim remained silent.

She could almost hear the anxiety churning in his thoughts. "We've done nothing wrong here. We just can't go any further than touching." Not strictly true, but he seemed to need the lie. She reached out her hand to place it on his knee, trying to reassure him.

He recoiled, falling off the bed, then scrambled up to pace, his bare feet slapping the puncheon floor.

Would the full truth be better?

Outside the cabin, Nuena trilled a whinny to another horse in greeting, and Wokweesi jumped onto the bed. His shadowed ears pricked in silhouette, and his tail curved tall and still. Jim stopped dead. A low growl rumbled from the dog's chest until Jim clicked a sharp command for silence. He grabbed his rifle and smooth-bore musket, hesitating a moment before handing Eva the musket. "Do you know how to use this?" he asked.

She nodded, realized he couldn't see, and said, "Yes." Enough to know I'd rather have the rifle, she thought.

After kneeling at the window, Jim peeked through the curtain. Pale moonlight streamed in, forming a wedge across the cabin floor. "String my bow," he whispered. Wokweesi's shining eyes never left Jim, and his panting came in fits and starts, his entire body alert.

Resisting the urge to ask questions, Eva fumbled in the dark, following through on his order and knocking over items stored in a corner.

"Shh!"

Eva froze, listening.

A distant coyote yip followed by a man's call sounded through the cabin timbers.

Jim laughed with relief, his shoulders relaxing, and he stood up, pulling the curtain aside and illuminating the mess Eva had made trying to find the bow. Wokweesi's tail gave a slow, cautious wag, and while his head fixed on his human, his eyes darted between Jim and Eva.

"Who is it?" Eva asked.

"My brother." Jim grinned when he looked over his shoulder at her. He stuck his head out the window and called out a lengthy response. An arrow thwacked into the side of the cabin, and Jim shouted what sounded like a mock insult before drawing his head back in. Eva handed him the musket. He moved to return the firearms to their places but paused, as if in sudden thought, before looking at her with a frown.

"What?"

"My brother is going to expect me to gift you."

"What do you mean, 'gift me?'"

"Brothers share wives; sisters share their husband. It's completely normal and expected. Like mouth kissing for you."

Eva stared at him in the darkness. "A) I'm not your wife, and B) Hell no."

For a moment, her phrasing distracted him. "Don't worry," he said, his voice harder than she'd ever heard. "I wouldn't do that to my brother."

Do *that*? she thought, outrage blossoming at the nape of her neck.

"Build up the fire," he said. "Don't come out unless I say."

Chapter 13

Jim

With the horses corralled and the rest of the men settled across the dogtrot, Jim held the door open for his brother to pass through. Eva knelt by the fire. Any child of the People would have known better than to build it as large as she had.

"You have a woman!" his brother said, interrupting Jim's irritated thought. "She must not mind your whiskers."

Eva stood up, and he gave her an appraising look, ears to tail and back again. Jim knew what his brother saw. A female, inferior in beauty to the women of the People, but serviceable.

Jim stroked his rough cheek. He had stopped plucking his facial hair soon after returning to Anglo society. Back in San Antonio, Pump had shown him how to shave what remained of his beard. Less painful, but it didn't last as long. He'd allowed his eyebrows to grow back, which had taken forever, but his brother made no comment about those. "Women here seem to like whiskers," Jim said.

"That's because they haven't seen a real man." The arrogance rolled off his tongue, natural, unthinking, thoroughly justified. "At least your hair is growing again. You looked like someone had died."

"Me. Apparently."

His brother's eyes twinkled as he moved toward the hearth, gently but bodily edging Eva to make room as if she weren't there.

Jim found it odd she hadn't anticipated welcoming him to the fire or preparing food. Instead, her blank face trailed their movements.

"Please bring my brother something to eat," he said in English. "And drink," he added for safety's sake. "And the same to the other men. And make sure they have extra wood for the fire." He wasn't used to thinking about these things when a woman was around to do them. Even Anglo women knew how to welcome guests.

Eyes blazing, Eva tilted her head and knitted her brow. "Aren't you going to introduce us?"

Surprised, his brother stopped talking when she spoke.

"Seems appropriate if I'm going to be sharing his bed tonight." Uncharacteristic sarcasm dripped from her words.

Jim frowned, lowering his voice unnecessarily as if his brother could divine meaning from his tone alone. "You won't be."

"Glad we're clear on that."

With perhaps more words on the tip of her tongue, Eva's jaw took on a stubborn quality, but Jim refocused on his brother. "She would like me to tell you her name is Eva." To Eva, he said, "This is my brother, Rutsima."

Rutsima stared down at Eva, then grinned at Jim. "She's a bold one. Not like the Anglo women we've had before, huh?"

Though Jim knew from prior conversations that she didn't speak Numu tekwapu — in fact, knew nothing of Numunuu ways — Eva smiled as if she understood, showing her teeth, but her eyes flattened to dull slate. "Hello," she said.

As she finally moved to fill a plate, Jim released the breath he didn't know he had been holding.

Despite fatigue visibly pulling at his shoulders, Rutsima shared the tidings of loved ones while he ate. Jim leaned toward him, eager to hear of a rival's mishap, and felt bittersweet about the marriage of a former boyhood lover. He was glad she had found happiness; the groom was a good man. More agonizing was the report of Huwuni's newborn. A baby that should have been his. And though his brother avoided the name… news of his beloved was also news of Tatua. His eyes narrowed to see only the fire in front of him, but he kept the muscles around his mouth relaxed. When he could do so politely, he asked a question, sending the gossip down a new path.

After finishing her tasks, Eva sat near him, eyes and ears glued to his brother's face. From the corner of his vision, he caught her mouthing the syllables, mimicking his brother's rhythm. Did she even realize she was doing it? In that moment, a glimmer of warmth rekindled toward her. He could think of nothing she had done that seemed devious. Their hands had grazed, their bodies had touched many times these past weeks, and nothing abnormal or unfortunate had happened to him. If she was going to harm him, she would have done so by now. She seemed to expect him to understand her, just as he expected her to know certain things without being told. His mind drifted, and he found himself wishing they had privacy to talk.

"Does your woman speak Spanish?" Rʉtsima stretched, yawning like a lion.

Jim knew what his brother wanted to ask her and realized he had put off a tough conversation for too long. In lieu of answering his brother's question, he explained how he had discovered her.

"You have not had her yet? She is in your home, but she is not your woman?" Rʉtsima's mouth hung open. "I don't understand."

"Things are done differently here. Just because she lives with me, she isn't my wife. There's more to it than that."

"What more could there be?" His brother's eyes traveled to Eva. "It's not like she's one of our women."

Jim placed both hands on his crossed knees and looked up at his brother sitting on the bench. "When we take enemy women, we can use them however we wish, yes?"

"Yes." This was self-evident.

"But among our people, would you take Hiitóo whenever you wanted?"

"No, of course not." Rʉtsima spat in disgust.

"I'm Anglo again. Anglo women are the women of my people now. Not my enemies' women."

Rutsima's lips puckered as if he tasted something bitter. "You're one of the People. You earned your place as my brother." His brother's voice rose slightly. "These womanly people can't be your people. You can't be both."

Jim's neck burned with shame, and his mind raced. Letting his gaze slide to the floor, he imagined himself riding away from here with Rutsima, Eva next to him, his neighbors' horses driven ahead of him. He should just take her and make her his first wife. No bride price needed, no family to convince of his merit. He'd return home with prizes in hand rather than as a spurned dog begging to be allowed near the fire.

Unbidden, Pump, his birth father's dear friend, intruded on his fantasy, unwelcome and insistent, reminding him of his promise — a promise that, at the time, had seemed inevitable and the only path forward to surviving among the Anglos. Plus, he owed his mentor. Jim would still be rotting away in that mission if not for Pump. A weight, made of obligation and honor, suspended from his heart, tethering him to this place. "I must try," he said. "I gave my word to stay. At least for a year."

Rutsima glowered. "Which is complete in the spring, isn't that right?" He surveyed the room, lip curled, as he spoke.

"Yes."

With a broad smile, Rutsima slapped his thigh; matters clearly settled. "Then ask her if she speaks Spanish, and I will invite her to share my bed."

Jim rubbed the side of his nose. "She has made a medicine that means she cannot lie with men."

At this, Rutsima's eyes widened. "Not possible. She's too young. Do Anglos even make medicine?"

Jim shrugged. "She says her people are different, not Anglo, and they seem to practice a different type of method for creating power."

"Is she a widow?"

"No, I don't think so. She says she's not."

The bridge of his brother's nose scrunched, and he peered at Jim from the side of his eye. "Are you sure she isn't telling you this, so she doesn't have to lie with you, but she can still stay here under your protection?"

Jim shook his head and peeked back at Eva. When their eyes met, she lifted her chin in question, but he ignored her. "She's given me no reason to disbelieve her."

His brother sighed, darted his own glance at Eva, and wagged his head before laughing and patting his cheeks. "I don't blame her. I wouldn't want to lie with an animal like you either. You stink like an Anglo, too."

Jim pretended anger, feinting a blow in the general direction of his unflinching brother, but was happy to be teased rather than facing Rutsima's rightful indignation. "I believe her," he said, sliding his eyes to hers again. "Taiboo ways are strange."

Rutsima inclined his head. This was true. "I'm not that attracted to her anyway. Maybe I will capture a prettier one tonight."

At those words, Jim lifted his eyes to the window. The moonlight had brightened to dawn.

Eva

Jim startled Eva when he shook her awake at midmorning to prepare food for the men, the animals already neglected by the late hour. He scowled down at her, then returned to his pallet with a huff, drawing the blanket over his back.

Eva's resentment at being treated like a servant warred with her commonsense regarding the reality of her circumstances. As she roamed about the homestead retrieving food items and completing the chores, she noticed most of the men had moved out of the stuffy cabin to bed down in the yard. Sleep had softened their fierce faces, but she tip-toed to avoid waking them.

With each passing moment, she fumed, but then the feeling dissipated like smoke through her fingers. Her situation was temporary. In fact, she could try to leave right now. She dropped the bucket where she stood and attempted to loop her strings. It didn't work, and Pump hadn't come back yet to train her. She would figure out the new trick another time. Nothing wrong with proven methods. Determined to find the particle vibrations, even if the effort split her head in two, Eva marched to the pecan tree, ignoring the man sleeping at its base. If this works, who cares if any of them see me leave? I've already disrupted this timeline as it is.

When she neared the would-be portal, her feet crunched over fallen and uncollected pecans. She positioned her hands on the trunk and took a deep breath. The next moment, long fingers encircled her ankle and broke her concentration. She followed the man's corded arm to his groggy face.

"Buenos días." His smile turned into a drowsy leer, the sheer size of him giving her pause.

Eva's mind slid effortlessly to Spanish, the lingua franca of Tejas and Comanchería. "Good morning." Gingerly, she tried to pull her leg from his grip. The last thing she needed was a tagalong.

With the speed of a rattlesnake strike, the man sat up, grasped her thigh behind the knee, then pulled her down on top of him, burying his face in her chest. Pushing the panic aside, Eva squirmed into a better position. With the heel of her palm, she struck him with everything she had in the tender spot beneath his nose. Then she tried to elbow his throat. Years had passed since she had last been in a ground fight, much less trained for one, and neither hit did as much damage as she had hoped. The first made him angry, and the second jab insulted him. More desperate now, and clearly outmatched, she patted at his waist, hunting for the knife she assumed he had.

He roared and flipped them both over. Blood dripped from his nose onto her face.

With her free hand, she reached for the tree. She would take him with her. She could get away from him at home.

He wrapped a hand around her neck and punched.

Chapter 14

Jim

Yelling and barking woke Jim from a deep slumber. With his brother's arrival, he had been sleeping soundly, relaxed for the first time in a long time by having family and friends near him. He was on his feet before his mind registered he was moving.

His brother beat him out the door. Outside, the rest of the party encircled Mopai, Jim's longtime friend and brother-in-arms, sitting astride someone. Jim saw the man's fist raised and realized as Mopai brought his arm down that the person below him was Eva. One of her shoes was off; her skirts were above her knees. When the strike landed, her legs stopped kicking. Mopai shifted to lower his breechcloth. The surrounding men jeered.

Jim and his brother rushed to pull Mopai off her, then his brother dragged the man aside, speaking urgently into his ear. Jim registered the mild protests and deep-throated 'yehh's of displeasure from the other men, their morning entertainment cut short. Eva lay stunned, barely conscious. Her hand seemed to have a mind of its own, searching the ground beside her. Jim pulled her skirts lower, anxious to touch her face, to reassure himself she was fine but knew the danger of showing concern for an Anglo. Nor did he have a moment to waste; instead, he stood over her, glowering at the rest of the men.

"Is this how you repay my hospitality?" he shouted.

"Is this how you treat a guest, Pasahòo Kwitapu̱? How was I supposed to know she's not just a slave? She's clearly Anglo." Mopai flung his hands out in an appeal to logic. He looked to the other men for validation. A few nodded; some crossed their arms.

None of the men would meet Jim's eye. Disapproval rolled toward him.

"Ru̱tsima tells me she's not a slave, but she's not your woman either. What is she then?" Mopai asked. It was clear what he thought of Jim's blatant incompetence.

Ru̱tsima struggled to clarify Eva's status. "Mopai, that's not what I said." Jim knew his brother had reluctantly grasped the nuances himself during what was a lengthy conversation. Now he was trying to explain it in a dove's egg in the middle of an argument.

Eva groaned beneath Jim. He wanted to take her into the cabin. Ignoring her pain and leaving her to lie in the dirt gutted him, but this needed to be settled first. He could not make an enemy here. To call attention to his otherness, especially after losing his status with his people, was to court death and future raids. His brother explained Eva's confusing foreign medicine to the group. With embellishments.

Mopai paled. The other men chuckled nervously at his expense. They would have been quick to follow his near mistake and knew it.

Jim could see the realization on the man's face as the full extent of what he had almost done to himself clicked into place, and on the eve of combat, too. The man could have erased his protective medicine in what would have been to him one thoughtless morning romp. Jim began to hope he had deflected Mopai's anger toward him, but then Mopai glared at Eva, his thoughts as clear as if he had spoken the words aloud. This woman had tried to harm him on purpose.

"She's dangerous. Why do you let her live?"

Jim's hope turned into something darker than fear for himself. "Nevertheless, she's under my protection." Behind him, the leaves rustled as Eva sat up. He looked to his brother, who read his mind and came to stand next to him in front of her.

Mopai stalked toward Jim. Jim stepped to meet him. Mopai was nearly as tall as him, but not quite.

"If you don't kill her, I will. Any man could be ruined by her."

Jim glared at Mopai in return. He wanted to punch him. He wanted to feel his throat beneath his squeezing hands.

Rutsima shoved between them. "Mopai, calm down. She didn't mean to hurt you."

"No? Then why did she come to me? I would never have tried to touch her otherwise." All three men looked at Eva. She sat with her back against the tree, hands spread along its trunk. She stared at the ground between her feet, her focus deep and inward, as if the men in front of her were no concern of hers. The next moment, she closed her eyes, then screwed them shut.

She looked odd. Maybe she was crazy and needed to be killed. No. Jim banished the thought before it even fully formed. Odd, but harmless.

"Why did you go to him, Eva?" he asked in Spanish, knowing she understood the common language.

Eva's eyes shot open. Annoyance, perhaps even disappointment, pulled at her face. She slid up the trunk until she stood. Blood dripped from her nose and over her cracked lip, and Jim noted the side of her eye was puffing. That lid would seal in a few hours.

"I didn't go to him," she said in English.

"He says you did."

"I came to the tree, not to him. Either way, does that make it okay to rape me?"

"Why…? Never mind, you need to apologize to him."

"Apologize to him?" Eva scoffed. "Never."

"You don't understand." Jim's frustration with her mounted. "He says you need to be killed. You intentionally tried to break his medicine with your own." Her story didn't make sense. He wanted to believe her, but this was a serious accusation. What could she have possibly needed at the tree?

As she struggled to answer, Jim crossed his arms, and the other men waited for her to speak. "You wouldn't believe me if I told you," she said. "But I didn't go to him. I went to the tree."

Jim studied her open face. Her exasperation spoke to the truth she seemed to believe.

"If you won't apologize, they will want retribution of some sort. Something to mark you as undesirable to protect other men from you. Probably cut off your nose, maybe your ears, and lips." He exaggerated about everything but the nose.

Eva gasped, the color draining from her face. At her expression, he lifted a brow and tilted his chin while she scanned the men arrayed around them. He imagined her counting, hunting for weapons on belts. She turned to Mopai. "¡Lo siento mucho, señor!" Eva made eye contact with each of the men. "Lo siento mucho, señores." Placing her hand over her heart, she bowed her head. When she lifted her face, terror and rage competed behind her eyes.

At her compliance, the dark fear frozen in his gut melted a little. Her ability to read the situation and adapt was critical to her safety. Now, her apology allowed Mopai to unruffle his feathers. Though mollified for the moment, he gazed at her with open hostility. Jim would need to watch him.

"I expect more of a nʉmʉnaitʉ, but obviously, things are different with Anglos." Significantly, Mopai spoke in Spanish rather than returning to Comanche. Jim chose to hear the ambiguous words as a neutral comment about Eva instead of the personal dig he knew Mopai intended. It would serve no one for him to take affront. His brother would be hard-pressed to take his side. A thread of confusion wound through him as he realized he would never have backed down from the insult three years ago when he was at the height of his power. No one would have dared.

"Trae comida a los hombres, por favor, Eva," Jim said. Eva's eyes narrowed. Don't cry, he thought. He willed her to hear him. Her face twisted, but she pushed from the tree to do as he bid and bring food. He watched in relief and approval as she strode away, shoulders back, head high. The cabin door slammed, and Jim feared for the leather hinges.

In the late afternoon, Rutsima challenged them all to a speed shooting contest. Jim glanced across the pasture to where Eva sat watching, and her presence reassured him. Though he knew she was perfectly safe, he could concentrate better if he could see her.

The loser of the last match stood ready with several arrows in his bow hand, as many as he could hold, points up. If anyone in the group shot more than him, he would be eliminated. He sent his first arrow high into the sky and then began nocking and shooting toward the ground target as quickly as possible. He landed two before his sky-bound arrow fell and buried its point into the dirt. Jim waited to the side. As he watched, a familiar anxiety squirmed through his gut, mixing with excited anticipation.

When it was Mopai's turn, he looked over his shoulder at Jim. "Nuena will be a nice addition to my herd. One benefit of you living among the Anglos is that not only, like them, will you take care of our horses until we are ready to collect them, but you'll get them trained up properly for us, too." It was a clever jab, and Jim kept his face passive until he could grin with good humor. Even his brother joined in the laughter.

"We'll see who's laughing at the end, my friend." All the losers would forfeit one pony to the winner. Jim did not intend to lose.

Mopai pointed toward the sky and drew his arm back to his bow's full extent. The arrow launched faster than an eye could follow, and he immediately pulled the next arrow up from the bundle in his bow hand. Nock. Shoot. Nock. Shoot. Nock. Shoot. Nock. Shoot. Thump. Mopai peered back at Jim, and the rest of the men cheered.

Rʉtsima clapped Jim on the back, indicating his turn, and Mopai slid to the side.

As he took his place, Jim looked down the field at Eva. She seemed to have been daydreaming but turned her eyes to him as if she sensed his gaze. Wokweesi lay at her feet. Between his fingers and the bow, he had arranged the arrows with perfect precision. Taking a deep breath, he focused on a cloud high above and released.

His mind cleared as he loaded each arrow and released in fluid motion one after another. When his periphery registered the end of his turn, three arrows decorated the target. His brother made sounds of sympathetic disappointment. It didn't matter; the game wasn't over. All that mattered was that he didn't lose this round altogether.

One by one, the contestants dropped from the game. When it was just Rʉtsima, Mopai, and Jim remaining, his brother whispered, "Don't worry, if I win, I will gift you your horse back."

Jim nodded. He appreciated his brother's kindness, but a chill ran down his back at the thought of needing his charity.

After all three shot again, Rutsima came in with one fewer arrow, and his brother bowed out with a scowl.

Mopai signaled for Jim to go ahead as the second-lowest score of the last round.

Jim stepped into the clearing. To loosen the tension building in his shoulders, he stretched his arms over his head, then reached to the side, jabbing out as he rolled his neck. He sought Eva and waved, and she waved in return. The men around him snickered.

"Let's go," Mopai said.

"Are you in such a hurry to build my herd for me?" Jim retorted with a smirk.

"Not likely." Mopai slouched back on his heel, a bored look on his face.

Jim peeked at Eva again and then turned to face the target. After sending the first arrow up, he raced to get the second nocked and released, sensing only his fingers and thumb, his arm, and the target in front of him. When he dropped his bow, there were four arrows in a decent formation. "Ha!" He pumped his arm in the air.

Mopai patted him on the shoulder. "Good shooting."

Jim inclined his head and stepped aside.

After getting into position, Mopai did nothing to delay and shot his arrow into the sky, sending four total in rapid succession. The returning arrow struck before he could get a fifth pulled. A tie.

They shot again. Again, the score was four to four, and the men groaned, but this time, Jim noticed Mopai had managed to get a fifth nocked. By the next round, he was certain Mopai would score five arrows, whereas Jim doubted he could load any faster. A modification to their gamble came to his mind.

"I have another wager, replacing this one, if you're interested?"

Mopai raised his eyebrows, listening.

"Horse race. Nʉena against your fastest horse. Winner takes all the forfeited horses from the shooting game we just played, plus either my horse or yours, depending on which of us loses the race."

After a moment, Mopai puckered his lips, eyes thoughtful. "We should make it more interesting than that. There's little skill in just running them," Mopai said. "We make an obstacle course. First man back to the beginning wins."

Rʉtsima and the rest of the men grinned in anticipation of Jim's answer; he didn't disappoint them.

"Tsaa," his brother said and led the design of a challenging series of tasks for the two men.

Jim whistled at Eva and pretended to drink from a dipper. After watching her leave to retrieve a bucket, Jim walked toward Mopai. The contenders stood shoulder-to-shoulder in companionable silence as they waited for the course to be laid out.

Mopai cleared his throat. "I'm sorry for what happened with your woman earlier."

Jim slid his eyes toward his boyhood friend.

Mopai stared straight ahead, face impassive, watching Eva move among the men. His mouth quirked. "Your not-your-woman woman," he said.

The corners of Jim's own mouth lifted. He nodded and grunted an acceptance of the man's apology. "I also regret what happened. It was poor hospitality. I will speak to her."

Mopai turned his head to look at Jim, concern fluttering behind his eyes. Before the man could voice his worry, Jim said, "She's harmless."

Mopai's locked attention never wavered. He did not appear convinced. After a moment, he said, "She reminds me of that woman we took not long before you left us."

Jim thought back but couldn't picture her.

When he didn't speak, Mopai continued, "Remember... the place with all the pigs that smelled so bad?"

Jim opened his mouth. "Ah! Yes." And he did. He remembered the woman they had captured. The stench of the place had lingered in his nose for a day. She even smelled of it, and they had tossed her in the river. Eva reminding Mopai of her puzzled Jim. They were of a similar build, he guessed, but otherwise looked completely different. He couldn't remember her face or the color of her hair, but he was sure they looked nothing alike. Jim thrust the memory away.

"Why do you keep this one? Seems risky, and she's not even that pretty."

Jim didn't know how to reply. He himself didn't understand why he kept her and tried to tick off the reasons against her staying. He could help her return to her people. She had healed. Because of her strange medicine, she wouldn't have sex with him. He trailed her with his eyes, taking in the tilt of her head, the lift of her hand. The fact was, he didn't want her to leave. At least, not yet. Not right now. He enjoyed her company.

After a moment, Jim shrugged. "She does the chores for me."

Eva stepped toward them, offering Mopai the dipper, but he stared above her head as if she wasn't there. When she gave up and moved on to Jim, Eva's eyes gleamed. She looked up into his face, and he held her gaze. Rather than taking the dipper, he cupped his hands around hers where it held the bowl and took a long drink, intent on proving to Mopai he trusted her. The hint of a smile turned a corner of her mouth.

When she moved away, Mopai's brow knit. "Perhaps since you are Anglo, her strange puha can't hurt you."

"Perhaps," Jim said. A chasm opened in his heart. He could tell his friend was genuinely trying to discover Eva's proper place within his worldview and meant no insult, but before he had been tricked by Tatua and sold back to the mission in San Antonio, Mopai would never have called Jim "Anglo."

The field before him disappeared, and he was thirteen again. With his bow in his sweaty hand, he sat astride his pony, and the moon shone on a tiny settlement. The older horse-warriors on either side taunted him, urging him to return to the cowardly Anglos, that he wasn't cut out to be one of the Nʉmʉnʉʉ. Without a word, he had gone into the tavern barn and pulled out each horse, one by one. Light and song spilled from the windows next door. A drunk exited to piss against the wall. Jim had frozen in place, leading the last horse. When he had realized the man couldn't see past his own feet, he had mounted and walked the horse to his party without a backward glance.

As Rʉtsima strode across the pasture toward them, the sun hanging low over his shoulder, the scene faded, bringing Jim to the present.

"All is ready," his brother said.

Chapter 15

Jim

Jim and Mopai trailed Rʉtsima as he pointed out each challenge in succession. When he asked if they understood the rules, they confirmed.

Others had saddled the horses, but Jim checked his tack, tightening here and there. When he mounted, he looked over at Mopai, who was taking his pony first through a left spin and then a right. Jim patted Nʉena's neck and crooned to her. Two men marked the starting line, and he and Mopai awaited the signal in taut anticipation, bows and arrows in their left hands, a lance in their right, their horses' manes and tails fluttering in the wind.

At a shout from Rʉtsima, Jim roared and kicked his heels. Nʉena's hooves dug into the turf, and she leapt into a gallop. He leaned over her neck, yelling encouragement in her ear. Mopai kept pace with him, their horses evenly matched. As they approached the first targets, Jim raised his lance until he came within range, then he launched it with deadly accuracy, his opponent's lance hitting a moment sooner. A distant cheer echoed toward them.

Ahead, two other men urged their ponies into a run, dragging weighted pieces of hide behind them.

Jim readied his bow. They had been given five arrows each, and four would go in this target. He nocked the first and drew back. Long ago, it had become second nature to match the rhythm of his horse, and he released on the crest, followed by immediately nocking and releasing his next arrow. Then Three. And Four. He hissed when the fourth skimmed the edge and drifted behind him like a twig down a stream.

He risked a peek at Mopai, who rode parallel beside him, all but a single arrow gone. Reaching the end of the pasture, they turned their horses with a knee and opposing heel. Hazy with dust and dry grass, the hoof-churned path lay before him. When they passed the designated point, they dismounted and ran along beside the ponies until the mark where they were free to remount at a run. Once reseated, Jim slipped his foot into a saddle loop and feigned death, throwing himself to the side, his head bouncing inches away from Nɨena's hooves. After a count of ten, he pulled himself up. In his periphery, Mopai whipped his pony with a quirt.

Without another glance, Jim dropped down into a rawhide sling hung from the cantle, his now horizontal body shielded by her belly, with only his leg remaining visible over her back. He watched for the approaching target and released his last arrow. He thought — he hoped — he hit but wasn't sure. Together, he and Mopai emerged from the awkward position. Jim leaned over Nɨena again, shouting and kicking his heels. He caught up the whip hanging from his wrist and struck her rump.

Farther ahead, a man he was supposed to grab up from the ground waited for him, arms raised. Jim barreled toward him, moving his bow to his right hand. As much as he dared, he slowed Nʉena, locked arms with the man, and veered his weight to the opposite side to assist him as he leapt up behind him. A thrill of success coursed through his veins, and he brought Nʉena back up to speed, turning his head to look at Mopai. They crossed the finish line at the same time.

Their audience whooped, jumping down the line. Half the colony could probably hear them. Jim sought Eva and found her eyes glued on him. Joy bubbled until he couldn't contain his grin. After he felt his companion dismount, Jim bent over the pommel and thumped Nʉena's neck, his hand coming away damp from her exertions, then peered over at Mopai.

They met on the ground for Rʉtsima's verdict. "You were both equal in every obstacle but the shooting. Mopai, you landed two arrows on the moving target. And you," he said, eying Jim, "had three. You both struck the target under your horses' necks."

Jim thrust his hands into the air, bow clasped, and whooped.

Mopai hung his head but then congratulated him. "Well done, Pasahòo."

Jim grasped his arm in return. "Thank you. Nʉena will be glad for the company. She has been lonely."

Mopai scowled but couldn't prevent a smile from breaking through his disappointment. "You know I took pity on you, right? You with your one-horse herd."

"Of course." Even Mopai's good-natured dig couldn't dampen Jim's mood.

Supper was cheerful as the men ate a well-earned meal lounging around the fire. Soon enough, it was time for them to prepare for battle, the most serious game of all. As he helped his brother finish dabbing on black war paint, envy slid inside Jim like a familiar snake awakening.

Mopai sat nearby, covering his chest in yellow.

Jim's indebtedness to Pump warred with his practical side. He should never have made that promise to him. Rutsima's open invitation to join the raid tempted him with a crooked finger. He didn't need to stay here.

Reluctantly, he scanned the homestead with his brother's eyes and saw a pitiful half-man living a half-life in his own filth without the sense to move to a clean campground. One who had forgotten everything he had been taught about honor or right and wrong. It was a testament to his brother's devotion that he was trying to rescue him.

When he squinted, he could see this land through Pump's eyes. He had relearned most Anglo customs, but he didn't prefer them, and they still confused him. His promise tugged at his neck, and he rubbed at it, jabbing a missed paint spot on his brother's face with his free hand.

Rutsima dodged away in annoyance, the whites of his eyes glowing against the black.

Jim handed the paint back to him. "Done," he said.

At the commotion, Mopai glanced at him, his hand blue from laying finger stripes down his face.

Dubious of Jim's handiwork, Rutsima frowned. "Do you have a mirror? I forgot mine."

Jim nodded and went to retrieve it from the cabin.

Next to the hearth, Eva sat on the bench, but she stood when he entered.

Now that they were alone, he let himself pity the sight of her eye and neck. "Are you okay?"

"I'm fine." Her eyes flashed.

"Did you eat?"

"Yes."

They stared at each other in silence.

Jim didn't know what to say. He wanted to comfort her but didn't know if she would welcome it. "I came in for the mirror."

Eva turned, picked it up from the washstand, and passed it to him. Their fingers grazed. Impulsively, he caught her wrist before she let go. At the contact, her eyes widened, her face shifting to the fear-struck face of another woman. He looked away until the memory faded, then took the mirror and brought her hand up. In the firelight, he saw fresh scrapes on her palm and kissed them with gentle lips. A single tear rolled down her cheek.

"I'm sorry, Eva," he whispered. His gut twisted as another tear pooled on her lashes, and her face turned red from suppressed feeling, her pain digging at the splinter in his heart. He cupped her unbruised cheek, then pulled her to him, where she buried her head in his chest. "I'm very sorry, notsaʔka." When he felt her shudder, he tilted her head up. Forehead to forehead, he said, "You can't cry right now. Later."

Eva squeezed her eyes shut and inhaled sharply, then drew back, nodding and sniffing, and wiped her face.

"You need to come out. You can't hide in here."

"I'm not hiding."

Jim cocked his head, brows raised. "Wash your face and follow me."

As they were leaving, he paused. He tried to think if there was anything else to warn her about. "Don't touch any of their things, especially their war shields, or we'll have a repeat of earlier."

Eva threw up her hands in mock surrender and obvious distaste. "Never would have crossed my mind."

As war leader, Rutsima brought out his pipe after the evening meal and filled it with tobacco, offering a piece to their guiding spiritual powers before lighting it. It moved from warrior to solemn horse-warrior, and when it reached Jim, he inhaled homesickness along with the smoke and closed his eyes. After exhaling, he stretched across Eva to return it to his brother.

When they danced, he let himself join them and felt as if he were treading on his heart with each turn and pound of his foot. Eva watched him, her eyes never leaving his body as he turned in front of her, and his head filled with the rhythmic, throbbing chants. His voice blended with the other men's, the only bit of himself that could join the raiding party tonight.

Just before the sun fully set, Rutsima deemed them ready, and they gathered their things to depart. Fireflies danced in the dusk.

"Anything you want me to tell our father?" Rutsima asked as he settled his buffalo-horned cap on his head.

Jim thought for a moment. "Just tell him I have not forgotten him."

"It will be good when you can tell him yourself," Rutsima said.

Jim nodded once but didn't reply. "Don't raid my neighbors," he said, jerking his chin toward San Felipe.

Rutsima cocked an eyebrow. "I don't make promises I don't want to keep, Brother. Besides, your 'neighbors' are so spread apart, it's hard to tell if they are your neighbors or *my* neighbors." With feral eagerness, he grinned, chuckling at his own joke.

Jim felt like he should laugh — wanted to laugh. It was funny. There was no good reason for his brother to pass over the farms and ranches nearby. They were plump and ready for harvest.

"After all, horses belong to those who can hold them," Rutsima said, stroking his pony's neck. He had refreshed the circles of red paint around its eyes and braided its tail for battle.

"True enough." Jim uncovered and handed up his brother's puha-infused war shield, its ring of feathers trembling in the night breeze. "At least skip the farm immediately down the road from me." Jim pointed in the direction of the man he had helped with the pen. "I know him, and he knows me."

His brother followed his finger. "We can get him another time."

Jim knew this was not a joke. In the coming months, Rutsima expected Jim to join him once and for all, leaving a trail of destruction in his wake. They both spoke as if his life here were temporary, this homestead a convenient base camp for raids. Jim thought he was undecided, but he was mostly unsure about his village's reception if he ever returned, and as much as Jim resisted Anglo ways, Pump had persuaded him that this farm was his only realistic option.

His brother's words stirred a deep unease in his chest. Raiding a man who had embraced him as a friend would not be easy.

Regardless, it was a creek to cross another day. Brushing his concerns aside, he placed his hand over Rutsima's beaded moccasin. "Good hunting."

His brother reached down for a firm shake, then glanced at Eva, who stood several paces behind Jim's shoulder and dipped his chin in a goodbye. Eva returned Rutsima's gesture, both of them unsure of the protocol for someone like her. Jim raised his hand to them all.

They whooped and saluted him with their bows and lances. Under his paint, Mopai glared at Eva every time he looked at her, but he lifted his arm high to Jim. He had refused anything from her hand and had preferred to eat his own trail food. Without a further sound or signal of farewell, he turned his pony.

With their departure, Eva's jaw relaxed, and she came to stand next to Jim. Together, they watched the group grow smaller under the moonlight until they rounded the bend.

"What does nᵻmᵻnaitᵻ mean?"

Jim lifted his brows, impressed with her pronunciation. "It means a person living as one of the People."

"I heard Mopai call you that."

Curious, Jim turned to her. "Yes."

"I thought you were considered one of the People," Eva said, tilting her head.

Jim mulled over how to answer. How did you describe being two things at once? "I am, and I'm not. I have full rights and honors. I can rise to be a leader of my people. But everyone knows I was not born Nᵻmᵻ. It rarely matters to most people. But sometimes, I must prove myself worthy beyond doubt."

"Do you feel you must be more Comanche than a Comanche?" He ignored her choice of words. When he didn't answer, she added, "Today's games seemed less of a game to you."

As he studied her face, he pondered her question. He would never have thought to phrase it like that. "Perhaps. Or perhaps I just want to be the best." He smiled his most arrogant smile, pleased she had been watching him.

"And what does Pasahòo Kwitapu̱ mean? That's your name, right?"

"Pigeon Dung." He paused for the laugh he knew would come and beamed when she delivered.

"Pigeon Dung?"

"It's not my formal name, not my secret name. It's just my name for everyday use."

"Ah, like a nickname," she said. The twilight had dissolved to complete darkness, and the mosquitoes were moving through breakfast and on to second breakfast and midmorning snack. After slapping her cheek, she turned on her heel and headed toward the cabin.

"Yes, a bit like a nickname." Jim reached the steps before her and ascended.

"And… why Pigeon Dung?"

"A bird shat on my head once, and there were people there to witness it. I was just 'boy' or 'little shit' before that. It was a step up for me. Most people just call me Pigeon or Pasahòo."

Eva gave him a pitying look.

"Ru̱tsima means 'Fall By Tripping,'" he said. He wished his brother were here for this conversation. They would speak in Spanish for his full benefit. "I think that's much worse, don't you? You can't control birds, but you can control your own feet."

Eva snickered, and he smiled to see her smiling again.

"Does Mopai mean asshole?" When he shook his head, the light left Eva's eyes.

"It means 'Owl.'"

"Owl? How did your brother get Fall By Tripping, and that asshole ended up with anything other than 'Asshole?'"

Jim had never heard an Anglo woman use such language. She's not Anglo, he remembered, correcting himself. He shrugged. Everyday names were ephemeral things. "You can call him Asshole if you like. If enough people join you, it'll stick." He sat next to her on the hearth bench. "Say it in English, and he'll never know."

Eva didn't respond to his quip.

"It could be worse," he continued. "Rɨtsima could be Pia Rɨtsima, which means Big Fall By Tripping. Or Kwitawooʔwooki, which means Barking Buttocks."

She seemed to chew over the names.

In the dim light, they stared at the dying coals together, but when she didn't move to add wood, he wondered if he would have to say something. With puckered lips, he waited. And waited. Neither spoke. Somewhere, a cricket chirruped in the corner, and Wokweesi sighed, laying his head on his crossed paws. Finally, out of patience, Jim decided that, yes, in fact, he would indeed have to say something. "One of us will need to build the fire back up because one of us has let it nearly die."

Eva turned her head to him. She swept her hand before her, leveling it at the hearth. "Be my guest."

At her tone, Jim squinted, irritation rising, and a long, baffling silence stretched between them.

Chapter 16

Jim

"It's your responsibility, not mine," Jim said.

Her face unreadable again, she stared ahead, jaw clenched, not looking at him. He had never seen her look stubborn like this. Once she could move without pain, she had been more than willing to help. He didn't know how to handle this insubordination. Not only were their roles clear, but she owed him her life. Should he beat her? He had seen husbands beat their wives. Very rarely, but it happened. Usually, a matron would beat her subordinates if necessary. Some Anglos definitely beat their wives. But she wasn't his wife. Or his captive. How did Anglos — wait... No, he reminded himself, she's not Anglo. How did someone like her repay life debts between a man and a woman? Sighing, he stretched a leg out straight. "Eva..."

She turned her head, pinning him with her eyes. This was about more than the dead fire; he should have guessed. Under her scrutiny, he lowered his gaze and shifted on the bench, then did the previously unthinkable to break the tension: gathered kindling and wood to build up the blaze. Within minutes, the familiar crackling and mesmerizing flames calmed him. He sat back on his heels. At a vicious thought that this might be a game to have her own way, he checked her face.

She stared dejectedly into the fire, tears streaming down her cheeks, her wounded eye swollen shut and darker than it had been when he had retrieved the mirror.

He pivoted on his foot and remained squatting in front of her, then placed a hand on her knee. She looked down at him. The fire picked out twinkling strands of light in her dark hair, and he could see the flames reflected in her shining eye.

After a moment, he held his hand open to her, and when she laid hers in it, he put his other hand on top. "You're safe. Mopai will not bother you again. I promise."

She nodded.

"It was a misunderstanding," he continued.

Eva pursed her lips and gave her head the briefest of shakes, eyes cutting to the side.

He didn't know how to interpret her reaction, but clearly, she disagreed. Mopai was a good man. A man of honor and a good horse-warrior. "I should have thought to clarify your status with all the men, not just my brother."

"My status being?"

"Unclear."

"Otherwise, fair game?"

"Well..." Jim shifted his weight. "Captives, yes, but it is considered rude to take you without my permission. He wouldn't have known if I intended to make you a wife or not. Though I am one of the People, not being born Nʉmʉ sometimes means warriors think they can take what they want from men like me because it's harder for me to do anything about it."

As she listened to what he said, he watched her face. "For wives, not fair game. I mean, not for the rest of the men. For my brother, yes. I share everything with him, and he with me." Her good eye widened. "But Mopai thought you went to him willingly. Captives aren't expected to be virtuous and faithful unless their captor intends to take them as a wife. He made an assumption. He has always treated me like a born Nʉmʉ and would never have insulted me like that on purpose."

Eva stared at him, her jaw pulsing. "So, to clarify, my being 'unclear' is the only thing that saved me?"

"No, you being unclear is what got you in trouble, and that's partially my fault. Your strange medicine saved both of us."

"And you didn't save me."

This suddenly felt like a trick question spoken like a declaration. He wasn't sure they were having the same conversation. "Of course, I saved you. My brother and I both saved you. Me a second time, I might add." Jim's temper rose.

"So, it's just okay to rape any woman any time and in front of God and everyone?" Eva threw her hands up, wrenching them from his own.

Jim tried to remain calm. "No, not anyone. I just said not —"

"I don't care what you just said. Would they have taken turns with me?" She waited for him to answer with an indignant look on her face.

"Maybe." Again, this felt like a trick question. "But only because you seemed available, and they didn't —"

"Look, my people don't rape women. It just doesn't happen."

She had interrupted him twice, and he took a deep breath for patience. His knees complained about the puncheon floor. As he stood up, he realized what she had said. "Anglos don't rape women?" Incredulity twisted his face. "What do you think —" Jim's thoughts went in several directions, and elders recited tribal history in his ear. "Do you have any idea what the Spanish have —"

"I didn't say Anglos or Span —"

Jim caught the back of her head and clapped a hand over her mouth. "That is the third time you have interrupted me. My people don't interrupt each other, even when they are arguing… especially when they are arguing." Had she not noticed he had been silent longer and longer before responding? He could feel her trying to bite his hand. Fitting. He smirked, which infuriated her. When she was still long enough, he cautiously moved away. "What were you going to say?"

Her one good eye was red and puffy. "I'm sorry. I will try not to interrupt." It seemed to take every effort for her to say that calmly.

Jim acknowledged her with a tilt of his head.

"I was saying: I didn't say Anglos or the Spanish don't rape. I know perfectly well they do. I said my people don't rape."

"And who are your people?"

She hesitated, but he could tell she knew. Without a doubt. It was on the tip of her tongue. She just needed to open her mouth. He waited. For the first time since he had found her, she looked calculating, weighing and discarding pieces of information as she bit her lower lip. "My people are the Lux Libera. They live far from here, very, very far."

"I have never heard of the Lux Libera."

"I know. I would be very shocked if you had."

Jim reflected on their interactions the last weeks and studied her face. She wasn't telling him everything, but she was telling him the truth. None of the Anglo women, captive or free, had ever spoken as she had or known so little of even the common things between Nʉmʉnʉʉ or Mexicans, let alone Anglos. "Sounds Latin," he finally said. His recognition seemed to surprise her, so he explained. "I had just started learning Latin before we left Tennessee. And I've been dragged to enough masses since I returned to recognize the sound."

Eva bobbed her head. "You're correct. It means 'Free Light.'"

Jim listened, waiting for more. None was forthcoming.

"How many women have you raped?" she asked.

Blinking, Jim drew his chin back at her question. He had still been hoping for more explanation from her. "I don't know. I haven't kept count."

Eva's face crumpled in disgust and disappointment.

"Rape's a strong word," he said. He had never suffered this sort of accusation from someone regarding normal behavior. In fact, exploits were necessary and worthy of boasting about. They kept enemies at bay. His people had been on the receiving end many years ago. It was every man's duty to make sure that never happened again. He had always thought of himself as a war shield, protecting his people, and he imagined threading his arms through the straps of his old medicine shield now, the weight of it as real as if it still existed. "How else do you take revenge on an enemy?" he asked. "Especially when they do the same to our women. Their men deserve it. If the women are lucky, they make more Numunuu. They can even become wives."

Eva's mouth hung open. "What about the women?"

"What about the women?" Confusion mixed with inexplicable guilt, burning his chest. "It has nothing to do with the women. It has everything to do with the men. In fact, if the women cooperate, that's all that happens to them."

"And if they don't?" Eva cringed as if an ax were about to fall.

Jim pointed to her eye. "Or worse."

"Do I deserve it?"

"No!" Jim's frustration startled her, making her jump. "You are not my enemy's woman." How else could he explain?

"But until three years ago, Anglo women were enemy women to you. Now they're not? What changed? Do they suddenly have feelings? Can they suddenly experience pain? How are enemy women different from your women? Does any woman deserve it? How come you didn't rape me the moment you found me?"

Eva's questions rained down on him with a force he could not defend against. He had no answer. He couldn't explain why it had been different; it just had. Things were different now. He was navigating two completely different worlds.

"This hurts." Eva pointed at her eye. "This hurts." Her throat. "If you had not come when you did, this would have hurt. All of this. Inside." She circled her belly. "All women bleed the same."

She pressed on the splinter in his heart. Faces cowered beneath him, memories unbidden. A quieter voice inside him countered that pain was entirely the point. He couldn't take her direct gaze and looked away, peering into the fire for answers that weren't there.

"There are unspoken rules. It's not just random," Jim said. "I haven't raped you or even expected anything from you because I haven't known exactly what was custom here. Among my people, unmarried women are the ones who approach men for lovemaking... secretly, of course, though the village usually knows everyone's business. But a man waits for the woman. It would be ill-mannered of me to treat you any other way. I tried to treat you how I would have treated you if you were a woman in my village. And definitely never like a captive. I don't know what an Anglo man would have done with you if he had found you. The rules are different here. I know that."

"This isn't about Anglo customs or Nʉmʉnʉʉ customs. I'm asking you to simplify your rules. Don't make it about men and men's honor anymore." Eva extended her hand, but he stared at it for a moment before taking it. She pulled him down to sit beside her and peered up at him. "It's the women you are hurting. Individual women. Not 'enemies.' Not their men. Not just someone's sister or daughter or mother or aunt. They have names. It should be enough." She started crying again, silent pain sliding down her face to hang from her chin.

Jim cupped her unbruised cheek and wiped away the tears that kept coming. He thought of the captive women in his memory, but they all looked like Eva now. He thought of his older sister and what he had witnessed, what he had gone on to do as the years passed. Memories he had bundled away now spilled out like clothing from an overstuffed bag. More Comanche than a Comanche.

Jim bent his head and brought her hands to his mouth, then gazed into her eyes, his own tears threatening.

"Your word is important to you, is it not?" Eva asked.

Jim nodded, unsure he could safely give voice.

"Promise me. Promise me you will never force another woman."

Throat swelling, Jim swallowed and thought of his brother's parting words: I don't make promises I don't want to keep. Out of necessity, he had made a promise to Pump he now regretted. He swept a lock of damp hair behind Eva's ear.

Could he promise? Could he ever return to his people and keep that promise? How would he control his captives? It had never been a lust of his. He had enjoyed it once he had gotten used to it, but he didn't yearn for it. Would the other men tease him? He thought of his brothers. His friends. Would he lose their respect? Or could he embrace being merely Nʉmʉnaitʉ? He was no longer a boy trying to prove himself a man of the People. Jim followed a tear down the side of her nose and over her lips. He lifted it off with the tip of his finger and rubbed the wetness with his thumb.

Would he ever be able to harden his heart in those moments as he had before? He silenced the voice in his head, taking his heart out and turning it over in his mind. He didn't think so. Jim willed his heart to be hard, but it ignored him. A queasiness took its place, knowing that all the future faces would look like Eva's, that the faces haunting his conflicted heart for the last year or more would never rest. He focused on her and saw fear creeping in. He was taking too long to deliberate, but Jim finally knew the answer to a hidden question that had taken root the moment he had returned to Anglo society, and which had grown to a size he could no longer ignore. He kissed her fingers again, tasting salt.

"Yes. I give you my word." The splinter pulled free, leaving a deep tenderness behind.

Chapter 17

Eva

Jim slept on the floor that night. Eva suspected he was afraid to sleep in the bed with her. She settled down with her back to the hearth, facing the wall, and as she tried to sleep, she imagined the raid taking place somewhere in the colony. Throughout the night, she pushed at the corn shuck mattress, rearranging lumps, only to kick off the blankets, then untwist them again when she got cold.

In the late morning, she woke to find Jim and Wokweesi long gone and the fire dead. She didn't know how to interpret that, but today unfolded before her like a new white sheet. No actual harm had come to her yesterday, and now that it was just her and Jim again, her body was relaxing.

It was easy enough to shrug off the warrior's attack, to fall back into a solid belief that he wasn't real — that he could hurt her, yes, but in the sense that an avalanche might if you didn't have the sense to get out of the way. She had been in scrapes before, but always with Tophe by her side. To approach the tree unarmed, without a single thought regarding the seasoned warrior asleep at its base, had been the height of stupidity. Not just stupid. Reckless and impatient. In the end, she bundled the experience away as a lesson learned, a warning against hubris.

Eva spent the morning at the corral, watching a small herd of eight horses getting to know each other. They had seemingly sprung from thin air overnight. Briefly, she tried to form a portal on the pecan tree but gave it up for lost. Even in her panicked state with Mopai, she hadn't heard the strings, and the morning had brought no change.

By mid-afternoon, Jim had not returned, and she wondered if he had gone to break a horse for a neighbor, remembering he had mentioned such a task. After finding something to eat, she had done the bare minimum of the work Jim had delegated to her and now had stretched out, napping on the porch, or rather, the gallery, as he called it. She felt his moccasined footfalls through the floorboards before she heard him walking through the breezeway. When he sat at her feet, she peered at him for a moment with her one good eye before sitting upright.

"Where have you been?" she asked.

"I finished making something for you." He placed a black strap in her lap, and she fought the reflex to toss it away when she saw the black scales.

As she ran her finger over the skin, she discerned the subtle black and brown bands for the first time. He'd threaded the belt through the loop of a sheath.

"This is my spare knife, which is now yours."

Eva turned the scabbard over in her hands, studying the patterned rows of blue and white seed beads along the side housing the sharp edge and letting the long, thin fringe run through her fingertips. "Did you make this sheath, too?" she asked.

"No, my sister did. I just added a ribbon of snakeskin to her decoration so it would match your new belt."

She withdrew the blade, hefted the weight and balance of it, and tested the edge with her thumb. Warmth blossomed through her core at his thoughtful gift, her chest swelling, and she locked eyes with him. "Thank you. It's beautiful."

"You're welcome. Here, I'll help you put it on." They stood, and he reached around her as she spread her arms. He positioned it with great care, lingering along her waist, and she smiled up at him. When he met her eyes and mirrored her smile, her fears about his fears of touching her disappeared. He tightened the belt slowly before securing the laces, then rested his hands on her hips.

His face grew serious. "I want you to be able to defend yourself next time."

"I should've been able to defend myself this time." Eva let her anger at herself leak through her lips. "I've been trained; I was just rusty. I usually kill from a distance."

"No," Jim said. He shook his head, then spoke again more emphatically, "No. Mopai is an experienced horse-warrior, twice your weight and strength. There was nothing you could have done. I've never seen a woman escape from a Nʉmʉ man when he was ready for her. If you had tried to kill him, he would have killed you. If you had killed him,

I would not have been able to stop them from killing *you*. They would not have made it a quick death."

Eva's thoughts tangled around the threat. "Then how do I defend myself?"

"If it is an Anglo man, kill him. But for my people, I recommend, very much, you bluff. You should intend to kill if necessary — the bluff must not look like a bluff — but only follow through if you absolutely must." His hands tightened around her waist. "They respect courage. If you pull your knife against a Numu man, and you threaten convincingly, if you draw some blood but don't kill him — he should back off." He drew her hips toward him until their bodies brushed. "But you don't show fear. Ever."

"And if none of that stops a Numu man, what then? Do I kill him?"

"Only if no one else is around to witness, and it is the best of bad choices." Jim laid his forehead on hers and closed his eyes. "Would you have killed him if you had found his knife?"

"Easily."

His eyes squeezed, and his hands cupped her buttocks, drawing her closer. She wrapped her arms around his back and laid her head on his chest, but then, just as he pulled himself away, she noticed part of him pressing into her belly. Coals sparked inside her, but she took a wise step back to increase the distance further. She'd made a vow. Her feelings couldn't be real. Shouldn't be.

To lighten the mood, she peeked down at her new blade and said, "We should have a knife-throwing contest."

Jim grinned.

She pointed at her swollen eye. "You might stand a chance of beating me."

"Is that so?"

"It is."

"Lead the way, sir," he said in a falsetto mimic of her previous shooting challenge to him.

*   *   *

Multiverse Copy
Petersburg, Virginia, United States, 1858

Water dripped down the alley walls and puddled in the gaps and missing cobblestones near Eva's feet. The rain had cleared, but now the humidity rose in a noxious cloud from the refuse piled around her. She crouched in the shadows, waiting for Tophe to lure his new friend within striking distance. A rat scurried under her skirt, over her foot, and out the other side. She bit her knuckle to keep from squealing in surprise. Rats didn't bother her as much as they did Tophe, but show her the person who wouldn't have been startled by a rodent entering their clothes. He would have had a good laugh at her expense.

Carriages and carts clattered by in the street, and people passed across the alley entrance without glancing in her direction. Even if they had looked, they wouldn't have seen her in the gloom.

Abruptly, Tophe and a gentleman rounded the corner, with Tophe pulling at his sleeve to guide him farther in and to a stop. The gentleman was laughing at something Tophe had said, and Tophe bent down to pretend to tie his shoelace. That was Eva's cue.

After rising on silent haunches, she threw her knife and struck the man in the throat, followed swiftly with one in the chest. Tophe caught him and pulled him behind a stack of empty crates while Eva scanned the street. No one had noticed a thing. It didn't matter if anyone had; they would be gone before someone could discover the body, much less apprehend them.

Eva retrieved her knives and took her time wiping them carefully on the man's shirt, then held each up to inspect before returning them to their sheaths. She didn't always use knives, but they were probably her favorite.

"He was quite good this time, actually," Tophe said.

"Oh?" Eva stood and brushed off her skirts.

"Yes, I was shocked. I mean, Booth's always been good-looking, but he really could act. Excellent swordsmanship — for a play, at least. He had a harem of women in the front row swooning over him."

Eva gazed at the man's face. She reached down to close his eyes and then reevaluated his appearance. His hair had a nice, tousled wave to it. Other women might call him handsome, but not being keen on mustaches herself, she looked at Tophe and shrugged.

Without another word, they moved as one to reenter the street. She accepted his arm and squinted in the sunlight, shading her eyes. They joined the throng and proceeded down the streets of Petersburg. It was not far to a cemetery with a secluded tree and home to the True line, but they took their time as if they had no place else to be.

—ℓℓ—

Elder Roberts met them at the sanctum of Axis Mundi as they exited the gigantic, ancient ash some had nicknamed Yggdrasil, though it was too holy for any single word. It went by many names, but Eva preferred that one. He lifted his brows. For him, they had left and returned to the same moment.

"No problems," Tophe said.

Elder Roberts nodded. He had expected nothing less.

"He was an excellent actor in that version."

Eva laughed, surprised Tophe was still on that topic.

"What? He was. Do you know how many of his terrible plays I have sat through in other timelines? Baise moi. I was beginning to think I should stand up in time to get your knife in my back. Put me out of my misery."

Elder Roberts' eyes crinkled. "Well, thank goodness his good acting saved one of our Menders."

The three of them strode together across the sloping lawn toward the pavilion. As Tophe had cultivated a budding friendship with their target, he and Eva had been gone for a few days. Now back at the sanctum, Eva was starving for a satisfying meal. The boarding house where they had lodged had disgusting food. She was reasonably sure the widow running it had murdered her husband with her lousy cooking.

"I have some good news I wanted to share with you after you returned," Elder Roberts said.

Eva's hopes soared.

"If you can forgo showers and food for a bit longer, the council would like to meet with you now."

Eva and Tophe clasped hands but avoided looking at each other. "Of course," he replied for them both. They passed a class of novitiates practicing takedowns. Most of them were children, some very young. A breeze funneled through the massive pavilion, hugging Eva's skirts to her legs and carrying doves into the rafters.

Ahead, the council house floated in an enormous oak, one of many in an expanding circle that faded into a forest of primordial trees. Sunlight streamed down in variegated strands of rippling light. She remembered the first time she had been brought here, aged just twelve years. Her head craned back to take in the lofty canopy, which supported elevated platforms and elaborate multi-room tree houses connected by suspension bridges, spiral staircases, and rope ladders. When she'd asked how this could be, her recruiter realized a difference between Eva's birth timeline and the True line of Axis Mundi. The Romans and Christian missionaries had never chopped down the sacred groves of the ancient Germanic peoples in the True line. They were still alive. The recruiter's hand had swept up in a proud arc to the sky. Here, a raft of holy space drifted in a river of time.

For Eva, joy always bubbled when she took in the exquisite combination of metals blended seamlessly with the natural outlines of the oaks and ashes. Decorated with nods to traditional patterns and motifs, the additions gave the impression of having grown from the trees themselves. Nothing quite like it existed in any other timeline, and its untouched survival through the 20th century only confirmed Axis Mundi's sacredness for her and every other member of Lux Libera.

Elder Roberts led the way into an elevator. His knees no longer appreciated long walks up staircases. From the top, it was a short walk to the chamber. A panel of six men and women waited for them. Elder Roberts took his place at the table, completing the set of seven.

Eva and Tophe stood respectfully before them and inclined at the waist, both hands across their bellies. They kept their eyes downcast.

"We have been very pleased with your work, Sister Eva and Brother Christophe," Elder Nnaji said.

Now they had been addressed, Eva and Tophe lifted their gazes.

"Your mimics of John Wilkes Booth's mugging death have been exemplary," she continued. "Each thread has aligned more perfectly with the True line, and you have achieved them without additional entanglements."

Eva smiled at her words, and Tophe's shoulders squared as his chest swelled with pride. She knew what he was hoping for; she hoped for the same.

"We would like you to switch your focus for the time being. We have several jobs for you in Charlemagne's court."

Eva's heart sank. It wasn't that she minded the new assignment. It could be exciting, but it was less than she wanted. Tophe sighed as if he wished to speak but remained silent. She cut her eyes to him, but he stared straight ahead. When they were dismissed, they bowed, and Tophe marched out of the room, hands behind his back. Eva doubled her pace to catch up.

Without slowing down, Tophe took the stairs two at a time. It wasn't until they reached the ground that she could walk beside him again. He glanced down at her and wagged his head. "We're ready to lead, not just be grunts."

"I know," she said, disappointment eating at her. "It'll happen for us. I know it will. We just have to be patient."

After a moment, he nodded and shook out his arms.

"And can you please slow down?"

Tophe over-corrected with exaggerated, snail-paced strides.

Eva rolled her eyes.

"What? You asked me to slow down," he said, tossing his hands up in mock confusion.

Her stomach couldn't wait any longer, so she left him behind.

"Now, who's walking too fast?" he shouted after her. He caught up and crushed her shoulders in a sideways hug. She punched him in the chest, smirking, and he let go to clutch his heart as if wounded.

Chapter 18

Eva

Jim's Farm

Jim and Eva studied the bumper crop of cotton, flourishing despite ample weeds. Several rows were denuded — yesterday's work — but the field might as well have been untouched. The morning bit crisply, and Wokweesi made his patrol rounds. With some rot starting to show, Eva suspected they were pushing the edge of optimal harvest season.

"Remind me again why we have to do this," Eva said. They each held empty tow sacks nearly as big as herself. Nasty cuts and scratches stung whenever she flexed her fingers, and she wished, for the thousandth time, for a pair of goddamn gloves. At least her face had fully healed.

Jim glanced down at her. "I'm wondering the same thing." Neither of them moved. "Do we have enough meat?" he asked.

"Yes. Do you have any dirty linens that need washing?" she replied.

"No."

"Rock, Paper, Scissors? I win, we don't do it?" Two days before, she had taught him the game to get out of a different chore. Instead of treating her like a servant, Jim had kept her with him most every day since his brother had left, and they had increasingly ignored the farm together in favor of more enjoyable pursuits. Today, though, he didn't respond and seemed to be thinking, miles away.

After he remained silent, she sighed and took a step toward where they had left off yesterday, but Jim grabbed her arm and stopped her. When she turned to him, his eyes searched hers.

Moving a strand of hair behind her ear, he opened his mouth and said, "Come wi —" Within the next heartbeat, his words seemed to freeze in his throat, and his gaze shifted over her head as she heard the rattle of a wagon.

Eva turned to peer over her shoulder. Pump had returned! With company, it appeared. She turned back to Jim, who was scowling. He threw down his sack, muttering in Comanche, and brushed her side as he passed. For a moment, Eva watched his retreating back, then followed. The tips of her wet boots peeked out from under her skirts as she walked. Blades of damp straw covered them, and the bottom edge of her dress soaked up the dew.

Jim stood below Pump, who still sat on the seat of his buckboard, reins in hand. She could see them arguing. Jim lowered his head, tossed his arms, and stalked away. Pump slapped the reins once, nodded to her, unsmiling, as she approached, and his team continued toward the barn. Two men sat on the tailgate of the wagon, feet dangling. Eva raised her hand as they went by, and they returned her greeting as they trundled away.

By the time Eva returned to the cotton rows, Jim had started picking again, mumbling to himself in a mixture of English and Comanche. When he heard her approaching, he lifted his eyes. "I told him no slaves." He pulled four bolls in quick succession and deposited them in his bag.

Eva cocked her head, both confused and curious about his reaction. "Are you an abolitionist?"

"I don't know what that means." He stuffed another handful in his sack.

"It means you want to abolish slavery. Make it illegal." Eva plucked her first few bolls and rolled the cotton between her fingers, feeling the seeds.

"No, of course not."

Disappointment dropped into her chest. She hadn't expected a different answer, but it still weighed heavily.

When the silence grew, Jim stood up straight. "Why?"

"I'm just wondering why it bothers you so much to have slaves helping us. Is it because you know what it's like to be a slave?"

Jim pushed his hair back, eyes turning thoughtful. "I was only a captive as long as I acted like a captive. As soon as I proved my worth, I was considered one of the People." He bent to collect another handful. "Race doesn't matter to the Nʉmʉnʉʉ; it's about loyalty and accepting a superior way of life. Anyone is capable of it." He shoved the cotton bolls into his sack. "Anglos kill their captives when they try to prove their worth." Jim's face turned angry again. "I watched my Anglo father beat a slave to death once. The man had defied him somehow, repeatedly. He could have been a great horse-warrior among the People. It's unjust."

The logic of his argument walked a line as fine as a silk thread.

"So, why not support abolishing slavery?"

Frowning, Jim stopped picking. "How would a community function without slaves?"

Quite well, she thought. How could she describe slave-free societies to him?

"Look at this homestead," he continued. He pointed at the field, the barn, the cabin. "There is more pointless work here than the two of us could ever hope to do. Among the People, who would look after the vast herds on the plains?"

Unable to follow his reasoning, she asked, "If you know there is more work here than you can handle, why are you pushing so hard against Pump?"

Jim stared at the ground, his heart clearly divided in two. "This crop, this homestead, is important to Pump, and he wants it to be important to me. I'm true to my word, the promise I made to give this a real go." He shook his bag, shifting the cotton to the bottom. "But I won't be their Anglo overseer just to please him."

By this point, the three visitors joined them, and Pump led the two men deeper into the field to start at an opposite corner.

That night, Eva's back ached in places she didn't know she had muscles. She examined the cuts on her fingers; most would heal easily, but one probably needed a stitch. Jim helped her clean and bandage it. Her neck and cheeks warmed as he gently mended her hands with his rough ones. When he finished, he allowed her to tend to his own cuts. She sensed him studying her face; her hands wanted to wander, but she forced them to stick to their task.

Supper was quiet, with Pump and Jim barely exchanging a word. The other two men, Caesar and Kitch, spoke in hushed tones between themselves. When they were done eating, Jim escorted them to the barn and didn't return.

Pump simmered in silence across from Eva. Apparently unwilling to bite his tongue any longer, he said, "This year's crop yield was the best since the colony was founded, and Jim got a pittance planted."

Eva met his eyes, not knowing how to reply, then slid her gaze elsewhere. This wasn't her fight. For her part, she would happily walk away from this place as soon as she could. But then an image of Jim's hands, his careful touch, came to mind. Well, maybe not happily, she thought. Or too soon.

Pump seemed to remember who he was talking to. "Never mind," he said, shaking his head. "I shouldn't expect you to understand."

"Jim would be happier returning to his people."

Profound sadness pulled on his heavy jowls. "I know it," he said to the ground. He flicked the dregs of his coffee into the fire. "I'm afraid to ask where the new horses came from. Lucky for him, I don't recognize any of them."

"Can I ask you a question?" she said, ignoring his comment.

"Shoot." His eyes reflected the light. "Pass me my pipe first, though, if you would be so kind."

Eva rolled her questions in the palm of her hand and flattened them out into a statement. "You've seen lots of futures where economies function without slaves."

He affirmed with a flick of his pipe stem, then packed a large pinch of tobacco.

"Until recently…" she relinquished her thought for a moment. Pump glanced up at her and then lit the bowl, puffing with his eyes focused down his nose. She continued, "When I was a child, slavery had long been abolished in my birth timeline… at least in my country. Growing up, I was taught it was wrong, and I still believe it's wrong, even after joining Lux Libera. I think timelines are better without it, even if they're not the True line, even if they're not real."

Pump moved to sit on the ground with his back to the log, legs stretched in front of him. His eyebrows rose slightly when she didn't speak for a moment, though he remained silent.

"As a Lux Libera, the question of slavery has been irrelevant. Timelines are set. The Fated can't choose whether they are master or slave." Eva remembered the many variations of suffering she had seen in every refraction, every thread. "But now, having met you," she continued, gesturing toward him.

He dipped his head in acknowledgment.

"… I no longer know what to believe." Her initial epiphany had faded from that night when Jim had returned from the Allens with honey. Pump had planted seeds of doubt, to be sure, but she seesawed between truths: one moment, Eva knew she had overreacted, and he was deluded; the next, Eva believed everything he had told her, especially when she was around Jim. Most of her day was spent with Jim. "If we say, for argument's sake, that everyone, not just Lux Libera, has free will, how can you stand by and condone slavery?"

"Ah," he said, now that they had finally reached her question. He shrugged. "This is the reality I live in."

She frowned at the weak answer.

"Do you know what ends slavery in most timelines?" he asked.

Eva could think of several factors, but nothing she could mark out as "most," and after a moment, she lifted a shoulder.

"Machines," he replied.

"But what about the abolitionists?"

"Oh, they play their role, but they are only successful when slavery is breathing its dying breath, and they can push it over, sometimes with war, if necessary. Each generation has slaves who seize freedom for themselves and reformed oppressors who work to improve society for more people, but so long as there is a need for free or cheap labor… morality doesn't have much to do with it. They have to wait for alternative ways to present themselves that will meet the needs of their community." He took a long draw from his pipe. "Women won't near freedom until appliances are invented," he added.

"But that doesn't answer my question. Do you approve of slavery, then?"

"No, I don't. It's why I'm a trader now. I came here as a planter, with my own slaves, just like Jim's father, but over the years, my travels made it harder and harder on my conscience. I finally freed my slaves and took up a new profession." He pointed at her with his pipe stem. "Luckily, I'm in a territory where it's not illegal yet to free your slaves. And let me tell you, my wife was hopping mad. She's still not gotten over it, if I'm being perfectly honest. Angered my neighbors as well. But what is every other planter going to do? They can't all quit their livelihoods and become traders. Something else needs to replace it. I don't make near the living I did before."

Eva stared into the fire. She wondered where Jim was — he had been gone a long time — then she thought about the options for men in this era, in this colony. Land meant everything.

"With cotton, specifically," Pump continued, "it'll be a hundred years before someone invents a machine that can do what the slaves do now. The mills in the northeast and Britain are ravenous beasts, and the demand for cloth increases every year. The slaves will be free on *paper only* in thirty years. It'll take another ninety for the next baby step to be taken when affordable cotton-picking machines become available." He threw up his hands. "Until then… I do the best I can."

"So, your choice is to do nothing."

At her words, Pump straightened his spine, and the fire sparked off his dark eyes.

Chapter 19

Eva

"My community is fully aware of my views. What more would you have me do, darlin'? You tell me, and I'll do it tomorrow. I'll either be dead or senile before I can vote for Lincoln or join the Union Army. Should I knock on every door and tell the man of the house to let his slaves go free?"

"Yes," she said.

Pump quirked an eyebrow and stared at her over his spectacles. "I know you're not that naïve. People will follow the example you lead, not the words you say. Arguing only makes them dig deeper into their hole."

"Underground railroad."

"If the opportunity presents itself, yes," Pump said.

"Otherwise, stay comfortable."

He clenched his jaw. "I think you're trying to say, 'stay safe.'"

Eva chewed her upper lip.

"Do you have any idea how afraid Anglos are of slave uprisings? Not only could I lead hundreds of people to their deaths, but my entire family might be slaughtered by an angry mob. At the very least, they would have to watch me be executed by authorities."

Eva turned away, irritated with him. "You don't know that."

He picked up his foot and laid it across his ankle. "You're right. I don't know that, but I'd rather choose the path that doesn't eventually branch off to certain death for more than just myself if it's all the same to you. Because it's too early for an uprising. You've seen the successful ones. Are all the pieces in place here? Are there enough people who feel the same way we do?"

Eva inhaled through her nose and narrowed her eyes. "No."

Pump inclined his head and opened his hand.

"Your convictions haven't kept you from using slave labor today," she said.

"I've told Jim he can pay the men for their work here. I borrowed Caesar and Kitch from the McMullens. They're good people. Mr. McMullen lets them keep anything they earn when he lends them out."

"Good people. How can they be good people if they own slaves?" The words sat like solid things in her mouth.

Pump nodded at the oxymoron. "I'm not unsympathetic to that sentiment. Perhaps I should rephrase: They are good people to other Anglos. They'll bend over backward to help a neighbor." He studied her for a moment. "Is that so different from Comanches being good people to other Comanches but exploiting and abusing their neighbors?"

"But at what point is it different? Because it feels different... maybe not now, but when they are being nearly wiped out in timelines like these and confined to reservations… that definitely feels different. Can a people look out for their own to such an extreme that they are no longer good people?"

Pump didn't seem to have a ready answer to that, and he gnawed on his pipe stem, eyes distant. After a while, he said, "I sleep easier at night knowing I've helped the person next to me, including the slaves I freed, rather than sacrificing for people I don't really know, like the Comanches. And for the Negro slaves in this colony, what real power do I have to change anything if I'm not a power broker? In my experience, the people with power win the power because they are interested in the power itself, not necessarily in making change. Change only happens if it aligns with their goal of hanging on to power."

Eva squinted at him. "That seems a very cynical view."

"And yours seems arbitrary to me. It's a luxury for you to judge me from the point of view of a world that has solved this problem and can pretend to have a conscience. If you had come even farther from the future to me, say from the twenty-second century, you would be chastising me for eating meat and exploiting animals. Technology solves those problems and creates new ones as it does so."

Eva gritted her teeth. His argument didn't sit well with her.

"How many of us are truly free?" he continued. "Take Jim. He grew up in a very rigid society with a slave class. Every Anglo thinks the wild Indians live free of any restraints. Nothing could be further from the truth. They have codes of honor, strict roles and expectations for both men and women, extensive unspoken rules and taboos. There's a give and take in every community. I'm not sure any human is truly free when they live together, especially when survival is a daily battle. Community comes first for them. No one chooses their role, and no one questions it. Anglos and their own slaves aren't that dissimilar. Our communities are just structured differently."

"That's not the same thing at all," Eva said. His words didn't entirely square with what Jim had told her.

"No? The need for cheap labor will never fully disappear. At least not in any timeline I've ever visited. The actors may switch roles; those who are slaves in this world are masters in another. But the codes, customs, and laws change to veil slavery from society, and everyone pretends it's something else. People tell themselves what they want to hear, why it's all so needed and justified and right so they can sleep at night. Nobody wants to look too closely at how their clothes are made or why their food is so cheap. They just aren't called slaves anymore. Sometimes they're called sharecroppers or prisoners or migrants or factory workers or debtors or bondsmen or indentured servants or serfs or peons or coolies… I could go on. You know I could. What are the good people doing in those times to fix their societies?"

Smoke drifted toward Eva, and she moved closer to Pump to escape it. "But those people often have the possibility of improving their situation. The Anglos' slaves are born into slavery with no more hope of changing their lot than the horses in the master's stable. Their children will be born slaves, and their children's children."

"Well, you have me there. I won't deny it. That's the abhorrently efficient bit of chattel slavery," Pump said, biting down on his pipe stem with a loud clack. "You been to the worlds where people are classed by eye color?" Pump asked.

Eva creased her brow. "No."

"Interesting places. Sometimes brown eyes are the people in charge. Sometimes purple. Sometimes blue or green, like yours." He banged out the spent contents of his pipe against the log.

After she crossed her legs, she rested her chin in her hand, elbow on knee, and worried a piece of venison trapped between her back molars. They fell silent, each thinking their own thoughts. For Eva, it was strange to have an opinion about a timeline, any timeline other than Axis Mundi and the True line. Such musings were entirely irrelevant to the Lux Libera belief system, and no Mender worth their salt ever wasted energy wondering about the morality of the Fated. It just wasn't a thing; there were no moral compasses in these worlds because they didn't exist. They were just reflections. Now, however, she found herself unsettled rather than neutral. She cared.

"You gotten your ability to travel back yet, gal?" Pump pulled his legs up and draped his hands over his bent knees. "That's actually the question I thought you were going to ask me: when can I train you?"

She tilted her chin, peered at him from under her brows, then shook her head, frowning. Frustration ate at her. Why hadn't she gotten her ability back? What was wrong with her?

Pump smiled to himself like he knew a secret.

"What?"

"Something tells me you ain't completely miserable having to wait a little bit longer."

As if on cue, Jim stepped into the firelight. He said a curt goodnight to Pump and locked eyes with Eva. Saying goodnight as well, she stood to accompany him into the cabin. When she peeked back at the older man still sitting at the fire, he grinned at her.

"Stop," she mouthed. She considered returning just to prove him wrong, but the lure of laying her aching body down was too strong.

It took another day and a half to pull in the rest of the crop. By morning, Jim's temper had cooled, and he and Pump were back on genial terms. Even Kitch and Caesar warmed up and contributed to the conversation or traded turns with Pump singing a work song. Toward the final rows, though, nobody felt like talking or singing anymore. To celebrate the end of the meager harvest, Eva doled out the last of the honey to them all.

After Jim paid the men for their work, Pump hitched the horses to his buckboard, and Kitch and Caesar hopped onto the tailgate. Eva walked over to thank them for their help, holding out her hand.

Wary looks came into both men's eyes, and they glanced as one at Jim and Pump before looking back at her. They shook it in quick succession as if it would burn them, avoiding eye contact. "You're welcome, ma'am," Caesar said.

Eva could sense she had misstepped. Her hand suddenly sweaty, she rubbed it on her skirt without thinking. Shadows passed over their faces, and Eva realized what it looked like. "I... safe travels," she finished. She could feel her cheeks turning red and backed away to tell Pump goodbye.

Jim took in her face and raised his eyebrows until she gave her head the barest of shakes. It's nothing.

Pump stuck out his hand, and Jim shook it firmly, then Eva embraced him.

"Thank you for your help. We wouldn't have gotten it in without you," Jim said. The older man accepted Jim's near-apology with good grace. "I'm glad to have it done," Jim added.

Pump blew out in mutual relief and nodded. He swabbed his scalp, put his hat back on, and climbed to the seat, picking up the reins. "Well, I best get these men back home. After I get it processed at the McMullen's gin, I'll be back to help you cart it to San Felipe."

Wokweesi escorted the wagon until it was out of sight, but before they even rounded the bend, Jim was rummaging in the rafters of the dogtrot. Eva walked up the steps and stood underneath him. "What are you doing?"

Instead of answering, he handed down a muslin-wrapped side of bacon, salt pork, and a small quantity of dried venison. She took each and set them on the worktable in the breezeway; then, he descended the ladder. "I'm gathering provisions for Kitch and Caesar. Don't mind putting my old partner's pork to better use."

Eva felt her heart lift a little. "What for?"

"I've given them directions to the Saltwater Tribes. They thought that sounded preferable to heading to Mexico."

"What are the Saltwater Tribes?"

"Help me get a good passel of corn and beans packed up for them to pick up later." He turned, and she followed him to the corn crib. "The Saltwater Tribes are escaped slaves living out north northwest of here. They have villages like their original homes in Africa, and they are slaves no more."

Eva imagined Kitch's and Caesar's hopes rising on learning of their existence, but she coughed at a further thought. "They might be better off if they go to Mexico." She held a bag open as Jim scooped beans, but he paused to regard her from his crouched position.

"Oh? Why?"

"Won't the Nʉmʉnʉʉ make war on them?" she asked when what she really wanted to say was, "Because the Anglos will be making war on them both."

"Three years ago, we had a peace treaty with them. I'm assuming it will still be safe. I've taught them Nʉmʉ tekwapʉ phrases that should help." Jim contemplated the amount in the sack. "We should pack a bit more. They didn't know if they would try to take their families or come back for them with warriors."

"How will they remember everything? I'm assuming they can't read."

Jim's eyes crinkled at her ignorance. "They'll remember. Writing weakens the memory."

Eva pursed her lips and lifted a brow. Not in her experience.

"Think about it," he said. "If blind men have stronger hearing, don't you think it's possible for people who must remember everything in their heads to have excellent memories?"

She conceded the point. "Let's go with them," Eva said, changing the subject. Adventure called to her. "You could show them the way."

At her words, Jim's face lit up, but he immediately crushed the suggestion. "I've already thought that through. The owners may suspect me when they go missing, but they won't be able to prove anything if I'm still here on the farm. And I can't do that to Pump. If we leave, we pretty much can't come back."

Would that be so bad? Eva thought as she tied up the sacking. She knew leaving this place was what Jim really wanted. Wait, what was she thinking? She had to be here when March rolled around. The mission. Tophe. El Copano and Goliad. Even if she got her ability back, only punishment awaited her if she returned to the sanctum unsuccessful. "Right," Eva said. "Are you going to give them horses?"

Jim froze in place, clearly torn at her question. "Hadn't crossed my mind." He darted his eyes in the remuda's direction, then refocused on Eva. "I should.

It'll give them a better chance. But it'll go way worse for them if they're caught." He scratched the back of his head. "I'll give them the choice."

Chapter 20

Eva

A crescent moon had climbed high when Wokweesi growled low in his chest. Eva could hear the footsteps of two men walking up onto the dogtrot. Jim shushed the dog, rose from his pallet by the fire, and opened the door. Caesar, trailed by Kitch, entered the small room, and they removed their hats while Eva threw a blanket around her shoulders.

All remained standing as Jim had them recite his directions and the Comanche phrases he'd taught them. Kitch stumbled over the pronunciation, but Caesar remembered them perfectly. Eva breathed a little easier about their odds of success.

"Remember, every Nʉmʉ man feels obligated to offer you lodging, food, even protection if you ask for it like I've taught you. Even to their most bitter enemy," Jim said.

The men nodded, their confidence visibly increasing.

"Did you decide to take your families?"

Caesar and Kitch shared a look, and then Caesar said, "Nah, sir, it's better to come back for them."

It couldn't have been an easy decision. Unspoken were the fears of traveling with women and children across hostile Indian territories, the hardships of journeying overland to a place they may or may not find, not to mention what might happen to their loved ones while they were gone. Eva could see they were placing a lot of trust and hope in a man who didn't look all that different from their master.

"I have two horses you can take."

Both men's faces registered shock and then huge smiles.

"But think it through," Jim said. "If you're caught with them...." It was unnecessary to finish that sentence.

"We'll take our chances," Kitch said without hesitation. "Thank you."

Jim inclined his head. Only Eva knew how much it cost him to give up two of those ponies, but he had breezily told her he could always get more. Jim shifted his gaze to her.

Neither man had looked at Eva until that moment, but they both darted glances at her, so she smiled. As one, they dipped their heads, eyes shuttered. "Ma'am," Caesar said.

Formalities concluded, Jim moved to the door. "No saddles, unfortunately." Both men shrugged, indicating it wouldn't be a problem, and followed him out of the cabin. Jim continued as he thought of new advice. "Don't make a fire until you reach...."

As Eva settled by the hearth to wait, his voice became too faint for her to hear. A sudden, intense yearning to go west with them surprised her. She hadn't been stuck in one place for so long since she was a child.

When Jim returned, the men safely on their way, he sat beside her on the bench, thigh pressed to hers. Several minutes ticked by while he stared into the fire, lost in thought. She imagined he saw the trail leading away from here in the flames.

"I know you've made your promise to Pump, but you mentioned once before that you hadn't been rescued. What did you mean? Why did you return here at all?"

The light in Jim's eyes burned away the reflections, and his jaw hardened. She could see the pulse in his throat. At the sight, a shiver crawled up her spine.

He didn't speak for a long time but pulled at the pant seam near his knee, rolling the coarse fabric between his fingers. Eva watched his hand and let her eyes move up the ropey arm so close to hers.

"There was a woman — Huwuni — I intended to make my wife, but another man wanted her, too. His name was Tatua." He leaned forward, resting his forearms on his thighs, then clasped his hands, the knuckles showing white. "One day, he invited me on a raid with his friend and some Wichita. We were to travel far down into Mexico and meet a larger party of raiders. We would camp in the hills and attack the villages there throughout the summer." Abruptly, he stood, propelled to his feet by evident emotion, and began to pace, the soft hairs of his chest glittering as he moved.

"As we passed San Antonio, they tricked and bound me. Ended up with this scar from that day." Jim pointed to his temple. "Took me into Mission Concepción and sold me to the priests for some horses. Tatua, the bastard, got rid of me and added to his herd to boot." Jim plopped onto the floor with his knees up and feet crossed, arms draped.

"The priests kept me confined for months, not knowing what to do with me. Every time they let me out, I tried to escape. They wanted to convert me before they let me go. Pump heard about me and came to see if I was his best friend's son. He'd never stopped hoping my sisters and I would be returned someday." Jim smiled as he met her eyes. "He was very happy to find me."

After a moment, his grin faded. "By that time, I knew Huwuni must have married Tatua. I was already losing heart at returning, and Pump convinced me I could have a future among the Anglos. He found me a place here." Sitting at Eva's feet, Jim stared through her legs at a distance only he could see, then looked back up at her.

"When Rutsima found me, through sheer dumb luck, he told me Tatua claimed I had been killed." Jim's fists clenched and unclenched. "I was no captive to be sold. No one owned me anymore. *He* certainly didn't own me. He might as well have murdered me. My father and brothers cut their hair; my mothers and sisters cut their breasts. They burned my possessions and gave my horses away." Jim's eyes shimmered, and his face reddened, but he paused and drew in a deep, quaking breath.

Eva winced at his descriptions, remembering a time her own overwhelming grief had needed physical evidence.

"Months later, Tatua's friend let it slip what they had done. Most people were angry with him, and he feared retribution from my family. He took Huwuni, and they say he hid with the Waco for a time before joining another band. My father, my brothers, my true friend, they discussed going to San Antonio to rescue me, but it would have been too difficult to enter the town unchallenged, much less to find me."

They sat in silence, listening to the fire crackle. Wokweesi came and stretched out on his side between them, baking his head. He pushed his paws against Jim's feet to support an elaborate stretch.

"She's had a baby," Jim said. "My brother told me last time he was here. Their bands camped together for a season."

Eva gripped the bench beneath her. A strange feeling crept into her heart. The baby poured cold-blooded satisfaction on her jealousy, but pain slid down Jim's shoulders and puddled on the floor around him. "I'm sorry," she said, then knelt before him.

Jim sighed. "I plan to go back as soon as I'm free. I hate it here more and more," he whispered. Eva must have let her face speak too plainly because he hastened to add, "Except for you. You've made it more bearable." His mouth moved to say more, but he stopped.

Heat blossomed inside her at his words, but she dumped icy water on the kindling. It was unthinkable. She couldn't stay with him.

Sanctum, Axis Mundi, the True line, 1995

A man and a woman stood naked on the amphitheater floor, blood running down their legs. The woman hunched over her scalpeled belly, holding it in place. Behind them, the council sat on a dais, but the couple faced the audience, and Yggdrasil sheltered them all. Eva looked at the rainbow of individuals surrounding her. Many were friends she knew well, and the novitiates clustered in rows at the front. Rarely were all the people of Lux Libera rallied within the sanctum of Axis Mundi.

Tophe's jaw pulsed in his ashen face. She reached for his hand, but he had it curled into a fist. He wagged his head as if to deny what was happening, and his eyes were rimmed red. She wrapped her hand around the back of his.

Elder Gulpilil rose to address the gathering as silence rippled across the stands. All stood in unison, eyes attentive, ears open, mouths shut. "You know why we are gathered here today. It is with a very heavy heart we have passed judgment on Sister Sakura and Brother Enrique." He paused in his pronouncement, scanning the ranks lined up before him.

"Sterilization, their punishment for fornication, was carried out this morning," he continued. The woman on the stage wept openly; the man at her side stood erect, granite-faced. Tears rolled down Eva's cheeks, but she dashed them aside and shot a glance up at Tophe.

"They also stand accused of apostasy and have been found guilty. We are assembled to witness their expulsion from our community, committing them into the Abyss. They will be forever separated from God and the True line."

Elder Gulpilil returned to his seat, and Elder Roberts stood, bowed to Elder Nnaji, and then, at her nod, walked with ceremonial dignity to stand before the couple. A Brother approached him, bearing a sacramental knife. Elder Roberts lifted the blade from its pillow and hoisted it above his head as he pivoted to face the watchers. He slowly withdrew the knife from its sheath and lowered his arms.

"I mark these apostates so that all may know their crimes."

At that moment, Sakura's courage failed her, and she turned to run. Two men seized her, dragged her back, and held her in place. Enrique's face twisted into a rictus of torment, but he forced his eyes away from her to stare over the crowd.

Eva wished she could stretch beyond the people and hold Sakura's hand. Disbelief, anger, betrayal, and love warred inside her.

Elder Roberts turned to Sakura, who shouted and struggled before he even raised his arm. Within seconds, her cries slid to screams of agony. When he backed away, a large X had been carved across her forehead. Enrique's face glistened with tears.

Elder Roberts took a cloth from the Brother and wiped the blade. Blood ran down Sakura's cheeks and dripped onto her breasts. He turned to her companion.

Enrique adjusted his stance, planting his feet and squaring his shoulders. No sound came from him, and when Elder Roberts moved aside to clean the knife, Enrique glared at them all from where he stood. Eva could see no trace of remorse, and she shut her eyes to his plight, shaking her head, yet wanting to understand how he could have committed such a heinous act or waver in his faith when he knew the truth. Enrique was a good person, a best friend. It didn't make sense.

More tears threatened, but she would not let them fall, and when she opened her eyes, Eva glanced toward the novitiates, glad they could learn this hard lesson young, so they could avoid this fate. With mouths slightly agape, they kept an unwavering focus on the couple before them as their instructors muttered into their ears.

Elder Roberts returned to his seat, and Elder Nnaji rose, spreading her mahogany arms, wrinkled as the great ash tree, and casting her voice to reach the farthest members. "Brothers and Sisters. In times like these, we must recall our mission and purpose. These two have allowed themselves to be led astray by their own false notions."

She scanned the novitiates with a piercing gaze, and after a significant moment, Elder Nnaji pounded her fist onto the table. "We are at war. Only through repairing the world can we separate the evil of matter from the light of God."

Focusing the power of her words down the line of her arm, she directed a finger at the couple before her. "Anything, be it denying the sacred texts or engaging in procreative acts that add to the materialism of this world — anything that delays the day we are reunited with the Source in eternal bliss, is another day longer that we, the Free Lights, remain tied to this accidental creation of space and time, and another day it is allowed to keep expanding, unchecked."

Elder Nnaji's words burrowed into Eva.

"We will now recite the Admonishments," she continued. Eva's mouth moved along with everyone else's, but Tophe yelled the chants, his voice deepened by emotion. Enrique's shoulders slumped, and Sakura bent double, arms and legs trembling, but a deep calm settled over the congregants. To Eva, they seemed united. Justice served on a square plate.

Elder Nnaji descended from the dais and went to stand before the couple. She spoke to them for a moment, and Enrique responded, but Eva was too far away to catch his words. Sakura stared at the Elder's feet and swayed while Enrique shivered violently and uncontrollably. The muscles in his arms and chest flexed as he held his hands tightly balled.

Without another word, Elder Nnaji escorted the condemned to Yggdrasil. The men restraining Sakura allowed Enrique to pick her up and carry her in his arms, fresh blood running down his legs. Eva's heart tugged as she watched him kiss the clear skin at the top of her forehead.

Suddenly, Tophe's hand opened to Eva. She had been digging her nails into the tops of his fingers without realizing it. Sakura wrapped her arms around Enrique's neck and laid her cheek on his shoulder, then he limped, hips and knees stiff, to follow the Elder.

When they reached the tree, Elder Nnaji placed her palm upon its trunk, where the bark dissolved into a black portal unlike any Eva had ever traveled through. She gasped at the swallowing darkness.

Enrique turned to face his people. "They're lying to you!" he said. The combined force of pain, disillusionment, and heartbreak hurled his words through the ranks. His gory mask locked eyes with Tophe and others in the throng, one by one. No one moved to silence him. There was no need.

Without turning, he stepped backward with Sakura into the Abyss and disappeared.

Chapter 21

Eva

Jim's Farm

The following week, shortly after noon, Pump arrived, intending to take the cotton to market the next day. Eva greeted him at the buckboard as he was climbing down.

"Where's Jim?" he asked.

"He left yesterday to hunt."

Pump's eyes widened, a sudden thought seeming to strike him. "Do you feel like you can travel again? I could train you while he's gone." He winked. "Show you Lux Libera doesn't know every trick."

Eva stiffened, uneasy. Would this be considered heresy? To use "nothing" to travel, as Pump claimed. She wasn't sure. Though she had tried to do so on her own, those efforts had felt like fantasy — nothing truly sinful, especially since they had never worked. Eva had only ever traveled through trees and had been told it was the only way. To learn anything different smelled and tasted transgressive, like harnessing an evil power.

But one question ate at her. In truth, it had been eating at her since the day Pump had revealed himself as a traveler. Was he telling the truth? Either Pump was a liar and a fraud, or Lux Libera was wrong. There could be no in-between; his simple existence challenged her beliefs. With only one way to find out the truth, her curiosity prevailed, and she swept away her fears of committing a sin.

"Honestly, I haven't tried in several days." With every previous attempt having failed, it had begun to feel pointless. For a moment, she focused inward, where she stood, seeing if she could sense any improvement. As if through an ear stuffed with cotton, she seemed to hear... something... could feel... something. She walked to the pecan tree and placed her hands on its wide trunk. With her eyes closed, she sensed Pump come to stand beside her, his heavy boots rustling the fallen leaves and crunching shells, but then she refocused, running her fingers along the bark. Deeper and deeper, she peered into the nature of the tree, and after several minutes, it shimmered, then solidified.

Relief washed over her, and she laughed out loud. Sweat beaded her upper lip, but Eva could feel an opening. She had pushed a hole through a wall that was thinning.

"That a girl!" Pump thumped her between the shoulders. "How did that feel? Looks like it took a lot out of you."

Eva crouched over her knees, gasping. Needing to sit for a moment, she turned and slid her back down the tree.

"Let me unhitch the team while you rest," Pump said.

As Eva worked to slow her breathing, she pinched up the dirt and ran handfuls through her palms like an hourglass. An enormous weight, worry so tangible it had seemed clawed and black-feathered, had flown from her shoulders. She had suspected her brain needed time to heal, but without access to Lux Libera's doctors, she had only guessed and worried. Now, she had hope of a full recovery, and by the time Pump returned, she was breathing normally again.

"Okay, my dear. Better?"

Eva nodded.

"Good. Now, you may not be able to do this until your strength is back, but I can at least give you the theory."

She stood and brushed off her seat. "Ready."

"Basically, you're gonna form a portal out of the moisture and gases in the air. As you can probably guess, this works better here inland of the coast than it does, say, farther out west where it's drier. But you can still do it."

Eva squinted and tilted her head.

"Here, let me demonstrate." Pump cupped his hands in front of him as if he held a ball. Intense concentration settled on his features. Abruptly, he broke off and said, "You don't have to put your hands like this, but I like to. Gives me a defined space to connect with." She gave a thumbs up, and he returned to his meditation. In a shimmering instant, he appeared two feet to the side.

At the look on her face, Pump slapped his knee. Eva's mouth hung open. The simplicity floored her, and her heart beat double-time. So many possibilities opened; so many restrictions lifted. Why had she not been taught this?

"I think for you," he said, "you'll want to practice with the tree at first. Imagine the moisture flowing up the trunk rather than the tree itself."

At Pump's encouragement, she rested her hands on the tree and pictured the water trickling up its roots to the canopy above, a lazy river of sap. The tiny hole she had punctured in her senses widened, and the tree shimmered a little longer than before.

Fatigue descended on her without warning, and every muscle weakened; every thought slowed. The portal sealed as she fell away and sunk to the ground. Pump knelt at her side and placed a hand on her back.

"I think that's probably enough for today," he said, chuckling. "But do you get the idea?"

"Yes," she said, then puffed her cheeks.

"Eventually, you won't need anything at all. The tree is just a crutch now. Let's get you up on the gallery."

She draped an arm around his shoulders, and he helped her to stand. Once he had her seated on the breezeway bench, he joined her, sitting hip-to-hip, and took off his hat.

What else had Lux Libera hidden from her? Despite her body feeling like lead, her mind bounded from thought to thought.

"I can see your wheels turning, gal," Pump said.

She spun to him. "I believe you now. I think I had talked myself back into thinking this is just a shadow world, that Jim's not... real." Even as she said the words, she knew they weren't true anymore, hadn't been true for a while, but couldn't have pointed to the hour or day she had stopped believing.

Pump leaned back, mouth round. "No one who has seen the two of you together would believe for one second you think Jim isn't real."

Eva's neck grew hot. "I need to. It's better that way."

"It's hard to ignore a truth once you know it."

Eva squeezed her eyes shut and pressed the back of her head against the wall.

"May I ask you a delicate question?" Pump said. When Eva lifted her hand, he said, "Have you and Jim…." He rubbed the stubble at the base of his scalp and waved his arm.

She shook her head and looked at him. "It's forbidden, and I would lose my ability to trav—" She sat up straight, allowing her last word to trail. "You're married."

He smiled, clearly happy she had connected the dots herself.

Heat flooded her from head to toe, followed quickly by shame as she thought of Jim. She nudged him aside to reflect on later.

"I didn't really believe you until you traveled right in front of me. I don't know what to think anymore, but if timelines were truly immutable, I wouldn't be able to change them. My own thread, I think, is like the weft of a piece of cloth. I've been weaving in and out of the warp all this time and thinking I was something different. Either I'm Fated as well, or nobody is."

Pump shrugged. "Nobody knows. Not really. We can only guess. Anyone who tells you they have all the answers is lying to themselves — at best... or trying to control others at worst."

Eva tapped the back of her head against the log wall. She gazed out over the yard but saw the sanctum.

"There are shadow worlds, gal, where the creations are automatons. I've been to them. They're the ones we build in our imaginations. Our books, poems, plays, songs... They all exist in a dimension somewhere. So, then, the question is, do our creations feel? Should we be very careful what we imagine?"

It was almost too much to take in. Eva was still grappling with her reality crumbling. Pump had cracked her world like a tea-crazed egg, and now he was peeling the shell away. "So, are you saying we are like gods, creating worlds?"

"No, I'm saying we are God. Or, more precisely, that we're made *of* God. God's consciousness is split into an infinity of infinite pieces. We're each a little individual speck of God, living through our own point of view and limited by our bodies and the rules of our worlds. You, me, that tree, the rocks under the porch, the sun — all of it, all of us, all the particles, right?... all together — we're made out of God. God is all that there is. We're God who has forgotten It is dreaming in order to experience."

Fear oozed from the top of her skull, down her spine, and turned her guts to water. "That's blasphemy. God can't be creation, nor is creation infinite. God is outside of creation."

"It's not that different from what Lux Libera teaches, is it?" Pump asked. "It's a common teaching in many worlds, going by different names, like Tikkun Olam for one. The vessel of God's creation broke into innumerable pieces, and the essence of God became entangled with the unholy matter of the material vessel itself. Your job has been to separate and mend the holy from the unholy, right?"

Eva sucked in a breath and nodded.

"I'm saying there are two key differences where they're getting it wrong. One," he said, holding up a finger, "God doesn't want it repaired. This is God's eternity, and it's infinite. We exist because everything exists; every possibility exists for God to experience anything other than nothingness. Our own individual consciousnesses are individual bits of God doing that experiencing. Even Lux Libera exists because it is a possibility for it to exist. God is amusing Itself."

"And the second?" Eva asked.

Pump added his next finger to the first. "Lux Libera puts God outside of Its creation. I'm saying that the essence of God *is* creation. Lux Libera wants to end space-time, wants to end creation. They're trying to end God without realizing it... or even realizing that such a thing is impossible."

The floor dropped from her feet. She folded forward with her head in her hands. "I don't know if I find this liberating or terrifying," she mumbled between her fingers. "It means every evil exists somewhere, as well as every good. Glorious, perfect timelines and hell-scapes... and then everything in between. Infinite copies of every conceivable world." Her eyes stung. "We haven't been bringing anything toward unity; we've just been creating more derivations. I've mended nothing." If these revelations hadn't gutted her to the core, she might have laughed at the irony. Her sole purpose had been to end creation, not multiply it.

"Correct. We are creators in our own right. Every time we make a choice, both outcomes are created, including a new soul. We're conscious of only one outcome. Our copy is conscious of the other. But the us that is us made the choice that we experienced."

"But the threads I've combined... is one set of the consciousnesses lost?"

"I don't know. Maybe they're just new threads. Would you want to take that chance, though? You wouldn't know which would survive. It's one reason I couldn't remain a Lux Libera and escaped instead. My conscience wouldn't let me stay."

Eva cradled her head in her hands. "I've been killing people. So many people." Different faces, copies of the same face, moved through her mind's eye. Too many to remember or count. All that blood shed for nothing. "Our mission has been futile." Eva didn't know where to put the horror. It spilled over both hands. How could she clean it up without spreading the filth?

Pump didn't respond for a long time. When she met his eyes, the concern on his face crushed her chest. The air in her lungs crystallized, and she sent her gaze to the middle distance — anywhere but him.

"Lux Libera's mission may be futile, but I don't believe choosing good when you have the opportunity is. We aren't able to change much, but we can still do what we can. I don't know if this is the Truth, Eva. It just makes sense to me with everything I have experienced and pieced together. You have to figure these things out for yourself. Don't let anyone tell you they have all the answers."

"How have I never seen these other worlds that would be so, so different? These heavens and hells? Or automaton worlds."

"Did you ever have the freedom to choose where you went?"

"No." Some of Eva's horror sparked into rage.

Jim appeared mid-afternoon with a doe strapped to his horse and a rock squirrel dangling from his saddle. Wokweesi dodged hooves, nosing his catch as it bounced in front of him. While Pump helped him dress and butcher both, Eva deserted for a walk by the river. She ignored the irritated glance Jim tossed her way. He would expect her back soon to fry up the raw venison steaks.

Her legs took her a greater distance than she had ever been along the bank. She stooped to gather flat rocks for skipping, but her anxiety bubbled over. She picked up the largest stone at hand and threw it as far across the river as she could, then bent to pick up another and launched it farther. On the third, she screamed. The rage exploded from her chest, wild wings tethered to her heart. She wept jagged, uncontrollable sobs. She wished she had never known. Part of her wanted to kill Pump for the briefest of moments. Her rage searched for a target, but it kept fluttering home.

She couldn't go back to the cabin. Not like this. She walked until her legs tired, and she sat down, miles from the farm, letting the tears come and burying her head in her skirts. Grief over her lost birth family, now real, never shadows, consumed her, and she envisioned the tangle of her lifeline weaving in and out of Axis Mundi, hopelessly obscuring the path home to her people, to her birth world and time. The sun slipped closer and closer to the horizon, but Eva couldn't bring herself to care. Fresh tears welled when she thought of Tophe and her friends. What was she going to do with her life? Could she return to Axis Mundi and pretend? Where else could she go?

Would Lux Libera send someone to hunt her down like Sakura and Enrique? Her mind seized at the thought. Terror forced her to stand and pace. What would happen to Jim? Could she live here in peace with him? She couldn't stay at this homestead past March, and she still didn't know who had planted the second beacon or if its existence was a complete accident by a sloppy scout, a leftover relic from a different mission. They could easily find her amongst the Comanche, but would they think to look?

The mission dangled over her head like a sword by a frayed string. She couldn't go through with it now. Should she try to stop Tophe? She rebelled at the notion, bile rising in her throat. She couldn't betray him like that. But could she stand by, knowing what would happen if she did nothing? If she didn't show up, he would assume her lost. Would Lux Libera search for her or give her up for dead? If she tried to stop Tophe, they would definitely know she was an apostate.

Fear rolled down her cheeks, and her very bones quivered. Twilight illuminated the trees around her, haloing everything with a golden light. The temperature plummeted, and gooseflesh raised the fine hairs on her arms as she shivered. Under the sheltering skirt of an ancient magnolia, she laid down, curled on her side. She just wanted the world to stop. After a time, no more tears came, and they dried on her face in salty trails. Her body conformed to the ground beneath her like molten lead, and Eva stared at the moon as it dawned red-gold and engorged on the horizon, every crater visible. She had no desire to move ever again.

Chapter 22

Jim

The butchering had been cleaned up, and the salted steaks sat on a board waiting for Eva. Pump dried his hands with a cloth and pulled out his pipe. Jim's stomach rumbled along with his annoyance. Eva had already shirked processing his kill, and the sun would be setting soon.

He spitted the squirrel and propped it above the coals. He'd let Wokweesi have most of it. It was his kill anyway.

"I think we'll get a pretty good price," Pump said, "from what I've heard from other planters. Fifteen cents a pound."

Jim kept forgetting what they were doing tomorrow. He grunted.

"With the weather turning cold, we need to round up your hogs and get them processed."

"No need. Let them live. I won't eat them."

Pump took several long drags on his pipe and scratched his neck but didn't respond.

Jim felt the older man studying him.

"The McMullens want me to pass an invitation on to you."

Interest piqued, Jim glanced up from the squirrel and raised his eyebrows.

"They're hosting a dance Saturday to celebrate the end of the harvest," Pump said. "You can introduce Eva to everyone. They even have a caller coming, and Andrew Wilson is gonna play his fiddle."

Jim enjoyed dancing as much as raiding, and the thought of Eva on his arm took away any reticence about attending an Anglo gathering. She'd be the prettiest woman there.

As Jim warmed to the idea, Pump's ready smile broadened.

"How many days is that from now?" Jim asked.

Pump counted on his fingers. "Six."

"What should I tell people about Eva?"

For a moment, Pump gazed into the distance, chin in his hand. "I haven't quite figured that out. I've been thinking about it. Maybe your fiancée? You met in San Antone. If you intend to marry, people will overlook a little indiscretion here on the frontier."

Pump's suggestion that he lie about how she came here distracted Jim. He had just been wondering, for her sake, how to explain her unattached status. He rubbed his knuckle across the stubble on his cheek and nodded. "I'll ask her. See what she thinks."

"Speaking of the McMullens, Kitch and Caesar have disappeared. You wouldn't happen to know anything about that, would you?"

Jim kept his face relaxed. "Oh?"

Pump peered at him over his spectacles. "You don't fool me, boy."

Rather than make eye contact, Jim rotated the spit.

"I don't judge you for it," Pump finally said. "But you should know that they beat Caesar's wife and Kitch's sister half to death to find out where they went. They said the Saltwater Tribes."

"They might feel it's worth the beating in the long run."

Pump shook his head. "They've taken Caesar's two children into the house and threatened to sell them."

Jim grimaced. As if in a bad dream, he imagined a rope pulling through his fingers, dropping the person he was trying to save. Flexing his palms, he was surprised he didn't feel the burns.

"What's done is done," Pump continued. "I know your heart was in the right place. I'm not even sure you did wrong. It's just that the price is so damn high."

"Do the McMullens suspect me?"

"No."

Neither said anything for a long while. Jim thought about Caesar and Kitch on the trail; they had a good chance. He wouldn't regret it if they didn't but wondered what their women thought. He tested the squirrel, scorching himself in the process, then popped the piece in his mouth and sucked his fingers. Not his favorite meat. He laid it to the side to cool, and Wokweesi materialized from behind a log.

Jim's stomach complained again, and he realized the sun had well and truly set, the night wind causing the fire to throw sparks. His annoyance turned to worry. Where was Eva? Glancing at Pump, he could see the older man beginning to have the same thoughts.

"She needed some time to think," Pump said, answering his unasked question.

"Why?" They had been getting along this week… no miscommunications or misunderstandings. In fact, she made a great training partner, and they had fallen into an easy rhythm. Worry twisted his thoughts, and Jim replayed every conversation from before he had left to go hunting.

"Some hard memories came back to her today," Pump said.

"What?" Jim's ears pricked, concern and curiosity battling. He thought back to arriving home from the hunt. She had left with no explanation.

"She should be the one to tell you."

Jim didn't know how to interpret that. A tendril of anxiety curled through his intestines.

For several minutes, they sat listening to the night and the fire, supper forgotten. Jim debated searching for her. The moon rose a handsbreadth above the trees.

Just as he stood to get his rifle, he heard footsteps approaching. Wokweesi left the circle, tail wagging, and Eva stepped into the light.

Jim surveyed her from head to toe, concern growing to alarm. Her skirts were wet and muddy, her braid disheveled, and her face streaked and dirty. Bits of feathery cypress needles pressed into her arms and hung in her hair.

Her eyes pinned him in place. "I can tell you who I am."

ele

Once Eva had convinced Jim that the mess he saw was self-inflicted, his next words boiled over. "What do you mean you can tell me who you are?"

Eva bristled, hearing accusation rather than vented anxiety in his heated tone.

Pump took the opportunity to cook the steaks. He seemed to be acting on the supposition that food would help moods.

She described her history with Lux Libera as succinctly as she could manage. Without preamble, words spilled from Eva's mouth, flowing from her soul in an unstoppable rush. Jim's face morphed from confusion to disbelief to wariness and back again. She stumbled over her old beliefs as she spelled out her new ones, which only confused him more. Some parts required giving him a crash course in physics and cosmology and defining words she had known since childhood — none of which he seemed to grasp.

"If you could cut something in half," she said. "And half again and again and again until it was the smallest possible thing that couldn't be cut, you'd see a filament of energy, a tiny string, just a snippet, entangled, woven into the world around it like a cloth. I can disentangle individual filaments, loop the snippets to themselves, and move them, including myself, between dimensions. It's like the string of a fiddle. The way it vibrates makes it real, determines what it will be and how it will act in time and space. When I re-tune the strings, I change their properties."

Jim's mouth gaped as he slowly shook his head from side to side, and his unblinking focus never left her face. It was as if she had been speaking to him in Chinese, and her heart faltered. She inhaled sharply and looked to Pump for help. Pump's eyes widened. He had been feigning surprise, confusion, and skepticism, along with Jim, as he rotated the venison over the fire. Eva barreled past his need for secrecy.

"Show him how you can travel, Pump."

Jim scrunched his forehead. "Pump?" His eyes darted from his friend back to her, filled with scorn. "What do you take me for?" When she didn't answer, he pulled a hard mask over his features. "Show me yourself, Eva."

"I can't," she said. "I'm still too weak from my injury. It's why I'm even still here."

Hurt veiled his face for the blink of an eye. She would have missed it if she had not known him so well.

Desperation made her voice rise. "Help me, Pump!"

Pump sighed, holding Eva's gaze. His head seemed to twitch in indecision, but then he stood and formed his hands. The air shimmered, and in an instant, he plopped beside Jim.

With an unmanly squeal, Jim leapt to his feet and fell backward over the log. Wokweesi barked and growled at the humans, at the darkness, at the fire. Jim scrambled, backing away to a safe distance.

It took a moment for his tongue to find English words. "I should kill you both for sorcery," Jim said, panting. Eva hoped that was fear talking.

"It's not sorcery, Jim," Pump said.

Jim scanned his friend, his mentor, boots to bald head as if he had never seen him in his life.

"Eva and I were born with this ability. It's a sense, like hearing or taste."

"This is my puha, Jim," Eva said.

"No… no…" he said, jabbing a finger at her. "That's not how medicine works. Your power didn't come from a dream. You aren't sharing secrets between a spirit and yourself or following the restrictions they impose on you. I see now I misunderstood you." His chest no longer heaved, but an eerie calm seemed to settle over him. "Your puha never made sense."

With his last words sounding ominous, Eva wasn't sure if this was progress or not. He stared dumbstruck at Pump.

"You know me, Jim," Pump said. "I'm still the same person. My ability to travel can't hurt you." He raised his hands, palms out, to soothe as he explained. "It's just a different way to move. I can travel anywhere in space in this dimension, but I can also go to other dimensions anywhere along their timelines. Once I am there, though, I can only move around in space and be carried along by the stream of time, just like here. It gives me no other powers. Eva is the same."

Jim slid wide eyes to her, reminding her very much of a cornered wolf. She nodded, trying to reassure him, but he seemed incapable of hearing, much less comprehending Pump's words. They bounced off the younger man as if he held a war shield.

"Why are you here?" Jim asked, his tone hollow.

A chilly gulf opened between them. Eva kicked herself for her selfish impulsiveness. She had been so angry that she needed to share it and let it overflow onto him.

"I'm here for the Angel of Goliad."

"Who?" Pump and Jim asked together.

"Her name is different in other timelines, but here she is known as Francisca Alavez. She will save many men during the Goliad Massacre in March. I'm here to stop her."

Pump's face crumpled, and his eyes narrowed.

Eva settled back on her heel. "*Was* here to stop her," she amended. Why was he looking at her like that? He knew what she was. She hadn't known the truth.

"What do you mean by 'stop her?'" Jim asked. "And what's the Goliad Massacre?"

"Exactly what it sounds like," Pump answered for her. "She's an assassin of sorts. And as for Goliad, it's no place you want to be come March, boy."

Eva winced. She had never, ever thought of herself that way; indeed, she had *stopped* many assassins. She saw Jim putting the pieces together. All the pieces about her that had never fit together quite right.

"But why would you want to do that?"

"Because her man kills her in the True line. My partner Tophe and I are to recreate those circumstances as best we can."

Pump stared at his feet, shaking his head, hands on hips. He shifted his weight from one foot to another.

Jim stood as still as a stone. His attention remained on her, his lips a thin line across his face.

Eva's heart fluttered, and she dropped her eyes. "I'm not going to do it anymore," she said. "I want out. I renounce my vow. I renounce the Admonishments." She stared at Jim's chest, unable to meet his stony gaze another moment. She hoped he understood what she meant. "I renounce my people." She risked a glimpse up, but he no longer looked at her.

"I need to think," he said, leaving without a backward glance, and Wokweesi rose to join him. The steaks Pump had cooked lay cold and uneaten.

Eva moved to follow him, but Pump grabbed her arm.

"He feels like he was standing in the middle of a stampede. You dumped a century or more of learning on him, never taking a breath or preparing him the least little bit. What did you expect would happen, honey?"

"I— I—" She didn't know what she had been thinking, knew only that she couldn't contain all the pain within herself, had wanted him to understand her, to see her, to be a witness maybe, or a refuge. What had she done? She covered her mouth with her hand.

"He just needs to clear his head," Pump said.

"How can you be so sure?" An abyss opened beneath her all over again, and her vision blurred.

"He didn't tell you to leave."

Chapter 23

Eva

Eva lay curled into a tight ball on Jim's bed. She had never been so scared or unsure in her life and didn't know how long she had laid there, wondering where he had gone. Hours had passed, but dawn was still in the distant future. Unable to take the agonizing uncertainty until morning, she threw the blanket over her shoulders and pulled her boots on without lacing them.

Silently, she slipped through the door, tiptoeing past the storeroom across the dogtrot where Pump slept on the floor. She searched the breezeway, the brush arbor, and the outdoor kitchen, then walked to the pecan tree. The moon waxed nearly full, giving the yard a ghostly light. At the corral, she listened to the horses. They grew restless as she stood there, so she moved on. She thought she had seen Nuena but couldn't be sure and headed to the barn.

After stepping out of the moonlight and into the pitch-black shadows, Eva halted, ears straining. She crept toward the hayloft, the one place she thought Jim might have bedded down. When she climbed the ladder and reached the top, her heart stopped at the realization that this hadn't been such a good idea,

half-expecting to find a knife at her throat. As Eva
lowered her foot a rung, she felt breath on her face,
and Jim's nose came into focus. She startled, freezing
in place, eye-to-eye with him. He gazed at her, silent,
his face unreadable in the darkness.

"I have come to you," she said, echoing his words
from the night he had comforted her, her voice barely
above a whisper. She swallowed. "In secret." Her heart
opened to him, and such a longing flowed from her
that she was sure he would be drenched by it. "I want
no other man." The moment she said it, she knew it
was true.

He didn't move, and her heart sank, but then he
closed his eyes and pressed his forehead against hers,
inhaling. He touched her hand, and she took the last
steps up into the loft, then knelt in front of him, his
chest inches from hers.

"I would never —"

Jim put his thumb on her lips, fingers cupping her
jaw. "Shh…" he said. "I don't understand most of
what you told me, but I trust Pump, and I trust you,
too. You've had months to harm me, and you have
done nothing but bring me good. The rest…." He
paused, exploring her cheek. "The rest can wait 'til
morning." He drew his thumb across her lips again.

Tiny slivers of moonlight shone through the
chinks, and his musk made of afternoons on
horseback filled the small space. The sweet-smelling
straw rustled beneath their knees. She wished she
could see his face better.

The next moment, he buried his head in her neck
and wrapped his arms around her. She clung to

him. Fear. Anger. Love. She craved to swallow him whole. Grief erupted even as the starved desire she had suppressed gnawed at her.

Jim felt her face and kissed away the tears. "You and I are the same." His voice choked with emotion. "We will be as one now, notsaʔka." He drew her chemise over her head, and she fumbled with his laces. "Here," he said and untied them himself as she took off her boots. He spread the blanket and pulled her down with him.

Anxiety coursed through her.

Jim kneaded her back, her hips, and her legs. He seemed to want to squeeze the fear out of her.

"I'm not afraid of you," she whispered.

As if listening to her breathing, he paused. "What are you afraid of?" he whispered back. He kissed a path across her breast and placed his head on her chest.

She knew he could hear her heartbeat and forced herself to relax, smelling his hair and pressing her lips to the top of his head. She thought she might be able to pick his scent out blindfolded.

His hand cupped her breast and then traveled down her hip. He took her nipple in his mouth and pressed softly between her legs.

After turning from her people before witnesses, she held no desire for second thoughts. She felt him hard against her thigh and rolled onto her side to open herself. "I'm afraid of nothing."

He grinned like a wolf. "We're well-matched," he said. His fingers stroked her, gently circling, then bearing down and stretching.

Though it hurt, she pushed against his fingers and sent her hand across his broad back, memorizing his shoulder and arm. She longed to kiss his mouth.

With each approach, Eva did her best not to wince; with each release, she softened. He nuzzled her neck, then bit down lightly as he pushed into her again.

Before her mind could decide which pain to focus on, he returned to caressing. She dug her fingernails into his shoulder as her need became more insistent.

After a moment, he rolled on top of her. "Look at me, notsaʔka. No fear." The deep notes of his voice pinned her in place.

Eva fixed her eyes on him, and then he entered in one hard, burning thrust. Her eyes watered, but she didn't blink. At the pain of his rocking hips, she raked down his spine and across his buttocks. He shuddered, closed his eyes, and stopped moving. She smiled at his reaction. When he started again, the burning eased, and she whispered, "Look at me."

He forced his eyes open. Eva dragged her nails across him again, and he caught one of her hands and pulled it above her head. "Don't."

She wiggled underneath him.

He growled and dropped the entire mass of his body onto her. "I'm not ready yet. *You're* not ready yet." His warm breath caressed her ear, his scent filling her nose.

As the pain increased with the lack of movement, she squirmed. His eye screwed shut against her cheek, and she wrapped her arms and legs around him, forcing herself to be patient. After a moment, he kissed her neck and eased the burning once more, taking his time with her, waiting for her to catch up.

For a brief instant, Eva floated above herself, unable to believe what she was doing. The next, she could no longer think, only feel. "I need you," she breathed.

He surrendered, touching something deep inside her, and she thought she would burst from aching for him. Every nerve from her tail to her scalp came alive. She gasped in surprise, and Jim answered her with a groan.

She melted underneath him, never wanting him to leave her, marveling that she was really here, with him inside her, in this moment. He relaxed, propping some of his weight on his arms. She circled her legs around his hips again, locking him in place. He chuckled in her ear.

"Let's do it again," she said.

He laughed louder this time. "I need a moment." He rolled onto his side, releasing a heavy breath, and she turned to face him, throwing her leg over his thigh.

"It will never hurt like that between us again," he said. "At least, after you heal, it won't." He played with the heaviness of one of her breasts and kissed her shoulder. "But I intend to have you again before that," he said, his eyes returning to hers, his feral grin glittering in the moonlight. He nipped her nose, and she shivered, pulling his blanket over them both.

As he curled her hair behind her ear, he grew serious. "You are my woman now, Eva. You belong to me. Now and forever." His eyes seemed to scan her face for understanding.

Without hesitation, she placed her forehead on his. "And you are my man, James McCullough. You belong to me," she said. "Now and forever."

Pale sunlight needled through the shingles and chinks of the hay loft. Eva heard Pump below, noisily talking to himself and hitching his team to the wagon.

"Sure am looking forward to this trip to San Felipe today. To SAN FELIPE to take COTTON to MARKET." Harnesses rattled and banged, and the buckboard tailgate was unlatched, dropped, and slammed shut again, marking his words with syncopated emphasis.

Eva turned her head to Jim. It was still quite early in the morning. He smiled at her in their drowsy cocoon, then put a finger over her lips and slid inside her. She gasped, and he put his hand over her mouth, bringing his lips next to her ear. "Don't make a sound." He rocked silently, slowly, and deeply. She wrapped herself around him. He had made love to her twice more during the night, and she had been less tender and responded to him faster each time. He watched her face. The next moment, he stopped without finishing, and she protested with her eyes, but he lifted his hand from her mouth and shook his head.

"Good morning, Pump!" he shouted over his shoulder.

"Well, good morning, Jim! Glad you could join us. Are you planning to go to San Felipe today? And would you, by any chance, know where Eva is?"

"Good morning, Pump," Eva called down.

"Ah, good morning to you, too, my dear! Will you also be joining us?"

Jim raised his eyebrows, echoing the question.

"What about the animals?" she asked, just to Jim.

"We'll keep the chickens in the coop and put out extra food for the others. Just need to make sure the water troughs aren't empty when we get back late tonight. Even if we stay overnight in town, they should be fine." He nuzzled her shoulder. "I'd rather have you with me than leave you here."

"Yes, I'm going, too," Eva yelled.

"Then get a shift on you two. Time's a-wasting." She heard him leave the barn. Reluctance pulled her back into the hay, where she shut her eyes for a moment, then tugged him down beside her. She wanted to trace the tattoos on his chest and ask him what they meant.

"We need to go," he said, kissing her on the nose and then her chin. "Once we get this cotton moved and can shoo Pump along, we can stay in bed as long as you want."

The comforting drone of the hooves, buckboard, and harness combined with the muffling screen of their cotton mattress allowed Eva and Jim to travel in style. Pump had needed to make a couple of trips to the McMullens' gin, but one wagonload worth was all that was left after the seeds had been removed. Wokweesi followed at a trot, tongue lolling. Occasionally, he darted into the brush, returning to catch up at a run when he fell behind.

"The first time I've ever preferred a wagon ride to a horse," Jim said. His hand caressed her thigh under her skirts, and he jostled against her as they hit a rough patch.

"Heh, we'll make an Anglo of you yet, as Pump would say," she said.

Jim scowled in mock indignation.

Eva played with the fabric of his shirt. "What does notsaʔka mean? It doesn't mean something terrible like 'Thick Waist' or 'Misses When Shooting,' does it?"

Jim laughed and appeared tempted for a moment but chose the truth. "No, nothing like that. It means something like 'sweetheart.'" His hand moved to her belly. "Your waist is perfect," he said, giving it a squeeze, "but Misses When Shooting is not a bad name for you." His eyes twinkled.

"Maybe in the beginning, but not anymore," she said, thinking of their last close round.

His grin widened. "True enough. I'm afraid you will put me to shame soon." After a shared moment of listening to the wagon wheels turn, Jim asked, "Your hair — you painted it black before you came here? For your mission to Goliad?" When Eva nodded, he laced his fingers through her hair at the roots. "I prefer your real color. It reminds me of honey."

She laid her head in the crook of his arm, ignoring the twinge of anxiety Goliad brought up in her. Jim added a second blanket over them, and she snuggled closer to his warmth. Against a backdrop of gray sky, a caracara sailed the thermals overhead, and she watched until she grew too drowsy, closing her eyes to let the wheels lull her to sleep. Eventually, Jim's hand stilled, and he snored softly in her ear.

Chapter 24

Eva

San Felipe de Austin

E va noticed the warmth first and then that the buckboard had stopped. She stretched, basking in the full sun on a chilly day, pleased the clouds had parted. Jim removed his arm from underneath her, sat up, and pulled her skirts down over her calves before Pump's head could pop over the end of the cotton mound.

Curious to see the town of San Felipe de Austin, Eva glanced around her. They had parked at the exchange amongst many other cotton wagons. Jim leapt to the ground and then turned to help her down. Groups of men stood clumped in small cliques outside the office.

"Old Pumphrey Brunet, about time we saw your face in town." A man peeled himself from his companions and extended a hand.

"Horatio! You know you can't be rid of me," Pump said, smiling as he shook with both of his.

"And I see you have Comanche Jim with you," Horatio said with a little less enthusiasm.

Jim bobbed a cordial greeting. "Mr. Chriesman." He put his arm around Eva and pulled her an inch closer, which caused Horatio's attention to shift to her.

"Ma'am," he said, tipping his hat.

With no thought to how Jim's action looked, giddiness filled Eva's heart to be claimed by her man, however subtly. Her mind reeled with the newness of it all. She, *Eva*, was someone's wife, and she was *loved*.

While Pump dominated the conversation, Horatio surveyed her, his eyes darting out from the corners to scan her head to toe. She wondered what he saw. Standing there on the edges, Eva remembered being sent as a child through the connecting back rooms of a beauty parlor and into the barbershop next door to retrieve a Coke for her birth mother, who was having her hair done. The men had all stopped and stared when she entered their small sanctuary. Eva shifted her feet, feeling like a hen in a fox house.

"There's talk of Johnson and Grant gathering volunteers to invade Matamoros once all the Mexican troops are expelled," Pump was saying.

"I think that's possible before the year is out. They can't expect to take our slaves and livelihood away without a fight," Horatio said. "Mexico City will have to take local rule more seriously."

"Why would they? Seems to me they'll have every reason to send more soldiers," another man said. He stood wide-legged, arms clasped above the elbows, and spit voluminously to the side.

If they only knew, Eva thought. They didn't realize Mexico would declare them all to be pirates at the end of the following month. "Remind me to tell you about the Grass Fight," Eva muttered to Jim, who cocked an eyebrow in reply.

At Eva's whisper, Pump focused on her and pulled a slip of paper from his pocket. "Just a moment, gentlemen," he said as he stepped aside with her.

"Why don't you take this down to the W. C. White & Company Store? Just hand it to the clerk, and they'll fill our order," he instructed in muted tones. "You can wait there or come back here. They'll put it on Jim's credit."

"I'd rather her stay put with us, Pump," Jim whispered.

Pump's brow creased. "She'll be fine, Jim. She can take care of getting supplies while we get our cotton weighed. Who knows how long we'll be here jawin'?"

Eva, too, was surprised by her husband's reaction.

After a moment of studying the direction she needed to walk, Jim consented.

She placed a hand on his arm and went on tiptoe to speak into his ear. "No one knows me here, but I look like I belong. This is what I'm good at." She pecked him on the cheek. "I won't call attention to myself."

A few men turned their heads in her direction, distracted by the kiss, before returning to their debate.

"You were saying?" Jim asked. "I believe they are very aware of you."

Pump gave her directions, and she set off. When she cast a glance back, Jim was watching her. She waved. He raised his hand and returned to the circle of men. She wondered when they would start weighing the cotton.

Eva's heels echoed as she strode down the wooden boardwalks lining the main avenues. She passed rough cabins and finer establishments, and curiosity led her to peek inside open windows. Between the buildings, she glimpsed plazas laid out in the fashion of a Mexican town. Hooves churned the mud in the streets, and her nose told her most of it was muck. Men tipped their hats as they crossed paths, but she encountered few women. Several of the Anglos dressed in various pieces of buckskin, though of a cruder sort than Jim's. At the ferry, she paused to watch the raftsmen guiding more cotton wagons across the Brazos and listened to the ring of a hammer on iron in the distance. Laughter and the clack of billiard balls drifted to her from a tavern. Overall, new construction spoke of genteel aspirations smoothing over fading roughness.

When she pushed open the general store door, a bell rang overhead. Corrie ten Boom's ghost greeted her from behind her watch counter until Eva's eyes adjusted to the interior. The next moment, the woman she had murdered dissolved into a male grocer with oiled hair and a pointed mustache. As she took a breath to slow her heart, she scanned the dim shop. Behind the counter, bottles and packages lined the shelves above the man's head, threatening to topple in places.

"Welcome, miss. I don't believe I've seen you before. Newly arrived?"

"Good day," Eva said, dipping, suddenly aware her rebozo shawl was missing, and her head was bare. She hadn't thought about it since she had traveled with Tophe. It must be somewhere along the creek bed. "Um, yes," she replied and lowered her eyes.

"Whereabouts from?"

Eva flailed, realizing she had not put in the time to create a back story. She probably shouldn't say she was living with Jim. "New Orleans. I came up on the steamboat yesterday."

"Beautiful city. New people come from New Orleans all the time."

"Yes, or I should say, oui, monsieur." She forced a laugh at her own joke, then remembered the shopping list and handed it over to him.

The clerk smiled wider. "Let's see what you have here, and then we'll open you an account." He ran the stub of a pencil down Pump's list. "Yep, we have everything in stock. Would you like a copy of the *Texas Gazette*? There's also a new paper that started up just last month, the *Telegraph and Texas Register*." Eva stopped herself from saying yes to both and told him, "No, thank you," instead. She didn't know how much money Jim had. She could always come back.

"So," the clerk said as he scooped flour from a barrel, "what brings you to town?"

"I'm visiting a friend," she said, running her fingers over a nearby bolt of cloth.

"Oh? Who?"

His question caught her as if she had just taken a bite of food, and her hand froze in place. San Felipe was too small to make up a name. Truth was best. "James McCullough."

The smile left the clerk's eyes. "Comanche Jim?"

"I usually just call him Jim," she replied. Her face hardened, and she willed it to soften.

"Are these items for you or for him?"

Eva dropped the pretense. "They're for both of us."

He stood up, and a puff of flour sprinkled his hand when he shoved the scoop back into the mound. "Will you be paying with your own funds?"

When she shook her head, he ran his eyes over her and lingered on her uncovered, half-dyed hair. "I'm sorry, my dear, but Mr. McCullough does not have credit with us. I believe he may have intended to send you to Townsend's."

While he gave her directions, Eva's face burned. She stood apart from herself for a moment and recalled a time when an unconscious shadow couldn't have embarrassed her.

"We, I mean they, Pump and Jim, just brought a wagonload of cotton to the exchange today."

His eyes relit with interest. "Well, you're welcome to return with cash in hand. I don't want you to misunderstand me, miss… ma'am. I like Jim just fine. I'll be happy to extend him credit if he is now making an income." His words mollified her until he said, "I'm glad to hear he's applying himself. He seemed just about ruined for civilization last time I saw him." His jaw and shoulders relaxed. "Tell you what. How about I just hold on to your list? I can fill it when you… or Jim… returns with cash."

Eva reached out and gently pulled the paper from his hands. "Thank you kindly, but I should check and see what Jim would prefer."

The corners of the clerk's mouth lifted, tight-lipped, and he nodded. "All right," he said, placing his hands on the countertop.

She turned to leave just as the bell rang over the door, and Jim stepped in.

Chapter 25

Eva

"The hell I don't," Jim said. Eva had pulled him outside so they could speak privately. He pushed past her and barreled into the store. Wokweesi followed him, darting out of the way when the door grazed his hip. Eva caught it before it slammed.

"Walter, I hear I don't have credit here. What the hell did I do with you and Pump at this very counter? And my finances? As if that's any of your goddamned business."

Walter's mouth dropped open. Perhaps too alarmed to notice the dog, his eyes remained riveted to Jim's, and he took a half step back.

Eva hovered in the doorway but then moved to stand by her husband.

"I'm sorry," Walter said. "You'll have to forgive me. I've just realized I had forgotten we had done that."

Jim glared at the clerk, jaw ticking and face darkening.

Walter's brows rose, and he stuttered, "If you'll hand me your list, ma'am, I'll be glad to fill it right now." He shifted his attention to Eva, arm outstretched.

ell

Back outside, Wokweesi trotted away, and Jim stood for a moment with his hands on his hips, collecting himself. He opened his mouth to say something, shut it, then tightened his lips, shaking his head.

"Why didn't we just go to another store?" Eva asked.

"Because that's what he wants. He doesn't trust me. I'll get the same treatment at the other two places. He extended credit to me as a favor to Pump. Pump wasn't with you, and it's easy to tell my woman to go away," he said, waving across her body.

Eva debated asking a question. She had already been thinking about how she — correction — how _they_ would make their way in the world. Everything Eva had ever had as an adult had come from Lux Libera. She owned nothing of her own. "Out of curiosity," she asked, "what is the state of our finances?"

Jim appeared to blink at her use of the plural possessive. She watched him roll a question over in his head, answer it for himself, and say, "The state of our finances is fine. Pump set me up with a little bit of money, and I inherited everything from my former partner, who had inherited everything from his former partner. No family, either of them." He leaned back on his heels, eyes distant. "We do need the cotton money, though, to make the land dues." When he glanced toward the shop door, his face hardened again, and he said, "I've never wished I'd planted more cotton than I do right now." His eyes shone with the same competitive gleam she saw when they trained. Not wanting to spend the rest of her days farming, she hoped that wish was fleeting.

Across the street, she noted a huddle of three boys stealing peeks at Jim. Their hands flew in a hand-clapping choosing game, and the loser was compelled to cross the street. He waited for a cart to roll by, then proceeded with downcast eyes, his hands in his pockets.

Jim seemed to come out of his own thoughts when he alerted to the boy. He fixed a stern mouth, but his eyes crinkled as he drew himself up to his full height, then peered down at the boy who stepped before him.

"Excuse me, sir?"

Jim let a moment pass before he replied. "Yes?"

"Are you the man who lived with wild Indians?"

"No," Jim said, allowing the boy to be crestfallen before he continued. "There's no such thing. I lived among the Nʉmʉnʉʉ."

The boy's brow scrunched as he mouthed the strange word.

"The Comanches," Jim filled in for him.

"Oh!" His face cleared. "That's why they call you Comanche Jim. We weren't sure." The boy pointed at his friends.

Jim followed his gaze. "Yes, people call me that. I prefer Jim."

"Can you teach us how to shoot a bow and arrow?"

Eva's heart melted at the hope on his face, then she checked Jim's reaction.

His lips pursed as he stifled a smile. "I think you would need to ask your mothers first," he said. "Also, I live several hours from town."

The boy hopped in place, face beaming. "We'll ask them! Thank you, Com… Jim" He ran back to his friends, dodging passersby. Eva guessed the boys were about eight years old.

Jim offered his arm to Eva, a wide grin lighting his eyes, and she hooked her hand on his elbow as they strolled down the boardwalk. "He forgot to ask me where I live. They always forget to ask."

"Always? How often has that happened?"

He shrugged. "Maybe five times. Happened in San Antonio, too. Sometimes they want to learn to 'ride like a Comanche.'"

"You're famous. You must have quite the fan club, then," she said.

Jim tilted his chin. "Fan club?"

"Not fan," she said, miming. "Fan like fanatic. It means you have admirers."

Jim laughed. "That I do. Them I don't mind," he said, smile fading. "There's a fine line between famous and infamous. Pump said that to me early on. It fits."

Throughout the rest of the day, Eva observed people darting glances at Jim. The enslaved woman at the tavern served Pump and Eva first and then sloshed Jim's blue shell-edged bowl as she set it down with a shaky hand. Most matrons threw acid-tipped daggers into his back, but a high-status young lady studied him with veiled interest. The men — Anglo, Negro, Tejano, and German alike — evaluated him from a wary distance, a cautious watching and waiting.

It seemed to Eva several had made up their minds long ago. Jim's shoulders sat around his ears, and she resisted reaching out to smooth the fine hairs on the back of his neck.

With the cotton weighed and paying out at about $230 — an enormous sum for their tiny harvest — and store-bought packages under arms, Jim's head turned in the direction of home. Pump was giving Eva the story of every settler they passed when she ran into Jim's back. He had stopped on the boardwalk and was glaring at a group of people coming out of the municipal building across the street.

"Tonkawas," he said, his face souring enough that he spat.

Eva and Pump exchanged concern.

"They're filthy. I can smell them from here." Jim's lip curled.

It was the first time he had ever looked ugly to her. Eva stared at him.

"What?" he asked, irritated.

"Do you not see the irony? You've been called a filthy Indian before," she said, gesturing at him with her hand. "And after the day you've had today?"

"I don't know the word irony, but I take your meaning. But in this case, they actually are filthy. Look at them!"

Eva cast her eyes across the street in order to humor him. She saw Tonkawas, who appeared as clean as she was.

"But more importantly, they eat people."

"They do not!" Eva said, scandalized at what had to be propaganda.

"They absolutely do. I've seen it with my own eyes." He pointed at both his eyeballs. At her skepticism, he said, "Look, one of our horse-warriors fell behind when we were being chased by Tonkawas, and they captured him. As soon as we were able, we turned back to rescue him. When we sneaked up on their camp that night, they had chopped off his arms and legs and bashed in his forehead. They were roasting one of his legs and eating the other. Not only was our friend doomed to wander the afterlife lost, but they were eating him, too. Eating him!" he said again as if she needed further clarification. Jim shuddered in disgust. He bounced on the balls of his feet, vengeance for his long-murdered friend in his eyes.

"Why do they eat people?" Eva asked.

"They think they can get the warrior's power. And mutilating him keeps him from journeying to the lands beyond the Sun. They do that part on purpose."

"Don't the Nᵾmᵾnᵾᵾ mutilate enemy warriors, too?"

Jim didn't answer for a moment, his focus unwavering. "We don't eat people. Ever. You don't get puha from eating people. And everyone knows that once you eat people, you develop a taste for it."

"That's not what I asked," she said.

"And if that's not the worst of it, they're allied with Anglos."

Pump had been watching the Tonkawas, but at this, he turned to Jim. "What's wrong with being allied with the Anglos?"

"Anglos are foolish to have Tonkawas as friends. Like warming a snake under your shirt."

Though Eva couldn't know if it would happen here, she thought of the possible reservation in Oklahoma to which the friendly Tonkawas might be driven after years of service and cooperation with the Anglos and despite the protests of frontiersmen and Texas Rangers. They would be surrounded by enemy tribes eager to settle old scores and might be cut down to just over one hundred survivors. Her heart sank. You may have it backward in this timeline, my love, she thought.

Jim shuttered his expression and continued walking. By that time, the Tonkawas had noticed them staring, and they followed Jim with their eyes. A younger man about Jim's age made what Eva assumed was a rude gesture behind his back. She was relieved Jim hadn't seen it.

Pump and Eva kept their distance the rest of the way to the buckboard.

"That was Plácido and some of his family," Pump said under his breath.

Eva glanced over her shoulder at the Tonkawas, their retreating backs already farther down the boardwalk. She had heard the name before but couldn't recall his importance to history in any variation.

"A good man," Pump continued. "I tried introducing him to Jim when we first returned from San Antonio, but he nearly gutted the fella right there on the spot. Would have if I hadn't intervened.

Plácido ran out of the building before Jim could get an arrow strung."

"Plácido… Plácido… why do I know that name?" Beyond what Eva remembered from the Texas history lessons of her birth timeline, she had only ever been briefed on the Native Tribes when they affected her mission as a Lux Libera Mender. Her knowledge was spotty, especially for the present year of 1835. If they had been further forward in time, decades away, she would have been on firmer ground.

"He's the head chief of all the Tonkawas. He and his men are critical to the defense of the Anglo settlements against all the hostile tribes of the plains, especially the Comanche. Without them, without their knowledge and skills, we'd be overrun. If our line plays out like other lines I've visited, he and his people will be our steadfast allies for over fifty years."

"And are they cannibals like Jim said?"

Pump lifted a shoulder. "I believe so, though I haven't witnessed it myself." With a tired hand, he rubbed the back of his neck. "I've known nothing but friendship from the Tonkawas. Shame Jim can't see past his blood feud with them."

When they arrived at the buckboard, they found Wokweesi sound asleep underneath. With the cotton gone, the ride was going to be rougher. As she climbed up behind Jim, he said, "Good thing I didn't plant any more. We would've had to make two trips."

Chapter 26

Eva

Sanctum, Axis Mundi, True line

Black and white stones battled on the game board in front of Eva. She tugged at her hair from the roots and looked up at Sakura. "Why did I ever agree to play you again?"

A serene smile spread across her friend's lips, her eyes glittering. She shrugged but didn't say a word.

Eva noticed her leg jiggling and tucked it behind her ankle. The smell of mown grass floated up to them through their open window, and she heard the whir of lawn equipment in the distance. Groaning, she passed Sakura a black stone. Sakura made another move without hesitation. Devoid of hope, Eva studied the Go board as a matter of course but then handed over her final prisoner.

"Listen, I will only play Gomoku with you from now on. Go is too hard," Eva said as they pinched up their stones and dropped them in bags.

"You said that last time."

"When's your next mission?" Eva asked. As she tried to close the lid of the tattered game box, it split, so she stood up to find tape in their desk.

"Tomorrow. Enrique's supposed to be picking up my mended kimono for me right now. Should be here any minute. We're going to the Imperial Colonies of Europe."

"Oh, fun! New Tokyo or New Kyoto?"

"New Kyoto. New Tokyo isn't part of the West Spain Trading Company in that world."

A faint whistling drifted to them from the long hall. Knowing it was Tophe approaching, Eva said, "Let's see if Enrique wants to play a round of spades before dinner. I'm sure Tophe will be up for it."

"Speak of the devil," Sakura said when Tophe appeared in the doorway.

"What?" Tophe asked, eyebrows raised.

"I was just asking Sakura if she thought she and Enrique might want to play a round of spades before we go to dinner."

"I'm in!"

"Told you," Eva said to Sakura.

"Eva and I have been unstoppable lately," Tophe said. He lowered himself to sit cross-legged next to the coffee table.

"Ah, I see," Sakura said. "Payback."

"No, not at all," Eva said.

"You're such a sore loser, Eva," Sakura said and laughed, looking to Tophe for confirmation.

"Absolument."

Eva rolled her eyes. "I'll get the cards." She opened her trunk. "I can shuffle and deal out while we wait."

Tophe moved to her bunk.

"Hey, shoes off. How many times do I have to tell you?" Eva asked as she shook the cards from their box.

"Meh meh meh meh meh meh meh," he mimicked but complied. He sighed as he leaned back and closed his eyes. "Merde, I'm still exhausted. I even slept last night."

"Well, we were awake for nearly fifty-six hours straight. Takes a day or two to recover," Eva said.

"No more war zones, okay?"

"You'll have to take that up with the council," Sakura said.

"When we get our promotion," he said, lifting his arm from across his eyes and rolling his head toward Eva, "no more war zones. There are plenty of other options. With hotels. And cafes."

"Do you know where I want to return to?" Eva asked. "Rome." The cards riffled between her arched palms. "Ancient Rome, I mean."

"Republic or Empire?" Sakura asked.

"Either. I found both delightful."

Tophe wrinkled his nose. "That's because you weren't the one playing bodyguard to the patrician lady."

Eva pointed at him, the split deck in her hand. "Tell me that wasn't the softest bed you've ever slept in. Even for a slave."

Tophe stuck out his lower lip and lifted a shoulder. "I recall mine being made of coarser stuff."

"And the food." Eva inhaled in ecstasy, closing her eyes.

"Again. Not the same experience," Tophe said. "The table-scrap pottage our host served the slaves had been boiling continuously since the time of the previous emperor, I'm sure."

"Was that during the Third Servile War?" Sakura asked.

"No, that was on the mission to end Nero's reign. The Third Servile War was during the Republic." She reshuffled the cards and dealt the first hand. "And, on a different timeline mission, we were there several years before the slave revolt. I convinced the Editor to turn his thumb in Spartacus' favor with my womanly charms. We were there so that the Third Servile War could happen just like in the True line."

Not for the first time, Eva reflected on the immense power concentrated in that one man, the Editor. From his balcony in the Colosseum, he gazed down, hand aloft, and decided the fates of human beings in the gory arena below. Would he choose mercy or death? The crowd would roar, hoping to sway his judgment, but in the end, he controlled the outcome. An upturned thumb: Life. A downturned one... swift execution. How like the Elders, she thought, sitting on their dais, determining so many lifelines, including hers. Most days, the knowledge gave her comfort.

"Ah, yes, that's right," Sakura said. "That's why I had it in my head."

"The Games were something to see," Eva said. "The fights. The blood. The thousands of screaming spectators. Even the beasts. The victories were rarely predictable." She stretched her arms above her head, yawning. "Quite entertaining."

Tophe started to snore, and Eva tossed a pen at him. He rolled onto his back, arm draped across his face.

"You would think shadow worlds wouldn't feel so... alive," Sakura said.

"Hey," Enrique said from the doorway.

Sakura stood to greet him. "Gracias," she said as she took a brown paper package from his hands.

"Elizabeth told me to tell you she couldn't get the blood stain out completely," he said in Spanish. "But your new obi should cover it, and you can only see it if you know where to look."

Sakura pressed her lips together, disappointed.

"Espadas?" Eva asked, gesturing to the four piles before her and his empty seat.

Enrique chuckled. "Do I have a choice?"

"No," Tophe said, removing his arm from his eyes and sitting up. He rubbed his face and mussed his hair. He didn't bother to smooth it down.

Eva fanned her cards and arranged them by suit, then looked up at Tophe, who had settled across from her. He raised his eyebrows. "Four," she said.

He examined his cards, lips puckered. "Four," he echoed, snapping his hand shut.

"Eight?" Enrique's eyes widened as he wrote the bid, head shaking. He put the pencil down and picked up his own cards. "I bid four. Sakura?"

Sakura wagged her head back and forth, undecided. "Two."

"Okay," Enrique said. "Fourteen bid. Some people — not us — are going to miss their bid."

Sakura led with an ace.

"Ouf," Tophe said.

Sakura grinned at him, unrepentant.

"Hey, have either of you run into yourself in a timeline?" Enrique asked as he gathered up the trick and laid the next card.

"No, of course not," Tophe said.

Eva shook her head, agreeing with her partner. Their friend's words walked up her spine. Even discussing the question was forbidden. "Have you?" she asked, unable to stop herself.

Enrique and Sakura's eyes met and fluttered apart. Tophe moved cards around in his hand.

"No, I was just wondering," Enrique said.

Tophe collected the trick. "It's never crossed my mind."

"I've just been thinking lately… since I have free will, what would talking to myself be like? Would I know what I was about to say?"

"Probably," Tophe said.

"But wouldn't that mean I didn't have free will if I could predict what my copy would say? Or maybe I wouldn't be able to predict what my copy would say because I have free will, and they don't?"

Tophe shifted in his seated position, frowning, but remained focused on his cards. "I have no idea. You should probably ask one of the theologians."

Enrique and Sakura shared a longer look until Enrique glanced at Eva and broke it off. A heaviness filled the room, and Eva chewed her cuticle while she decided which card to play next. The lawn equipment had stopped running, and the sunlight waned. She hid her hand, stood up to flip on the overhead light, and took a deep, savoring breath at the window before shutting it.

"Bastard," Tophe said as Enrique gathered up another trick. Sakura giggled, and the pensive mood dissipated.

Eva knew before the final hand that they had lost.

"You overbid," Tophe said, only half-teasing.

Eva hung her head in mock shame. "It was nice while it lasted. Our winning streak."

Tophe scratched the back of his head and said, "I need to grab something from my room. I'll meet you at the dining hall."

Eva nodded, packing the worn cards away. Turning from her trunk, she saw Enrique whispering into Sakura's ear.

Sakura blushed, their fingers twining. Sakura's eye caught her gaze, and they pulled away from each other. "Ready?" she asked.

Jim's Farm

Three limestone pebbles balanced on the log in front of Eva. She added a fourth to the row, thinking of Sakura. A metate and mano with a bag of dried corn lay beside her, untouched, as she listened to the river. She was so absorbed she didn't hear Jim's footsteps behind her and jumped when he touched her shoulder.

"Ʉnha hakai nʉʉsuka?" How are you, he asked.

"Tsaatʉ," Good, she said. "Ʉnha hakai nʉʉsuka?"

He tweaked her pronunciation and smiled. "I'm good, too." He sat beside her with his knees up and searched through the rocks near the mealing stone. "I see we won't go hungry tonight," he said, selecting a flat stone the size of her palm and skipping it across the water.

She stared at the sack of corn and saw her friend's obi wrapped in brown paper. "I miss my people," she finally said. "Some of them are dead. Worse than dead, actually."

Jim skipped a second rock and looked over at her. "What's worse than dead?"

"Alive in a dark place, but not able to die."

Jim sighed, face serious. In his gaze, Eva saw his murdered friend, mutilated and wandering the afterlife. "Do you want to go back to your people?" he asked after a bit, voice guarded.

Eva placed another pebble on the log and then another. "I can't."

Jim turned to face her. "But would you want to if you could?"

She couldn't meet his eyes. "I feel as dirty as you believe the Tonkawas to be. Going back would mean swallowing the filth and being fine with it. But I miss my friends. They are my family. Were my family. And they have no idea they're dirty. They would feel justified in… sending me to the Abyss. They would cut out my…" she hunted for the word she thought he would know, "womb before they did, though, for making love to you. And it would break their hearts to do it."

Jim's face drained of color. "This is what your vow meant?"

"Yes," she said. "I had always been taught I would lose my ability to travel if I did what was forbidden."

"How do your people have babies?"

"They don't. They find children who have the ability to travel and take them to Axis Mundi for training. Recruits leave their birth families behind."

Jim shook his head. "Nʉmʉnʉʉ women are not able to have very many children. Each child is precious to us. We would never keep our women from having babies. In fact, a pregnant woman is all the more valuable as a bride."

Eva blew through her nose with bitter irony. "Both our people kidnap children. For the same reason." She closed her eyes and thought of her parents. She couldn't remember their faces anymore, just their hair.

"Can your people find you?" Jim asked.

"I don't know. I don't think so. There's no reason for them to know what has happened between us or that I am an apostate, so I don't believe they are hunting for me yet." At his look of confusion, she explained what apostate meant.

"And you have until March and Goliad before they suspect anything?"

"Yes."

"We should go to my people," he said. "Neither of us is happy with the life here."

It was what she wanted more than anything, but thoughts of Tophe complicated matters. "I think I need to save Francisca from Tophe." She heard the doom in her voice.

"That seems like a bad idea."

"I know."

"You will have to kill him."

Eva pulled her knees up and buried her face. "I don't think I can. He's my entire family."

Jim put a hand on her back and then scooted closer, so they sat hip to hip. He kissed her shoulder. The silence drew out in a long stream that joined the river and carried her thoughts away. Her mind and heart were empty. There were no more tears to shed.

"Speaking of wombs and babies…"

When he didn't continue, she turned her head to him. "Yes?"

"Are you able to have children?" His eyes scanned the other bank, and the skin of his jaw drew tight.

"I don't see why I wouldn't be able to," she said, her brow creasing. "I've always been pretty regular." Eva had never pictured herself as a mother after she joined Lux Libera. She had always liked children, but it had never been a possibility. She imagined his baby growing inside her, a spark of warmth in her belly, and it comforted her.

"It's just that you haven't bled since you came here."

Eva tucked her lips to hide her amusement. "I have, twice. I'm due again soon."

Jim's face froze, and she saw thoughts racing behind his eyes. He sounded a little panicky when he said, "I'm… I'm going to tell you what happens in my village, and then you tell me what has been happening with you."

Chapter 27

Eva

E va lifted her eyebrows and pursed her lips tighter. She inclined her head for him to continue.

"In my village, when a woman starts to bleed, she stays in her own kahni or goes to her elderly parents' home. She does not touch any of the men or any of the men's things. If someone needs something from her kahni, she will throw it out. She will return at the end after she has cleaned herself."

She nodded again, unsurprised.

Jim waited for her to explain herself.

"Oh," she said, realizing it was her turn. "I use a menstrual cup. I just happened to be wearing it because I was at the end of my cycle when I came here. It's in the cabin. I can show it to you."

With wide eyes, Jim stared sidelong at her, mouth open, but didn't respond.

"I have a small, thin cup," she said, demonstrating with her hands, "that I can put inside me to catch the blood. I just dump the blood in the outhouse." At the shock on Jim's face, she added, "It's very discreet. You would never know."

"I didn't know. That's the problem." Jim's features tick-tocked between disgust and anger.

Eva's own temper stirred, and she took a breath. It had never occurred to her that he would have an opinion or expect her to conform to something so personal. "Why is that a problem? I don't see how it's been any of your business... at least until now." She thought she knew what he was going to say, and it was probably going to involve puha.

"Because your power cancels out my power when you're bleeding. I can't hunt. You put me at risk of being killed," Jim said. His voice rose. "You've touched everything in my cabin!"

"Have you had any trouble hunting?" Eva asked, as calmly as she could.

Jim chewed the side of his mouth and studied the river.

"Have we gone hungry? Haven't we had so much meat that we've been drying the extra? We have enough meat to last for months!" Eva grabbed a handful of pebbles and launched them into the water one by one. "When we have been training, have you been shooting poorly? If anything," she said, poking him in the shoulder, "I've been *improving you* because you have someone to compete against." With extra force, she threw an entire handful that scattered like birdshot.

Jim remained silent for a long time, but his breathing slowed. "I have had no trouble."

Eva dusted her hands. "Women's cycles are nothing to be afraid of. They won't cancel out your power. Or, at the very least, please believe that mine won't cancel out yours." She put a hand on his arm, and he looked at it. "There's nothing dirty about it. It's very clean and washes away easily. We deal with animal blood all the time." She clutched his biceps. "Anglo and Mexican women don't hide away. Neither do Lux Libera. I won't sequester myself like a Nʉmʉ woman when I am bleeding. That's non-negotiable."

Jim's head jerked at her tone, and his jaw clenched. She sensed she had overplayed her hand. "You underestimate a woman's power." His eyes searched hers. "Do you not realize you are powerful enough to kill a rattlesnake if you spit on it? It has nothing to do with being unclean. Just look at how weak Anglo men are. And Mexicans. You may have a more… contained… solution, but women separating themselves is practical. You must follow the women's customs, regardless of how you feel about it. Even if you don't affect me, other men's lives are too important to risk." Jim turned his head from her.

Eva dropped her hand, dug her fingers into the silt, and changed tactics. "I think the good news, remember, is that I should be able to have children." When he didn't respond, she added, "I'm not bleeding right now."

Though he softened, his eyes stayed glued to the far bank.

She leaned into him. After a moment, he leaned back, and she laid her head on his shoulder.

He stared down at her but didn't say anything. When he finally nodded, she decided to interpret that as an armistice or, at least, a ceasefire.

"You're right about one thing," he said after a while, his voice soft. "You're not bleeding right now. That's the real reason I came to find you in the first place." He kissed her neck and caught her earlobe between his teeth, growling in her ear.

The rumble traveled all the way to her toes. She pulled away, the sensation too intense.

He reached under her skirts, and she found him beneath his breechcloth. When he was ready, he moved her to straddle his lap, pushing deep inside her. He held her to himself, unmoving, and sighed into her chest. She squeezed around him, and he chuckled, pulling his arms more tightly around her in answer.

Eva rocked her hips and cupped his face with her hands. "May I kiss you?" After a moment of hesitation, he consented. She pressed her lips to his, and he pressed back. She surprised him by darting her tongue, but then he touched his tongue to hers in return.

When she pulled away, he smiled at her. "The rocks hurt," he said. "I have a better idea."

She stood up from him, and he led her to the cypress tree, pressing her back against the trunk. He kissed her on the mouth again, but this time with confidence and enthusiasm. She laced her fingers through his hair, and his hand found her breast. She could smell the earthy water trapped between the roots at her feet, and it mixed with his scent, intoxicating her.

He spun her to face the tree. Confused, she tried to turn, but he held her shoulder in place, nuzzling her neck. As he kissed her hairline, her scalp lit up, and a frisson shot straight to her core. He lifted her skirts and, understanding his intention, she pushed her hips toward him, her desire for him growing. He found her entrance and pulled her to him. Without warning, an urgent need for him consumed her; his touch was the only thing that could overshadow her loss, her anxiety, and her anger. She didn't want him to be gentle. She thrust back toward him, and he responded in kind, murmuring approval.

When they were finished, Eva felt every bone had melted away and said, "I could have done that forever." She rested her cheek against the bark.

"I could tell," Jim said, adjusting his clothing. "Unfortunately, I can't." He wrapped his arms around her and kissed the back of her neck. "I just have to content myself with doing it again as soon as possible."

Eva laughed and settled back against him, savoring his warmth, his arms around her, his lips on her neck — his entire being enveloping her. She closed her eyes.

Jim paused in his kisses, his breath hitching. After a moment, he whispered, "I think I was meant to find you that day."

That night, in their bed, Eva traced his tattoos in the flickering firelight. "Do all Nʉmʉnʉʉ tattoo?" she asked.

"No. Many of the northern bands don't. My eldest brother doesn't have any." Jim pointed above his left breast. "But Rʉtsima has a black star right here."

"Does this mean anything?"

Jim glanced down at his chest, just below his right shoulder. "That's where a Tonkawa's arrow went in. I killed him with my knife."

Eva quirked an eyebrow, and he returned her gaze. His eyes followed her fingers as they traveled to the scar on his side.

"And this one?"

"An Apache's knife when they attacked our village. I killed him, too." A smile played at his lips, and his eyes gleamed. He took a deep breath, his chest expanding under her hand.

"What about this one?" Eva touched a place on his left shoulder. "Why is it not tattooed?"

Jim's gaze faltered, and he dropped his eyes. "That's from a captive woman who resisted me."

Eva's heart stopped. "Did you kil..." she asked, reluctant to finish her question.

Jim nodded.

Eva studied his face, and his eyes blinked as he stared through her chest. He brushed his hand down her hip.

"She was brave," she said. "She deserved a tattoo, too."

Jim's jaw tightened, and he squeezed her thigh.

She brought her lips to the unadorned scar and kissed it as if it were a holy thing, a living memorial. When she pulled away, she saw a tear leak from the corner of his eye.

"I wish my scars were visible for you to kiss," she said.

The corners of his mouth lifted, and his eye dried as quickly as it had teared. "I would kiss them."

Eva rubbed a hand over his chest, unable to take the intensity of his gaze. "When you raided, did you always kill everyone you didn't take captive?"

"No," he said, shaking his head and drawing a trail down her arm.

She imagined he saw settlements and farms mapped across her body.

"Usually, we only killed for revenge or if they tried to fight us, but many times, we liked to see how close we could sneak to the house and then jump out and scare the people. We would chase them indoors and carry off their animals in broad daylight." He grinned at the memory. "Sometimes, if they were especially brave, we might leave them alone. It just depended on our mood."

Though it felt wrong, Eva giggled. She could picture Jim crouched in a pen, waiting for someone to come milk the cow simply so he could send them running. "What about dogs?"

"Dogs didn't bother us. We just gave them meat. They were our best friends after that. We didn't always take captives, either. Often, we didn't want to bother with the extra work and were only interested in horses." He turned serious eyes back to her. "One time, we came across a family that was so poor and miserable, we couldn't believe humans could live like that. They lived in a hole in the ground like prairie dogs. They had no animals and seemed trapped where they were. We killed them so they wouldn't starve." He grimaced. "I'm sure their ghosts don't thank us for it."

"No, I suspect they don't," Eva said.

Jim tilted his chin. "Of everyone we ever raided, we probably should have taken some of them captive, but at the time... we thought they were ugly and skinny."

Silence followed those words. As each minute stretched longer than the last, their dark humor gave way to remorse so heavy it filled the space between them.

Eva rose from the bed and gathered a fingertip of soot. When she settled again next to Jim, she drew a rayed circle around his unadorned scar. A midnight sun.

"She fought back," she said.

Jim nodded, shutting his eyes, but seeing everything.

Chapter 28

Jim

The morning of the dance, Jim woke Eva with a kiss. They had packed the night before, and all was ready except for breakfast and last-minute chores. He rolled out of bed and rummaged in a box, then handed Eva a blue ribbon. "For your hair," he said. "It matches your eyes." Back in San Felipe, he had bought it on a whim when he had returned to the store for their order. Now, he watched her face for her reaction, scanning every detail of her expression.

When Eva ran her finger over the satin and smiled, the knot that had formed in his stomach released.

"Thank you," she said. "I will look beautiful in it tonight."

For a moment, nostalgia snagged him as he remembered Hʉwʉni. The women in his village would be painting the tops of their ears red for an occasion like this. He imagined his former love next to Eva on the bed and compared his feelings for them both. Hʉwʉni, features indistinct, turned her baby in its cradleboard to face him. He let her fade away, Tatua waiting for her in the distance. Even at their strongest, his feelings for her had never been the same as what he felt for Eva. No lover's had. Beautiful, prestigious Hʉwʉni would have been an excellent first wife as he rose in power, but he didn't recall ever feeling like her friend.

Eva laid back on her side, eyes closed. Jim slapped her rear twice and said, "Come on, tsaanʉʉmai. Time to get up." He bent down and placed his mouth next to her ear. "That means lazy."

Eva cracked an eye open. "I'm not lazy; I'm tired. Someone has been keeping me awake every night for the last week. How do you have the energy?"

Jim propped on an elbow beside her head. "I'm sorry. Should I stop?" His grin made a lie of his tone.

Without warning, she straddled him and growled, pecking his lips. She reminded him of a mountain lioness. "No," she said. "You should not stop."

He hardened beneath her and moved his hands over her broad hips, imagining a baby inside her. Soon, he hoped. "You'll get a break tonight."

"Why? What do you mean?"

"The men and women will sleep separately so that more people can fit. Women in the house. Men in the barn."

Eva frowned. "Then I will have to make this count." She kissed him again, long and lingering, then jerked away and dismounted. "Come on, tsaanʉʉmai. Now, who's the lazy one?"

He lunged to pull her on top of him, but she dodged out of reach. For a second, he debated chasing her down, but it was true. They needed to leave soon.

Jim chose the perfect horse for Eva, a bay gelding he had discovered to be unflappable, slow, and responsive. Jim imagined some Anglo or Tejana lady somewhere missing her fine, well-trained horse, and he dearly hoped the woman wouldn't be at the dance tonight. In the Mexican fashion, he had branded his new herd and managed to lay his own over the gelding's old one without noticeable misalignment. For many of the horses, his mark was the first they had endured. He did it for no other reason than to conceal their origin. Most Anglos had a hard time telling the difference between individual animals.

Eva traveled beside him, lost in her own thoughts. As she rode astride, her skirts hitched up to her lean thighs, and he stole glances at her loveliness. He didn't have a lady's saddle for her, and he knew that might be a problem when they reached the McMullens'. Amused, he pictured their faces at the sight of Eva "riding like a Comanche," and the image filled him with pride and, even, anticipation.

He peered down at himself, checking his attire. Eva had helped him clean his buckskin shirt and leggings two days prior with yellow clay. At the last dance, he had dressed like an Anglo. He ran a finger over the loosening beadwork on his chest and the delicate fringe under his arms. The feather in his lengthening chestnut hair fluttered in the breeze.

His movement caught Eva's attention. "You look very handsome," she said.

Her words and admiring eyes swelled his heart. "I feel like a man again," he said, thinking of all the good she had brought him. Over the many months since his return, he had forgotten himself, who he was, who he should be. Before Eva arrived, he would have felt trepidation at the thought of attending another Anglo party, of not fitting in no matter how hard he tried, but she made him feel brave and rebellious again. His desire for Numunuu approval crisped into focus as Anglo society's faded. He saw the colors of his future painted before him on the road, but the outlines had been redrawn the night his brother had found him.

Besides, he thought, it would be stupid to pass up a chance to feast and dance.

When they reached the drive to the McMullen plantation, Jim marveled at the vast, empty fields of harvested cotton. Six weeks' work at least. He had viewed the landscape with ignorant, naïve eyes during his last visit. Now, he scanned the rows with a new appreciation for the labor that went into the plowing, planting, weeding, and harvesting. Enslaved harvesters had gathered every single white fiber, turning the summer snow into green, barren rows.

Eva surveyed the plantation in a similar manner and examined her fingers. "If I never pick another boll of cotton, it will be too soon," she said. "You know, giant machines did the harvesting in my childhood timeline. They always missed a lot, leaving dirty dregs in the fields, and it looked like a hurricane had blown through, but even with the waste, it's better than people doing it."

Disdain curled in his nose. They were not meant for this life. He might feel differently if the People had never adopted him, but why would any man want to be a slave to the land just to earn metal to buy more seed and start all over again? It made no sense.

The drive opened onto a wide, meadowy expanse leading to the plantation house and a bare, slave-swept yard as hard-packed as his own. Lines of wagons and carriages were parked near the house, and horses had been let loose to mingle with the McMullen's herd. Wokweesi found the plantation's dogs, his upright tail waving in cautious greeting.

The house, a dogtrot much like Jim's own, was new, its boards still fresh-cut and golden. Pump had told him it boasted four large rooms with rich furnishings imported from the United States and an adjacent winter kitchen. It even had a spacious loft for storage and extra sleeping space. A generous summer kitchen sat farther behind, along with slave quarters and all the other little outbuildings of a prosperous, self-sufficient plantation. Though not new, the barn where the dance was to be held made Jim's own look like a shed.

Children ran amok in a chasing game while their parents chatted in gender-segregated groups. The women were up on the gallery, and the men milled about the yard, though a wife stood next to her man here and there, and several young men kept unattached ladies company deeper within the breezeway.

Their arrival remained unnoticed in the buzz of activity until two women on the gallery covered their mouths at the sight of Eva. Before the gossip spread, she dismounted, and her skirts fell into place. She seemed oblivious, and Jim grinned to himself, pleased.

Eva helped him unsaddle their horses, and then they walked together to the knots of men. "Did you see some of the women's faces when I rode up?" Eva whispered. "You could hear them gasping from the drive."

"Want a sidesaddle?" Jim asked, worried he had misread her.

Eva snorted in contempt.

"Jim, welcome!" A man strode toward him, hands outstretched, and Jim's spirit rose to greet Mr. McMullen.

He matched his handshake with his own firm one. "Thank you, sir. We're glad to come and are looking forward to the dance." He cupped Eva's elbow. "May I present to you my new wife, Eva? We met in San Antonio."

Eva darted her eyes at him, and her brow crinkled, setting Jim adrift before she cleared her features. They hadn't gotten their stories straight. Mr. McMullen either politely ignored or didn't notice Eva's face, saying only, "Pleased to make your acquaintance, my dear. I'm very glad to hear Jim has taken a wife and such a pretty one at that."

Eva blushed, basking under the compliment, and bobbed a curtsy as well as any Anglo lady. "It's very nice to meet you as well, sir. I hear we have you to thank for ginning our cotton." She glanced up at Jim, and he relaxed, proud of the woman standing beside him.

"Happy to do it. Happy to do it," Mr. McMullen said. "Let me lead you to my wife so she can make you welcome."

Eva followed on the heels of their host with Jim right behind her, his hand on her waist. Though it would have been simpler to go around the crowd, Mr. McMullen wove his way through the cliques, stopping here and there to give a clap on a shoulder or to drop a droll comment. Everyone offered a warm smile to their host.

Up on the gallery, the hostess held court with her own coterie, which opened like a pair of calico wings as they approached. Many of the women smiled, but most of their eyes shuttered as they watched Eva, their scrutiny reminding her of the wary coyotes who'd visited the edge of their farm one evening.

When Mr. McMullen made the introduction, Mrs. McMullen said, "Please, call me Hortensia, my dear."

Eva inclined her head as Hortensia introduced her to each of the women in turn. Mr. McMullen pulled on Jim's sleeve, and the men took their leave.

"Now... San Antonio, my Thomas said?" Hortensia exchanged a look with her companions. "I heard you came in by way of New Orleans just this past week."

Eva's mind raced. "Yes, I was visiting family before I joined Jim, but we met in San Antonio when he first returned."

One of the other women, Lily, asked, "And how are you finding Jim's farm and married life?" Her gaze traveled up Eva's dress from stain to tear to fraying hole and landed on her strange, two-toned hair. Suspicion puckered her lips, but pity reigned. For the first time, having been without a full-length mirror, Eva registered the state of her appearance.

"I'm finding it just fine. Jim is a good man to me," Eva replied.

Doubt flitted behind Lily's eyes, and the chorus of women vibrated beside her.

"Were you married by Father Muldoon? Or one of the new Protestant ministers?" Hortensia asked.

"Neither," Eva said. "We were married back in San Antonio before he left, and I've only now been able to join him."

"It's so strange we haven't heard of you before," the older woman said.

Eva shrugged. "Jim's a very private man, but I can assure you I exist."

The returning smiles of the women ran warm and cool, like milk swirling in coffee.

"Bless your heart, honey. Don't you have a sunbonnet?" another woman blurted. "You're as brown as a nut." Frowning, the woman let her concern-filled eyes drift to Jim in the yard below.

Eva demurred, unable to say anything, but no, she didn't have a sunbonnet.

The small talk moved to other gossip, and Eva wiped her upper lip. This particular spotlight burned too hot for someone used to working in the shadows. The original role for her aborted mission had been that of a Mexican officer's wife, but now, she had no script to follow, no costume to protect her, no intelligence to fall back on.

An enslaved woman brought a tray of drinks, and Eva took one with gratitude. At the sight of the server, one of the women asked Hortensia, "Have you found your missing slaves yet?"

"No." Hortensia sighed, frustration clear on her face. "I had Moses beat both those girls again, but they wouldn't tell him anything else. I don't believe they know where the Saltwater Tribes are."

The woman carrying the tray proceeded through the guests, unflinching, face blank.

"I've sent the children back out of the house. No sense in selling them right now. Besides, Thomas doesn't have the heart." She trilled a laugh, resentment leaking through the veneer. "It really falls to me to instill the discipline."

Eva wished she could say something to the serving woman, but she would be just as likely to bring more trouble on her head. After a moment, Eva caught Jim's eye, but he turned back to his conversation. He stood, legs spread and back relaxed, taller than he had seemed in San Felipe. She excused herself from the ladies and drifted to her husband. She would be glad when the dancing started, but she suspected it was still several hours away.

Jim smiled at her when she sidled up next to him. She laced her arm through his, and he leaned closer, squeezing her hand between his brawny biceps and chest. He had never looked more handsome to her.

Pump commanded center-stage. "Ah! Eva!" He turned to the man beside him. "Hiram, have you met Jim's fiancée?"

Jim shifted in place, bringing his hand up to cover hers. "Actually, she's my wife. We're married now."

Pump coughed, his eyes sliding to Eva's. "Yes, of course, I misspoke. Jim's *wife*." He straightened the line of his vest and checked his buttons.

Eva wondered what other tangles in their story threatened to unravel.

Chapter 29

Eva

McMullen's Farm

"And where's Jane, Pump?" Jim asked.

"Betsie Hornsby's having her baby, and she's gone to attend her," Pump replied. "As my wife likes to say, 'New babes mind nobody's schedule but their own.'"

The other man snorted. "Have I told you about the time my gal was birthing one of ours at the same time the milk cow was having trouble birthing a calf? This was before y'all joined us in the colony. Coulda used Jane that day, I tell you what. I tried to get my wife to come into the barn where I could tend them both, but she would have none of it!"

Eva cringed inside but plastered a smile on her face. Surely, he wasn't serious, she thought.

When the conversation shifted, Jim bent down and whispered in her ear, "I would never make you give birth in a barn."

The men's talk ranged from the typical complaints of a farmer to slave troubles to politics, and Eva's eyes glazed over, her legs tiring from standing in one spot.

Just as she was searching for a place to sit, Hortensia called the guests to supper in the backyard. Blankets were scattered around picnic-style, and a long table held a smorgasbord of Southern cooking. Corn dodgers, light and fluffy. Fried beef and chicken. Mashed potatoes. Various greens: collard and turnip. Catfish. Gravy. Boiled okra and tomatoes. Squash. Beans. And pie. Lots of peach and pecan pie. Each dish signaled the plantation's wealth and success, and the dogs circled underneath.

Eva's mouth watered, and Jim studied her face. "You look like I've been starving you," he said under his breath.

"I'm sorry," she said. "I've had a steady diet of venison, beans, and ash cakes. I don't know how to make any of this stuff, and I love all of it. My mom cooked this way." Eva envisioned killing one of the hens at home. Jim did eat eggs, but he could take 'em or leave 'em. When she was back to full traveling strength, the first thing she was going to do was pop into different timelines until she could find a restaurant.

Abruptly, the fantasy burst as soon as it had come. She couldn't walk into the sanctum currency bank and get whatever she needed anymore. Or costumes. Eva shoved that depressing train of thought off the tracks. Right now, she was here to have fun.

"I see I'll need to sacrifice a chicken to your stomach," Jim said.

Eva swallowed, still gazing at the laden table. "Probably."

When they found empty places on a blanket with two other couples, Eva lowered herself as she balanced her plate. She had piled it to an unladylike proportion, but she didn't care. Who knew when she would eat like this again? If Pump's wife knew how to cook like this, Eva would take him up on his offer of lessons. Come to think of it… she could always ask Mrs. McMullen if she might learn from her cook. She wondered how that request would be received.

Though Eva would have preferred to sit cross-legged, she placed her legs to the side and perched on her hip, and though she would have liked to inhale her food and go back for more, she took small bites.

Jim smirked, his eyes crinkling. "It is good," he said into her ear. "Maybe one of these women could teach you. I wouldn't mind eating like this sometimes."

She pushed her bite into her cheek. "Way ahead of you."

"My people don't eat birds normally unless we're desperate. Never turkey — makes one cowardly," he said, wagging his eyebrows. "Though I remember food like this when I was small. We had a cook like the McMullen's."

"Cowardly?" Eva asked.

"Anglos are never more cowardly than after they've had their Christmas dinners."

Eva choked on her mouthful.

"It's true."

"Shhh!" Eva glanced around their blanket. The men they sat with chatted between themselves, and their wives were busy coaxing small children to take bites from their plates. The children favored their chasing game. Both couples were poor, young farming families.

One of the men turned to Jim. "Tom says you're good at breaking horses."

Jim swallowed and nodded.

Eva half-listened as her husband dispensed advice. Midway through her plate, Eva realized with dismay that her eyes had been bigger than her stomach and started in on her pie before it was too late. One of the children pointed out that he shouldn't have to keep coming by for any more bites. He should be able to eat his pie, too. Eva apologized to the mother and put down her fork.

"Oh, honey, please eat your dessert." The boy had already run off again. "He knows the rules," she said. "I'll just remind him that grownups can do what they want."

When she was done with her pie and mourning her leftovers, Jim picked it up without pausing his discussion and began eating what she couldn't. During an interval, while the other two men were talking, he grinned at her. "You just knew to get extra for me."

His head jerked up an instant later, and Eva caught the turn of the conversation.

"I've heard the same. Just over a fortnight ago, Comanches were definitely in the area. The Jones family lost all their horses. Luckily, no one was killed. They slept through it. Never heard a thing."

Eva dared a glance at Jim. His face, now still and calm, had assumed a blank expression of disinterest. The men and their wives had been welcoming in the brief time they had been on the blanket together, but that could change.

"Jim, you lived with the Comansh. You got any advice? Any way we can thwart the buggers?" one of the men asked.

"Roy!" his wife said. "Language."

Roy muttered an apology out of the side of his mouth and waited for Jim's reply.

Jim took a halting breath, and his gaze turned inward. She could sense him trying to come up with a helpful answer. "The Nʉmʉnʉʉ are fierce warriors. They will kill you if you try to put up a fight." He checked over his shoulder in the direction of little ears. "They will carry off your children, maybe your wives."

"We know that," the other man said.

Jim rubbed his finger along the side of his nose, his shoulders rising. "If you have enough ammunition, and you're a good shot, you can scare them off, but they're just as likely to throw firebrands on your house and burn you out."

The women's eyes widened in alarm.

"Are you saying we can do nothing to protect ourselves?" Roy asked.

"I'm saying it's better to let them have your horses. Use oxen instead."

The men leaned back, their jaws hardening, eyes flinty.

Jim continued, "We — They often skip farms that don't have horses. It's easier to hit a farm with women and children *and* horses."

"Why do they take the women and children?" one of the wives asked.

Complicated answers scrolled through Jim's eyes. Moments passed before he said, "They need slaves."

The women frowned, unsatisfied. Eva knew what must be running through their imaginations, and they wanted him to confirm their worst fears.

"What about treaties?" one of the men asked.

Jim wagged his head and lifted an upturned palm. "The Nʉmʉnʉʉ will make treaties, but a treaty with one band isn't a treaty with another. Plus, any man who plans a raid is a war leader. It's the only way to earn wealth and influence. The elders can't always keep the young men from wanting to build their herds and reputations, even if peace has been declared."

"So, they can't be trusted to keep treaties," the man said, spitting on the words.

Jim's eyes sparked. "No, that's not what I said. A Nʉmʉ man will never break his word, but he can't control other men." Jim jabbed his fork in the direction of San Felipe. "The Anglos will think they have secured a treaty with all the Nʉmʉnʉʉ for their whole colony, but the individual Nʉmʉnʉʉ band will believe they have a treaty with just themselves and the men and families they have dealt with."

The men shook their heads. Eva wasn't sure if they didn't agree with Jim's assessment, the Nʉmʉnʉʉ worldview, or were simply disappointed.

"What really chaps my hide is that if you can get them to talk and not just kill you straight out, they expect gifts," the other man said.

Jim shrugged. "Well, it's their territory. If you want to stay here, you need to pay tribute. That's how they see it. They're allowing you to live here."

"That's something I don't understand," Roy said. "They think they own all this land, but they haven't done a thing to improve it. There's plenty of land for everyone, Comansh and Anglo."

"They don't think they own it," Jim said. "No one can own the land."

"Exactly. They have no right to demand tribute from us for something they don't even own."

Jim's mouth clamped shut, and Eva could see him wrestling to express a completely different way of interacting with nature.

Before he could untangle what he wanted to say, Roy said, "Well, I thank you kindly for your advice, such as it is." He shifted in his seat as if he had more to add and scanned the blankets arrayed around them. When he turned back, he said, "I can see you're an honest fellow. I feel I should tell you that there's some that think you're giving information to the Comansh on who to attack. Some even say you've joined raids in the area."

"I'm aware," Jim said, his face stony. "It is untrue. Thank you for your warning."

Eva knew he walked a thin line. He'd told her he'd shared no information with his brother, and he'd even directed him away from certain farms, but also… his brother had yet to request such intelligence.

"Where do you live?" Eva asked. The husbands and their wives stiffened, their eyes finding their spouses' in silent communication. She thought only to gather information for Jim that might protect them in the future. In answer, they gestured in the general direction of the northeast, opposite Jim's own farm. Little did they know they would have been safer being next-door neighbors. The warm, congenial atmosphere evaporated, and the couples made their excuses and left, supper finished.

Jim and Eva remained on the blanket. He stared down at her.

Plates clattered around them as people began cleaning up. "I'm sorry," Eva said.

He didn't reply for a beat. "It can't be helped. It's too easy to say the wrong thing. They all want to ask me questions but hate me for the answers."

While Eva assisted the other women with folding the blankets, Mr. McMullen stole Jim away. Upon returning, her husband wore new shoes.

"How do you like them?" Jim displayed each foot to her.

"Dashing. Where'd you get them?" she asked as she admired the worn, wooden-heeled leather boots.

"Thomas," Jim said. "Now I can stomp my way through the dance like a proper Anglo."

Eva had never seen him desire to take on an Anglo trait.

"It's hard to get the same effect with moccasins," he added.

Eva peered down at her own feet.

"Yours will be perfect," he said.

As guests trickled toward the barn, the fiddler tuned his instrument, his fingers running nimble scales in a purling line. Bits of different songs started and stopped abruptly, and someone laughed. Excitement fluttered in Eva's stomach; she had no idea what to expect. She had danced in European courts and hoped the style was similar. "I don't know if I know these dances."

"Don't worry. There are some basic, repetitive steps, and the caller will tell us what to do," Jim said. "I've only been to one other dance since I returned, and I did fine. And this time, I have boots." His eyes sparkled like a five-year-old's.

A smooth-planked dance floor had been laid out in the barn. In prime viewing location, children sat in the hayloft with their feet dangling over the side. The setting sun streamed over her shoulder, illuminating the interior as the temperature dropped. Enslaved people dispelled shadows in corners with well-placed lanterns. Under their soft glow, work-worn masks fell away to reveal the hidden, youthful faces that must have first stepped foot into this harsh land. The smell of burning lard candles mingled with sweet hay and manure. Eva watched a blushing boy ask for the first dance, his lady of choice nodding, eyes glued to his feet.

"I remember my mother loving to dance," Jim said. "I used to be one of those little boys in the loft."

After the fiddler played a final string of notes, he nodded to the caller perched alongside him on a haystack. The people formed long lines facing each other, and Jim took Eva's hand to lead her to the end. Two sets of lines ran the length of the barn. The fiddler plucked and worried his strings, fighting the temperature changes that stole his tuning.

"Ladies and gents, find your partner," the caller said, his deep voice filling the space.

Chapter 30

Eva

E va stood across from Jim. To the puzzlement of their neighbors, he demonstrated the basic steps they assumed she should already know. Her limbs relaxed when she recognized them as descendants of dances she had done many times before. Some of the names were even the same.

The fiddler lifted his bow, and the couples bowed to each other. He drew down on the first notes of "Tam Lin," and the dancers bounced in place, finding the rhythm. Some stomped and clapped in time.

"Gents, balance and swing your neighbors." The reel of the fiddle competed with the caller's sing-song commands.

Jim turned to the other woman in their group of four, and Eva lost half a beat turning to the man. They brought their hands together at shoulder height, then he tipped toward her and leaned away, the single stomp of their collective boots reverberating through the rafters. The man pulled her back to him, hip to hip, arm extended, his hand pressing firmly against the small of her back. She leaned into his hand, allowing them to spin faster, and he smiled down at her with pure joy.

Her heart flew with her feet. All worries, all thoughts of any kind, disappeared, and her body became one with the music and the rhythm.

"Long lines go forward and back."

Eva joined hands with her neighbors on either side. She slammed her boots down, imitating the people around her as she stomped to meet Jim in the middle. He smiled ear to ear and winked at her. She wanted to kiss him.

"Ladies, left-hand chain; ladies, allemande left."

The men whooped around her and clapped in time as she took Jim's female neighbor by the hand. She traveled to Jim's side of the line, and he spun her around to send her back across. She clasped hands with Jim's neighbor again, and they pulled against each other in a tight spin.

"Gents, swing your partner."

She skipped to Jim, and he spun her, eyes fixed on her face. He positioned her hip against him with the indecency of shameless familiarity. She blushed, a thrill racing up her spine, and he grinned.

"Ladies, left-hand chain; Star all the way around."

Eva passed Jim's female neighbor through the middle, spun around her own male neighbor, and they all returned to the center to join hands in a star. On the release, Jim and Eva shifted down a position, and their neighbors slid up a place, forming a new group of four with the next in line, repeating the sequence.

They flowed through the steps until the couples needed no reminder from the caller, and the music carried them. The fiddle urged them faster. The caller clapped his hands in rhythm, and Eva's feet moved with the effortless grace of an experienced dancer. Jim beamed at her, and Eva eagerly pressed herself to him every time they came together. Her breath quickened, hard and fast, and the dancers around her perspired despite the chill. When they cast off at the end of the line, Jim spun them until the lines caught them up again to make the next group of four, and another couple took their place.

Just when she thought she would have to step away to catch her breath, the music slowed and stopped. She curtsied to Jim, and he bowed to her, his smile hungry.

Eva led Jim outside, passing a table of refreshments near the doorway. The cool night bathed her sweaty face, and she spread her arms. Eva gasped when he tugged her into the shadows and stole a kiss. Laughing, she stole one right back, then pushed off his chest with both hands. Their behavior was a little too public for Anglos or Nʉmʉnʉʉ, but neither of them could help it.

To the side of the barn, the slaves formed their own dancing lines with a drummer keeping time to the fiddle in the barn. Laughter from both groups mixed in her ears. Some of the enslaved women milled about fetching things for the Anglo guests, but most of them, men and women, danced unencumbered, their work suspended for the evening.

For the third song, Eva's original neighbor approached her, introduced himself as "Adam," and asked if she would like to dance. She glanced up at

Jim. She'd rather dance with him all night, knowing he could read the preference in her eyes.

"It's custom to dance with different partners," Jim said. His arm around her tightened even as he turned a blank face to her.

She accepted Adam's hand, and they lined up to dance "Garryowen." Her partner guided her as she learned the new steps. When they spun, she looked over his shoulder.

"Keep your eyes on mine," he said. His own dropped to Eva's lips and her chest. He squeezed her tighter, and his hand traveled lower down her back with each repetition. By the middle, she reached back to reposition his hand higher each time. She forced a laugh, and his eyes glittered, creasing around the edges. Uncomfortable, her vision strayed away from his; at his insistent reminder, she concentrated on his nose. When she crossed paths with Jim, she relaxed in his arms but had to compel her hand to release his when they parted.

Though Eva had been part of a celibate society, she had acted the coquette on countless missions. But that was what it had been: an act. An act with a script and mindless shadows for counterparts. Now, because she was aware, this man was real in a way she had never experienced before.

Her next partners were polite, including an old widower with a long, white beard who shuffled through the steps but stomped and yelled like the younger fellows. He twirled her in a slow walking circle, his attention somewhere above her shoulder. His hands held her as light as a butterfly, and their bodies hovered inches from each other. Eva could have balanced a teacup on her head.

"Thank you, my dear." He cupped Eva's hand between both of his and squinted a happy double-blink at her. His cheeks sunk around empty gums. She bobbed her head eye-to-eye with him and hoped he would ask her to dance again.

As the night wore on, Eva danced with Jim, and some of the other men returned for repeat dances. Though perfect gentlemen during their first rounds, they grew bolder. They stole squeezes here and pinches there. Their hands brushed her breasts, and their smiles slid to leers, reminding her of Mopai's attack under the pecan tree. Her hands dampened, and she pulled back to leave space between them. She kept her demeanor light, placating. She pleaded and admonished, but their arms drew all the tighter, and their groins pressed into her thigh.

Unable to face the next dance, Eva turned down invitations. She watched Jim weave in time with his partner, wishing she stood in the woman's place. The refreshment table lay emptier as she passed it on her way outside, and she allowed the darkness to swallow her. As she stopped to look at the moon, Eva's legs, no longer light and nimble, seemed to drop roots. Suddenly, she heard footsteps behind her and groaned when she saw the boldest of her dance partners.

He swayed, and she took a step back. He caught her up to spin in time with the music flowing overhead. Fear drove a laugh from her throat. When he stopped twirling, he held her off the ground and bent to kiss her, crushing her ribs. She pushed against his chest and leaned back, cringing from his lips. Her thoughts flew to Jim.

"I could eat you up. You're the prettiest little thing I've seen in a long time." His breath smelled of whiskey, and she wrinkled her nose, turning her head in disgust. He dragged her farther from the light of the barn and into the deep darkness. "Let's go someplace more private. Don't worry. I have money to pay." His fingers gathered her skirts by the handful.

Eva drew her knife and placed it under his chin. "This is what we're going to do," she said. "You're going to let me leave, and you're not going to follow."

His lips spread, showing teeth, and his eyes crossed as he peered at her blade. He set Eva down, but his grip tightened around her upper arm. He towered over her as the other hand sped to haul in her skirts.

Eva pressed her knife until she drew blood.

He froze.

"Let go," she said through her teeth. The man's hand remained around her upper arm. They hung at a standstill, the autumn breeze swirling across her exposed thighs.

With the music winding down, his eyes snapped into focus, and he released her, anger painted across his face. "Anyone can see what you are. How dare you turn your nose up at me?"

Eva ignored him and walked as calmly as she could to the safety of the barn. Ahead, Hortensia's back was to her, and Jim passed their hostess in the doorway on his way out. Catching sight of her husband, Eva wanted to sink to the ground. The next moment, he found her, and his eyes darted to her hand. She still clutched her knife. She turned, discreetly wiping it on the inside of her skirt.

Jim crouched beside her. "What happened? Are you harmed?"

Eva scanned the area. They were alone until the man walked past, dabbing at his chin with his handkerchief. He stowed the bloody cloth back in his pocket and disappeared into the mill of guests.

Jim followed him with his eyes, and Eva grabbed his arm before he could launch into action. "Stop," she whispered. "I can't kill him, and you can't kill him. He didn't touch me. He just thought he could." Her words warred against Jim's expectations of himself.

He closed his eyes and inhaled.

"This isn't about you," she said. "I put him in his place. He won't bother me again. No one saw."

Jim pulled her to him, crushing her head into his chest. "I don't promise I won't kill him later."

Eva assumed he wasn't joking, but chose to treat it as such. "Let's go back inside," she mumbled into his chest, lips pressed against a decorative red mescal bean.

He gave her a tighter hug, then placed his forehead against hers. When he turned toward the dance, he offered her his arm. "You are the most beautiful woman here. It's no wonder other men are circling. But I will be your only dance partner for the rest of the night."

"Yes, please," she said, squeezing the hand he had placed on top of hers. "I no longer feel obligated to the 'change partners' custom."

Only a few dances remained. The caller croaked the steps between sips from his cup, voice hoarse and words slurring.

As they turned in place, Jim whispered in Eva's ear, "We can still enjoy this." He tilted his head and raised his brows, half question, half statement.

She nodded, willing herself to hear only the music and feel only his hands.

Each stomp loosened her muscles; every holler lifted her mood. She ignored the stolen touches from the other men as if they were gnats. Jim held her eyes whenever they parted, and Eva gazed over her neighbor's shoulder until she found Jim again whenever they turned away.

During the last dance, enslaved women appeared to clean up the refreshments, signaling bedtime and the end of festivities. Eva kissed Jim goodnight and ignored the looks they received. She followed Hortensia to the house with the other female guests.

Like wolves in a pack, the women filed inside, choosing their places on the floors, the sofas, the beds, and the loft. Hortensia pulled her aside. The older woman dropped her congenial mask to reveal white, hot indignation, and Eva took a step back, her lungs forgetting how to breathe.

"I saw you go into the field with Mr. Brown, *Mrs.* McCullough. You are obviously not who you are pretending to be, but I will not allow you to corrupt the young women who are guests in our home or to conduct more business with the men."

Eva's mouth fell open. "It's not what it looked like —"

Hortensia's nostrils flared. "Don't you dare answer back to me, girl. I don't know what you take me for, but I'm not a fool. No decent woman would ever marry Jim McCullough — if indeed you are even married. Your stories don't line up. They make no sense at all, and I'm ashamed of Pump trying to cover for you. What Jim does with you is his own business, and Lord knows my husband has spent a great deal of time helping him, against my better judgment, I might add, but Jim should never have brought you into a good, Christian gathering."

Eva's face ignited with anger, embarrassment, and shame, none of them justified except the first. "I did not have sex with Mr. Brown."

Her hostess gasped in shock at her direct language. Eyes narrowed and lips righteous, she said, "That is not what I hear Mr. Brown is saying, and I have it on good authority some of the other bachelors are expecting to be able to take their turn."

Angry tears pricked. Eva would not, absolutely would not, let them spill. Her throat swelled as she shoved them back. "That is a bald-faced lie. If you check under his chin, you will see where the point of my knife delivered my refusal for me."

Hortensia reared back, uncertain. Her jaw reset. "Regardless, it's too late to sort out tonight. You will sleep on the floor of my room, and you will be escorted to the privy if you need to use it."

Eva bristled at the thought of being under this woman's nose as if she were some sort of criminal but then thought better of it. She might need her protection, especially if she needed to relieve herself during the night. Daring a glance toward the barn, she listened to temptation arguing for them to leave but then shut her ears to it. What irreparable damage would running away cause? She didn't know how far the gossip had traveled — perhaps the situation was salvageable? At that thought, she complied without further protest.

The sun peeped over the horizon. Jim had tossed and turned, restless without Eva next to him, and he decided to get up and check on the horses. The party had been asleep for only a handful of hours. He shivered as he walked up the side of the house, and his breath steamed. He calculated the horse wealth here for the taking with the owners exhausted and drunk. With less relish, he thought of all the women and children. In his fantasy, it would be a legendary prize, a tale told for years to come.

As he approached the front gallery, Jim heard soft, feminine voices. It seemed he wasn't the only one who didn't feel like sleeping. He froze when he heard the words, "Have you ever seen such white trash? He treats her no better than a squaw. Just look at her."

Hugging the wall, he crept to the corner, heart in his throat.

"Well, and did you see when he took her food away? The poor thing."

"Don't feel too sorry for her. I heard this afternoon that she's a whore from New Orleans. Who else would take up with Comanche Jim? Passing themselves off as married. He's not even trying to act civilized anymore. Did you see the way he's dressed?"

The other woman clicked her tongue. "There's no telling what horrors he visits on her."

With a shrug in her voice, the first woman said, "I'm sure she doesn't mind. She went off in the field with Mr. Brown."

"She did not!"

"Hortensia saw her. The audacity! Can you imagine? She had to put her on the floor of her own room so she could keep an eye on her because the slut had made arrangements with all the other bachelors."

Jim's ears roared. He stepped into view and marched across the outside of the railing to the entrance steps. He rested on the rail in front of them and crossed his arms. At his stony mask, their faces drained of color, leaving them pastier than usual.

"You were saying?" he said. "Please continue."

The two women, both young, stared up at him, speechless.

When they didn't respond, he leaned down into their faces. "For one thing, 'squaw' isn't a Nʉmʉnʉʉ word. Don't ever use it again," he hissed. "For another, what you are saying is untrue. If you didn't see it for yourself, it's gossip."

The whites of the women's eyes showed, and he felt an old, feral viciousness flare up. He tamped it down and stood up straight.

"You don't seem to be able to say it to my face. Can you say it to Mrs. McCullough's?"

The women didn't move. He wasn't even sure they were breathing. He stared at them for a moment longer before pushing away from the railing. With each step, he regretted the confrontation. By afternoon, they would say he had threatened to scalp them alive.

He knocked on the first door, not knowing which was the McMullen's bedroom. A drowsy, middle-aged woman squinted at him with one eye. She hesitated, suspicious, but pointed him in the right direction down the lantern-lit breezeway.

When the correct door opened, he told the woman answering he was there to collect Eva. She smirked and shut the door. Jim leaned against the dogtrot wall, imagining Eva putting on her clothes. When she stepped out, her lashes clumped beneath her bloodshot eyes in black, wet points. Her lips parted to speak, but he interrupted her. "I know. We're leaving."

Hortensia emerged and followed them like a warden escorting a prisoner from her jurisdiction. As the woman's footsteps fell behind them, Jim's vision narrowed. Out of earshot of the gallery, he turned to their hostess, anger heavy on his tongue, but his wife beat him to it.

Eva stood nose to nose with Hortensia. "Any decent woman would be lucky to have Jim for a husband. He's kind and honorable to the point of keeping his word to Pump, even though it's killing his soul, and he's a good provider. I've never gone hungry or cold since I've been with him, despite appearances," she said, looking down at her dress.

"And he has protected me more than once. How we came to be together is none of your business. But know this: we are married before the eyes of God, and that's all that should matter."

Hortensia opened her mouth to retort, but Eva barreled through.

"I never gave any of the men here the slightest encouragement, and the fact that they thought I was available to them because I was with Jim says more about their character than mine."

Jim's neck flushed with shame. He had not connected that her association with him endangered her.

"The only reason Mr. Brown isn't lying gutted in your field right now is because I chose mercy, and so did Jim."

Hortensia's mouth hung open at Eva's ferocious tone.

"This is no kind of hospitality," Eva growled in a dig Jim knew would strike home. "When you see the cut under Mr. Brown's chin, you will know you owe me an apology. I dare you to look."

Hortensia shut her mouth and swallowed. "I will," she said. "You can rest assured of that." Spite clung to each word, but Jim watched self-doubt creep into the older woman's eyes.

He took Eva's arm. She drew breath to say more, but he wanted this to end. "Please give Mr. McMullen our regards and appreciation for the fine supper and dancing. He has been nothing but kind to me. Tell him he will find his boots in the hayloft." He hauled Eva around to walk the rest of the way beside him. She jerked her arm out of his grasp but clutched his hand, lacing her fingers through his. Mrs. McMullen's footsteps echoed down the breezeway behind them, and Jim thought his fingers would go numb before they reached their horses.

Chapter 31

Eva

The ride home was long and silent. Neither felt like talking; their hearts weighed too heavy. Jim's only words were to tell her his people didn't whore their women like Anglos. They never even gifted them to non-Comanches. The misunderstanding would never have happened in his village.

Such a distinction, Eva knew, would have been lost on most monogamous Anglos. For white people, women with multiple partners became irredeemably fallen, reduced to being fit for nothing more than selling their bodies for money. In contrast, though Comanches might gift their woman to a brother or a true friend, for them, sex was not something to be shared, much less bought, outside that close circle. Unmentioned by Jim were the women of no value, the non-Comanche captives never taken as wives, who, while not exactly for sale, were available for use as long as a man asked the owner first.

Eva, who had witnessed a spectrum of social structures across countless timelines, had no bias toward one particular custom over another unless it affected her personally. In response, she nodded dully, trusting Jim and trusting in her abilities to protect herself no matter what situation she found herself in. Staying with Jim came with risks, but leaving his side, even to build a new life in a more modern time, had become unthinkable.

Back at the cabin, they moved like automatons through the chores, ate some dried meat, and went to bed with the afternoon sun still up. Jim curled his body around Eva, and they slept straight through until morning.

Eva woke to Jim whistling tunelessly from somewhere outside the cabin, and she thought of Tophe, who could whistle a bird down from a tree. "Which song is that?" she shouted to him.

"Tam Lin," came his reply. "Why? Can't you tell?"

Eva smiled as he returned to his monotonous droning when she didn't answer. She stretched and burrowed into the bedding. Her conflict-induced headache from the previous day had disappeared, and her emotions were under control. Things no longer seemed as dismal as they had the night before. Eva pushed the blankets off but then had second thoughts when a gust from the tundra blew over her legs. "Come back to bed," she called.

Jim's whistling paused for a moment, but he didn't respond. When he started whistling again, Eva added, "I'm cold." She heard his footsteps, and he opened the door. He held his hands in front of him like awkward claws, and she registered they were covered to the wrist in blood and feathers.

"Are you absolutely sure you want me to do that?"

She sat up in surprise. "What are you doing?"

"We're going to figure out how to make fried chicken. It can't be that hard."

"For breakfast?"

Jim shrugged.

Cold forgotten, she rose to the challenge.

After Eva dressed, she watched him finish plucking the bird. She had never seen it done in person and reflected that most of her missions had been in the upper echelons of society, the power centers. If she had bothered to look, she would have had plenty of opportunities to see a real, live chicken-plucking, but the rich are always shielded from the dirty things of life.

They chopped and dusted the pieces in cornmeal and salt. "You know we'll need to fry this in hog fat, right?" Eva asked.

Jim pursed his lips together but waved a hand.

When several golden-brown pieces of chicken were sitting in pooling grease on a plate, Jim said, "That happened really fast."

"Go ahead." Eva opened her palm to him. "You first."

"We made this for you, remember?"

"Don't warriors get the first bite?"

"Warriors are entitled to the last bite." Jim turned a leg over and sniffed it. "Same time?"

"Deal," Eva said as she picked up a piece. When she bit down, she could tell immediately that the texture was wrong. Pausing her teeth halfway, not wanting to commit, she looked at Jim. Blood ran down the sides of his mouth, and he grimaced around his bite.

She released her teeth and wiped her lips. "You told me you've eaten raw buffalo."

"Mmhm," he said, taking his chicken out as well. "You haven't lived until you've had fresh, warm liver with gallbladder juice squirted all over it. Children fight over it. This is different, though."

Eva studied the plate. "I think I can just cover it in the pot with water and stew it."

"Okay," Jim said, tossing his piece back on the dish and wiping his fingers. "Well, that was fun. What do we want to do now?"

"Let's feed the animals and go for a long ride."

"Deal."

The rest of the day, Jim took her places she had never been on the farm: a secluded stream with a waterfall and a beaver dam, a stand of majestic oaks, the ground underneath churned rough by the domestic hogs allowed to roam free, and the arroyo where Wokweesi had found her. The dog, who had been ranging in and out of sight, went straight for her crumpled rebozo, now firmly molded to tangles of greenbrier. Water had passed through it many times, and Eva thought back to the rainstorms they'd had since she'd arrived, including one that would have counted as a tropical storm. She pulled it loose, shook out the filth, and ran her fingers along the tassels. The fabric was still soft and fine despite the snags. With a last flick of her wrist, she wrapped it over her head as if she were headed to mass, and Jim laughed.

"Too bad we didn't find it in time for the dance."

"Wouldn't have made a difference," she said bitterly. "Even if it had been a lady's hat in the Anglo style."

"I'm sorry." He kicked a rock into the creek, and the lines of his face followed it downward.

She shook her head and walked toward him, laying her palms on his chest. "It's me that's sorry. I never understood how important status could be until I didn't have any. You needed a woman who could raise your standing in the Anglo community. If anything, I've made your situation worse."

"No," he said, cupping her face between his hands. "That would only matter to me if I cared about creating a life here. I don't anymore. The dance made it clear we'll never be welcome. I'll finish out my time for the sake of Pump, keep the animals alive, but then we will be free to return to my people. The best use of our time between now and then is catching any wild horses that enter our property. Maybe we'll get lucky and catch a stallion." His teeth gleamed. "We'll take those with us and trade everything else we can for as many horses as we can get." Jim closed his eyes, and his body hummed.

"What do you see?"

"My triumphant return," he said, eyes still closed before refocusing on Eva. "But first, we'll get you material for a decent dress. We should've bought cloth while we were in town. We have the money. I just didn't think of it." He rubbed his hands down her arms. "It's not fitting for you to be dressed in rags. They're only going to get worse over the next months until we can get you proper clothing at home."

"One problem: I don't know how to sew."

"How do you not know how to sew?" he asked. "What do women do in your time? You don't know how to do anything."

"First, I'm not like normal women in any time. My days were spent learning different languages and how to kill people." When she said it out loud, she realized it wasn't only practical survival skills she was missing. "I also wasn't taught science or advanced math or literature or art or philosophy or any other academic subject besides histories and theology."

Jim wrinkled his nose at the academic arts but huffed in consternation at the others. "You're worse than a child. You wouldn't survive a day alone on the plains or as an Anglo — and that's saying something."

"Hey, I knew how to start a fire before I came here."

"Without a flint and steel?" When she tucked in her lips, he said, "I'll show you how. We should make a list."

"Write it down? On a list? Like an Anglo?" She feigned shock.

"I know. This is what you've brought me to." He tapped his temple. "But no need. I have it all in here. I'm titling it 'Eva's Won't Die Cold And Hungry Lessons.'" His face grew serious. "Now that I think about it, I do need to teach you many things before we return to my people, or it will not go well for you with the women."

Eva sighed. Women were proving harder to earn respect from than men.

When they approached the cabin, Pump's buckboard was parked outside. Jim turned his face to Eva, worry at the potential confrontation etching his features. She had no idea how their friend had taken their abrupt abandonment of the McMullen's party. Better to get it over with, she thought, kicking her horse into a trot.

Pump sat in their cabin with a nice fire going, her stew bubbling merrily, and his head enveloped in a fog of pipe smoke. He swiveled to them when they entered.

"I come bearing peace offerings," he said. Concern and exhaustion pinched his eyes, and his skin hung saggy and gray. He handed Eva a packet. "Mrs. McMullen sent you an apology and receipts for every dish served at the supper. She took them down by hand herself as her cook recited the steps." At her confusion, he added, "Jim told me as we were bedding down how much you enjoyed the food and that you wanted to learn."

Eva's heart opened a crack, and she hadn't even read the note yet.

Jim's face, on the other hand, contained a storm. A few recipes, or receipts, as they were called here, were not going to mend things with him.

"I was fit to be tied when I heard what everyone was saying about you… and Mr. Brown." His voice trailed off as his face turned beet red. "And why you left at first light. I went at once to Mrs. McMullen and set her straight. She can be a hard woman when she feels righteous, but she's also a woman who will admit when she's wrong if someone can get her to see it. Hortensia's kind at the core."

The door to Eva's heart slammed shut when she remembered the mistreated enslaved people.

Pump read her face and lifted a hand. "I won't defend what she's done to her slave women, but that's a perfect example of her righteousness getting in the way of her doing the right thing. Unless she feels like she has been wronged morally or someone's acting immorally within her realm of influence, she's a kind and thoughtful woman. You saw the slaves dancing that night. They had their own harvest feast with all the fixings at her encouragement and blessing."

Eva fumed. Comparing her minor conflict with their daily lives or inflating Hortensia's kindness at other times was absurd. Yearly parties could never make up for daily pain.

"The point is, she knows your friendship is important to me," he said, addressing Jim. "And she values my word regarding your character and Eva's. She was already having her own doubts about Mr. Brown, and when he woke, she had her husband examine his chin. She dressed him down in front of all the guests in no uncertain terms. She knows your reputation was tarnished under her roof and at her hand, and she has taken it upon herself to help you enter society respectably. Every guest there was chastised."

Eva glanced at Jim, his face unreadable as he stared at the floor.

"Mrs. McMullen is used to ruling the roost," Pump continued. "She is the best ally you could wish for in our community."

When neither of them spoke, Pump filled the silence with his anxiety. "There is still a place and a path forward for you here."

Jim gazed at Pump for a long time. Given their happy planning that afternoon, Eva thought she knew where his opinions lay. Without looking at her, he said, "What's the note say, Eva?"

Eva snapped the wax seal and opened the intricately folded letter.

> *My dear Mrs. McCullough,*
>
> *It is with the heaviest of hearts that I write to you. I am appalled at my behavior and ashamed I assumed the worst of you without more evidence than my own notions and idle gossip. Mr. Brown's behavior was inexcusable and not befitting a gentleman, and he will be struck from our future guest lists.*
>
> *Our esteemed friend, Mr. Brunet, spoke passionately to me in defense of your virtue, Mrs. McCullough, despite the unusual circumstances of your arrival. I recognize now that life has dealt you a very hard hand, and despite all of your obstacles in life, you managed to guard your virtue jealously.*

Mr. McMullen and myself are overjoyed at the news that Mr. McCullough has found himself a wife. We have felt nothing but Christian charity toward your husband and wish to extend the same to you. As Mr. Brunet will have delivered to you, you will see upon opening a collection of receipts instructing you in the making of the dishes, which you so enjoyed during your stay with us. If you would like direct instruction from our cook, you have only to ask, and we will be happy to host you in our home once again.

Much as my husband has taken it upon himself to help your husband be successful in his return to productive citizenry, I, too, hope you will allow me to help you enter into respectable society without further hurdles. As a start toward that effort, I hope you will accept an invitation to come to my home for a fitting for two new dresses, one for work and one for special occasions. It is my gift to you in the hopes that you will forgive me.

I remain yours truly,

Mrs. Thomas McMullen

Eva heard Jim snort at Hortensia's phrasing. "Productive citizenry," he muttered. Nevertheless, his jaw softened, and his shoulders relaxed.

"What did you tell her, Pump?" The letter mystified Eva.

"That you grew up very poor in New Orleans, and your parents had a hard time marrying you off. Your father forced you to dye your hair and tried to sell you to a brothel, but you escaped before he could make good on his plans. You made it to San Felipe in September by your own honest sweat, but you were starving and wandering the land when Jim found you and took you in."

Jim's face broke into astonished admiration at Pump's inventiveness.

"I explained you grew to love each other," he continued, "and that though you had not been married in a church yet, you had married yourselves before God with appropriate oaths, and that I never knew a man as honorable at keeping his word as Jim." Pump smiled. "It helps that Mrs. McMullen is a romantic underneath that corset."

Chapter 32

Eva

After Pump's visit, Jim redoubled his efforts to teach Eva to speak Comanche. What before had been a game was now serious business.

Eva sat back on her heels, task at her knees. Jim was having her stretch a de-fleshed rabbit's skin and rubbing its own brain into it to keep it soft until it dried. He had told her every animal had exactly the right-sized brain for tanning its own skin. A moment ago, she had pulled too tightly too soon, and now there was a small, thinning hole toward the edge. She grimaced and peeked at Jim to see if he had noticed. He was focused on braiding rawhide.

"So," he said, continuing the current language lesson, "family words end in -hpʉ, like 'father' is a-hpʉ, and 'mother' is pia-hpʉ. Then there's 'husband': kuma-hpʉ… That's me." He grinned. "It's also Rʉtsima and my other brothers to you."

"So, I call your brothers 'husband?'" Eva pictured a complicated family tree in her head. Between learning a foreign language and practicing a new skill with her hands, her mind concentrated on immediate matters rather than any implications for her future. It was a simple word, nothing more, labeled and cataloged with all the others.

He nodded without looking up. "Yes. You will call us all 'husband,' but you belong to me. The word for 'brother-in-law' is for me with your brothers. 'Sister-in-law' is for my sisters to you. You will be 'sister' to my brothers' wives." He jerked twice at the rawhide straps with both hands, then stepped on the braid and pulled, tightening and straightening. "Words that can be grouped together tend to have the same ending." He put his work down. "How are you doing?"

Eva gestured at the hole.

"It seems good otherwise. Keep working it. Everyone puts a hole in their first one. Be glad you're not learning as a captive and getting beaten for it by some mean, old matron."

"Are all the women mean to captives?"

"No, of course not," Jim said, leaning forward on his leg. "Some women are kind; some are very cruel. Some women get jealous of their husband's attention to a captive, or they've lost a husband or a son to an Anglo, or they're short-tempered with everyone and take it out on the weakest. It's not easy for females who are captured when they're already women. They are the lowest members of the band, and some have it worse than others. But there are good and bad mistresses, just like with Anglos." He picked up three new straps and ran them through his fingers. "You won't be a captive with a mistress, but you'll have to make your place in the jabbing order all the same, and none of the women will be happy if you ruin a buffalo hide."

Eva's mouth quirked. "Do you mean 'pecking order?'"

"Yes, the pecking order of women," Jim corrected.

Eva squinted at her pruney fingers. She liked these new skills about as much as she had liked the Anglo chores. Enjoyable at first, learning a new thing, but she didn't need much of an imagination to see her days could end up being spent scraping hide. "Let's leave time to shoot this afternoon."

"Say that in Nʉmʉ tekwapʉ̲."

Eva searched the tiny dictionary in her head. "We horse afternoon," she said in Comanche.

Jim laughed and restructured the sentence for her with all the missing words, and she repeated it. He bobbed his head, impressed. "You're doing well with the whispered sounds. They're usually difficult for Anglos."

Eva glowed. "After the fourth language, every next one is easier."

"Four?" Jim's head jerked up. "How many languages do you speak?"

Eva paused in her rubbing. "Well, that depends on what you count. I speak French and Spanish, including Latin American Spanish, like a native, and of course, English from various time periods." She turned back to her rabbit skin. "My German is quite good. I'm passable in Dutch. Passable in Greek, better in Latin. Some Russian. Oh, Norwegian and Old Norse," she added, holding up a finger. She glanced over her shoulder at him. "I picked those up as well, along with Icelandic. Swedish, I haven't used enough for it to come easily. Would love to learn Finnish or Hungarian."

Jim stared at her.

Eva hid a smile when he gave his head a shake. "Nɨmɨ tekwapɨ is a nice challenge," she said. "There seem to be four different ways to say the same thing."

Without warning, a wave of homesickness crashed over her, and she stood to lift her head above it. To distract herself as the sensation flowed through her chest, she watched the horses milling in the distance, seeing instead her Lux Libera friends gathered in their cozy dormitory lounge and Tophe sprawled on the sofa beside her, feet in her lap. They would quiz each other before vocabulary tests. When she could breathe again, she put her hands on the small of her back and stretched. "I think it's dry," she said, referring to the skin.

"I'll check in a moment." Jim's gaze remained absorbed with his own task.

Eva walked to the water bucket, washed her hands, and scooped a drink with the dipper. The icy water slid to her stomach, and she shivered. Jim straddled the bench with his back to her. After returning the dipper, she arranged her hands in front of herself.

Concentrating, she imagined the air within her circle, little droplets of moisture and floating gases. She peered deeper into the elements and farther still. The vibrating strings played their eternal symphony, every tone and vibration forming the unique properties of its nature. In a breath, she joined each loop to itself in a cascading ouroboros and stepped inside, reopening them the next instant behind Jim and wrapping her arms around him.

Without a sound, Jim flipped her over his shoulder. She thudded onto the puncheon floor of the dogtrot, her lungs compressing and Jim's knee digging into her belly. One hand pushed down on her chest while the other gripped his knife. Eva tried to take a breath, but no air would come.

He lifted from her in horror and collapsed back against the bench, the seat slamming into the wall. He ran his fingers through his hair and shut his eyes, chest heaving.

Eva chuckled.

His eyes flew open. "I nearly killed you."

"No, you didn't."

Jim looked away, frowning.

"I've never been able to sneak up on you like that," she said, pleased with her joke. Jim had shown her how to roll her feet while stalking prey. Though she had done plenty of sneaking as a Mender and had been practicing the more advanced techniques Jim had shown her, he had been impossible to surprise.

"You cheated."

"I used my skills to my advantage," she countered.

Jim rolled his eyes.

Eva noticed his sweaty, pale face and began to feel repentant.

"I'm sorry," she said, sitting up. Contrite, she crawled to him and straddled his lap. He straightened his legs to accommodate her. Once settled, she licked a finger and smoothed the eyebrow above his right eye — the one that always swept upward — then kissed his forehead. "I need more hand-to-hand combat training."

"How about, let's not sneak up on Jim using sorcery?"

"Well, that's less fun, but okay, I promise not to sneak up on you using sorcery."

"No," he said, his eyes narrowing. "Promise not to sneak up on me using space jumping or traveling or your abilities or whatever other words you use to describe what you just did."

Eva stuck her lower lip out, and Jim raised an eyebrow. When she didn't respond, he pinched at her waist in a rough tickle.

"All right, all right, I promise."

Jim's face remained dark. "Also, promise not to come up behind any Numu warrior like that, even without jumping," he said. "He will kill you."

Eva tilted her head. "If I sneak up on another man, it will be with the intent of killing *him*. He won't live long enough to fight back."

Jim pressed his lips together in a flat line and blew through his nose.

She lifted her hands to ward off his next words. "I take your point. In all seriousness, I need to improve my combat skills. In the past, I've usually killed from a distance. All novices are taught basic martial arts, but I never used them much." Mopai's sun-haloed face flashed in her mind's eye. "I've never needed to defend myself at close quarters as often as I have here."

Jim studied her until his color returned, and his chest rose and fell with normal breaths. "Yes, you're right. It's a good idea. I will add wrestling to the 'Keep Eva Alive' list."

"Oh, it's the 'Keep Eva Alive' list now, is it?"

"It's also the 'Things Every Child Knows But Eva Needs To Learn So That She Doesn't Do Stupid Things Anymore' list, but that's too long to say."

Eva lifted his shirt to place her cold hands on his belly.

He gasped in surprise and tackled her. Within moments, he held both her wrists to the floor. "First lesson?" he asked. "Get out of this pin."

Eva tried to pull her arms from his grip and then wiggled her hips, straining against him.

He leered down at her. "Eventually, I'll have to let go of one of your wrists if I want to do anything else to you. That will be your chance." He moved his hand to her throat. "Now, what do you do?"

When she drew back to send a mock punch to his face, her elbow hit the floor. He sat up straight and rose out of the path of her fist, which ended below his collarbone.

"Now what?" he asked.

Eva kneed him in the back and bucked. He smirked. She drove an elbow toward his groin, stopping before striking.

"You could. It might distract me for a moment, but it will probably make me mad." He lifted his fist and punched down toward her eye, tapping her on the face where Mopai had struck. He released her other wrist and used both fists to graze her cheeks with alternating strikes.

"Okay," she said. "I get the idea."

"From this position, you don't want to start a fight with me. You can't win. You have to concentrate on getting out from under me."

Eva thought as he waited.

He moved his hands back around her throat. "Find one of my little fingers."

She took hold of both.

"Good. Now pretend to bend them back. They will break, but that could also just make me mad. I might stick my thumbs in your eyes if you did that to me."

Eva bared her teeth at the thought. "Well, what else can I do?"

"You want to force my arm to bend at the elbow." Jim positioned her hands and showed her where to press. "See how my arm goes back?"

She nodded.

"Now, at the same time, you're going to hook this foot," he patted her left, "around my foot. Then put your other foot right up under your bottom and push off. You're going to roll me, and then you'll be on top."

Eva struggled to find the right angles, but as Jim repositioned her and had her try over and over again, she managed to break his mounted position. Out of breath, she threw up her hands in triumph.

He beamed up at her. "Tsaa, nicely done."

Eva felt him hardening beneath her. "I'm not going to learn very much if you don't stay focused."

"That is going to be a challenge." He put his hands around her waist. "I'm worn out."

"You're worn out?"

"Let's take a quick break inside the cabin, and then we can continue," he said.

"Inside the cabin? You mean in the bed."

"Yes," Jim said, mouth spreading wide.

"Only if you say: 'Always on Top, please join me in my bed for a quick break' in Nʉmʉ tekwapʉ̠."

"'Always on Top?'" He cocked his head to the side. "Are you giving yourself a Nʉmʉ name?"

"Perfect, right? Accurate for so many reasons."

Chapter 33

Eva

The next day found them at the McMullen's plantation. Eva had planned to travel alone, but Jim preferred to join for the visit. And so, they were both perched on Hortensia's stiff horsehair settee across from their hostess, who was trying to put them at ease with non-stop small talk. Outside, Wokweesi whined at the door.

Jim shifted his legs, then shifted them again and took a sip of coffee. Eva placed a calming hand on his knee.

Taking pity on him, Hortensia glanced over her shoulder and lifted a finger. "Clarissa, please go and fetch Mr. McMullen. I'm sure Mr. McCullough would like to join him today while we busy ourselves with ladies' matters." Her words sent the enslaved woman at her elbow off to search.

Jim's shoulders relaxed, and his thigh sank next to Eva's.

"Thank you, ma'am," he said, standing up. "I'll just wait outside for Tom and let you two get on with it." He gave Eva a reassuring nod, which she answered with her own.

"Of course. Your wife will be in good hands. I'm sure you and my Thomas have much to talk about."

With Jim out of the room, the atmosphere lightened considerably. Absent of men, this became Hortensia's sole domain once again.

"Now, my dear, I can't tell you how pleased I am that you have come. We started off on the wrong foot, and I aim to mend that mistake."

Eva gave her a warm smile. "I do appreciate your charity, Mrs. McMullen." She looked down at her travesty of a dress. "I certainly need new clothing." Already torn from her fall down the cliff, her colorful skirts and embroidered Mexican blouse had long since faded, threadbare from repeated washings with harsh lye soap.

"Well, and I certainly love new dresses myself. It is a pleasure to have an excuse to design two for you. We'll take your measurements when Clarissa returns," she said, picking up a biscuit and slathering it with butter.

Eva bit into her second. "Could I have the receipt for biscuits as well?"

"Oh, yes, of course," Hortensia said. "When we're done here, we'll take you down to the kitchen to meet Cook." She took a ladylike nibble and swallowed. "I should warn you, though, she can be quite gruff. She will act as if you are wasting her time, but deep down, she was enormously flattered to learn how much you enjoyed her food."

Eva raised an eyebrow.

"Flattery will get you everywhere with her," Hortensia added.

Eva snickered, stopped herself from saying, "Okay," and instead said, "I'm looking forward to meeting her."

When Clarissa returned, Eva removed her clothing down to her chemise. She held out her arms as the woman wrapped a cloth tape measure around her bust and her waist. Clarissa called out the numbers to Hortensia, who wrote them down on a piece of old brown paper sacking.

"I believe we need circle skirts for... modesty while riding," Hortensia said. "Unless Jim will be purchasing you a sidesaddle soon?"

"No, no plans for a new saddle at the moment," Eva said. "But may I ask? What is a circle skirt?"

"It is cut to be very full and will cover your legs when you sit astride. But honestly, my dear, it is unsafe for you to ride in a skirt at all with no sidesaddle."

"Bonnet, too, Miss Hortensia?" Clarissa asked, cutting into her mistress's admonishment and fingering Eva's hair.

"Most assuredly, yes," she replied, gazing at Eva, pencil to lips. "Sunbonnet to match the work dress, and a hat from town to go with the best dress. What do you think?" This last was asked of Clarissa, not Eva.

"Yes'm, I think that will do nicely," she said, measuring Eva's crown.

"Let's see your boots, gal," Hortensia said. When Eva turned her feet on display, showing the soles, her hostess said, "Still very serviceable."

"I'm thinking the sturdy brown for the work dress, and then that nice blue we still have some of… from your Easter dress two years ago," Clarissa said.

"Is there enough?" Hortensia rested a fist on her ample hip.

"Yes'm, I believe so."

Eva wondered if it was the same brown fabric Clarissa was wearing. Cloth like that laughed in the face of farm chores. She refrained from reaching out to touch it.

"You will look so lovely at your wedding, Eva," Hortensia said.

Clarissa paused her here-and-there touches to take a step back, knuckling her chin in thought. A smile played on Clarissa's lips, and Eva saw her new blue dress taking form in the woman's eyes.

"I don't think Jim and I are planning on getting married again," Eva said, her vision tunneling a little bit.

"Yes, Pump told me you two had married yourselves," Hortensia said. "And while Jim might be excused for not knowing any better, now that your union is common knowledge, we need to make it official."

Eva opened her mouth to protest but stopped when Clarissa looked at her out of the side of her eye and sucked her teeth in warning.

With the next breath, Hortensia stood and took both of Eva's hands. "You're currently living in sin, my dear. We must remedy this as soon as possible." Her soft eyes blunted the sting from her words. "You at least need to perform a civil marriage before a judge, and Mexican law requires Father Muldoon to solemnize your union in the eyes of the Catholic Church. He should be back in San Felipe by Easter."

Eva knew without asking that Jim would refuse to be married by a minister or priest, and she doubted he would care about colonial laws. She had no idea if she could convince him to change his mind, especially since he had no plans to stay, but she was sure he would want to visit Pump whenever he wished and still be welcome in society. A darker thought pushed into her mind: was she taking this woman's charity under false pretenses? No. She brushed the concern away. This was reparation. Hortensia may be placing strings on the gift, but she would not feel obligated to be her puppet.

"I'll have to see what I can get Jim to agree to. He has different notions of marriage… and you know how men are," she said. One good thing about this era, she could blame her own reluctance or strategic lack of opinions on her man's wishes.

At her words, Hortensia's agitation spun higher. "If you have any children, they will be bastards. It really is not up for discussion. I will have Thomas speak with your husband."

Eva bowed her head in submission. "Yes, I'm sure you're right."

Clarissa tucked her lips and stared at the floor, clearly immune to Eva's act, but Hortensia released a breath and brightened.

To change the subject, Eva asked, "Do you have any children, Mrs. McMullen?"

Clarissa's brow furrowed, and Hortensia's face clouded. "No, unfortunately. I've had several, but none have survived past the age of three."

"Oh, I'm so sorry, ma'am. I didn't know."

Hortensia fluttered her hands. "No, no, my dear. How could you have known? We women all have things we must be brave about. It does not bother me you asked." She sat back down in her chair. "I have a question for you, though, if you don't mind my prying?"

Eva bobbed her head.

"How is it you never learned to cook or sew? I would have thought even a poor girl, or I should say, especially a poor girl, would learn how to do both at an early age."

Clarissa's ears seemed to grow two inches, curiosity eating her up. Eva imagined she had been the subject of much juicy speculation since the dance.

"Oh, that's easily answered. My mother died when I was very young, and my father raised me. He knew none of the womanly arts, and we lived on charity. I only knew how to cook corn and beans, and all my clothes were cast-offs from other women. We could never have afforded material, even if I had known how to sew."

"What did your father do?"

"Drank and gambled. Money rarely made it home."

Clarissa tsked, and Hortensia's mouth rounded. "Well, you're here now," she said, "and in better circumstances, I am sure. Bless your heart, dear."

That should appease the gossip gods, Eva thought, relieved to have salvaged the room's mood.

The winter kitchen lay a short walk down the dogtrot. Warmth billowed through the doorway when they entered, and a tiny woman, bent at the waist, stirred a large kettle. At the disturbance, she levered herself upright, scowling, and instantly transferred her displeasure with the contents of the pot to the intruders.

"Good morning, Miss Hortensia," Cook said, voice flat, words clipped. She glanced back at her task.

"Sorry to disturb you, Cook. This is Mrs. James McCullough, who we wrote the receipts for the other day. She is hoping you can show her how to cook some of the dishes or at least talk her through the finer points."

Cook's face remained unchanged.

Eva resisted the urge to hide behind Hortensia.

After a long moment, Cook smacked her lips. "Yes, ma'am."

Hortensia gave them both a smile before leaving but then turned back as the door shut. "I'll be in the parlor when you are done," she said through the crack.

Faced with Cook's direct stare, Eva fought the compulsion to drop her eyes. The elderly woman's snow-white hair and wizened face reminded her too much of Elder Nnaji. As Cook scrutinized her from head to toe, Eva straightened her shoulders and cast her eyes to the floor, clutching her skirts to keep from bowing.

Cook broke the silence. "I hear you're the gal who's taken up with that Injun fella." The west coast of Africa tuned her voice.

"Yes, ma'am," she said. "Jim is his name."

Cook's face crinkled into a crepe-paper smile, then she opened her arms. "Come here, child."

Eva approached her, uncertain of the sudden mood shift, and found herself in a fierce hug.

When Cook released her, she said, "Now, you give that to that man of yours from me. Otherwise, mind you, that didn't happen. I have my reputation to maintain."

Mystified, Eva mimed locking her lips.

Cook pulled out two stools for them to sit at her worktable and dropped her voice to a whisper. "Tell me about Kitch and Caesar, when they came to your house."

The heavens opened. Of course. Kitch and Caesar. "They came late that night, and we gave them supplies for the journey and two horses. Jim taught them Comanche phrases that should help them pass safely through their territory."

Cook puckered her lips in surprised satisfaction, her ancient eyes twinkling. "And do you know where the Saltwater Tribes are?"

"Only that they're north northwest of here. Many days away."

Cook's eyes unfocused. Eva imagined her mind flying over the piney woods and open plains to join them.

"They hoped to come back for their families," Eva said.

Cook returned to her. "We'll just have to wait and see. We'll just have to wait and see." She slapped the table with both hands. "Now, time's a-wasting. I have too much to do to sit here wagging tongues. What can I teach you?"

Eva pulled out the receipts Cook had dictated to Hortensia. "I have some questions."

Chapter 34

Eva

If efficiency formed Cook's bones, energy coursed through her veins. Fresh commands followed on the heels of the previous ones, and she expected Eva to respond to her clipped instructions without delay. Elder Njani faded behind Cook's own personality. She seized Eva by the wrist and guided her hand to feel the different temperatures within the hearth and at its edges.

"On the fried chicken," Eva said, "Jim and I tried to make it again, with egg and flour this time, but it was still raw. It looked nice on the outside, though."

"Grease too hot." Cook demonstrated the ideal flame height and skillet distance.

Eva committed the image to memory. Unexpectedly, she thought of Tophe in the dining hall, choosing a fried chicken leg. It had been his favorite, and he'd throw an extra piece on her plate when he came back from getting seconds, knowing she liked it, too. Cook's version beat the cafeteria's sorry excuse for fried chicken with a stick.

"Who taught you how to cook?"

"The cook at the first house I was taken to, many, many years ago. I've always worked in the house," she said. Her face softened.

"How old were you? When you were first captured."

"About twelve. Woman enough, but still a child." Her eyes gazed over Eva's shoulder.

Eva stopped herself from saying she, too, had been twelve when her whole life had changed. Their experiences could not have been more dissimilar. While accompanying wealthy buyers, she had seen slave ships and auction blocks in different timelines and had stood on the decks with a handkerchief to her nose, the ship's bowels composting the living. Children of every nation filled the holds, and the middle passage flowed backward between continents in some, but the suffering was the same. Eva wondered if Miss Hortensia knew how her property had been imported. She doubted it.

"How did you survive?" Eva pictured Cook chained as a young girl in her own excrement and vomit, unable to lie down for months. The words tumbled out unbidden, and she locked eyes with the table, ashamed. "I'm sorry. It was wrong of me to ask you that."

Cook's spirit no longer occupied the room with Eva. "I just did." She returned to her body and studied Eva, the whites of her eyes yellow ivory. "You just do. I wasn't ready to die where I sat. You'd be surprised what you can get used to."

Eva wasn't surprised. She had seen firsthand what humans, slave or free, could endure. Whether individuals or multitudes, they had just been shadows to her, their endurance simply unfeeling fate, an assigned role, a trick of the light, an illusion. Many times, she had ensured their suffering by killing their rebels and saviors. With horror, she counted the decades from this moment to an exact ship when Cook might have been twelve. Not in this timeline, but in others exactly like it. Gooseflesh crawled up her arms and down her spine. She wanted to weep.

Faraway again, Cook said, "There was a man next to me. He made me laugh when I tried to cry. Every day until he died, right before we landed."

Guilt shrunk Eva's voice to the barest whisper. "What is your name? The name your mother called you?"

Cook smiled. "Ifedayo. It means 'Love Has Become Joy.'"

"Beautiful." Eva pressed her lips together to dam her unworthy tears.

They sat in silence until Cook broke the spell, her face stern. "Anything else for you, gal?"

Eva shook her head. "No, ma'am," she said and lowered her gaze, hand over her heart. "Thank you for sharing your time with me today, Miss Ifedayo."

The wintry air cleansed Eva's face when she stepped out of the steamy kitchen. She wished it could wash her filthy soul. Past the barn and at the edge of a field, Jim stood with Mr. McMullen and another man. A small boy played in the dirt at their feet.

Needing to be near Jim, she glanced at the parlor door but walked down the gallery steps and across the yard. Wokweesi jogged toward her, tail wagging. As he jabbed his nose into her knee, she bent and scratched behind his ears. Jim lifted his chin when he saw her coming, and a smile spread over his face.

"We were just about to head to the house for a bite to eat," Jim said when she reached them. Eva nodded hello to the other men, and Mr. McMullen introduced her to his neighbor Samuel Carter and his son Jed.

"Pa, can I pet the calf?" the boy asked.

His father assented, and the adults headed to the house.

"I was just telling Jim here that I saved all your cottonseed for you to feed your stock this winter. I can send one of my boys round with it this coming week."

Eva thought about their poor, lonely ox. She'd had no idea it would eat cottonseed.

"And I'd like to enlist your help in convincing him to plant much more this coming spring."

Jim squeezed the hand she had looped through his arm.

"Yes, of course, Mr. McMullen," she said. "It seems this past year was good for everyone."

"That it was, my dear," he replied. "As you can see, cotton can be quite lucrative." His hand drew an arc, ending at his new house.

In her mind's eye, bloody fingers spun the white fibers into gold, and the filaments flew through the glazed windows and away to the northeast and England.

Mr. McMullen opened the door into the parlor, and Mrs. McMullen welcomed them to the fire. Eva scanned the room with bitter melancholy and thought of their sparse cabin at home. With all this comfort within reach, was it any wonder so many turned a blind eye in any timeline, including those where Mrs. McMullen's face was black and Clarissa's was white? Even she yearned for easy luxuries. Only a man like Jim could look at this operation and see himself as the slave. His envy lay elsewhere and at the expense of different people. And her? Who was she to judge? She'd done more harm than they could cause in all their lifetimes combined.

After some small talk, Hortensia led them into the dining room, where Clarissa laid out a light meal. Jim's laugh at things said by others papered over the hole in her heart. The men dominated the conversation while Eva contented herself with listening. Here and there, Mrs. McMullen added her comments like seasoning, but she was too much of a lady to over-salt. Eventually, Eva shook herself free of her depressing thoughts.

Mr. Carter told them about the siege of San Antonio at the end of November. Eva grinned up at Jim, knowing what was coming. He turned his head to her and raised his eyebrows in question, but she didn't reply.

"So Deaf Smith," Mr. Carter said, "he rides into camp and says, 'Fellas, the Mexican cavalry is escorting a heap of pack animals, and I think they're carrying pay for the army.'"

"Seems a reasonable guess," Mr. McMullen said.

"Well, Colonel Burleson, he orders Bowie to take our cavalry and get in the Mexican cavalry's way." Mr. Carter took a bite and swallowed. "So, while Bowie's keeping the cavalry busy, Jack takes our boys on foot, about a hundred of 'em, to seize the supply train." He snatched the air with his hands.

"Here are the two cavalries, fighting it out, and then they're having to get down on the ground with each other in the ravines and everything." Mr. Carter jabbed his knife at an imaginary Mexican soldier. "Well, that Mexican General Cos, he sees what's happening and sends out more cavalry with an artillery piece. So, now, our boys are caught in the middle. They've got Mexicans shooting at them from the left and Mexicans shooting at them from the right." He dipped and dodged.

Hortensia eyed the dirty fork in his hand with alarm. Clarissa stooped to blot the rug.

"Our boys managed to get free of the crossfire, but then they were pinned down under four separate attacks." He held up his fingers for emphasis. "Until reinforcements could arrive, led by Swisher. After all that, we only had four wounded, no dead," he said, smug. "Mexicans had three dead and *fourteen* wounded."

Eva leaned forward, smiling in anticipation. Jim peeked at her, brows drawn.

"But here's the best part," Mr. Carter said. "Well, not best for us. But anyway, our boys get about forty of these pack animals back to camp. They're getting ready to open up bags and bags of Mexican coin. Enough to swim in. And do you know what they found?"

His audience shook their heads. Eva tucked her lips.

"Grass! It was all grass to feed the army animals!"

Jim's eyes crinkled, and Tom barked a laugh.

"I know our side could use the money," Mr. Carter continued, "but it's too funny. They're calling it the Grass Fight."

"Someone should write an ode," Hortensia said.

Suddenly, Eva heard footsteps running down the dogtrot, and everyone's attention turned. The little boy, Jed, burst through the door, tears streaming down his cheeks.

"Pa, Pa, the calf got loose, and I can't get her to go back in."

Mr. Carter's neck flushed bright red, then he leapt from his seat and dashed out the door.

Thomas called after him, "It's not a problem, Sam. I'll just have Moses round her up." Without haste, he slid back and placed his napkin on the table. "I should go help calm things down."

For the next ten minutes, Hortensia took up the hostess mantle and filled the silence with Christmas plans. As she was telling Eva she should return for a fitting the following week, she stopped mid-sentence. They could hear a series of steady thwacks and a child's cry. Hortensia frowned, and they all peered out the window. Jed lay bare-bottomed, draped over his father's knee. Sam held a thin switch in his hand.

Disapproval scrawled over Hortensia's face, drawing deep lines. Eva's surprise doubled when she looked at Jim. His eyes burned.

"He should have waited to do that at home," Hortensia said. "There's no need to humiliate the boy in public."

Ah, Eva thought. Her reaction made more sense.

Hortensia trembled with indignation and left to intercede.

"And they call my people savages," Jim said when she was out of earshot. "The last time I was ever whipped with a switch on my behind was the day I was captured and my parents were killed. I had left something behind at the last campsite that morning. I don't even remember what."

"The Numunuu don't whip their children?"

"No, they prefer to lead by example. They'll sometimes use scary stories and threats, but they never hit them."

"The same for captive children?" Eva asked.

Jim folded and unfolded the napkin in front of him. "If they're still young... less than ten."

"You were eleven," Eva said. "And big for your age, I bet." When he looked away again, she studied the back of his head. His life before captivity, she was coming to learn, resided in a black box. He never spoke of his sisters or his birth parents unless directly asked, and Eva assumed it was too painful. Even the early days of his captivity were a touchy subject.

At some point, Jim had fully embraced being Numu. His survival had depended on it, and to do so, he had realigned his moral compass to a different set of coordinates, hiding away anything that couldn't be reconciled, like the deaths of his parents and the mistreatment of his oldest sister, and focusing on the best of his new people.

Jim stared out the window, silent. After a moment, he said, "One time, when my father was still my master, he called me into his teepee. He had gotten word I had hit a little girl, another captive. She and I had been arguing, and I had punched her in the stomach. As I stood before him, he sat there sharpening his knife. He reached out, quick as a snake, and grabbed me by my hair — made like he was going to cut off my head."

Eva's eyes traveled down his neck to the hairline scar.

"I never hit a female again." His eyes darted her way. "A Numu female, I mean." He turned his entire face to her. "More effective than a whipping."

"If you say so," Eva said.

Outside the window, Hortensia entreated Mr. Carter to end the punishment. Sam relented, and he threw the switch in the grass. Jed pulled up his pants, and she guided him toward the kitchen.

"My Numu father never beat me, though." Jim stood. "Let's say our goodbyes."

Chapter 35

Eva

Jim's Farm

T he next day was unseasonably warm, and they had ridden out to the oak grove to spend the afternoon. Eva spread blankets in the sun. Once settled, Jim laid beside her on his belly. Nearby, the horses grazed on the dormant grass, while Wokweesi snuffled in the mounds of fallen leaves where hogs had been foraging. Eva watched him sniff with a hurried frenzy, double-marking every tree.

At a mischievous thought, she looked down at Jim's dozing face. She knew he was possuming and bent down to take his earlobe between her teeth. He chuckled until she bit down.

"Anáa!" Jim said, rolling away from her. He stayed on his back and closed his eyes again. Without warning, his hand snaked out to grab her by the back of the neck, and he brought her head to his chest, then patted her hair. "There. Safe from your teeth. Go to sleep."

Eva wrapped her arms around him and draped a leg over his thighs. His chest rose and fell beneath her ear, and she matched her breathing to his own. She wondered if their heartbeats were in sync, too.

"There are probably farm things we should be doing to prepare for the spring…" Eva said. With a twist of anxiety, she worried that they would regret days like these if they ended up staying in the colony.

Jim shrugged. "Thomas gave me a list."

Eva imagined him wadding the paper into a ball and throwing it over his shoulder. A gust of wind ran through the trees, and when the boughs creaked behind them, she snuggled closer. When the air stilled again, she grew comfortable in the sun.

"Thomas also told me we need to get re-married."

"What did you say?"

"That my people would recognize our marriage, and I expected our marriage to be recognized by the Anglos."

Eva sat up. "You did?"

Jim's eyes snapped open. "Of course. Why would we need a Christian wedding? Neither of us is Christian."

"I'm just curious what his response was."

Jim shut his eyes. "I think Hortensia made him say something. Once he had done his duty, he dropped the subject."

"He didn't try to tell you that you aren't Comanche anymore?"

Jim cracked a lid. "No. He's a 'live and let live' kind of fellow. He likes helping people. Hortensia likes changing people."

Eva gazed out over the meadow, her arm on her knee.

"I also told him I didn't expect to stay after our year was up, but I hoped to be welcomed for visits in the future."

She hoped for the same. There were things she liked about this little farm she would miss when they left. Days like this. They were living in a luminous space between, enjoying the fat of the land but neglecting to feed the fields for the following year. If they stayed, they would have to fall into a pattern of work in order to survive.

"What did Thomas say?"

"That we would always be welcome in his home. That he hoped he had armed me with the knowledge to choose either life freely."

Eva smiled. Mr. McMullen's answer was unexpected. She thought of her dresses and the possible strings attached. "Do you think he'll tell Hortensia?"

He shook his head. "I think there's a lot he doesn't tell Hortensia. Besides, even if he did, she will assume you had no say in the matter." With those words, he settled back to resume his nap.

"When you're back with your people, will you go raiding in this area?"

Jim sighed, jaw tightening, then shook his head again, eyes still closed.

Eva let him be and stared up into the deep blue sky, rolling a sweet hackberry kernel between her teeth. She knew what hid beyond the Earth's atmosphere and wondered what Jim thought was out there, but refrained from asking. He snored, mouth cracked open. It was so tempting to take a piece of grass, and... no, she would be good.

After a few minutes, she nestled beside him again and touched his face with a soft fingertip to stop his snoring. He pulled her to him in his sleep, and she lay there listening to the day. Wokweesi came and stretched against her back. If only she could freeze time, she would never leave this moment.

Eva thought of the road ahead, time flowing under her feet, impossible to dam even if she blocked it with her body. Though she looked forward to a new life with Jim's people and the adventure that entailed, her worries swirled around more immediate concerns. What was she going to do about Tophe? When he finally arrived at El Copano in March, their original time and destination, she would have caught up to him in the time stream, but over one hundred miles would still separate them. For all that, the real problem was what to say to him, how to act. She had less than three months to figure out a solution, and her heart broke when she saw his face smiling at her in her mind's eye. He had been her other half, a brother in every way.

"I can hear you thinking, notsaʔka."

"I'm thinking of Tophe," Eva said.

He stiffened. "What about him?"

"All the same questions. Do I try to stop him? Do I disappear without a word? Do I try to save him from Lux Libera? What do I do about Lux Libera? Do I try to fight them?"

Jim rolled her on top of him. "You don't worry about any of those questions. You worry about being my nupetsu, my wife." He looked up at her, concern in his eyes. "The Texian war is not our war. What does it matter if you stop Tophe this time? Won't he continue his life?"

"But what if I could convince him of the truth — like Pump did for me? Tophe is a good man. He deserves to be free, to choose his own way." She laid her forehead against his and peered into his eyes.

"Is there another Eva somewhere wondering the same thing?"

Eva rolled off him. "I never believed so before. I thought I was unique. Perhaps there are an infinite number of Evas who can travel and are lying with their husbands on a blanket, worrying about their Tophes."

"If there are so many Evas and Jims and Tophes and Lux Liberas, and between them, they are all making all the choices possible, what does it matter?" he asked. "It all happens, does it not?"

"That's what Pump thinks." She watched a fat squirrel leap to another tree branch. "There must be worlds where the squirrels became the people," she said, gesturing at the canopy. "What would those be like?"

Jim grinned. "Lots of tree houses, I expect." He looked at the horses and Wokweesi. "What would a dog world be like? Or a horse world?"

"I've only ever seen timelines with humans. The worlds can be topsy-turvy, but it was always human people. Your enemy here would be your ally there," she said.

"There is no world where I'd be allied with a Tonkawa."

Eva laughed and poked a finger in his chest. "Not only that, but there are worlds where you are the cannibal."

Jim grabbed her hand and bit around her finger with a growl.

As he clamped down, Eva tugged, catching her knuckle.

He released her finger and said, "Nope, don't think so. Too tough."

With her imagination sparked, Eva put her sore finger to her lips. "Perhaps all the possibilities are just probabilities? The paths are laid out, every possible path, but it doesn't come into being until you choose. Like the tree," she said, pointing at the canopy, "all laid out, but the squirrel chooses which branch to run along, and everything else fades to the periphery."

Eva ran her eyes up from the trunk and down the winding branches to the leaves. "What if your 'fate' is the sum of your last two choices? It's not really fate, but your choices have narrowed because of the path you have taken." She lifted a finger and counted off in her head as she scanned the trees again.

A corner of Jim's mouth rose. "What are you doing?"

"Fibonacci's sequence. You add the last two numbers to get the next number in the line. So: 0+1=1, 1+1=2, 1+2=3."

Clearly unimpressed, Jim's face blanked. "I don't follow any of what you just said."

"But then," she said, holding up her hand for patience, "2+3=5, 3+5=8, 5+8=13, and so on. It's everywhere in nature." Eva turned her head to point up at the tree again. "Look, if the ground is one, and the trunk is one, what number do you see next?"

Jim followed her finger to the first split of the nearest tree's trunk. "Two."

"Now, imagine a straight, horizontal line and go up to the next branching. You see the three?"

"Mmm."

"The next is five," she said, her words coming faster with excitement.

He raised a brow, unsure. "And?"

Eva cast her gaze around the meadow, but it was too late in the year, and she didn't even know if they grew here yet. "It's easier to see on a sunflower. Anyway, what if our timelines grow like trees? We *do* have free will, but when we make a choice, it creates another set of branching points, and we make a new choice."

"Except for all the numbers you listed, I don't see how this is different than what you've been saying. I'm on a path. I come to a fork in the road. I choose to go down one instead of the other. And you think both choices, both me's doing opposite things, exist somewhere."

"I think I'm saying that all these branching choices exist as a hazy, unformed possibility, but then the branch solidifies under our little squirrel feet as we make our choices. Maybe it's a way that all possibilities can exist at once, but we still have the freedom to choose."

Jim chewed on a piece of grass, gaze distant for several moments. "But what about crazy worlds? Wouldn't those exist, too? Where you expect one thing, and something wrong happens instead?"

"A random world? Like if an anvil fell on our heads right now?"

"Yes, like that. Or other people's choices take away our own. That our squirrel feet have taken us to a certain choice, but then a hawk flies out of nowhere. Like they do. And…" Jim snatched at the air with his hand.

Eva brought her fingernails to her mouth. "I don't know." As she lay back across his chest, her thoughts twisted into a Gordian knot, then shifted to the Comanches and the narrowing choices they faced. Ones they didn't even know about yet.

Jim rubbed the crease between her eyes.

"In other timelines I've seen," she said, "the Nʉmʉnʉʉ are united with all the Tribes, even the Tonkawas, and they keep their lands safe for hundreds of years from now. I've also seen places where the people of this continent become the colonizers of the other lands across the sea, their cultures erasing all other indigenous ones before them, and much of the world speaks only Nʉmʉ tekwapʉ, Algonquian, or Lakȟótiyapi."

Jim cocked his head, alert. "And our timeline?"

Eva sat up. The words lay heavy in her mouth; she had been holding them for so long. "I can't say for sure, but the trajectory of this timeline points to the Anglos pushing the People onto a reservation in the

1870s, if not earlier. There may be just over 1500 of your people left by then."

It was Jim's turn to sit up, his eyes boring into hers. "Why haven't you told me this before?"

"Because I haven't been able to think of a way to change it that doesn't involve a lot of death or isn't too little, too late. You would have to unite all the horse tribes and all the settled tribes from here to as far north as you can go." She plucked at a fraying hole in her skirt, eyes on her lap.

Jim's mouth fell open, and his eyes widened.

"But the unification process must have started hundreds of years before now. In the timelines I've seen, the native people didn't have a mutual policy of torturing war captives to death, and... I'm guessing here... but I think they didn't have as many blood feuds because of it. Most importantly, they were willing to follow a single leader with trusted lieutenants from all the tribes. The allied tribes didn't raid each other but forged lasting treaties backed by the power of their combined might. The Europeans stayed east of the Appalachians and never pushed farther. Some lines even pushed the Europeans into the sea.

"The Nʉmʉnʉʉ in this timeline," she said, pointing at the ground, "are very fierce, as you know. Too much of their life requires war to sustain it. And the Anglos will eventually react forcefully and decisively to all the raiding. The Anglo soldiers will do unspeakable things to Nʉmʉnʉʉ women and children and old men in revenge, and the People will make good on a vow to do the same, tenfold, and more. Even when treaties are signed, the Nʉmʉnʉʉ won't be able to keep their young men from raiding, and the Anglos won't be able to keep their people from settling farther and farther into Nʉmʉnʉʉ territory. One great chief will ask Sam Houston to create a clear border, but Houston will tell him that if he could build a wall from the Red River to the Rio Grande so high that no Indian could scale it, the white people would go crazy trying to devise a means to get beyond it."

Eva shook her head. "Your people seem to have begun raiding the Anglos even earlier than I've seen in other timelines, and the Anglos are encroaching on your lands more aggressively. Great war leaders will keep your people free on the plains as long as they can. The last of your people will go onto the reservation because they can't find anything to eat, not because they are defeated. All the buffalo will be shot by the Americans in a handful of years."

Jim's face contorted. "All?" he asked, breathing the word. "That's not possible."

Eva's throat constricted, and she dropped her gaze, unable to hold eye contact. "I suspect one of your most influential leaders with the Anglos during the transition to the reservation, Quanah Parker, will not be able to be born in this line. Quanah's mother, Cynthia Ann Parker, should be captured this coming May, as in other timelines, but I imagine her family's fort is more prepared for raiders in a way that other Parker homes are not."

Jim pulled a mask over his features and stared at the horizon.

Until this conversation, Eva's knowledge of the future had felt abstract — something she needed to warn Jim about, but nothing to worry over. Possibilities, not certainties. They had decades to avoid anything that might come, and she could always leave, taking Jim and anyone they loved with her.

Yet, somewhere in the back of her mind, as mere probabilities converged into realities, she realized she was part of this time stream now. To make her life here meant building extensive relationships, and self-preservation would not be enough. Jim's pain became hers with every minute that passed. In that moment, she would have given anything to have been able to travel forward in this line, to see for herself what fate awaited the Comanches, to discover she was wrong and allay his fears.

At the sight of his face, she bit her lip. Her stomach clenched, and her next breath trembled. "To complicate things further, the People have not been living among the Europeans in this timeline, so they have been safe from the diseases that have decimated the Tonkawas and the Caddos and all the other friendly tribes, diseases that don't even exist in other lines. If you could somehow change the People's entire way of life to a peaceful, settled, cooperative one with Anglos, it would kill them as surely as the coming war. As it is, the diseases will reach them anyway in the coming decades. And if I urged you to make war on the Anglos while you still could, your people would kill people like Pump and Thomas McMullen and everyone they care about."

When she stopped speaking, they sat in silence for a long time. If she had dared to touch, he would have felt carved of stone. She wanted to tell him that anything was still possible. It was not fate. But she couldn't.

"All I see is death."

Chapter 36
Jim

"I wish you hadn't told me." Jim sat away from her, and a gust of wind blew between them.

Eva studied her lap, unable to meet his eyes. "I'm sorry."

He watched her pluck a piece of dry spear grass and lightly poke the sharp point into her fingertip.

"How do you know all this?" he asked.

"This isn't the first Angel of Goliad I've been tasked with killing. Or my first mission in a Tejas like this. And there have been others in later times when this land is called Texas."

He couldn't look at her anymore. After the initial feelings of horror, he didn't know what to feel. Or think. He careened between despair, grief, and the hope that she didn't know the complete future. He should be racing to his village without delay. With growing terror, he could see the approaching dust storm like a black wall on the horizon, and everyone he loved was unaware. But what could he say? No one would believe him. They would question his bravery and loyalty, especially with a new Anglo wife at his elbow.

He propped his arms on his knees and put his head in his hands. As the agony built in his chest, he pulled at his hair. He wanted to cut it off and wail in mourning. Any children and grandchildren he had with Eva would end their days on a...

"What is a reservation?" he asked.

"North of the Red River, there will — maybe — be a state called Oklahoma. You will have a small plot of land there for all the Comanche, Apache, and Kiowa."

"With the Apache?" he asked, incredulous. They weren't as bad as the Tonkawas, but there were still bloody scores to settle. "We have to share with two other Tribes?"

Eva nodded but clarified. "Not the Lipan Apache. The Kiowa-Apache."

"What?" he asked, still confused. "The dog-eaters?"

"Who?"

"The Kiowa." The Penateka band of Nʉmʉnʉʉ had never been allied with the Kiowa. It didn't make sense to him.

Eva shrugged. "Under the right circumstances, other bands will become close friends with the Kiowa in the coming decades. The United States will try to turn you all into farmers. If events continue to unfold as I have seen, Tejas will join the union in 1845 as the state of Texas, at which point, they will have the nation's power at their backs. American settlers will flow across the border in an unending stream."

"We might as well stay here."

"That's why Pump is trying so hard to convince you to be happy here."

Jim's world shrank again. "Why didn't he tell me?"

"Same reason I haven't been able to. Because he knew it would tear you up inside. And he can see how unhappy you are. Would it be better to live a long and unhappy life or a happy one with an... unhappy ending?"

Gall flooded his mouth. He hated her for a moment. Knowing emotions were heating his blood, Jim tried to put himself in Eva's place, in Pump's place, but it was too soon. He was too angry. That they would hide these things from him. That they had known. All this time. Time he could have been warning his people. Their double betrayal seared lines across his heart with a white-hot blade.

"Your people who survive are resilient. They don't stop being Nʉmʉnʉʉ. They find new ways to honor the old ways, and they grow, even in the face of other challenges," she said.

"What other challenges?" he heard himself ask.

Eva bit her lip and turned away.

"What other challenges?" he repeated, raising his voice.

"Like all the other Tribes, the Nʉmʉnʉʉ may have to weather forced assimilation. Their children might be taken away to be raised in boarding schools. The schools may mistreat them, even causing their deaths without explanation or acknowledgment. And their reservation lands might be broken up and stolen. The United States will probably not honor the treaties."

She squeezed her hands together, her voice lifting as if to offer some sort of silver lining. "In spite of all this, in the lines I've seen like this one, your people will preserve their history and identity. There are individuals who become renowned artists and scientists, warriors who distinguish themselves in the coming world wars...." Her voice dwindled when she dared to look at him.

Jim narrowed his eyes. He just wanted her to stop talking.

Eva stood, walked to one of the trees, and climbed it. She sat in the cradle of the first branch with her back to him and hugged her knees to herself. After a moment, he saw her bury her face in her skirts. Her tears made him angrier.

It was hard to imagine. His people were the most powerful force on the hills and plains, well-fed, wealthy, feared, and safe. He pictured the tens of thousands of bodies that would need to die to leave far less than 2,000 of his people.

He had always wondered if, when people died, they were reborn near the same place they had died. Would all his people be reborn as Anglos? If he thought back further, were the Tribes his people had pushed out of this land reborn as Nʉmʉnʉʉ? If every possibility existed, he thought bitterly, his theory was true somewhere, and it made him sick.

Jim watched the sun travel across the sky. His senses numbed to the enormity of the pain, and he packaged the knowledge away while he was still brave enough to touch it with his bare hands. Jim thought about what Eva had said about the other timelines. He wanted the knowledge to make him feel better, to maybe go there with everyone he loved, but those other Nʉmʉnʉʉ were strangers.

ele

Hours passed before Jim calmed down. He stood at the base of the tree.

Eva peered down at him, her face streaked red. She flushed deeper, her eyes skittering away. "I'm tired of crying. I never cried before I came to this world." She attempted a watery smile, but it crumpled, and fresh tears rolled down her cheeks. "I know too much. I've done too much. I don't know what to do with it all. I never want to hurt you. Or anybody. I'm sorry I told you."

He pulled himself into the tree and straddled the wide branch in front of her. "No. I needed to know. And I see that there would never be a right time to tell me."

"I was born Texan in my childhood timeline," she said. "My mother's Anglo ancestors pushed the Nʉmʉnʉʉ and other Tribes out. I don't know what to do with that either."

"And I was born Anglo and live as a Nʉmʉ," he said. "My Anglo parents and grandparents pushed out the native peoples in the states we moved through. My Anglo great-grandparents were transported here by force from Scotland by the English. My people pushed out the Wichita and the Apache from these lands. Others, too. I carry all of that." He wiped wet hair out of her face. "How far back do we go? Who lived here before those Tribes?"

"It's the scale," Eva said. "Like a torch set to a prairie, entire peoples are and will be cleansed away. It's already happened in the east."

Tongue-tied and overwhelmed, Jim skimmed a thumb across her cheeks. "All we can do is try to make the next right choice."

"You don't understand. I helped."

He put his hand under her chin and lifted her eyes. "Remember what I said to you the night you came to me? You and I are the same. We have both done things we regret that seemed right at the time."

"Is it even possible to make a 'right' choice without causing someone to suffer somewhere?" she asked.

"I don't know." He laced her fingers with his own. "Would we be bored if suffering didn't exist?" His joke fell flat even to his own ears.

She released his hands and dried her nose on her sleeve. "That's what I've wondered: is God bored? And if so, what does that mean about right and wrong?"

"I know I want to live in a world where people care about right and wrong, about honor," he said.

"And what about suffering?"

"We choose whether or not we suffer, but it's hard for me to imagine a world without pain." Would anything be able to move in such a world? To even take a step caused pain to a plant or an insect. Birth. Growth. Love and Loss. Death. All took or gave pain. "Every good thing seems to have its matching bad thing, don't you think? Life can't happen without death."

Eva shut her eyes and rolled her head. "What's the point of it all? What do you think happens when we die?" she asked.

Jim wondered if she had read his mind earlier. He told her his theory.

She twisted her mouth in thought. "The ancient Greeks said the dead had to drink from the river of forgetfulness, the Lethe, before they could be reborn. Pump said God forgets Itself. That we each are a single particle of God experiencing the world." She stuck a finger through a hole in her skirt and chuckled.

"What?"

"I was just picturing the river Lethe as a water park," she said. At his confusion, she explained, "Water parks are from my time. They are enormous man-made pools, like lakes, for swimming. And into these pools, they have long slides that people can ride down and splash into the deep water."

Jim pictured it in his mind. It sounded fantastical.

"What if we're like souls at the top of the water slides? We have to choose which slide we're going to take. Our choice will be our new life. Do we know ahead of time what lies at the end? Do we get to choose between options and then forget as we ride through the waters? Or are they all dark tunnels?"

He shook his head, bemused by her imagination. "I have a different question for you," he said. "Would you know me from all the other Jims that exist? Would I know you?"

"I want to believe that my soul would recognize yours no matter where it was in the multi-verse, even when you are no longer Jim, and I am no longer Eva."

Jim leaned forward and kissed her on the mouth. It still felt wrong to do so but in a delicious sort of way. He motioned for her to stand so they could trade places. He sat again, leaning against the broad trunk, and held her. Once they were comfortable, he noticed the sun touching the horizon. Jim rubbed his hands up and down Eva's pimply arms. It would be colder soon, but he wasn't ready to leave.

"I'm getting stronger," Eva said. "In my ability, I mean."

"Oh?"

"I think I might be able to jump you with me."

"You can do that?"

"Of course. How do you think I don't end up naked on the other end? Or that I create a portal in the first place?"

It took a moment for Jim to understand what she was saying. The idea was too exciting to be true. "Can you do it now? Can you put us on the blanket?"

"I can try, but we should stand. We'll need to step into the portal."

Eva rose to her feet and balanced on the branch in front of him. "Hold on to my waist," she said. "And don't let go, no matter what."

Her words brought him up short. He wouldn't have let go, but now that she had said don't, he worried his hands would let go of their own accord. And what would happen if he did let go? He dug his fingers into her dress.

"Ouch, easy," she said. "Actually, I can just use this tree if you would feel safer with me holding on to you?"

Jim scoffed, pride pricked. "This is fine. You need to practice the air method, anyway."

"Okay." She opened her hands, and the air shimmered in front of them like a heat mirage on the high plains. "Ready?"

Jim stared into the wavering pool, mesmerized. When he could respond, he nodded until he realized her back was to him. He cleared his throat. "Yes."

"Walk forward with me."

Jim's foot trailed hers. She disintegrated in front of him, and then his feet dropped to level ground on the blanket faster than his eye could see. He let go of her waist. An internal check told him he felt exactly the same as before they jumped, but he counted his fingers and wiggled his toes to be sure. Eva beamed over her shoulder at him.

"Can you take us and the horses home?" he asked, breathless with possibilities.

Eva grinned wider at his excitement. "Not yet, but soon. And I'll be able to do more than that — you'll be able to travel with me. Give me a few days. I'm gonna find you a waterpark."

Chapter 37

Jim

Jim's Farm

Jim watched Eva as she lifted the rifle stock to her shoulder and looked down the barrel. She had stuffed cotton into her ears, which he thought was a little silly, but she had been doing it every time she shot, and he was used to it now. Thankfully, she had stopped trying to get him to adopt the practice.

Eva squeezed the trigger, and the pan flashed. After a breath of delay, the shot echoed through the trees and down the river. Chips of rock flew off her target over two hundred yards away. A cloud of smoke engulfed her and then drifted toward the river. She rarely missed and could still be accurate several yards farther distant. His shots struck home about half the time.

She glanced back at him, and he handed her another ball and cartridge to load down the front of the barrel. With practiced ease, Eva tore the paper with her teeth. If he could get her to improve her stalking technique, she would be the ideal hunting partner. A quick peek in his pouch told him he'd need to cast more bullets soon.

Eva wore one of her new dresses, the brown one. He thought it made her look as drab as a sparrow and preferred the blue dress she had tucked away for special occasions, like a good Anglo woman. Her gray-green eyes turned as blue as the sky when she wore it for him. Wisely, she had ignored the sunbonnet and buried it at the bottom of his cedar chest. He had told her she would get nothing but a sunburn when they returned to his people if she tried to lighten her skin this winter.

As she raised the rifle to her shoulder again, Wokweesi barked. Jim peered back at the house and the rider approaching. His heart soared. Rʉtsima! Instantly, confusion replaced his initial joy. It was an uncommon time to raid, and his brother was alone. He took off at a run, with Eva close behind.

Rʉtsima pulled the saddle off his horse as they neared. His feet shuffled as he moved about his task, and his horse dripped with sweat. Jim locked eyes with Eva and jutted his chin toward the house. He reflected with satisfaction that he could trust her now to build up the fire and prepare for a guest without instruction. She would not shame him.

Rʉtsima freed his horse to join Jim's herd, and they embraced in a side hug around the enormous bundle in his arms. Jim took it from him.

"I'm glad to see you, but what brings you here?"

Anxiety pinched Rʉtsima's face, and he clasped Jim's upper arm. "Father is dying. He hopes to see you one last time. He wants his whole family around him before he leaves the village."

Jim furrowed his brow. His father was one of the strongest men he knew. Though the older warrior no longer went on raids, Jim had never been able to best him at wrestling, or much of anything for that matter. "Is he sick?"

"Yes. He's been weakening all summer. I should have told you last time I was here, but he seemed to be getting better." His brother turned toward the house. "None of Tatsiwóo's songs or cures have worked, and even Noyer's Beaver Ritual failed." He stopped walking and cupped Jim's shoulder. "You won't recognize him, I think. He's grown very old, very skinny, and he's become short-tempered when he can't manage the things he used to. His friends have said their goodbyes. It's just family that goes near him now. He is also angry that some people think he has broken an oath and is sick because of it."

"Our father would never break an oath," Jim said.

"The people that matter don't believe it. His friends have reassured him as much as he will let them."

Jim noted the sun. Most of the day was gone, and they would need to prepare. His mind tallied problems and solutions. Among his disjointed thoughts, he decided they could send animals to the Allens.

Though still chilly when they stepped into the cabin, Eva had a good fire going and bustled around the hearth, crouching over the kettle. She stood and turned a warm face their way. "Welcome, Husband," she said with a slight Anglo accent. Jim swelled with pride.

Rutsima's naked brows shot up in surprise. "Husband?" A wide smile spread across his face. "And she speaks like a person?"

Jim laughed in turn. "Yes, Eva and I are married now. And… she's learning."

After a moment, Eva passed his brother a bowl of stew and turned back to the kettle while Rutsima settled on the bench. Jim sat on the floor, wrapping his arms around his knees to leave room for her to work.

Abruptly, Rutsima's spoon hovered over his bowl, and his eyes filled with concern. "What about her strange medicine?" he asked, tilting his head at Eva.

"A misunderstanding. Her vow was not like our power, and she has been released from it."

Eva banged the spoon against the kettle and hung it on its hook.

Relief smoothed his brother's features, and he finished putting the bite in his mouth.

Jim sat quietly, determined to give his brother a chance to catch his breath. When he could contain his impatience no longer, and Rutsima was halfway through a second bowl, Jim peppered him with more questions. "Where are you camped?"

His brother swallowed and named a place two and a half days' ride from their cabin.

Jim ran the trail through his head. "What's in the bundle?"

"Buffalo robes. One for each of you." Rutsima grinned. "I thought you might still have your woman." He grinned wider. "I saw how you looked at her. Even if she wouldn't let you have her."

Jim blew out in genuine relief. A buffalo robe would shield them from the cold better than four Anglo coats. The overnight part of their trip would still be frigid, but it would be much more tolerable with proper protection.

"What happen?" Eva asked in broken Comanche.

"My father is sick." Jim enunciated each word and paused while she translated in her head. "We will go to him." His brother watched them with interest. Eva nodded and went back to what she was doing.

Over the next hour, Rutsima shared gossip from the village, though every half-hearted laugh he made revealed his thoughts remained at his father's bedside.

Finally, Jim and Eva left him to rest, so they could gather the things they'd need for the trip. As they moved about the farm together, they discussed getting the animals to the Allens. It made the most sense to take them when they departed at first light. It would only delay them about an hour.

While they worked, Jim noticed Eva's demeanor became more and more introspective. Just before he was going to say something, she asked, "Is your brother going to want me in his bed tonight?"

Jim cast his eyes to the cabin and grunted. "No, he's exhausted, and he's preoccupied with our father. He won't be in the mood."

Eva let out a breath.

Jim realized he didn't know how he felt about gifting her. On the one hand, he didn't mind, and he owed his brother the reciprocation, but on the other, seeds of selfishness or jealousy took root — feelings that had never been a problem for him. "None of my brothers will expect it during this trip home, given what's happening right now. Plus, they're in camp with their wives. If it was the summer, and you were accompanying us on a long raid, and their wives had stayed home, or I left you with one of my brothers while I was away, then...."

When he didn't continue, she asked, "Then what?"

"I don't know. Let's cross that creek when we get to it."

Eva's face clouded. Though she was no longer Anglo, she had been born so. He stopped her as she closed up a sack and placed his hands on her waist. "Please know that when brothers share wives, it is the deepest gesture of kinship and respect. It doesn't mean I don't love or value you. It means the opposite. You are my most prized possession that I gift only to those closest to me. They will marry you if I am killed and care for our children as if they were their own. In fact, they will call our children their sons and daughters."

Briefly, Eva dropped her eyes to the floor of the dogtrot. "I understand. I do. I've seen lots of different ways to live over the years, none of them perfect, and I see the value in the Nʉmʉ way, but I don't want to be your possession. I belong to you, but I don't *belong* to you. I want to come to you freely because I choose to. I want to be allowed to choose if I go to your brother or not."

Jim studied her earnest face and then pulled her close, resting his forehead against hers. She held his promise in her fist. "I will think of something."

"Thank you," she whispered and kissed him.

When she drew back, he sighed. "No more kissing on the lips, I'm afraid. At least until we're back here."

"Even in secret?"

"Only if we're sure we're alone. Which is hard in the village."

Eva frowned, jaw jutting forward.

Jim chuckled. "Don't worry. I can make it up to you in other ways," he said as he reached around, squeezing her bottom and nuzzling her neck. "We can go off together to hunt wild plums."

"In winter? That won't fool anyone."

"It never does."

She giggled but then stiffened at the sight of something behind him. He heard the jangling of harness and turned to look. "Two visitors in one day. Pump is not going to be pleased to find Rutsima here."

"At least it will save us leaving a note for him," she said.

"True."

Jim grabbed Eva's hand, and they walked down the steps. Pump set the brake and descended in one motion. His eyes brimmed with unshed tears.

"What's happened?" Eva asked. She opened her arms to him, and he enveloped her. Her eyes widened with fear over his shoulder.

"Pump, what's happened?" Jim's voice projected louder than he intended.

The older man released Eva. "The McMullen's plantation was raided. They were killed."

Jim's stomach fell, and Eva's hand flew to her mouth.

"When?" Jim asked. "Today? Last night?"

"No, we think two or three days ago, maybe four. The raiders are long gone. They took all the slaves and all the livestock. The slave quarters were burned."

"Was anyone else killed besides Tom and Hortensia?" Jim asked.

"No, just them." Pump sucked a ragged breath. The older man's tears pushed against a dam Jim feared would not hold. After lifting his hat, Pump dragged a hand over his scalp and down his face.

Eva took his arm and led him to the cabin. "Let's get you inside. You can tell us more while you have something to eat."

"You should know my brother is here," Jim said. Before the look of betrayal could settle on Pump's face, he added, "My father is dying, and he has called me home. We plan to be back here in a couple of weeks."

An odd look came over Pump's face, but he let Eva lead him, and Jim followed.

Inside the cabin, Jim made introductions to his brother. Rutsima's face shifted to a wooden mask, quiet and watchful. He looked like a different man.

Pump refused to sit at first until Eva convinced him to rest on the edge of the bed. It was warm in the cabin now, and she handed him a cup of coffee.

He waved away food, and his coffee sat in his hand, untouched.

"They are saying it was Comanches," Pump said.

Jim scoffed and translated for his brother. After a moment of backstory combined with the accusation, Rutsima sniffed loudly. "Ata-bitsi-nuu uruu-ma pahí-nu Yuniwat narumuʔikatu."

"He says non-Comanches attacked them, and I agree with him." He decided it was prudent not to translate Rutsima's name for Pump: Yuniwat. No Hair. "Were any scalps taken?" Jim asked.

"No, but there were plenty of arrows."

Jim translated again, and his brother looked as puzzled as Jim felt. "Most bands don't raid during the winter, at least not often. Maybe the Wichita? Or Kiowa?" At a thought, he asked if anyone was at war with the Anglos, but his brother shook his head and shrugged. "What were the arrows fletched with? How were they tied? Were they marked?" Jim asked.

"I don't know, but I don't think it was the Comanches or the Wichita or Kiowa," Pump said, his voice sparking against flint. "I believe it was the Saltwater Tribes." Pump's eyes ignited with unspoken emotion. His words flayed Jim alive, leaving him exposed and unsure. Disappointment, rage, and hate layered Pump's fiery gaze.

Chapter 38

Jim

E va bit her knuckle. His mentor's look passed as quickly as it had ignited, but left Jim scorched by feelings he wouldn't have expected to be directed at him.

His thoughts leapfrogged from one point to another. What Pump said made sense. Only the McMullens had been killed. All the men "taken." Livestock, not just horses. No scalps. They were wise to come in winter. Very risky for their people, but harder to follow. And if they had prepared with horses, buffalo robes…

Nausea replaced Jim's urge to rejoice when he saw Tom's face in his mind's eye. When Caesar and Kitch said they would return for their families, this wasn't what he had pictured. For a moment, he feared he would shame himself in front of them all. He took a deep breath and swallowed.

Pump darted his eyes at Eva, his mouth working against indecision, but then he seemed to make up his mind. "Hortensia's body was mutilated. They left Thomas alone. We don't know if it was done before… or after."

Firelight flickered over Eva's drained face, and dark shadows ringed her dry eyes, transforming her into an unblinking skull.

Jim translated, and Rutsima grunted in response. Mystery solved.

Pump took out his pipe, put it back in his pocket, and stared at the fire. After a moment, he turned to Jim. "People are saying you were involved in the attack as revenge for Hortensia's treatment of Eva."

"What?" Eva's mouth dropped open in shock, and she found Jim's eyes.

"It's why I came here as fast as I could. To warn you." Pump regarded Rutsima, whose blank face remained in place. "If you leave with your brother and return in two weeks from Comanche country, it will confirm their suspicions."

"Are you saying we should stay?" Weights descended upon Jim's shoulders, with filial duty sitting on one side and his promise to Pump on the other.

"With passions as high as they are, I don't know if I can dispel the rumors as easily as I have in the past." Reluctance appeared to stop Pump's tongue, and several moments passed as he worked it loose. "I think I'm telling you you need to go and not return." He removed his glasses to rub his eyes with fingers and thumb before pinching the bridge of his nose. Pump curled the wires back over his ears and looked at him.

Jim read profound sadness on his friend's face. Pump's mistake so many years ago had cost Jim's family their lives. That open wound had started to close but now was ripping apart again.

"I release you from your promise to me." Pump's words echoed around the cabin with the finality of a judge's sentence.

Jim took a step back, adrift. He scanned Pump, Eva, and back again. He should be happy. Free. It was what he wanted. But he didn't want to leave like this. From across the room, he could feel Eva's heart reaching out to him.

"You shouldn't wait until morning. You should leave as soon as you can. I'll take your animals to my place."

With those directives, Jim saw Eva shift to action, taking stock of the cabin. Everything would go now. Suddenly, she paused and focused on Pump. "Do you know about the Runaway Scrape and San Felipe being torched?"

"Yes, and with the tearaways we have in town, I think it's likely the citizens will set fire to their own city in this timeline before Sam Houston even orders it. I've already started burying valuables. I don't want to leave too early, but don't worry, honey, my family and I will be the first on the road north."

Eva visibly relaxed and left the cabin, but Jim froze, untethered, and the world accelerated without him.

Eva

There had been too much to do, too much to think of, too much to pack. Eva peered around the bare and dark cabin. She held a precious candle aloft and searched the corners and under the bed and table. Everything of use had been collected, and Jim waited outside with the men.

It came too abruptly, this parting. Eva didn't want to stay, but she wanted to have a chance to say goodbye, to have a few more luminous weeks alone with Jim. She felt robbed.

Hortensia and Tom crept into her thoughts. Eva could imagine their bodies well enough. As she closed her eyes, a tear leaked through. They were the first Fated ones she had ever acknowledged as real who had died, and she mourned for them almost as if they had been Lux Libera.

Eva's stomach twisted when she backtracked the forking paths of a lifetime of choices that led to their death. Which branch would have ended in a different outcome? She pictured the Saltwater Tribes as hawks swooping down on the plantation. If she held a weapon, would she shoot? The choice to save one was often the choice to destroy another. And which was more worthy?

Neither.

Both.

Jim's voice called to her. She rubbed the lone tear from her cheek and wiped her nose. Her soul contained only an empty reservoir now, a hollow cavity in which she could curl if she chose to, the despair acting as a filter on her heart. All her deeds camped beyond the soundproof door, too big to fit.

Breathing in deeply, she wanted to remember the smells. Wood smoke, furs, leather, metal, monotonous stew, skunky dog, the unique scent of her man. She gave herself one more moment to feel only through her senses and then clothed her heart and soul within her body once again. She snuffed the candle and left it on the bench.

When she stepped onto the dogtrot, she saw all the horses had been rounded up. Most were bridled with lead lines attached to a long rope that began with her gelding, and their baggage was spread across several backs. Pump had the ox tied to the back of his wagon and their chickens in crates. He was placing the rest of their salt pork in the bed.

The cold seeped into her bones, and her breath steamed in the moonlight. There was nothing left to do but leave.

Rutsima mounted his horse and politely ignored them as they said their goodbyes. Jim held out his hand, and Pump yanked him into a hug. As he embraced him, he whispered in Jim's ear. Jim bobbed his head, and then Pump thumped him on the back and pulled away. Tears threatened in both their eyes.

Pump turned to Eva and hugged her.

She inhaled softly. She would think of Pump when she smelled pipe smoke.

"Take care of Jim. You're good for him, and he's good for you," Pump said into the top of her hair.

Eva nodded.

He tightened his squeeze and released her, but held her elbows. "We will see each other again, Eva," he said, drilling into her with an intensity that would make it so. He repeated his words to Jim.

Jim gnawed his lip, eyes glued to the ground as he placed his hand on the small of her back. She could hear his breath catching.

Pump climbed onto his buckboard, and Jim escorted Eva to her gelding, Wokweesi at their heels. After she mounted, he handed up her buffalo robe and helped her arrange it around herself. Jim got onto his own horse, and when he was ready, he kicked Nʉena to a walk. Eva nudged her pony to follow, and the baggage creaked behind her. Rʉtsima would protect their rear. Eva gazed back one last time to Pump in his wagon. He saw her and raised a silhouetted arm. In answer, she brought her hand to her lips and sent him a kiss.

For a moment longer, Eva scanned the little farm, committing it to memory, then turned in her saddle to face the new, unexpected road ahead.

ele

The adventure continues in Book 2, *The Captive.*
Available HERE on Amazon!

If you enjoyed reading *The Mender*, I always appreciate reviews! They mean everything to independent authors like me. The Amazon search algorithm favors books with many reviews, which means more readers can find my work, and I can keep writing. Please consider leaving one on Amazon, Goodreads, or BookBub.

And I love, love, love hearing from readers! For links to contact me, view fun extras, leave a review, or purchase the next book, *The Captive*, please visit:

https://jennifermarchman.com/tmc

Reading a print copy? Use your phone's camera to follow the link:

Notes &
Acknowledgments

Full notes available at:
  jennifermarchman.com/authors-note/

I considered writing only about the people I am descended from, but I don't live in Norway, Germany, or the British Isles. I don't know those places. When I visited a cousin in Hønefoss, Norway, though it was the most beautiful landscape I had ever seen, my heart did not recognize the mountains.

I make my home in Texas. I have swum in Barton Springs Pool, where Jim took Eva to feel the water. I can imagine a Comanche raiding party laughing around a campfire in my backyard. A spring that never runs dry is located conveniently at the bottom of the hill from my home. To drive into west downtown Austin is to travel through a Tonkawa village before the Anglos forced the tribe to leave.

With some regularity, I cross the intersection of Braker Lane and Mopac Expressway, where Josiah Wilbarger, an early settler in Austin, was scalped and left for dead on an August day in 1832. After he revived, he tried to walk six miles to Reuben Hornsby's house but collapsed under a giant post oak tree. During the night, his deceased sister came to him in a vision and said, "Josiah, you are too weak to go by yourself. Remain here, and friends will come to take care of you before the setting sun."

Reuben's wife Sarah saw Josiah alive in a dream, woke her husband and the survivors from the attack who had escaped, and insisted they return to search for him. The men humored her if only to bury Josiah's body, but were shocked to find him alive where she had said he would be and able to stand. He survived another eleven years, something of a local celebrity, though his injury killed him in the end when he hit his thinning skull on a low door frame. I shiver whenever I cross the Braker Lane overpass and think of his ghostly beloved sister saving him.

As I travel south on Mopac, I can look to my right and see Mount Bonnell, over which a raiding party crisscrossed to escape with captives. They headed north, riding hard, back along the road I have just driven when it was still just a trail. When they stopped at a spring, a little brother begged his older sister to calm down, but she would not and was killed and scalped on a slight rise at Mopac and Spicewood Springs Road, now located beneath an office building and parking lot on Wood Hollow Drive. Her family, though heartbroken, mourned her death as the better, preferable outcome to life as a captive, even if they could have recovered her.

Nʉmʉnʉʉ Sookobitʉ. Comanchería. Tejas. Texas — different names for a rich, vast land, though there have been many more through the millennia. I live on the limestone balconies, gateway to what is now called the Texas Hill Country, and I was born on the Blackland Prairie. On an annual pilgrimage to Colorado, many Texans escape the August heat, and we pass through the Llano Estacado and Palo Duro Canyon, the Comanches' last refuge before the reservation period.

Though separated by time and differentiated by culture, humans worldwide are, quite literally and biologically, cousins, and I believe all the people who have walked the hills and plains of Texas are my people. Not directly, but collectively. The beautiful acts of great humanity, the desperate, vengeful brutalities, and everything in between are how we got to now. When discussing any society, romantics often focus only on the perfect, and enemies often remember only the savagery. Humans are both and always have been. Many of us have long memories regarding the wrongs other people have done to us and short ones concerning our own cruel deeds, but we need to remember it all and learn from both.

My characters are individuals. Each deviates from the ideal Anglo, the ideal Mexican, and the ideal Comanche, just like all humans in any society that holds up an ideal of what it means to be a good man or a good woman.

In the current political climate, it can be a controversial thing for a white woman to include non-white characters. I believe the alternative, an all-white cast, is far worse, perpetuating the sense that this land was open and free for the taking. It is difficult to write a story set in 1836 Texas and not include Comanches, Mexicans, Tonkawas, Tejanos, and Africans. That said, I have chosen a period in which the Comanches are at the height of their power, and I have steered clear of writing my main characters from anything other than the point of view of an Anglo or an Anglo captive.

Jim exists in an interesting space in time. Each people, Anglo and Comanche, are privy to only half his story. No one alive today can write authentically from his point of view, but I hope I've done him justice.

When using the sources listed below, I followed the example of Scott Zesch (*The Captured*, p. 304): "When two sources disagreed, I gave more credence to eyewitness testimony than hearsay, and to earlier rather than later sources."

Tikkun Olam

Tikkun Olam is an ancient concept in Judaism and comes from the earliest use of the phrase mip'nei tikkun ha-olam, which means "for the sake of repairing the world." As one can imagine, this concept has been picked apart, studied, prayed upon, argued over, retranslated, and reinterpreted by generations of faithful scholars. I have seen this phrase referenced in modern times as humanity's partnership with God to make the world a better place through good deeds. Interestingly, some older interpretations discuss returning the world to a state of spiritual bliss, effectively ending the material world. Both ideas inspired Lux Libera and Pump.

Dr. Steve Lundy, Department of Classics, University of Texas, helped with the translation of Lux Libera.

String Theory

For Eva's ability to travel between dimensions, I took inspiration from String Theory. Real physicists will scoff, but that's why my book is science fiction.

<u>Sources:</u>

Books:

- Greene, Brian. *The Elegant Universe: Superstrings, Hidden Dimensions, and the Quest for the Ultimate Theory.* New York: W.W. Norton, 2003.

- Greene, Brian. *The Hidden Reality: Parallel Universes and the Deep Laws of the Cosmos.* New York: Alfred A. Knopf, 2011.

Anglo Society

Living in Central Texas, the details of Anglo society were the easiest to research, and some I just knew from growing up here. Several of the Anglo names can be found on Austin's Old Three Hundred roster, including Pumphrey Brunet. Versions of both Jim's small cabin and the McMullen's larger house can be seen at the living history museums listed below.

The most enlightening factoid I learned while researching this book was exactly how lucrative the cotton business was based on how much a single man could be expected to pick in a day, how many pounds an acre could yield on average, and the price of cotton. Jim earned $230 from his measly harvest in 1835. Think about that for a little bit, what that kind of money meant at that time, and one begins to have a sick understanding of the greed-induced ruthlessness and moral equivocation regarding the use of slavery to maximize mind-boggling profits.

The dance Jim and Eva attend is a contra dance, and it's a lot of fun.

Sources:

Books:

- Keer, Jeffrey. *The Republic of Austin.* Austin: Waterloo Press, 2010.

- Moss, Helen. *Life in a Log Cabin: On the Texas Frontier.* Austin: Eakin Press, 1982.

Journals:

- Temin, Peter. "The Causes of Cotton-Price Fluctuations in the 1830s." The Review of Economics and Statistics 49, no. 4 (1967): 463-70. Accessed July 25, 2021. doi:10.2307/1928330.

Museums:

- Jourdan-Bachman Pioneer Farms in Austin, TX. https://www.pioneerfarms.org/

- San Felipe de Austin State Historic Site in San

Felipe, TX.
https://www.thc.texas.gov/historic-sites/san
-felipe-de-austin-state-historic-site

- Washington-on-the-Brazos State Historic
  Site in Washington, TX.
  https://www.thc.texas.gov/historic-sites/was
  hington-brazos-state-historic-site

Websites:
- Land Grants and Political Divisions,
  1821-1836.
  https://legacy.lib.utexas.edu/maps/atlas_texas
  /texas_land_grants.jpg

- Association, T. A. A. D. (n.d.). Traditional
  Austin Area Dance Association. TAADA.
  https://www.taada.us/

- Texas State History Society *Handbook of
  Texas* website:
  https://www.tshaonline.org/home

Comanche Captives

Originally, Eva was the only protagonist, but when
she met Jim, he insisted he wasn't Anglo. He would
not shut up about it or let me sleep until I recorded
his point of view, too.

I want to thank Prof. Joaquín Rivaya-Martínez
at Texas State University for his correspondence,
advice, and willingness to have a Zoom call to answer

my many questions. He specializes in Comanche captivity and generously shared two excellent articles with me.

I also relied upon Scott Zesch's *The Captured* and Clinton Smith's and Rachel Plummer's narratives. Most of Jim's experiences (both while living as a Comanche and being forcibly returned to Anglo society) can be found whole cloth, or as echoes, in the true life experiences of Rachel Plummer, Clinton Smith, Adolf Korn, Banc Babb, Dot Babb, Temple Friend, Minnie Caudle, Herman Lehmann (first taken as an Apache captive who then ran away to the Comanche), and (my favorite) Rudolph Fischer.

Of the nine, only Rudolph Fischer was able to return to his Nʉmʉ wives after being reunited with his German family. He lived out the rest of his days on the reservation as Quanah Parker's right-hand man. Adolf Korn, who survived breaking his leg, crawling from camp to camp, and hiding from his master while he healed, never did readjust to life among the whites and died a hermit in a cave near Mason, TX.

Over the generations, most Comanche captives were Mexican, and their accounts survive mainly in untranslated official Mexican government reports rather than in sensationalized personal narratives. Such documents are at the center of Prof. Rivaya-Martínez's research and hopefully will shed more light on the captive experience in the future.

Regardless of origin, it is interesting to note that some adopted men became more brutal to captives than Comanche-born men and women. I explored this a little with Kuhtu.

I took only one poetic license with Jim's story. While it is plausible Tatua could have sold Jim to the mission, it is not probable. But that's the fun of fiction and alternate timelines. A woman or a child would be sold by their owner for ransom (and that's sometimes why they were taken in the first place), but a fully integrated warrior would not have been. Such a man was no longer owned by anyone. Though a former captive might have to fight harder for status than a full-blood Comanche, they were not second-class citizens, and someone selling a free man would have been committing a heinous crime akin to murder.

It is also unlikely the mission would have been interested in buying a non-Catholic Anglo, and Jim's family wasn't around to lobby the government for his return. It was only during the transition to the reservation period that all captives and fully integrated former captives were forced to return to their birth families by the U.S. government. Prior to that, over the decades, some Peneteka chiefs worked toward ending the taking of captives and helped those they could return to their birth families. Other individual captives were hunted down by Texas Rangers and rescued, though not all were thankful for it, such as in the tragic case of Cynthia Ann Parker and her daughter Topᵤsana.

Sources:

Books:

- Smith, Clinton L., with Hunter, J. Marvin. *The Boy Captives.* 23rd ed. Distributed by Allen and Beth Smith, Campwood, TX, 2018.

- Zesch, Scott. *The Captured: A True Story of Abduction by Indians on the Texas Frontier.* New York: St. Martin's Press, 2004.

Websites:
- Full text of "Rachel Plummer narrative; a stirring narrative of adventure, hardship, and privation in the early days of Texas, depicting struggles with the Indians and other adventures." Accessed July 15, 2021. https://archive.org/stream/rachelplummerna r00park/rachelplummernar00park_djvu.txt

Articles:
- Rivaya-Martínez, Joaquín. "Becoming Comanches: Patterns of Captive Incorporation into Comanche Kinship Networks, 1820-1875." *In On the Borders of Love and Power: Families and Kinship in the Intercultural American Southwest,* edited by David Adams and Crista DeLuzio, 47-70. Berkeley: The University of California Press, 2012.

- Rivaya-Martínez, Joaquín. "The Captivity of Macario Leal: A Tejano among the Comanches, 1847-1854." *Southwestern Historical Quarterly* 117, no. 4 (April 2014): 372-402.

Numunuu (Comanche)

I want to thank Hawana Huwuni, an enrolled Comanche tribal member, for her careful reading of my manuscript not once, but twice. She was my first beta reader. Her feedback alerted me to things I needed to triple-check and gave me valuable insight into a Comanche woman's perspective. Some of Ohayaa's, Rutsima's, or Jim's words are hers.

I'd also like to thank Carney Saupitty, Jr., Cultural Specialist at the Comanche Museum and Cultural Center in Lawton, OK. He patiently answered all my questions over a series of phone calls, emails, and an hours-long in-person interview, including allowing me to bring my horse bow and teaching me to shoot Comanche-style, and finally, reading my manuscript.

I am indebted to both Mr. Saupitty and Ms. Hawana Huwuni for the time they spent with me.

I should also mention, in 2012, when I was writing a fourth-grade curriculum for Texas history, Jimmy W. Arterberry and Tomah E. Yeahquo, who were working for the Comanche Nation at the time, recommended two of my main sources to me.

At the time of this writing, Wallace and Hoebel's book (listed below) is considered the gold standard by the museum in Lawton, but it is not without its recognized flaws. The pre-reservation Comanches left no written records, and the Santa Fe Laboratory study, upon which their book is based, didn't occur until 1933 and was conducted by researchers of

European descent. Much of pre-reservation life was fading in memories by that time, and members of only a few bands were interviewed, so it's not an exhaustively representative collection of information. Additionally, the informants were only speaking from their own experience, their own family, and their own particular band with their own unique taboos and customs.

To this day, the Comanche Nation comprises individuals and individual families with their own family lore and traditions under the umbrella of what it means to be Comanche. Enrolled members may read my book and not recognize themselves or their family history in it. I humbly beg for their grace. At all times and to the best of my ability, I aligned my narrative, even to the smallest detail, with the Comanche Museum's research, narrative, exhibit collection, and recommended sources. The official narrative is that the Comanches were a patriarchy (though other modern Comanches may disagree). They were also highly individualistic, which opened space for my female characters to have a range of experiences along a continuum of more or lesser autonomy while still functioning within a patriarchy.

One criticism leveled against Wallace and Hoebel is that they misquoted their informants. For this reason, *Comanche Ethnography* became the most important source for me. It is simply the unedited field notes from the 1933 Santa Fe Laboratory study and a thick doorstop of a book. It was fascinating to read the source material for the Wallace and Hoebel book. Each informant's voice shines through unblended, direct, and sometimes contradictory amongst themselves. Kavanaugh does a wonderful job of footnoting the instances where the Wallace and Hoebel book contradicts the informants' original interviews.

My second favorite source was *The Life of Ten Bears*. This is a collection of oral histories collected by Ten Bear's great-great-grandson, Francis Joseph "Joe A" Attocknie. These are not "myths," but true historical tales, actual deeds done by real people. Reading these versions of accounts I had already read in other sources felt more like sitting around someone's kitchen table and an uncle saying, "Did you hear about the time...?" They are rich with a unique voice and full of humor.

Being Comanche: A Social History of an American Indian Community shed light on the importance of language within the broader Comanche community, and we know from captive narratives that an individual wasn't accepted until they could speak like a Person. Language is what turned a captive into a Comanche. While writing *The Mender*, I corresponded with the Comanche Language Department, but ultimately, they were stretched too thin to verify my translation choices. Mr. Saupitty and Ms. Hawana Huwuni provided some guidance, though any remaining mistakes are my own and unintentional.

I worked from four main sources approved by the Comanche Museum and Cultural Center:

<u>Sources:</u>

Main Books:

- Attocknie, Francis Joseph. *The Life of Ten Bears: Comanche Historical Narratives.* Edited by Thomas W. Kavanagh. Lincoln; London: University of Nebraska Press, 2016.

- Foster, Morris W. *Being Comanche: A Social History of an American Indian Community.* Tucson: The University of Arizona Press, 1991.

- Kavanagh, Thomas W., E. Adamson Hoebel, Waldo R. Wedel, Gustav G. Carlson, and Robert Harry Lowie. *Comanche Ethnography: Field Notes of E. Adamson Hoebel, Waldo R. Wedel, Gustav G. Carlson, and Robert H. Lowie.* Lincoln: University of Nebraska Press, 2008.

- Wallace, Ernest and Hoebel, E. Adamson. *The Comanches: Lords of the South Plains.* Norman: University of Oklahoma Press, 1986.

Dictionaries:

Books:

- Comanche Language and Cultural Preservation Committee, compiled. *Taa Nʉmʉ Tekwapʉ̱ʔha Tʉboopʉ̱ (Our Comanche Dictionary).* Lawton, OK: Comanche Language Department, 2017.

- Wistrand-Robinson, Lila, and James Armagost. *Comanche Dictionary and*

Grammar. Second ed. Dallas, TX: SIL
International Publications, 2012.

Website:
- "Search for a Word in the Comanche
  Language Dictionary." Comanche
  Dictionary. Accessed July 15, 2021.
  https://www.webonary.org/comanche/

- *Indigenous Languages Digital Archive:
  Comanche Nation.* Ilda Dictionary. (n.d.).
  Retrieved April 12, 2022, from
  https://mc.miamioh.edu/ilda-numu/

Additional Sources:
Books:
- Archer, Jane. *Texas Indian Myths and Legends.*
  Lanham: Republic of Texas Press, 2000.

- Gelo, Daniel J. and Pate, Wayne J. *Texas
  Indian Trails.* Lanham: Republic of Texas
  Press, 2003.

- Houser, Steve; Pelon, Linda; and Arterberry,
  Jimmy W. *Comanche Marker Trees of Texas.*
  College Station: Texas A&M University
  Press, 2016.

- Wistrand-Robinson, Lila and Armagost,
  James. *Comanche Dictionary and Grammar.*
  2nd ed. Dallas: SIL International
  Publications, 2012.

Websites:
- "Collections Search: National Museum of the American Indian." Collections Search | National Museum of the American Indian. Accessed July 15, 2021. https://americanindian.si.edu/explore/collect ions/search

Tickanwa-tic (Tonkawas)

The Tonkawas call themselves "Tickanwa-tic," which means "real people." The history of Anglo-Tonkawa relations is a complex one. Dunlay called it "cooperation and battlefield comradeship...always interwoven with mutual suspicion and fear and with contempt on the part of many whites." Both communities relied on each other for survival, and those who worked closely with individual Tonkawa warriors, particularly frontiersmen and Texas Rangers, considered them friends.

By 1835, on the plains, the Tonkawas were pariah among the other nomadic tribes, not only for their alleged cannibalism but also for their alliance with the Anglos. All friendly "reservation Indians" were driven from Texas in 1859, including the Tonkawas, who were discarded when they were no longer useful. They were settled near their traditional enemies in Indian Territory (Oklahoma), and on October 23, 1862, a group of Comanche, Delaware, Shawnee,

Wichita, Caddo, and other tribes attacked the Tonkawas, massacring all but about 150 individuals.

Readers may object to Jim's and my Comanche characters' attitudes toward the Tonkawas, but they are historically accurate. Additionally, of all the Anglo sins against the Native peoples of Texas, their mistreatment and betrayal of the Tonkawas must rank at the top of the list. It's an understatement to say that the Tonkawas got a raw deal from everyone. They deserve those crimes to be acknowledged, as well as to be remembered for their bravery and friendship.

Sources:

Books:

- Dunlay, Thomas W., "Friends and Allies: The Tonkawa Indians and The Anglo-Americans, 1823-1884" (1981). Great Plains Quarterly. 1904. https://digitalcommons.unl.edu/greatplainsq uarterly/1904

Websites:

- "Placido   (Unknown–1862)."   TSHA. Accessed February 28, 2022. https://www.tshaonline.org/handbook/entri es/placido

- "Tonkawa   Indians."   TSHA.   Accessed February 28, 2022. https://www.tshaonline.org/handbook/entri es/tonkawa-indians.

- "The Tonkawa Tribe Official Website!" The Tonkawa Tribe Official Website! Accessed

February 28, 2022.
http://www.tonkawatribe.com/

Miscellaneous

Corrie ten Boom was a real person during the Holocaust who chose compassion in the face of horror and great personal danger. Her memoir made a considerable impression on me in middle school.

- Boom, ten Corrie. *The Hiding Place.* Peabody, MA: Hendrickson Publishers, 2015.

Everything I know about horse archery I learned from my buddy and competitive horse archer (and now kok-boru player), Mike Sabo. I miss riding and shooting with him as much as I miss his horses, Joker (aka Nʉena) and Miss Buttons.

I'd also like to thank Mihai Cozmei, a world record-setting horse archer, for double-checking my arrow count on how many arrows a great horse archer could release during a shooting contest.

The Saltwater Tribes may or may not have been real. My middle son's U.S. history professor mentioned them in passing during one of his lectures, but could not point to a source when further questioned. Whether or not they were real in our own timeline, I've made them real in Jim's. I was also inspired by the podcast, *Seizing Freedom*. It was important to me that the enslaved characters in my book rescued themselves. Jim just pointed them in the right direction.

- Williams, Kidada E. *Seizing Freedom*. Accessed July 15, 2021. https://www.seizingfreedom.com/

Support the San Felipe de Austin Historic Site

The San Felipe de Austin Historic Site is preserving the history of early Texas. Please consider supporting their mission.

- https://www.thc.texas.gov/historic-sites/san -felipe-de-austin-state-historic-site

Beta Readers

Many thanks to my many beta readers! You made my novel better than I ever could have alone. I already mentioned Hawana read my manuscript twice, but I also want to give a special shout-out to Laura Irani and Linda Piazza for helping me do a final, months-long, fine-toothed combing. And, of course, to my mother — I lost count of how many times she read chapters for me.

Hawana Hɨwɨni
Lisa Griggs
Evan Marchman
Susan Holey
Ayla Marchman

Dunagan Marchman
Jen Philhower
John Arnn
Betsie Eikenberry
Chris Hedge
Carney C. Saupitty Jr. Tahquinterup
Diann Marchman
Rusty Marchman
Laura Irani
Linda Piazza
Laura Galan-Wells
Leilani Lamb
Bettye Hobbs
Pam Farris
Shiloh Ryker
April Aguren
Becki Throop
Jean M. Roberts
Karleen Mauldin
Deb Collins
Gail Holey
Joshua Bellin
Shannon McKinney
Kathryn Balitsos
Debi Leonadini

Translations

Spanish

Lo siento. — I am sorry.
Está acostumbrado a estar adentro. — He is used to being inside.
Indio — Indian, Native American (The preferred modern Spanish word is indígena, or indigenous, as it is in English).
Norteamericanos — North Americans
Buenos días — Good day, Good morning
¡Lo siento mucho, señor(senores)! — I'm so sorry, sir (sirs)!
Trae comida a los hombres, por favor. — Bring food to the men, please.
Gracias — Thank you
Espadas — Spades

French

Ma crotte — My dropping

Comme ça. — Like this.
On y va. — Let's go.
Qu'est-ce que c'est? — What is it?
Merde — Shit
Baise moi. — Fuck me.
Oui, monsieur. — Yes, sir.
Absolument. — Absolutely.

Nʉmʉ tekwapʉ̱ (Comanche)

For a detailed pronunciation guide, visit
jennifermarchman.com/translations/
(or the Comanche Language Department's website:
www.talkcomanche.org
At the time of this writing, there is no pronunciation
guide on their website, but I hope that changes in the
future.)

While writing *The Mender*, I corresponded
with the Comanche Language Department, but
ultimately, they were stretched too thin to verify my
translation choices. Mr. Saupitty and Ms. Hawana
Hʉwʉni provided some guidance, though any
remaining mistakes are my own and unintentional.

Dictionaries:

Books:

- Comanche Language and Cultural
  Preservation Committee, compiled. *Taa
  Nʉmʉ Tekwapʉ̱ʔha Tʉboopʉ̱ (Our Comanche
  Dictionary)*. Lawton, OK: Comanche
  Language Department, 2017.

- Wistrand-Robinson, Lila, and James

Armagost. *Comanche Dictionary and Grammar*. Second ed. Dallas, TX: SIL International Publications, 2012.

Websites:
- "Search for a Word in the Comanche Language Dictionary." Comanche Dictionary. Accessed July 15, 2021. https://www.webonary.org/comanche/

- *Indigenous Languages Digital Archive: Comanche Nation.* Ilda Dictionary. (n.d.). Retrieved April 12, 2022, from https://mc.miamioh.edu/ilda-numu/

Nɨmɨnɨɨ Sookobitɨ — Comanchería, Comanche Territory

Pasahòo — Pigeon

Tɨe Kahuu — Little Mouse (Tɨe Tseenaʔ son)

Yehh — Officially spelled "Yee" in the Comanche language, this is a word used only by men to express surprise, positive or negative. I chose to spell it as "Yehh" so that English-speaking readers would not read it with a long ee sound.

Hɨwɨni — Dawn

Tatua — Little Toe

Kuhtu — Coals in a fire (Jim's Haitsi)

Haitsi — True friend (special relationship between men, like brothers with same obligations and privileges)

Nɨmɨnaitɨ — Live as Comanche

Wokweesi* — Prickly pear cactus (Jim's dog)

Kaayʉkwitʉ — Cheater
Nʉena — Wind (Jim's horse)
Nʉmʉ tekwapʉ — Comanche language
Muubiwokweesi — Nose Full of Cactus/Cactus Nose
(Wokweesi's full name)
Tsaatʉ — Good
Nʉmʉ — Person
Nʉmʉnʉʉ — People
Esitoyanʉʉ — Mexican Captives
Hʉpenʉʉ — Timber People
Rʉtsima — Fall by Tripping (middle brother, closest
relationship to Jim)
Tsepuhtuhte — Lance with shepherd's crook
Hiitóo — Meadowlark (woman)
Puha — Power, Medicine
Taiboo — White person
Mopai — Owl
Tsaa — Good
Pasahòo Kwitapʉ — Pigeon Dung (Jim's full
Comanche name)
Kwitawooʔwooki — Barking Buttocks
Notsaʔka — Sweetheart
Nʉmʉnaitʉ — Person living as Comanche
Ʉnha hakai nʉʉsuka? — How are you?
Tsaanʉʉmai — lazy
Anáa — Ouch
Nʉpetsʉ — Wife
Quanah — Odor
Tatsiwóo — Old Buffalo (medicine man)
Noyer — Snake (beaver medicine man for
tuberculosis)
Ata-bitsi-nʉʉ   urʉʉ-ma   pahí-nu   Yuniwat

narɨmuʔikatɨ. — (Tell No Hair Non-Comanches attacked them).

> *I consulted several sources for the correct translation of prickly pear cactus, including Mr. Saupitty, Cultural Specialist at the Comanche Museum in Lawton Oklahoma. I chose to rely on *Our Comanche Dictionary*, 2017. Another word, Husi̱, was recommended to me, but *OCD* translates that as "spirit during peyote ceremony."

German

Nein — No
Scheisse — Shit
Ja, mein lieber. — Yes, my love.

Also by Jennifer Marchman

The Mender Trilogy

The Mender – Book 1
The Captive – Book 2
The Guardian – Book 3

Short Stories

"The Hunt"

The Accidental Time Travelers Collective, Volume One
- an anthology by 12 time-traveling authors
"Field and Flame" (a prequel to the Mender Trilogy)

―ℓℓ―

For an up-to-date list of Jennifer's publications visit:
https://jennifermarchman.com/alsoby

For new releases and other time travel happenings,
join Jennifer's mailing list, *The Time Mender Dispatch:
News from the Temporal Front,* at
jennifermarchman.com/list

About the Author

Jennifer Marchman lives in Austin, Texas, with her husband, three nearly grown children, and the two best dogs in the world. At different times, she has worn various authorial hats, including ghostwriter-memoirist, editor, curriculum writer, educational blogger, grant writer, and addicted social media over-sharer, but now, after many years, she's writing for pleasure.

Jennifer is a member of the Writers' League of Texas, the Historical Novel Society, and #TimeTravelAuthors in the Twitterverse. She enjoys flamenco dancing, is the proud owner of a white belt in jiu-jitsu, and wishes to compete internationally in mounted archery but lacks a ticket to Kazakhstan and a horse to practice on. She has toyed with the idea of picking up pottery again, but needs more hours in her day and a husband willing to install (for the fourth time) the necessary electrical outlet for a kiln that may likely go unused.

Though she is not sure, she probably would have run off at the age of twelve to be a time traveler — if the opportunity had presented itself.

Jennifer's debut novel, *The Mender*, is a 2022 finalist in the Writers' League of Texas Manuscript Contest.

Want to read more from the multiverse of *The Mender,* find pre-order links for new books, learn about Jennifer, join her reader group, or follow her on social media?

Visit her website at:
jennifermarchman.com

Made in the USA
Coppell, TX
02 November 2024